ALSO BY ELISABETH de MARIAFFI

How to Get Along with Women (stories)

THE DEVIL YOU KNOW

A NOVEL

ELISABETH de MARIAFFI

A TOUCHSTONE BOOK

PUBLISHED BY SIMON & SCHUSTER

NEW YORK   LONDON   TORONTO   SYDNEY   NEW DELHI

Touchstone
A Division of Simon & Schuster, Inc.
1230 Avenue of the Americas
New York, NY 10020

Epigraph excerpted with permission from *Celestial Navigation* by Paulette Jiles (McClelland & Stewart, 1984).

First Touchstone hardcover edition January 2015

TOUCHSTONE and colophon are registered trademarks of Simon & Schuster, Inc.

For information about special discounts for bulk purchases, please contact Simon & Schuster Special Sales at 1-866-506-1949 or business@simonandschuster.com.

The Simon & Schuster Speakers Bureau can bring authors to your live event. For more information or to book an event, contact the Simon & Schuster Speakers Bureau at 1-866-248-3049 or visit our website at www.simonspeakers.com.

Interior design by Claudia Martinez
Jacket design by Jason Heuer
Jacket photograph © plainpicture/Mohamad Itani

Manufactured in the United States of America

10 9 8 7 6 5 4 3 2 1

Library of Congress Cataloging-in-Publication Data

de Mariaffi, Elisabeth, 1973–
    The devil you know : a novel / Elisabeth de Mariaffi.—First Touchstone hardcover edition.
        pages cm
1. Women journalists—Fiction. 2. Murder—Investigation—Fiction. I. Title.
    PR9199.4.D427D48 2015
    813'.6—dc23
                            2014016059

ISBN 978-1-4767-7908-9
ISBN 978-1-4767-7910-2 (ebook)

FOR GEORGE

I USED TO BE PARANOID, THINKING SOMEONE
WAS AFTER ME, BUT IT WAS YOU
ALL ALONG.

Paulette Jiles, "Police Poems: I"

THE DEVIL YOU KNOW

PROLOGUE

The first time I saw him it was snowing.

I was standing next to the stove, under the band of light shining down from the range hood, picking through a bag of spinach leaves and throwing the mushy ones into the sink. Outside it was white and pretty and there was just a little frost on the windows, along the edges. The kitchen faced out onto a patchwork of dark backyards sewn together with skinny, faltering fence lines. It was about nine o'clock but I hadn't eaten dinner.

It was Sunday night, February 21, 1993. I have a sharp head for detail.

That winter I was a first-year reporter with a newsroom desk at a not-quite-national daily paper. Not even my own desk: I shared it with another new hire, a guy named Vinh Nguyen who sat out the overnights and left crumpled bags of Hickory Sticks in the pencil drawer. My mother loved and hated my job. She thought I got too close to it. Most news is bad news. Her opinion is that I lived a lot of bad news very closely as a child and enough is enough. When I was ten years old my best friend went missing and that's what she's talking about. You can look at this as *bad news* and it's the understatement of your lifetime. It's likely also the reason I started reporting the news. A balls-out way of handling trauma, wouldn't you say?

My mother admits this is true.

I'd come on board as a summer intern with a year of j-school to go, but the job came up and I wanted to be working. The *Free Press* prides itself on its name: free to print whatever will sell this week. Larger type than the other dailies and all-color photos. None of that makes the newsroom any less exciting, though. There's a soap-opera-addictive quality to the quick turnover. What will happen next? Reporters watch stories approach like heavy clouds. They roll up in fits and starts. The tension break is galvanizing.

A man named Paul Bernardo had been arrested four days earlier, and I'd spent the weekend camped out in front of his house in St. Catherines, watching the forensics team walk in and out the front door dressed in their disposable space suits. My job was to take notes on anything that looked promising.

It was a famous case. Bernardo had murdered two girls inside that house, teenagers he'd held captive for days before killing them.

The last girl, Kristen French, had gone missing back in the springtime—pulled into Bernardo's gold Nissan 240SX in broad daylight, in a church parking lot, near a busy street. These are things we are told can't happen. The police found her shoe, lying out in the open, as if there had been a struggle.

Kristen was the third in less than a year. Five months earlier, a fourteen-year-old named Terri Anderson had disappeared, her house only three blocks from the same church parking lot. Five months before that, Leslie Mahaffy, a girl from nearby Burlington, had also gone missing, but she was found within weeks, cut in pieces and the pieces encased in cement, in a nearby lake. One of the cement blocks had been too heavy to toss and lay resting near the shore. It was Leslie's retainer that helped them identify her body, what was left of it. She was in ninth grade.

When Kristen French disappeared, the community shut down. Girls walked home only in groups of four and five. No one went anywhere alone. St. Catherines isn't a big place. It's not a rough town. The house that Kristen grew up in was middle class and ordinary. They found her body later in the spring, curled and naked and left in a ditch.

News of Bernardo's arrest knocked the entire country to the ground. Back when I was in high school, the city had been haunted by a long, unsolved series of violent rapes. The media had given this attacker a nickname and the name was something I'd grown up with: the Scarborough Rapist, never caught, was front-section news for years. Now we learned that this, too, had been Paul Bernardo. The murders were only one part of a long, slow story that had taken years to roll in. He'd raped more girls than you could easily count.

In high school, the Scarborough Rapist was a thing we talked about, myself and my friends, teenaged girls. A presence larger than a real person, an eye that saw when you were alone and unguarded. Without knowing his name or what horror was to come, Paul Bernardo was the thing we thought about when we got on and off the bus in the evenings, or on our way home from dance class, or whenever a man walked behind us too long or too close.

I'd just spent my weekend watching his house from inside the locked doors of a blue hatchback. The part of the job my mother hates, on my behalf.

I wonder sometimes how much the thinking about it helps. I came home that night and stood in my apartment making dinner and listening for odd sounds, a creak on the stairs or hallway floorboards. You're alone on a dark street and the impulse is to keep checking: Is anyone following me? How about now? Your anxiety spikes, but then tapers off. The constant checking becomes your way of controlling the danger. If I keep looking behind me, into the dark, then there will never be anyone there. There can't be, because that's something that only happens in movies.

I figure it's the one time you forget. Your mind is busy with something else and for just a moment you relax. You're distracted by the smell of lilacs in someone's garden or the look of the moon or some other daytime anxiety. That's when he comes. And it's your fault, for not playing by the rules.

There's another way to look at this. Maybe it's your own fear that calls him to you. You've imagined him so easily and so often, stalking you in the dark or hiding in your closet or in the backseat of a car in the parking garage. It's like you want him. This fear sounds out into the night and somewhere, evil pricks its ears.

You're ready for him. You've spent a lifetime practicing.

At home in my kitchen, my fingers were slowly thawing out. There was a dull pain down through my teeth and I noticed how hard I was clenching my jaw, or maybe had been all day, thinking of these things, and I worked to focus on the task at hand: the spinach I was picking over, and the promise of hot food.

There were other factors about that first night I saw him, but they were things I couldn't put a finger on. The soft details. Things the police wanted me to know that hadn't registered. That's what they told me later, along with everything else. What sort of footwear did he have on? Boots or shoes, high or low, black or brown? Did the jacket have buttons or a zipper? Did I say he'd had both a hood and a cap? The hood pulled up or lying flat on his shoulders? I put their report, a thin yellow carbon, into the file box next to my desk where I keep all my other receipts and notes on stories.

I was living on my own for the first time and rode my bicycle from the office to assignments. I had to borrow a blue Plymouth beater from my boss so I could drive down to St. Catherines every day, to Bernardo's house. My boss was the news editor, Angie Cavallo. Angie stayed downtown and loaned me the car because she knew the stakeout would take a long time and would largely be boring. She'd placed her own dibs on the courtroom and the press meetings.

My apartment was part of a chopped-up house just off Gladstone, in a neighborhood that was cheap and problematic. I couldn't see Queen Street from my front door, but I could hear the sirens at night and the addicts yelling to one another, or to themselves. I had a side entrance off the street that led up a skinny flight of stairs. Inside my own door there was a hall and three rooms: to the right, the kitchen; to the left, the room where I lived and slept. Past the kitchen there was a bathroom with tiny black-and-white tiles all over the floor and wall, and a bathtub on legs where you could only take a shower. The tap had been co-opted, a long and slinky tube connecting it to a fixed showerhead above. Outside the kitchen a fire escape snaked up the exterior wall. Stairs from the back of the house and then a thin landing along my windows, then more steps to the third-floor apartment above. There were three guys living up there, Mexican medical students who always carried backpacks and avoided eye contact. One of them gave me a lift to the grocery store once, but he didn't wait or come back for me and I never learned his name.

The main floor entrance was off the next street, around the corner, and it was occupied by my landlord, a mute Spaniard with three cats that were never allowed out of the house. When I first came to see the apartment he brought a notepad out of his pocket and wrote down his questions for me: Job? Parents? Money? Man?

He had a clubfoot that dragged behind him when he walked. He was dysphonic mute. That means he can make some noises, but the noises are like swallowed whines. He sounded like a barn cat that had been abandoned by its mother and learned to make sounds by imitating the lambs.

On my level, the black metal landing surrounded the back of the house. I could climb out and save myself in case of emergency. Next to the refrigerator, a door and a dead bolt led out to the escape. This was my way out. There were metal bars on the outsides of the kitchen windows, so nothing out there could get in.

'd had a long, cold Sunday sitting in Angie's car down in St. Catherines. On the way home I cranked up the heat until my fingers unfroze and my grip on the steering wheel slackened. I was driving against traffic. Office people were heading home to the suburbs or all the way down to Hamilton for the night. I drove over the skyway, past the steel factory exhaust towers. A line of cars led into the factory for the night shift, and then again at Ford in Oakville. I left the car at Angie's place in the Annex and took the subway west and finally the Dufferin bus. There was an accident blocking the intersection at Dundas and the driver got out to buy himself a coffee while we were stopped, and I also got out and walked the last few blocks.

The heat from the car had worn off by this time. My bones were cold, and under my hat, my ears stung. There'd been a thaw a few days earlier but the snow was back in force now, falling heavily, and occasionally suddenly drifting in one direction or another with a gust of wind. Down your back or against your cheeks. It was cold enough that the snowflakes froze to my eyelashes and then melted there. I was in a hurry to get inside and crossed the bit of white lawn, diagonal, and snow got down inside my boots. Later, I couldn't remember whether or not the landlord had cleared the path to my door. It didn't occur to me to look for footprints.

I got home cold and hungry and put a pot of water and rice on the stove before I'd even taken off my jacket. Bits of snow fell on the floor and I stepped on them in my socks and then peeled the wet socks off and put on two new pairs, one on top of the other. I went back out into the hall and shook out my hat and coat and hung them on an old hook behind the door. In the kitchen, my hand went in and out of the spinach bag and the rustle of the cheap plastic gave me a little jump each time.

I didn't have any music on. The sound of the bag interrupted the other listening I was doing, a kind of keen attention through the quiet to whatever else is out there. Only nothing was there. This type of listening is common among women. You're alone and there's that baseline drone of electricity powering up your house, and your whole consciousness is taken up with witness to that noise, the hum of no humans. You catch your own hand moving out of the corner of your eye and it surprises you.

I had a tiny chunk of pecorino crotonese from Gasparro's that I planned to grate into the spinach and rice. I'd been in to pick up olives and flirt with the dark-haired son, who was newly married but enjoyed a little call-and-answer over the meat counter. The father and the uncle either shook their heads or joined in, depending on the day. They were gray-haired but not really elderly. There was a sway-back wooden chopping block in the center of the shop. They were busy at the block, wrapping loins and strip steaks, and the son told me they had to do the offal separately and scrub the block down so there would not be contamination. Between us, under the glass, a pile of calves' livers slouched and glistened.

I grated the cheese into a bowl. I was making myself hear things. Mice in the walls. The burble of water through the rads. Steam from the rice pushing up against the lid, the *click-click* of the pot as the lid rose and fell. Any floor creak sounds like something moving. It can't really happen if you've imagined it enough.

There was a scrape outside and the chime of something heavy rang off the metal fire escape and my heart flipped up. A heavy icicle falling from the eaves. A hardy raccoon. I turned my body to the window.

There were two black stumps on the snowy landing.

The stove light shone off the glass and made it hard to see anything else. I could see my own reflection, my own fridge and stove. One of my hands was full of spinach and I held it out in front of me with the fist tight and the raw leaves sticking out between all my knuckles. The stumps were not stumps. They were black boots.

One of the guys from upstairs. Right? If you forgot your key, you'd climb up the escape and try to get in some other way. I counted in my head, waiting for him to move on, a friendly knock, something. The boots just stayed there.

My breathing stopped and I squinted, but the window shone back only a pale and cloudy version of my own kitchen, like a wet painting folded in half. On one side of the glass, real white table, white wall, desk in a corner, two chairs. On the other, the mirage:

table, wall, desk, chairs, and under the stove light, girl, spinach-fisted, staring. For a moment I didn't recognize myself. I took two long steps forward.

Aggressive. Get off my escape. I could see the boots on the landing where a thin periphery from the streetlamp was casting some light. They ended at my kitchen table. Above that, my own long hair brushing my shoulders, the V of my sweater, my collarbone standing out white. In another yard, a cat or a raccoon screamed and the neighbor's motion sensor kicked on. The outside lit up all at once.

Replacing me, a man. Taller than me. Black hoodie, black jeans, stocking cap pulled down close over his ears. Eyes shadowed or else deep set, and his hands hanging there, huge and gloved, black against the snow balanced on the rail behind him. The raccoon scrambling across the top rail of the yard fence.

The light held for the count of five. Long enough for me to see him there, two feet from the window. For him to see me looking. Then it turned off, leaving just the white walls again, the hazy girl in the glass. There was a silhouette where I knew he must be standing, a few feet away at most, dancing spots where my eyes were trying to adjust to the sudden swell of brightness and then the dark again. The window between us. The silhouette becoming an outline, part of my eye's reckoning.

If he was still there.

I reached up and turned off the stove light. The spinach leaves fell all over the range, into the elements.

Nobody. My own reflection disappeared, but now the man was also gone. I went over and shut the kitchen door and shoved a chair up under the doorknob. Out in the night, I could see the shape of the thin bars on the outside of the windows, and beyond that only the snow-covered landing, the steps, the black railing. I was in the dark now.

What if he was somehow inside the house with me. Could he be inside? Or out there, watching me do this? I walked over to the window and knocked on it with a fist to warn him off and then pressed my forehead against the cold glass.

Outside, fat snowflakes were still drifting down against the fence. A little piece of moon came out from behind a cloud.

No one. No trace.

You're making this up, I said. Ridiculous.

I said it loud enough that someone would have heard me, if he was there, around the corner, just out of sight.

I know how to work myself up. Panic, and then it's nothing, and the relief of it is so good. There's no one there. There is no better feeling than suddenly realizing you're not going to die.

Outside was clean and gorgeous. I could see everyone's sloppy backyards, white and muffled. The raccoon was gone.

I looked down and saw the tracks: boot prints, all up and down the landing, the heavy marks in the snow where he'd stood and stared.

CHAPTER 1

On May 23, 1982, the week after she turned eleven, my friend Lianne Gagnon took the subway to St. George Station to practice running the two hundred at Varsity track and never came home. Sometimes I think I was supposed to meet her there. Sometimes what I think is we had a plan to meet—I used to run relay with her, never fast enough to be last leg, but they'd put me in second or third—only that day I didn't go, and Lianne stood around on the corner, waiting for me, until whatever happened next came along and happened.

I've had a few therapists, and my parents, tell me this isn't true, but it's a hard notion to shake. No one knows if she got to the track at all: maybe someone talked her into getting off the train early, or maybe she never even made it onto the platform. Kids didn't carry phones back then. These were the days before Paul Bernardo or the Scarborough Rapist. The next winter a little girl called Sharin' Morningstar Keenan would go missing from an Annex park. They found her a few weeks later stuffed in a fridge. People still remember that time as the moment the city changed. Up till then, Toronto was pretty safe. We used to ride bikes through Mount Pleasant Cemetery, all the way up to Yonge Street, and come home in the dark. They made you carry a quarter in case you needed to call home.

When I see it in my mind, Lianne is standing around near the track entrance at the corner of Bloor and Devonshire, waiting for someone (me), and that's when the guy notices her. He probably told her he had some running tips. He probably said he was a track coach and could help her with her time. That's how the cops painted it for us, later on. In the couple of days right after Lianne disappeared, my friend Cecilia Chan and I used to sit at the piano in her mother's classroom after school and tell each other how it happened, how it was raining and Bloor Street was empty, and a long black car drove up and pulled Lianne inside. Then Cecilia played "Jesus Loves Me" on the piano. That's the only song they taught her at Chinese Sunday School.

The other thing I picture, sometimes, is my bedroom closet in my parents' old house on Bessborough Drive. The year before, I'd grown a plate of penicillin in the back of the closet, hidden so my mother wouldn't know what I was up to and come and throw it away. Penicillin is just bread mold: Alexander Fleming was a slob who left old sandwiches lying around in his desk, and then one day—*poof!*—some mold got into his petri dish when he was away on vacation and killed a bunch of bacteria. (He made another startling wonder-drug discovery when his nose accidentally dripped into a different petri dish. You never hear about the stuff Fleming discovered on purpose.) I was growing the penicillin for a science fair, but once the bread got moldy I couldn't prove it had antibiotic properties because I didn't have ready access to bacteria. The closet was good and dark, though: easy to hide stuff in.

When I say I picture my closet, that's also because of the cops. When Lianne didn't come home for dinner, her dad drove down to Varsity to get her, but no one was there and the gate was locked. I guess he drove around for a few hours before they thought of calling the police. Everyone figured she was lost. I went to bed not knowing a thing, but later my parents told me her school picture was on the eleven o'clock news.

Right away, I had a terrible feeling, my mother said. Right here: she pushed a fist into the soft part of her stomach. We were getting ready for lunch when she told me this, so she stood there with her fist in her stomach for ten or twenty seconds, and then went back to setting the table.

The police called our house at two in the morning. My parents didn't want to wake me up, but the cop on the other end of the line wouldn't hang up until he'd asked me some questions. They had a class list and they were going through it alphabetically. I wasn't special: they were calling everyone. Lianne was my best friend and I wanted to be the first one they called. If anyone knew where Lianne was, it would be me, right? How could they not know that I should be first?

What they wanted to know was if Lianne was hiding in my closet. Did I know she was going downtown to practice for the track meet? Did I say I would meet her, and then forget?

This seemed possible, even though I wouldn't be eleven until November and I wasn't allowed to take the subway alone. I also wasn't allowed to take gymnastics, or throw myself out of trees the way Lianne did, hoping to break a bone so that she could have a cast and get everyone to sign it, like Sarah Harper did in the fifth grade. I know that the day before she disappeared, we wanted to help find a lost dog in the park and we'd both run home to ask. I wasn't allowed to do that, either.

The cop knew everything about me. He knew I ran relay with Lianne, and hurdles. He knew which corner store we stopped at on the way home from school when it was sunny out and we wanted to buy frozen cherry Lolas. It was like he'd been watching me and Lianne for months.

Questions the police asked me in the middle of the night:

Did I say I'd go to Varsity and run track with her, and then leave her there alone?

Or did she come home with me? Maybe we wanted to have a sleepover and didn't tell anyone. Were we afraid our parents would say no?

Was Lianne in my house right now?

I was standing in my parents' bedroom in the dark, with the curly phone cord wrapped around my wrist. No one put a light on. There were the red numbers shining out of my father's digital alarm clock next to the phone and a couple of skinny stripes of moonlight where the vertical blinds didn't match up. I imagined Lianne sitting in my closet, safe in the back shadows like the plate of bread mold, with her knees drawn up high against her chest and her red sneakers still on.

No, I told the cop.

You didn't see her today?

No.

You didn't play with her?

No.

Did you see her at the park?

I don't think so.

Did you go to the park today? Did you see her in your backyard?

No. I don't. I don't know.

If she's at your house, you're not in trouble. We're trying to find Lianne, we need to know where she is.

I didn't see her.

The way I can picture Lianne sitting in the closet, or standing around on the corner at the track entrance, those things are called confabulations. False memories, probably induced by a combination of guilt and suggestion. If you want to answer a question badly enough, your brain will supply the solution.

It's a strange thing to have to think about every spring.

Outside it's bright and cheerful and there'll be fat yellow dandelions in all the yards across the street, turning into white wishing puffs. I like to buy three or four bunches of cut hyacinths at a time from the Portuguese lady on the corner and rollerblade down the block with my hands full of them. Purple and pink and white: the whole room smells sweet and clean and I'm windburned from rushing around on wheels all afternoon. I mean, I have fun. I'm a fun girl, I'm good at it. Still, there's this piece of you, every May, that kind of wants to slit its wrists a little.

Lianne was the track star, not me. She went to the City's every year for sprints: one and two hundred, hurdles, plus a few jumps. My legs are long, so I was a good high jumper when I didn't panic and stop short of the bar. You have to think about the jump but not look at the bar. You can see this as a metaphor for your whole life: if you remember that you're jumping over something that could crash and hurt you, you probably won't do it.

The gym teacher always made me run distance in elementary school because I was tall and sturdy and could go for a long time. She was Czech. Her name was Mrs. Jacek; she wore black-stripe Adidas pants and her basic speaking voice was a loud yell.

You're big horse! Mrs. Jacek said, pleased both with me for being bigger than the other kids and with herself for noticing. I was five-foot-four in the fifth grade.

I wanted to be a hurdles all-star. I wanted to make that L-shape with my leg curved back and barely touch down before sailing off again. Lianne was five inches shorter than me and weighed eighty-three pounds. Every night I'd go to bed and pray to wake up four-foot-ten.

Varsity Stadium was where the high school girls went to train on Saturday mornings. If you showed up at the right time, the hurdles would be all set up and you could use them while the older girls cooled down. Lianne knew the coach from Jarvis Collegiate. He was a friend of her dad's, so he'd let us in and give us ice to suck on when it got hot.

I know what you're thinking, but it wasn't him. Track practice was canceled that weekend for a school camping trip, and there were lots of witnesses up in Algonquin Park with him when Lianne was abducted. This is a fact I learned from the newspaper.

Lucky son of a bitch, my father said. In the mornings he'd make me a soft-boiled egg and do the crossword while I combed the front section of the *Free Press*.

She was missing for twelve days. The newspaper reported on what the police had to say, which was not much. At school we learned *foul play*. Sometimes they'd find a witness, someone who'd seen her, or a girl of about the right age and description. Once there was an interview with a man who'd been walking home along Bloor with his groceries. He said it was hot, and he wanted to stop near the Varsity gate in the shade, but there was a man there and a little girl, talking.

Something seemed off, he said, but my hands were full. What could I do?

They never caught the guy, which is a shame, because they know who did it and traced him back to a rooming house in the east end. By that time he was long gone. He was an American, so there was speculation he slipped back across the border, or else disappeared somewhere up north. Sometimes his name still comes up in the news, like when one of the cops on that case gets promoted or dies. *Officer So-and-So was a meticulous investigator. He was frustrated throughout his career that police never managed to track down Robert Nelson Cameron, the suspected killer of eleven-year-old Lianne Gagnon.*

The school sent in some counselors to talk to us all for a day or so. That's something I know because there's a record of it, my mother says she signed a form. I don't remember anyone coming to our class. Up until they found her, I really believed Lianne would be okay. I had a dream one night that I was late for school, and walked up the empty stairwell and into the second-floor hall. It was wintertime, and there was a line of boots against the wall next to our classroom door, and Lianne's boots were there, too, and her coat, thrown across the hall floor, and I started running to see her because I knew she was back. I was a great believer in positive thinking. Later on, Cecilia Chan told me she didn't cry the day they found Lianne's body because she'd already guessed that Lianne was dead.

I never cried when Lianne was missing. I thought the only sure way to kill her was to slip, to let myself imagine for one second she might be dead. Every night I double-checked my closet. I got down on my hands and knees and crawled right inside so that I could see and touch the corners. I made sure my shoes were in a straight line at the very back, against the wall, so nothing else could fit behind them, then I crawled out and shut the accordion doors tight.

When I got into bed I said a little prayer over and over again: *Dear God, Thank you for everything you give me this day and every day. Please look after Lianne and keep her healthy and safe.* If I started to wave off into sleep I'd sit up and start over. I had to say the thank-you part first, so that I wouldn't seem spoiled and demanding. I needed God to do what I said. We knew enough, we knew she wasn't lost, we knew someone had taken her. I had a hard-nosed faith in the world. I wanted her back, damaged and alive.

On June 4, a lady named Alice May was walking her dog through the trails in Taylor Creek Park and found Lianne lying face-down in the mud. The dog found her. She wasn't wearing any shoes. Her body was all wrapped up in an Anheuser-Busch duffel bag and there was a leg sticking out of the bag. I read all of this in the newspaper. Where she was, who found her. There were other interviews: a Tamil family that lived in the same rooming house as Robert Nelson Cameron said they heard her screaming, but they were illegal and too afraid to call the police. Besides, who knows why a kid screams?

The way her body looked told the police a lot about what had happened. Last year I asked my mother how she could possibly have thought that was a good idea, letting me read the news.

There was a funeral that we all went to. I went along with Cecilia Chan, in the back of her mother's Pontiac, and we spent the whole ride there turned around in our seats, making faces at Alex Hsu in the car behind us. Alex sat next to me in class and we were going out in the way that fifth graders go out: so, barely talking but making each other miserable all the same. When you think about the shock of grief, the way a funeral is just a shit show for others to look in on, how you're not even in mourning yet, you can't be, but there's that immense pressure to look the part? That goes about a hundred times for kids, but with a hundred times less awareness. I'd never known a dead person. I'd been to two Jewish weddings where the brides wore hot pink and one regular wedding where my uncle married a Mexican girl and my father got drunk and did a hat dance. That was the closest I'd come to ritual. Cecilia's mother had to go to the funeral because she taught at the school and Lianne's little brother was in her class. It felt very similar to a field trip: we were there all together, with parent volunteers, and teachers telling us to please be serious.

In the course of the ceremony, the minister asked Lianne's friends to come and pay their last respects at the coffin and I got up and walked to the front of the church. The only other kids who came up were Alex Hsu and this Australian kid, Lachlan Armstrong. Neither of them had been particular friends of Lianne, so I was surprised. Later Mrs. Chan told me that the school principal had chosen just those two to represent Lianne's friends, because they were less likely to be traumatized. Once I was up there, I wished I hadn't gone. We were on stage. Lianne was dead and everyone thought I was trying to show off. I remember I was holding a red candle and the boys were standing next to me moving their feet around and making a noise against the thin carpet. I looked down and Lianne was lying there in her Christmas dress, polished white and still.

That last part is another confabulation. She screamed and screamed, and he stuffed an old shirt in her mouth and then he strangled her until her neck broke. The casket must have been closed.

W here were my own parents in all this? They got up with me on the funeral morning and my father ironed my navy-blue dress and then he went to work. My mother had a fierce self-protective instinct. A firm believer in auto-determination. That means she thought I'd better learn to deal with this on my own. She'd seen a lot of harsh things growing up in northern Ontario and then as a teenager alone in Toronto that she'd never gotten over. When I asked her, last year, why they had allowed me to spend months reading the details of my friend's rape and murder in the daily newspaper, she said: We couldn't stop you.

It's likely that she really does think this. I was a precocious reader and following the story would have given me a sense of control over what had happened. Knowledge is power, right? There's a basic neglect inherent to this style of parenting. I was a small adult from an early age. The same therapist who explained what *confabulation* means also advised me to never read the news when it's about little girls getting abducted, or older girls like me getting raped or killed. She told me this while I was in j-school.

I write those newspaper stories, I said.

She shrugged. That's all about control, too.

All through high school I could barely cope with riding the bus, even during the day, because out in Scarborough that's where girls were getting raped. At bus stops.

I walked everywhere. It's like when you go to a movie: they talk about suspension of disbelief. I don't have any disbelief, it's in permanent suspension. The good thing about working in the newsroom is at least now I'm the first to know. Any kind of awful thing humans do to one another seems plausible to me.

It must have been a tremendous relief for my parents when Cecilia's family offered to take me to Lianne's funeral along with them. There's not a lot of reality wiggle room at an event like that. Kids' funerals tread a funny line: people bring flowers and teddy bears and balloons and everybody eats cake afterward. It's a lot like a baby shower, except for the horror. It was a well-publicized case, so the church was packed with strangers.

After the memorial we drove to Mount Pleasant Cemetery and watched them lower the coffin into the ground. The funeral director gave all the kids white flowers. You were supposed to toss the flowers onto the coffin as it was going down. There was a ring of children standing around the grave. Some of them were Lianne's real friends from school and some of them were her cousins from Quebec, and some of them were just kids who'd read the story in the newspaper but didn't know her at all, and we were all standing there holding the same pretty white carnations. I was counting the faces in each row and how many rows there were and doing multiplication. In my own hand, the flower stems pressed tight against the insides of my knuckles so I couldn't lose them and then it was too late: the coffin was already down and a couple of men with spades were throwing great shovelfuls of dirt onto it. We'd spent all morning waiting. The dirt knocked the other kids' carnations off. The flowers looked like dirty Kleenexes, like someone had kicked over a garbage can.

I don't know what I was thinking. I wanted my flowers to be there, too, I guess, and then a second later Cecilia's mother was yanking me out of the hole by one arm. They thought I'd done it on purpose. This was the story that went home to my mother, that I'd thrown myself into the grave with Lianne. You can see that's the way adults would tell it, too.

After they pulled me out, people left a respectful distance between me and them. When I noticed that, I walked a little slower. No one even tried to brush the dirt off me.

CHAPTER 2

After Lianne's funeral my parents sold our house and we moved to a different, bigger house where my mother could feel like I was safe. Except what she didn't count on is that bigger spaces make you feel more vulnerable, not less. The safest place you can be is inside a shoebox, a tiny space that's just for you. If you can reach one hand out and touch a wall, and reach the other hand out and touch a different wall, then you know for certain no one else is in that small place with you and you are just fine.

The house on Inglewood had three stories for the three of us, three bathrooms, a laundry chute that used to be a dumbwaiter and fell in a straight path from my own bathroom on the third floor right down to the stone-floor basement. Two televisions. Sliding doors to the backyard, a big square of land with an engineered waterfall in one corner as a landscape feature. My parents still live in that house, but they pulled out the waterfall a few years ago. In the summer you could hear it trickling all day through the kitchen window. My mother said it made her crazy. It made her think she had to pee.

There's a big front porch with a couple of chairs on it, and my mother sat outside most of that first summer rocking in her seat like a sentry. That was the year everybody's mother changed. Every kid I knew suddenly had more rules to follow, an earlier bedtime. We didn't play hide-and-seek after dinner because if you were hiding and it suddenly got dark, something bad could happen to you. Every kid was under surveillance. My mother had never seemed to me like other parents, but now that difference multiplied: she'd go missing for a few hours at a time, without telling us where she was off to or even that she was leaving. I can't say for sure what triggered this. She was different from the get-go, so maybe it was what happened to Lianne, or maybe it was just a mid-life thing. Those little escapes were consistent with her personality in general. She's not always predictable. The day before Lianne disappeared, I'd run home to ask if we could help find a lost dog, but I found the front door locked. My mother was in the living room, arguing with someone I couldn't see. She saw me out on the steps and sent me to my room. As a kid, you don't really question things like that. Odd to imagine your parents as their own entities, moving through the world.

The alley from the next street over opens up right across the street from our house. One night I was sitting on the steps with my father, eating baked potatoes off plates on our knees. We'd been waiting for her to come home and make dinner but once it got dark I guess my father gave up and turned on the oven himself.

Your mother's okay, he said. He'd scrubbed the potatoes over the sink, then wrapped them up in foil with butter and chives already inside them. I hadn't asked where my mother was, and it made me happy that he'd supplied the answer. We didn't need to have a discussion about it.

It was the end of August and maybe nine o'clock at night. My father's hair was very blond and cut close to his head, short, the way you expect a dad to look, with just a tiny lick of a curl behind his ear. I was focused on the task of cutting into my potato without tipping the plate on my lap. I imagined the plate tipping and my potato rolling off and then bonking down the steps, *bonk bonk,* and down the path into the gutter. My father scooped some sour cream off his own potato and put it onto mine.

There was no streetlight over the entrance to the alleyway. It was the first night where you really needed a sweater, and I pulled the hood on my sweatshirt up over my ponytail. There was a scuffling sound like a kid falling off a fence or someone kicking at stones. I looked up and my mother came walking out of the alley, alone. Her jean jacket was open like it wasn't cold at all. She saw us and walked straight up the steps anyway.

No rapists in there? my father said, as though we bumped into my mother, casually like this, practically every day. He didn't say: Why were you in the alley at night? Or, Where have you been? Or even, Have you had dinner?

None, my mother said. No rapists at all. She smiled sharply. The smile was there and then done. When she went inside, the screen door smacked closed behind her. My father chewed his potato.

These days she's more settled. She fits inside her own skin. There's a theory that women in their thirties are naturally inclined to recklessness. A woman that age has more in common with a teen-aged boy than anyone else: she's reeling on hormone-drive. The sound of her biology isn't a ticking clock, it's a motor, revving up. I don't know if this explains it, or if it's a simple equation involving distance from a traumatic event. I can tell you my mother turns forty this year.

She's a bookkeeper by trade and works freelance out of a tiny, gold-painted office on the second floor of the house. There's a business card with her name, Annie Jones, also in gold. This is fixed to the door with painter's tape, instead of a sign. Her window faces the back garden. One day she's up there wearing a pantsuit and a pair of killer heels and the next day she's all ripped jeans and a T-shirt. This has less to do with client meetings than it does with just put-ting whatever she wants on her body at any given time. She's math-minded, in the same way that she would always prefer a yes-or-no answer to any question. The details of the situation take a back-seat to definitiveness. I guess she started chasing down deadbeat patients for my father's dental practice when I was a kid and took a shine to solving money problems. Her certification all came from night school. I can't imagine her working in an office or for any kind of boss.

Sunday mornings we'll bike over to the St. Lawrence Flea together, down the long sweeping spin of the Mount Pleasant Extension. She dyes her hair so it's brighter somehow and it comes flying out of her blue bike helmet, coppery in the sunlight. We jump off close to the lakeshore and lock up and get busy touching all the merchandise. Since I moved out she's keen to buy me things, house-ish things, or else sensible clothing such as cashmere turtlenecks or warm winter boots.

Burberry! Who got rid of this?

The vendors see my mother coming and get sad eyes. I like to leave her to it. She has a lot of stamina for arguing. This time she handed me an entire ensemble folded in on itself inside a white plastic grocery bag.

Ten bucks, she said. It was early February, but one of those days that warms up so much you almost believe it's going to be spring. Kids throw down their winter jackets and commit themselves to hopscotch.

I opened the bag: black turtleneck, classic belted trench coat.

No one will know I'm a reporter now! I said. Wait. Did you get me a deerstalker? I don't know if I can solve mysteries without my deerstalker.

Har.

I slipped my arms into the trench and opened up just one side suggestively, then sidled closer to my mother:

Would you like to buy an O?

There's a few antique dealers but in other respects it's just your standard flea market.

Audio cassettes and vintage Snoopy piggy banks, embroidered tablecloths, plates with pictures on them. Who wouldn't want a gravy boat with a picture of the *Bluenose* on it? Paper stalls with racks of old *Life* magazine covers wrapped up in their plastic sleeves: Marilyn and Jackie Kennedy and the moon landing. Stacks of romance novels and Agatha Christies. Royal Wedding memorabilia. Vintage porn and true crime.

Here's a stat for you. I held up a paperback and waved it at my mother: Women are voracious true crime readers. No word of a lie. Much more so than men.

She came over and took the book from me, then laid it back on the pile.

So, the men are doing all the serial killing, but the women are reading about it?

Not what you expect, is it? I said.

My mother had her fingers on the black spine of a copy of *Helter Skelter*. She flipped it up and flashed the cover at me.

I knew a guy once, she said. Who used to say he'd met him.

The True Story of the Manson Murders, I read. *Number One True Crime Bestseller of All Time!* I reached out for the book. Friend of a friend?

Of a friend of a friend, my mother said. I imagine it was all lies. She went back to browsing.

Think we live vicariously? I said. Reading it, I mean.

Sometimes I just throw this shit out there because it feels good. Because, hey, look at us, out for a Sunday stroll and chatting it up about gruesome murders and whatnot. I dug into my purse for fifty cents and reached the coins over to the book vendor, a tall guy with a comb-over and baby-fine gray stubble. He clicked open his cash can and threw the money in. There was a hundred-dollar bill Scotch-taped to the inside of the lid and I asked him what for.

Counterfeit, he said. So I remember what they look like. He leaned across the table and straightened the little rows of books. He had long, elegant fingers.

Your serial killer name is The Librarian, I told him.

I slid *Helter Skelter* into my purse and we moved on to the next booth, old paintings and ponchos hanging from a wire.

———

My friend David Patton moved me into my bachelor. He borrowed his mom's minivan and we packed it with all my stuff: books and papers and Goodwill buy-the-pound vintage. My mother had given me a plastic laundry basket filled with packaged food: spaghetti, canned tomatoes, peanut butter, applesauce. In the housewares department I owned three coffee mugs, a teapot that I thought was an antique but later turned out to be from Ikea, and a cast-iron fry pan. This paucity of assets must have seemed strong evidence that I didn't need help moving, and my parents didn't offer any. I think they were instead offering subconscious discouragement regarding my plan to live all by my lonesome. I could have moved all my worldly belongings in two cab rides—maybe even just one. But David had his mom's Caravan. So.

The original plan had not been for me to live out in Parkdale on my own. My friend Melissa and I were meant to share an apartment up in the Annex. She had a line on a nice one at College and Borden. Her father owns a bunch of cosmetic surgery clinics, so she comes from money. Only then Melissa quit her summer job to go see a few Grateful Dead shows and never came back. Her dad found her in a parking lot outside of Nashville, painstakingly carving I Need A Miracle signs into some shim wood she'd found. This is a thing she was doing for money, and I guess it's better than some of the alternatives. She had some kind of breakdown on the way home and ended up in the hospital on lithium. When I told David that, he said the same thing happened to his cousin Helen when she was twenty. Just the lithium part, unrelated to Jerry Garcia and his timeless music.

It's really common, he said. Girls go crazy all the time.

As it turned out, I loved bachelor life. You walk into your own tiny space at the end of the day and everything you see here is yours. There's no joint decision making and no explaining anything. On Saturday mornings I turned off the answering machine until 2:00 p.m., to feel independent of social connections. Sometimes it kills you. It's excellent to force your own hand. Then you know for sure you don't need anyone.

You think David's my boyfriend, but he's not. He's been my friend since forever. He's been my friend since we were kids. David Patton was just this kid I used to babysit. He's still got the same mess of dirty blond hair over his eyes all the time—back then because he was a kid, and now because he's trying to look hard-edged and a little broken. He wants his hair to make a girl think of Kurt Cobain, and maybe get the two of them, Kurt and David, confused for a moment. He's also still got the same five freckles across the bridge of his nose, plus a few extra in the sun. These detract from the grunge persona and a girl (me) is careful not to mention them too much. The year David turned thirteen he grew about seven inches in two months and did nothing but eat sandwiches. So today he stands six-foot-two, which is a solid five inches taller than me, but I still have the power because once upon a time I was the boss and somewhere inside we both remember that.

I was David's babysitter for a little over a year, starting about a year or so after Lianne disappeared. I was in seventh grade and David was in the fifth. That's not much of an age difference, but his mother didn't think he was old enough to be home alone yet. David was an only child and I was an only child and it's my understanding that those kinds of parents either worry about you too much or too little.

In those days David really did whatever I said. If I said, You know what's cool? We should make shoes out of cardboard and walk downtown. We should draw a game of hopscotch onto the bathroom floor with the paint from your paint-by-numbers. We should make Chef Boyardee ravioli on apple-juice can stoves in the backyard. We should make potato-chip-peanut-butter sandwiches with sweet pickles on the side. Then David would totally want to do those things. We didn't go to the same school and neither of us had any brothers or sisters. How was he to know I wasn't on the cutting edge of pop culture?

David's mother had blond hair and a chunky body, but she wore a lot of headbands and did aerobics in the basement. Sometimes she called me over just to take David to McDonald's so she could be alone in the house. She had a husband, Graham, who'd set the whole thing up. I guess he got to chatting my mom up in line at the grocery store one day and when he found out she had a daughter, voilà, I got the job. My mother didn't normally allow me to baby-sit for strangers. I looked on it as a reprieve from the post-Lianne lockdown. Graham Patton was never there when I arrived, but he came back with David's mother late at night and offered to drive me home, even though I only lived a few blocks away. He said he didn't want me walking home in the dark.

The fathers always drove you home and they were the ones you knew the least. The whole world tells you to never get into a stranger's car—unless you're babysitting his ten-year-old. I climbed into Graham Patton's station wagon with my fuzzy white winter coat wrapped around my chest and zipped, and he gave me five or ten dollars in my hand. He had a brown beard. He drove along making small talk, trying to get me chatting.

Why don't you tell me what you're doing at school, Evie?

He had a weird, repetitive way of using my name. Six or seven times per car ride.

Hi there, Evie. You look like you're ready to go home, Evie. Well, Evie, was Santa good to you? Did you get just what you asked for?

Maybe he was trying to show that he knew who I was. In the small space of the moving car, it felt intimate, like a hand against the back of my neck. A hard thing to articulate.

David said his father was a teacher at a high school in the east end. He taught industrial arts but he was really a photographer. He offered to take my picture more than once, which was appealing enough for a girl my age, but then one time I overheard my mother make a snide and raucous joke about Graham Patton getting the ninth-grade girls to sit pretty for the photographer. He and David's mother split up a long time ago now.

If I ever have kids, I'll tell my husband just to shut the fuck up in the car with the babysitter: she's probably afraid of him.

wasn't afraid of my own father. My dad is a pretty decent guy. He cooks and does the laundry and stuff. He's a dentist but he works for the public health clinic, fixing teeth for little kids or old people with no money. You could say he didn't get into it for the money. Most of his patients don't speak any English. He doesn't golf: he's more of a canoeing-type dentist, if you know what I mean. He's spry. He has a wiry look, and most but not all of his hair. In the fall he still climbs up the side of the house to put on the storm windows and he can hold himself there pretty easily with one hand while he does the work with the other. So he's doing well enough for a man just shy of his fifties. He's got a few deep lines in his face that make it richer when he frowns or laughs.

When I was little, my mother stayed home to look after me. She was the kind of mother who made peanut-butter-and-sprouts sandwiches. Instead of jam. We always had jars of fermenting yogurt in the stairwell to the basement, covered over with cloth and elastic bands. I had a playroom and another room down there, a crawl-space art room where I was allowed to paint on anything, walls, floor, ceiling, whatever. Other kids liked my house because of stuff like that and despite the weird food. When I was six I went over to my friend Melissa's for dinner. Her parents had a TV on the kitchen counter and we ate Velveeta-stuffed hotdogs. The cheese came already right inside the hotdog. They were like smoky miracles.

I didn't have grandparents around because my father was from Vancouver. My mother's family was all up north. She grew up in a place called Chapleau that was full of French people and lumberjacks. Near Quebec but not in it. She lived up there in the woods like Laura Ingalls, only with parents who were crazy. She told stories about them like she was the lost sister of the Brothers Grimm. They were hungry most of the time because there were six kids, which is why she only ever wanted one child: so she could feed that one kid peanut butter and sprouts and be generally sane.

Her family had a garden and they'd tent over the vegetables because the season was short, she said. So the tent helped keep the ground warm for long enough to get at least a few green things, beans and snap peas. Carrots and turnips and potatoes you could have without much work.

She had four sisters and a brother who was the youngest, and all the girls looked after him. He didn't have his own bed because he was an accidental baby and there was no more room, so he took turns sleeping in the sisters' beds every night. The brother's name was Sully. He died when he was six and my mother was ten because he had pneumonia and the weather was too bad to get any doctors or for the father to get into town for medicine. The next year her oldest sister went through the ice with her boyfriend, on his Ski-Doo. The sister was sixteen and should already have known better, but not much to do out there in wintertime. People drink.

Her parents had wicked fights.

Her father came out of the woods with whatever he'd managed to shoot. Mostly it was birds but sometimes it was rabbits, and if you didn't want to eat it they beat the shit out of you, because that's all there was to it.

My mother, mostly, she said. My father was always sorry if he hit you. Later on, he was sorry.

When he fought with her mother sometimes he hit her, too, and then locked himself in the car. To keep away from her. He had three copies of *Guns & Ammo Magazine* and an old *Auto Trader* that he kept in the glove compartment so he could switch gears from fighting. Her mother chased him out there, so he locked the door to keep himself inside the car and her out.

One time she was out there in her nightgown, my mother said, and just her slippers on in all this snow, and she takes a chunk of firewood and smashes in the headlights of the car while he's in there.

And my father's sitting there, doing the *Guns & Ammo* crossword or whatever. He was whistling.

When she was sixteen my mother moved down to Toronto by hitching a ride with her teacher. I don't know if the teacher knew she was running away. Maybe he did. Maybe he thought it couldn't be worse. When I was a kid I thought all teachers were nice and he was just doing her a favor and driving her someplace like grown-ups do. Now I figure she must have had some trade worked out with him.

She lived in bad places. She lived in one place with about ten other kids. Two rooms plus a kitchen.

I got to sleep on a real bed, on legs, she said, with three other girls, because I paid ten bucks extra a month. In the middle of the night someone would flip on the light switch and the whole floor was moving, like a wave. It was cockroaches. There were other kids who had to sleep on the floor with them. For ten bucks less.

I can't imagine my mother living like this. Once a June bug got into the house and she had to lay a sheet of paper over top of it before she could step down, so that she didn't have to watch her own foot coming down on the thing. It succumbed to a loud and crunchy death and my mother stood there, wringing her hands. She walked away, leaving the paper stuck to the floor.

When Lianne died I think we all went into shock in our own way, and my dad's way was to stop touching me or holding my hand when we walked down the street, something he would have always done before. Or, at least, that's the before that I remember. Something about having to explain that grown men do this stuff to little girls, or having to think about it every day, or watching me comb the papers and get more and more informed. Something about that must have upset him, or made him afraid he'd upset me. I still wanted to sit on his lap, but I didn't want to. Part of that was just me getting older. That divided feeling you get at that age, what other people think of as normal growing up. It's easy to pathologize it.

My mother seized up, too, but in a different way. She needed a lot more things after Lianne happened. Her hand was always on my shoulder. Whether this was new anxiety, or tied to her own childhood, or just because I was an only child, felt unclear.

In the last few years she seems more herself again. More like the peanut-butter-and-sprouts version than the wanders-out-of-an-alley version. She's got a vegetable garden and it's a thing she spends time on. When I was small we always had chives and snap peas at least. I'd hide out in the garden, crouching down and eating them off the vine before breakfast, then come into the house with pea-green fingers, my breath smelling mysteriously of onions.

Who can eat chives before breakfast? my mother said.

Fat cabbages, but their hearts split and filled up with jellied moth larvae. We never ate one. I notice in the new garden she hasn't bothered with these, leaning to black-eyed Susans and daylilies, pretty things that grow regardless, whether or not anyone is watching them. She grew those cabbages for years.

M y mother and I left the flea market and walked along Front Street in the sunshine. I had the new trench coat draped over my arm and I folded it over and wrapped the sweater around it. To keep things from getting wrinkled, I guess, although I only had the grocery bag to carry it all in anyway. My mother had her bike helmet clipped to the side of her purse and it smacked against her hip every time she took a long step forward.

You want a Jewish brunch? she said. Sometimes after the flea we break up the long uphill ride by market hopping. St. Lawrence to Kensington, which is pretty close to where I live now, anyway. We'll go into the Free Times for blintzes if it strikes us.

I shook my head.

Cold lemonade? she said. Free samples at Global Cheese?

My mother strapped the helmet around her chin.

Put yours on, she said. My own helmet was locked against my bike and I reached down and unhooked the U-lock and slid it carefully into a slot on the back rack. We coasted west on Wellington before climbing the hill at Spadina. I had the bag of clothes in my front basket and it bounced up and threatened to make a break for it every time I hit a crack in the pavement. My purse hung across my body and by the time we got to the top I had a thick band of sweat under the strap, from my shoulder to my hip. February thaw.

She locked up but I just stood there with my legs straddling the bike.

Which street did you live on, again? I said. On Brunswick, right? When you met Dad.

Brunswick, she said. She pointed across College Street. Up past the medical building. That wasn't there then, she said. Up next to the parkette. Number 102.

You're on my walk to work, I said. I took the copy of *Helter Skelter* back out of my purse and turned it over in my hands. I might just go get a coffee.

She clipped the helmet to her bike lock.

You have to thread it through, I said. So that it's locked on.

No one is going to steal this helmet, my mother said. She stood back a moment, then slid the key back into the lock and rejigged the helmet anyway.

I, for one, could eat a blintz, she said. Three, in fact. Sure you're not coming?

I'm sure, I said. Sorry.

It's not a sorry thing. She gave me a quick salute, then nodded toward the book. Just be kind to yourself. You know why women read that stuff.

I know, I know. Vicarious living.

Don't kid yourself, she said. It's so we learn how to get away.

CHAPTER 3

I need you to compile some stats.

I'd been sitting in my cubicle at work, filling in the blanks in an article about city zoning issues infringing on existing businesses on St. Clair West. Newbie reporters are like caulking: stuffed into the cracks for the City page, or Lifestyle, or wherever the holes are big enough to be noticed on a daily basis.

Angie Cavallo was the news editor, this second-generation Italian tough cookie who kind of clawed her way through the glass ceiling. She didn't so much break through as smash it with her skull. Then she crumpled a beer can on her forehead. Angie wrote the Page Three Opinion column and did more than her fair share of violent-crime reporting. It was also her job to assign me as required.

She leaned over the cubicle wall. She was eating an apple fritter out of a box and bits of white icing fell off the doughnut and onto my shoe.

I want to do a feature on women's safety, she said. When Did Toronto The Good Go Bad? Go down to the archives, get together a dateline of every girl who's gone missing since '83. That Keenan girl right through to now, to the girl in Burlington and Kristen French last year.

Two summers before, a girl had gone missing near Niagara Falls. When she turned up later, it was her chopped-up body they found, in cement blocks in the lake. That's who Angie meant by *the girl in Burlington*. Leslie Mahaffy. Kind of her own fault: she'd missed her curfew and gotten locked out of the house. There are remarkably few places for a fifteen-year-old to go at three in the morning. She probably sat out on her own curb in the middle of the night. Tough love. The wrong person offered to give her a lift and she said yes.

This new girl—Kristen French—was from the same area and that always makes everyone nervous. Her tenth-grade school picture was on all the news reports: brown hair, big smile, blue background. It's hard not to think about Lianne whenever stuff like this happens. Things got all mixed up in my brain, and I started thinking how much Kristen and Lianne really looked alike. I guess any smiling girl looks basically the same, if you think about it.

Those last two aren't really the city, I said. More like St. Catherines.

Still counts, Angie said. She wrapped the doughnut up in a napkin and squeezed hard to compress it back into the little box. She closed up the box and dropped it on the floor. Then she stepped on it.

So I won't eat the rest, she said. She looked down at the smashed box for a second and then bent low to pick it up again, letting it play back and forth in her hands in a contemplative way. Also do another list. From, say, 1960 to '82. Just to show the trend. Maybe we can make a chart or a graph or something.

That's a whole lot of time in the basement, I said. The archives were in the bottom of the *Free Press* building, in a kind of infinite, windowless room. I looked from the smashed doughnut box back to Angie. What did I ever do to you?

Get started down there, she said. Find something interesting, maybe I can get you better research privileges.

What about the Scarborough Rapist? I said. That's not exactly missing girls. Still counts?

Sidebar, Angie said. See what you can find. She turned away, then stopped and handed me what was left of the apple fritter.

For God's sake, she said. Save me from myself, would you?

B asically what Angie wanted was a dead-girls feature. Which is awesome, for obvious reasons. There are two categories: solved cases and cold cases. The cold cases are interesting but you have to watch how far down into the news file you read. As you go back in time, there's less care for the reader's soul. There's a six-year-old who was killed in 1980, two years before Lianne. I know it happened but I've never read about her. It's a case I've been encouraged to avoid. I generally catch myself just in time. I have a mental list of stories to steer clear of, as handed down to me by the therapist and my mother and David over time.

A lot of what I did for the *Free Press* was background research. Statistics. The archives were my playroom. Whenever you see a feature article that has a split byline—by Walter Smith, with files from Joe Blow and Arlene Black? My job was the "with files from." I liked to think of myself as a context provider. You end up looking at a lot of lists.

Report Femicide, that's a good one. Femicide started keeping track of women killed by their intimate partners—husbands, boyfriends, ex-boyfriends—after the shooting in Montreal, at the engineering school. I haven't run a stats analysis on this, but I can tell you just by eyeballing it, having a boyfriend who hits you makes you way more likely to get killed. And if you're going to get killed, chances are it'll be via stabbing. Among violent ex-boyfriends, stabbing is numero uno.

It's more about damage than death. It's hitting with a knife. It's about wrecking the thing you can't have. Death is a side effect of the wrecking.

The '80s had their fair share of dead girls, it turns out.

Sharin' Morningstar Keenan in 1983. That one they found stuffed in the fridge, after a long morning on the last day of a house-to-house search. She was in the last room they saw before lunch break. One of the cops stopped to talk to a neighbor in the hall and his partner noticed that a corner of the carpet was jammed up against the fridge. He almost missed it.

The room was empty, he said. The bed was made. I just went to open the fridge like you would. Casually.

The door was jammed and he could only open it a few inches.

Right away, he said. Right away I saw a garbage bag with a white shirt in it. I thought, Who keeps their laundry in the fridge? The little light didn't go on inside, when I opened it. So I had to force it a little more, you know, and then I saw her hair.

You can't believe how shiny her hair was, he said.

Sometimes I don't stop myself in time.

M ost of the time I was down in the basement, I was on my own. Sometimes you got another newbie reporter doing someone else's research, or else one of the veteran columnists—newsbrats, guys who grew up writing stories. They don't like anyone else touching their byline. Angie was only like that about her column. She'd come down here and stretch out on the cold linoleum when it was hot in the summer. The floors were speckled and smelled vaguely of bleach. In the winter there was that smell of burning dust as the heat burned through the ductwork. It wasn't a social space. There was no library coziness. It was a warehouse for old stories.

The door opened onto a set of work tables, set loosely in rows. Most of these held microfilm readers, but a few had computers sitting on them: boxy, plastic monitors on top and the motherboards hidden underneath, off to one side where you wouldn't kick them by accident. The archive spanned back, far behind the desks. Rows and rows of those gray, metal shelves you expect to see at the hardware store or in the tool room at an auto body shop, only instead of jars of nuts and bolts and piles of cleaning rags, these shelves had a hundred years of newspaper records sitting on them in microfilm canisters. There were a few freestanding rolling ladders, so you could reach the top shelves. Overhead fluorescent lights, but I liked to leave them off. A big room like that feels emptier with the lights on. I had a camping headlamp that I used to comb the stacks. It was my claim to fame: other reporters walked into this giant dark room and saw only my roving spotlight, searching for a file. When I sat down at a film reader, I brought a clip light from my desk upstairs and lit up just the area I was working in.

We all had our thing. My deskmate Vinh found an old wheel-chair somewhere in the building and dragged it down here and it was the only chair he'd sit in. He wheeled around in tight circles and smoked cigars while he worked. He wouldn't answer any questions. You'd say: Are you looking for World Series stats? And he'd just wheel around left or right, puffing away.

Clockwise means Yes, he told me upstairs. Counterclockwise means No.

The building's giant furnace sat in the mechanical room right next door. So there's the gurgle of the oil tank and the furnace thrums on and then the hot water moving up through all the pipes. I told Angie that when I was little I thought wolves lived in our basement at home and I'd run up the steps two at a time before they could grab me by the heels.

Then when I was twelve, I said, I read in *Tiger Beat* that Madonna grew up imagining devils lived in her basement. So she also ran up the stairs two at a time.

What are you guys, twins? she said.

Angie started working for the *Free Press* when she was a teenager. She walked into the mailroom on a Friday afternoon and never went back to school the next Monday morning. It was 1961, when people did stuff like that and got away with it. If I'd set out to impress her, dropping out of j-school and taking the job at the *Press* was kind of the best thing I could have done. Angie must have been in her late forties somewhere, but I found it hard to know for sure. She really came of age in the newsroom, so she walked and talked a lot like a guy. She wore golf shirts. The year before I met her, she'd gone to this Bulgarian cosmetician in Cumberland Court who tattooed permanent eyeliner onto her eyelids with a shaky hand—the result was a little slurry, like Angie had woken up hungover and put her makeup on too fast. You could say this made it more natural looking.

'd moved from Sharin' Morningstar Keenan in 1983 up to Nicole Morin in 1985 when the archive door swung open and Angie came belting in. All the overhead fluorescents flickered and shone on at once. She flashed me some jazz hands.

Welcome to the Information Superhighway, she said. I'm setting you up with Nexis access.

I had a vague idea of what that meant.

Necks and asses? I said. Or necks and axes?

Stop your smart-assery and pull up a chair, Angie said.

LexisNexis was thought of as the single best resource for filed news of any kind. That's most of what I knew about it.

Which table? I said. There were five computers. I pointed between them with an unsure finger.

Doesn't matter, Angie said. You can get to it off any computer. Here, at home, wherever. That's why it's so good. You just need a subscription and a password.

I dragged over my desk chair. It was heavier than I thought and the legs squealed and scraped along the floor.

Like a membership? I said.

Like a club, Angie said. Okay. She reached around to the back of the computer at the next table and switched it on. The Lexis half is legal docs, she said. The Nexis half is hard news. There was a little hum and a quick text scroll across the screen before it settled into start-up mode and the Windows 3.1 logo came up and held. They've got sources all over the world, Angie said. I don't even know how many sources. Tens of thousands. Records going back over a hundred years.

So I can use this at home, I said. In my kitchen? Info-to-go?

Pay-for-play, Angie said. Most subscribers are lawyers, police, media. Big corporations with dollars to spend on getting it right.

The computer shone a welcome screen at us and Angie fumbled around with the mouse till the pointer sat over the LexisNexis icon. She clicked a few times and a new welcome screen appeared.

I got a feeling this winter's going to be high impact, Angie said. Something's coming. She wrote out a bunch of numbers and letters on a scrap of paper and handed it to me. There's your password. You change it to something private. Go ahead, I'm not looking.

She pushed back slightly and let me lean into the blank screen. I went through the motions of password modification and hit Login. The search window opened up black and wide and empty. A bright green cursor blinked at me, waiting.

Okay, Angie said. What do you wanna know?

You want me to ask it a question?

It runs on keywords. Just throw in a few words, like a library search.

Angie Cavallo, I typed. *Toronto Free Press Date Of Birth.*

Good luck, she said. I don't release that information.

The screen filled and scrolled down fast, a block of green text.

The hell you don't, I said. What is all this? The list rushed down, screen after screen. What the fuck is going on? I said.

Here, Angie said. Hit some buttons. Hit the F-buttons.

Which one?

I don't know. Just keep hitting them till something works.

The screen froze.

```
FEBRUARY 8 1993: Angie Cavallo: Bell rate hike off the
    mark
FEBRUARY 3 1993: Angie Cavallo: These ladies don't
    speak for me
FEBRUARY 1 1993: Angie Cavallo: Job starts up: get
    back to work
JANUARY 29 1993: Angie Cavallo: Hard times at Toronto
    High for teachers' union
JANUARY 27 1993: Angie Cavallo: Shame-faced smokers?
    We're not gonna take it
```

JANUARY 25 1993: Angie Cavallo: Let cops get the job done
JANUARY 21 1993: Angie Cavallo: Windy City parents
   strong-arm school

See? Angie said. It's just the column. Nice try.

I looked at my hands on the keyboard. I had an old desktop in my kitchen that I'd used for school assignments, but no one was on-line in a big way. The Internet was something you read about, or wrote about, in the newspaper. David talked about bulletin boards sometimes and it's true that I'd been given an e-mail address at the paper; they even paid for dial-up service so that I could check it from home, but I almost never did. Mostly people used a fax machine.

How do I start over?

Angie leaned over me and pressed F10 down hard. Nothing happened. She hit it staccato about thirty times in a row.

Really? I said. This is how you're doing research?

Angie leaned harder on the F10. She put some shoulder in it. The screen stayed frozen.

Vaffancul, she said.

The big door swung open and Vinh walked in.

Look who's here! I said.

He moved with a hunch to his neck, like someone who spends too much time sitting down. I gave him a big smile and he glanced over one shoulder to see if someone else had walked in right behind him, undetected. Someone I would normally smile at.

What do you know about computers? I said.

I got a thing I forgot to file, Vinh said. He waved a box of film at us, then dropped down into his wheelchair and pushed himself across the room to the stacks. We sat and watched him file the item and spin the chair back toward the door.

Don't run away, Angie said. You know how to fix this?

What'd you do? Crash? Vinh rolled over slowly, his hands on the push-rims of the chair.

It's frozen, I said.

Man, you crashed on a search? You probably broke the Internet!

He reached around to the back of the machine and turned it off and then on again. The hum came up, and the pale blue Windows logo. Vinh got up from the wheelchair.

What would you ladies do without me?

Where do I log on again? I said. I pointed at Vinh: Shut up, I'm not asking you.

I'm gonna stay and watch, Vinh said. He came in close behind me, his elbow hard on my shoulder until I shrugged him off. He had one arm on either side of me, fighting for keyboard space.

What's your password? he said.

Fuck off.

For real, you want to log on or what?

I tried to move my body in such a way that he couldn't see what I was typing.

E-V-I-E? That's what you came up with?

I opened the Nexis window. The cursor blinked at me.

What about like this, I said. *Angie Cavallo editor years old*.

Put a search limit on, Vinh said. So she's the subject, not the author. Right there. See? There.

You still on this? Angie said. Five bucks says you get nothing.

Except when it doesn't, I said. Except when five bucks says: Here you go, Evie.

The screen expanded to show a small list, still green-on-black:

```
NEXIS SEARCH: SUBJECT, ANGIE CAVALLO EDITOR YEARS OLD
MAY 31 1992: Free Press takes home production awards,
   writers prize
MAY 5 1992: Free Press columnists Cavallo, Perry get
   nod on award list
```

Did you win last year? I said. No, wait. Don't spoil it for me. I hit the arrows on the keyboard until the entry for May 31, 1992, lit up, reversing to show black type on a small, green, highlighted field.

And go, I said.

FREE PRESS, MAY 31, 1992

Free Press staffers went home happy last night after the National Newspaper Awards ceremony, with production teams earning top marks for Special Project and Presentation, and news editor Angie Cavallo walking away with a Gold Award in the Column category. A self-described "lifer," 55-year-old Cavallo has been working the news beat at the *Free Press* for more than 30 years. This is her seventh NNA win and her twelfth nomination.

I could get used to this, I said.

Fifty-five! Vinh said. Shit, Angie, you're looking okay. You still get laid? He gestured to his chair with one hand. You want the wheelchair, you go ahead and use it anytime you like.

You want me to get laid in your wheelchair? Angie said. That's so sweet. Now fuck off back to the newsroom.

The door shut behind him and I started a new search.

Look, Ma, I said. And I'm not even crashing the system.

Of all the guys to help you out, Angie said. That guy's a pig. I don't like to give him an inch.

He's only got an inch, I said. Maybe two.

I typed new parameters into the search window: *Vinh Nguyen public masturbation.*

Atta girl, Angie said.

Nothing? I said. Impossible.

I got up and threw myself into the wheelchair to get it rolling.

Okay, Angie said. School's out. You still need to come down here sometimes. You want images, you want context, this is still your best bet.

Whew, I said. It's pretty glamorous here in the basement. I pushed back with my feet and the chair took me rocketing backward ten feet or so. I'd hate to give all this up.

CHAPTER 4

David and I came busting down the street toward home. He'd come to pick me up after my day in the archives and now we were waving our arms in the air and arguing. Houses in my part of town are old and most of them were split up into apartments or rooming houses at one time or another. If you take a walk around inside any of them you'll find they've all been altered the same ways: stairwells capped off and ceilings lowered to save on heating costs. So where there were these gorgeous fourteen-foot ceilings, now you've got cardboard ceiling tiles at maybe eight feet. Keeps you warm but makes for poor circulation, and you can tell by looking at the size of the icicles hanging from every eave. Broad-based and dripping.

It was the icicles that got us going. We were arguing about the state of the Earth.

It's not worse, I said. You just don't remember. When I was nine there was a thaw every year in January and again in February. Now-ish, I said. We'd throw our jackets on the stairs and skip rope at recess. There was no ice. We were sweating, I said.

Nah, David said. That was his whole argument. Two weeks ago when we were snowed in you told me *that* was normal for February, he said.

Because it's *February,* I said.

The gutters were running. I had a pair of red-striped mittens in one hand and I took off my hat and shoved them inside so I'd have less to carry. We'd been raiding the cash-and-carry line up at Hikers Anonymous, and I had two chocolate-mint PowerBars jammed in my pocket. David had a flask of Wild Turkey and we were doing a fine job taking turns with it. We walked down through the High Park zoo, breaking off chunks of the bars and feeding the animals. It's true that for a llama, or even a yak, chocolate mint is not as natural a food source as peanut butter flavor might have been. Beggars can't be choosers.

We took a left at the Queensway and wandered up to where it turns into Queen Street proper. The light was all behind us now. There was a fried chicken shop run by Jamaicans at the bottom of Roncesvalles and a few junk stores that sold antiques but only the chicken place was open. The sun was heading west to the suburbs and beyond. Around the corner from my house there was a parkette with a little bench and an old grocery cart with its wheels stuck in the slushy mud. I pulled it out and told David to hop in.

I'm too heavy for you.

Who you calling a weakling, weakling? I said.

I threw down the hat-and-mitts combo I'd been carrying around and braced myself against the cart handle. David climbed over the bottom end. I had to bear down with all my weight to keep the thing from tipping but once he was in I got him going okay.

We're on a downslope! I yelled. Jesus, I hope I don't let go!

Okay, now turn around and go back up, David said. Repeat! Repeat! A hundred push-ups!

I swung hard on the cart handle to turn it around but the weight was too much and it threw the whole thing off-kilter. The cart went over fast. David just lay there on the sidewalk with his eyes closed.

Are you dead? I said. I couldn't breathe.

You're laughing! David said. My head is cracked! You cracked my head. Stop laughing. I'm dead now and this is sad.

He got up and I made a big fuss of brushing the old road salt off his peacoat.

Too late, David said. I know what you're made of. He ran a hand down through my hair and left it there a moment, his fingers resting against my neck and shoulder. I focused on his ear to avoid eye contact. I could see the edge of my house just to the right of him, out of the corner of my eye. There was a row of spindly cedars along the fence line and they shook slightly.

Wait, I said. What's that.

What?

There's someone there. I stepped back and away from David. Just there. I pointed to where the fence disappeared into the backyard. Some guy. Like a homeless guy or something. He went in behind the trees there.

That's wind. David put his hand up and caught a few drops of water coming off the overhead maple. There's a breeze, he said. See?

The temperature dropped overnight. In the morning I stood in the bathroom pushing Tylenol down my throat and swallowing hard. The icicles had regained their shape and hung sharp in front of the window. I left for the newsroom and almost tripped over my hat on the way out. It was lying on the outer doorstep, soaked through and frozen. I remembered throwing them all down in the park, close by, when it was so warm the day before: the hat and the striped mittens. Had I picked them up again? The mittens weren't there. I put the hat inside on a rad to dry and sank my hands deep into my pockets for the walk to the streetcar.

The *Free Press* building is down near the bottom of Yonge Street, which means a fifteen-minute ride on the King car for me to get to work on a good day. The sidewalks had frozen over again so quickly that between my house and the streetcar stop I could skate along on my boot soles, and I did. On the way in, we stopped at University and a pregnant woman ran for the car and slid. She fell flat out on her belly and I watched from my seat as a couple of nice-looking old men helped her up. She got on the streetcar and sat across from me with both hands clutching her stomach and a look of quiet terror.

O kay—so is *this* February weather now?
 I'd called David from my desk.

It's not better, he said. It's not because it keeps changing. Do you get it? The ground needs to freeze and stay frozen.

Or thaw and stay thawed, I said. That's my vote. Are you still tree-climbing this summer?

A few years earlier he'd spent a summer in Junior Rangers planting trees. With the encroaching pressure from his mother around A Sensible Business Degree: Why David Should Get One, he'd been looking at escaping the city for another forestry gig come spring.

I can pick up a firefighting contract, he said. Wildfires. They fly you in via helicopter.

Where?

Northern Quebec. Or else Labrador.

I was quiet for a minute.

I'd still live in camp, he said. But the money's way better. Wanna come plant trees? Take a break from the Don Jail Daily?

I didn't answer that, either.

Hey, I said. I found the hat. Thanks.

What hat?

My hat. I left my hat and mittens at the park before I tried to grocery-kill you. Remember? You left the hat at my doorstep? But no mittens. Or else someone took them.

Not me, David said. I mean, I didn't leave you anything.

I could hear him turn on the kitchen tap on his end of the line. The rush of water hitting the bottom of the steel sink and the change in pressure when he switched the faucet to spray.

That's weird then, I said.

Nah, anyone will do that. Put the hat at the closest doorstep.

Like when you're out walking and someone's hung a baby shoe they found up on the fence, or on a fire hydrant or something. He was banging around the kitchen, dropping cutlery into a drawer with more cutlery already inside. Maybe you lost it right in front of the house, he said. Lucky.

Are you making breakfast still? I said. It's like one o'clock. I've been at work for five hours.

Think about the summer, David said. Working vacation. Write an exposé.

What if I'm urgently needed at the Don Jail?

I figure I'm irresistible in uniform, David said. But don't worry. I'll fight you off.

I came home balancing a tray of leftover muffins and white-bread sandwiches from a meeting I hadn't even gone to. The muffins had been left in the little kitchen on my floor at work. They had a clear plastic dome for a lid that clicked soundly into place. I thought that in itself was worth the price of admission on claiming the leftovers.

When I was a Girl Guide as a kid, we had this trick of weighing down our camping hats with those little plastic tags that seal up bags of bread from the grocery store. Not twist ties. We all saved those bread tags and clipped them up along the edge of our hats, fifty or sixty of them at a time, so that the wind couldn't blow the hats away. Today if I see a bread tag lying in the street, it's everything I can do not to lean down and pick it up and bring it home. There's a part of my brain that just kicks in. They're very useful. So I have a long and resolute history when it comes to collecting garbage. When I'm old, little children will see me coming and say, Here comes Crazy Bread Tag Lady.

I came into the kitchen and set my new muffin dome down on the table and switched on the light. Something red caught my eye, just outside the window on the fire escape. The color stood out against the ice. My red-striped mittens. They were laid out carefully, like an X. I cracked the lock on the emergency door and stepped outside. The temperature had fallen steadily all day. It was cool and slippery. The water from a long row of melting icicles had frozen slick on the landing. I held on to the rail and slid out to where the mittens were and brought them inside. They were dry and clean.

I think it's sweet, David said. He leaned his forehead against my kitchen window. You have a secret admirer.

It's creepy, I said.

It's just one of the guys upstairs. Where were they, he said. Just there?

Don't you think it's weird? I came over to the window but didn't lean as closely in. Looking at the fire escape made me want to keep my distance. Whoever found my mittens must have been watching us fool around in the park, I said. Then he watched to see what house I went into.

He didn't catch much action then, David said. Aside from my near-death. He pressed his hands against the glass and pushed backward. Maybe someone likes you, Evie. I mean, who wouldn't, right?

He had a way of holding his head down but looking up at me that sometimes made me want to jump up and down a little bit and sometimes just made me want to punch him.

That's the last thing I want to hear right now, I said.

I went over to the kitchen counter and opened up the cabinet. There were a few things sitting in the dish rack in the sink and I started stacking them up, pulling the plates and cups out of the rack and setting them in the cupboard. I turned back to David.

Then this guy waits a whole day to climb up onto my fire escape and leave them there in the creepiest way possible? Why not put them in the mailbox? Or leave them in the doorway with the hat? Or—now get this—how about ring the doorbell?

David turned around and put a hand on my shoulder.

Look, he said. It's definitely one of the guys upstairs. Why don't you ask them?

I pulled the mittens onto my hands and looked down at them. They'd been lost on a wet day. I opened my mouth to tell David what I thought, that they looked so clean when I found them, laid out like a gift. Like someone had washed them for me. I splayed the thumbs in and out. My hands looked like Pac-Man's hungry mouth.

I don't want to encourage anybody, I said.

CHAPTER 5

Your standard workday as low-man at a daily newspaper is engineered to start early and end late. This inspires loyalty. It's like Stockholm syndrome. Get ready to be there for fourteen hours, even if you're only scheduled for half a shift. Even if at first glance it looks like the world's easiest day, and actually you're just dropping by to pick up your paycheck before you go to your friend's cottage for the weekend. There are too many variables. Who can say what will happen next?

I controlled this aspect by showing up later than I should. I got up the next day and put on my weird, clean mittens and then took them off again and shoved them into my bag. In case sometime later the cold made me really desperate. Most days, Angie was too busy with her own stuff to come looking for me until around ten, so it was safe enough if I rolled in by that time; anyway, part of the reporter beat is to know the city. She'd told me that herself: Walk everywhere, learn the neighborhoods, pay attention. Get to know the local zoo—hookers, junkies, everybody. Hookers and junkies, especially.

It was a nice enough day and I zigzagged to work, walking up along Dundas and then through Kensington Market. I bought a sugary cappuccino in a Styrofoam cup from the corner shop, figuring I could drink it out in the bracing freshness of February and wander back down Spadina. It was cold but not impossible. I wondered if it would be worse to sit out on a park bench or on the frozen sidewalk. When I was a kid my mother was convinced that sitting on a cold sidewalk would give you a kidney infection. I was the only child standing up through the whole Santa Claus parade. Everyone else sat on the curb.

The sidewalk in Kensington is filthy in any season. On Baldwin Street a few stragglers emptied out of a second-floor booze can, a dark-haired woman in jeans and army boots wearing a full-length fur coat and dragging her boyfriend along behind her. The boyfriend was heavy-eyed. He had a cadet's cap on his head and a professional coat of pink lipstick across his mouth. Short, light blond hair stuck out straight from under the hat and at the back of his neck. He had a Russian look that suited him and the woman grabbed his cap and refused to give it back until he kissed her. It was 9:00 a.m. A good time had by all.

I'd been inside the same after-hours club a few times in the past year. Once to report on a shooting and a couple of other times as a patron. There's an inherent drinking culture that the *Free Press* has in common with all other news sources on the planet. That's another loyalty and/or hostage thing and it's easy to get caught up, especially when you're all on deadline and it's been a long week. Or even just a long day. It's after midnight and you're jacked on cheap coffee and hours of closely examining the worst that humanity has to offer. The impulse is to break out of the bunker. With your compatriots, of course. By now they're the only ones who could possibly understand you anyway. Which is fine and good if you're a 180-pound guy who can hold his liquor, but some of us lady journalists need to take it easy. It's possible to forget that part. All of this tightens the knot. Less like a job and more like the best, most secret club you could belong to. You think you're a grown-up but life turns out to be high school with money.

There's another way into journalism, which is to take a better reporting job at a smaller paper. David and I have talked about this, and that's why he thinks it's a good idea to dangle Labrador in front of my nose. Where I'm "with files from" in Toronto, I could jump to writing editorials and features in an outport town.

Except features on what? I said. Bears versus campers? Moose collisions?

I'll have you know that moose are a really serious problem, David said. He cited several instances of moose-related drama from his tree-planting experience. And don't even get me started on bears. A good bear attack? That's worth at least three street corner drug busts. Take a look at the inside of a bear's jaws. Have you ever seen a bear chase something down? Those fuckers are fast.

Part of his vehemence had to do with saving me from myself, working this job that pushed trauma up under my nose every day. Saving my heart, he called it. The other part had to do with the fact that David knew me well enough to wonder where the work might take me. Geographically, I mean. So that part was really about saving his own heart, and we didn't talk about it.

We've spent a lot of energy being friends. I've baked cupcakes on David's birthday every year since he turned fifteen. I'm lousy at it but there's a secret. You put marshmallow fluff in the frosting. The frosting is basically fluff, with chocolate or cherry syrup added in for color and whatnot. That's the whole key right there: not the kind of ingredient you'd ever expect, but it makes all the difference in the world.

I make the cupcakes because David's mother melts down every year on his birthday. I don't know if this is a thing she also did when he was small and his father was still in the picture, or if it has something to do with the fission of his nuclear family. One time we walked in after school and found his mother wearing the same aerobics outfit she'd put on first thing in the morning, maniacally doing jumping jacks and sobbing in front of the television in the basement. She'd spent an entire day doing exercise videos, one after another after another. I was in the tenth grade, David was in eighth, and Graham Patton had been gone for six months. That's why I relate her craziness to the family breakdown, although it's possible

I'd just grown old enough to pay attention. Who knows how many other days she'd driven herself into the ground?

David knows the blast is coming. He's helpless to stop it. This is because it comes in the form of a perfection explosion and any insinuation that her efforts do not, in fact, equal perfection feeds right back into the cycle. How do you ask someone to stop being so damn nice to you? The explosions aren't limited to birthdays, but it's the special times that really shine in a person's memory.

I used to go and ride out the birthday dinner with David, to keep him company. His mother spends three days planning some elaborate meal: duck à l'orange or nasi goreng, sheer white Pavlova with a candle stuck fast in the heart-shaped meringue. By the time dinner rolls around, she's so worked up about calories and fat grams and whether or not this will be David's favorite day on Earth ever, she can't even swallow. She sits through the entire meal, watching David try to eat and apologizing.

I'm sorry. I'm so sorry, is it good? I made this for you. I'm so sorry. I don't want to draw attention to myself. You eat, just eat. Is it good?

Like that. With more wine and crying.

The last time I was at the table was a couple of years ago. David tried to give her an out: You don't have to go to all this trouble. If it upsets you. Why bother?

He meant this in the best possible way. He meant, Why do this to yourself? But also, Why do this in my name?

The Why bother? put her over the edge.

You're right, she said. You're right why bother. Why bother?

The next moment her plate was flying against the kitchen wall. This was so sudden. I'd never seen her throw anything. I'd never seen her throw a ball in the park. The plate bounced and smashed on the tile floor. She grabbed David's plate and then mine, one after another. David jumped up and tried to hold her down, hold her shoulders. Every wood spindle of the back of my chair pressed hard into my spine. Duck skin and sticky sauce everywhere, and his mother in disaster mode, wailing. You do a thing that can't be undone and it's devastating.

After that, he asked me to skip the dinner. He comes over later, or else I show up there, once his mother is sleeping. Nothing special. What David actually wants is a quiet, pleasant marker of his aging process. He probably actually wants nothing but I can't bear it. Enter Evie and her fluff cupcake.

David has a way with his mother, where he can get her calmed down if they're alone.

No one's angry, no one's mad. You're okay. It's okay. His hand against her forehead, smoothing back her hair. You can see why he wants to disappear, to go off and fight fires in the Labrador woods. I've seen him feed her, one bite at a time, off his own plate.

I crossed College and walked up Brunswick Avenue—the street my own mother lived on when she first came to the city and met my dad. As far as the local zoo is concerned, Brunswick is pretty centrally located. I've heard a lot of stories about that time, and now that we were neighbors, in a time-warp kind of way, I was surprised at how often I found myself on her street. I walked by the house all the time, heading to the market or work or up to Bloor Street or whatever. Her third house in the city, technically, but the first two were hostels and didn't last. There was an industrial building on the corner and her house, number 102, was the next place beyond that, attached on one side to the house next door.

There's a parkette there, too, on the corner at Ulster, rimmed on two sides with that old-style, black-painted iron fencing. Waist-high. It's got a playground at one end and a cement wading pool at the other—the same kind we had at my public school when I was a kid. The water pours out a giant tap in the middle of the pool, and the cement slopes down on all sides into the center. This makes entering the water nice and gradual, like a concrete beach, or a giant version of those European shower stalls that have no doors. It's like a massive foot bath. I found a free bench down closer to the playground. The bench was cold enough to make my kidneys feel prematurely troubled.

Brunswick isn't a bad street these days, but I could still see two condoms in the gutter from where I was sitting, and I wouldn't recommend walking through the sandpit in your bare feet unless you're looking for an easy path to communicable disease. Stepping Stones to Hepatitis: A Visit to Margaret Fairley Park.

You go out of your way to become a respected writer, and they name a park after you in a neighborhood of addicts.

There were two girls in the playground, both under six. The bigger one was a master at the monkey bars. She whipped back and forth, skinny legs kicking momentum. Her hands were red from the cold of the bars. The smaller one was named Jenny and she just sat under the jungle gym and cried. Sometimes the sister's legs accidentally kicked her as they went by and then she cried louder. Jenny and her gymnast sister had a fat white mother waiting for them on the opposite bench, smoking a cigarette and wearing a black *Dirty Dancing* sweatshirt under a hooded parka. She had a purple bandana around her neck. In the frozen sandpit there was a blond baby in a puffy green snowsuit staggering around with a Filipina nanny holding on to her two hands at all times.

So that's reflective of what you've got down there: rows of town houses, some of them painted, mainly concrete steps and porches, some of them still operating as rooming houses and some of them occupied by lawyers with pagers and landscape architects. And nannies.

I left my empty cup on the bench and crossed over to have a little walk around. When I looked back, Jenny had left her spot under the monkey bars and was using my coffee cup as a snow scoop. She was making a row of tiny castles, like we were at the beach and this was hot summertime.

Brunswick was as permanent as it got for my mother, until she hooked up with my dad. Her old house bordered on an alley that ran along behind Ulster Street. There was a rooming-house look to it. It probably had four bedrooms. You could fit twenty-five homeless kids in a house that size, on floor mattresses. Maybe it's just that moving out on my own had made it more comfortable for me to like her. Or to find her intriguing, as a human. That happens. I'd never given the place a second thought when I was younger, but now if I was walking by, I tried to picture my mother, seventeen and standing on the porch with a kerchief tied around her hair.

I knew she used to clean houses for money, no contract, just under-the-table cash. She'd worked out a deal with a guy named Nathan Laskin who ran some frat houses and unofficial residences for professional students at U of T: Xi Psi Phi for dentists, Phi Delta Phi for lawyers, Alpha Epsilon Pi for Jews. This was when fraternities were respectable and not just drug nests. Or, at least, not known to be drug nests.

Nathan had made a deal with whoever was supposed to actually be in charge of fraternity administration. He was basically a subcontractor. This allowed him to avoid the bureaucratic nightmare of official hiring and wage policies. It also allowed him to cut corners and save a few bucks here or there, by feeding cheap pork liver to the orthodox guys and saying it was beef, or hiring teenaged girls to keep house and clean toilets. Enter my mother and her dust cloth.

To hear my mother tell it, Nathan Laskin was practically a savior, because while the rest of her roommates were out panhandling or stealing fifty-cent items from Honest Ed for resale on the corner, she'd get up every afternoon and go clean Victorian houses in the nicest part of town. The frat houses were shit holes, of course, being occupied by a bunch of young guys who'd never learned to pick their own underwear off the floor, but it kept her from turning tricks, which it's been suggested is how the other girls were making a living. I'm sure Nathan Laskin made a few offers of that variety, but my mother was okay to proceed without a wage increase, so they stuck to the original terms.

Living in that place was more or less a refugee culture. None of the kids who slept there were from the city, and all of them came from situations that needed escaping. Most of them were from the suburbs, Scarborough or Milton, although there were a few from as far up as Barrie and Midland. My mother was the only one from the way-north. She found the house by hanging around the bus station and other places lost kids go. She'd talk to anyone under twenty-one and see what they knew about Toronto.

When you're living with a bunch of beggars and thieves, no one is taking care of themselves. The reason is a) no time for that and b) no one knows how, anyway. Sometimes when my mother tells her stories, the Brunswick house seems filled with artistry and a kind of familial solidarity. She's also referred to it as a rat's nest. She paid the extra ten bucks a month to sleep up high, away from the cockroaches, but also away from the other rats.

She lived there a year. The guy who took the rent money made her nervous.

Something wrong with him, my mother said. At first we just thought he smoked too much pot. He stared at you too hard if you talked to him. He had a smile that made him look slow-minded.

But he wasn't, she said. He had a devious intelligence.

This is the thing with collecting housemates at the bus station. You get all kinds. There's no good sorting method.

He'd catch mice in glue traps and play with them like a cat.

Some of the other girls had stories, my mother said. You didn't want to be in the house with him. Once I walked into the kitchen and he was in there, alone. He had a mouse glued down and he stepped on it, one limb at a time. Listening to it scream.

It took her a long time to make enough money to leave.

So my mother woke up every day as early as she could and got dressed and left before anyone else was even awake. The frats were generally up around St. George and Bloor, which is about a ten-to-fifteen minute walk, depending on the length of your stride. She walked up there and ate some breakfast out of the frat house fridge and then got going on scrubbing and washing things. She did one house every day, six days a week. On the seventh day, she sat in a coffeehouse all day and ate chocolate cake for lunch.

Being young and living like that, you don't have a lot of the things that other teenagers have. I'm not talking about bicycles and record players so much as the other stuff, the things your mom looks after for you, like doctor's appointments and green vegetables and the right kind of coat for wintertime. Soft mittens.

So one day my mother wakes up sore and can't pee, and she's afraid to tell any of her friends because they'll just say she has syphilis, which she knows for a fact is flat-out impossible. Almost impossible. She gets up and goes to work anyway, and every day, it gets just a little bit worse. Seventeen is an optimistic and powerless age. You think you'll be walking down the street one day and Richard Avedon will jump out with his camera and discover you. The lottery is like a life plan you've put on hold, until you have a spare buck to buy your winning ticket. Things are good or bad, sure. But more than that, they're inevitable. If something hurts, you just let it hurt. You wait for it to go away, because what else is there to do?

Then one day she's at Xi Psi Phi, scraping out the sink with Old Dutch and she has to pee, and what she pees is blood.

I don't know if it's because I was sick, or because of the sight of that blood, she said. I fell over. Right there in the bathroom. Out cold.

And that's where my father the dental student comes in and finds her and figures out that she needs some antibiotics. Her kidneys were infected, and those things turn nasty if you don't treat them.

What are the chances of a nice dental student falling for a teenaged maid? My father was from the other side of the country and his own mother had died when he was a kid. There was no opportunity for mother-in-law-type disapproval. Lucky for me. They got married in six weeks.

I turned and walked back through the park, in part so I could check in on Jenny and the snow castles. Her sister had come off the monkey bars and they were making cakes and pies, using tiny icicles for the candles. It was a careful endeavor and they whispered instructions back and forth. I gave the tops of my legs a rub and my brain a little dead-girl pep talk. The other reason I was stalling about going in to work. The baby and her nanny had left the park a few minutes earlier. The girls' mother was asleep on her bench. A pocket full of candy says I could have walked off with the two of them, Jenny and her sister, in a heartbeat. Because that's how it happens. You just need one adult to look away, and another one to look too closely.

CHAPTER 6

Someone had left a bag of equipment sitting all over my desk.
I unzipped the bag and found a Pentax 35mm with a strap
and a few other technical items I wasn't sure of. A light meter,
maybe. A battery charger. I cracked a black plastic oval open and
found it full of tiny canisters of film. Next to the bag there was a
yellow sticky note with Angie's writing on it: Where the hell are
you?

I walked into her office.

I've been doing some thinking, I said.

Think in the newsroom, Angie said. At nine in the morning
like they pay you for. She had her head down in the previous day's
A-section. I waved the camera bag.

What's all this?

It's for your dead girls, she said. On your way home, swing up
and take a few shots of gravestones. See if you can find someone
relevant.

I do everything around here.

We could use a stock photo, she said. But my impression is you
like fresh air. Plus you may as well learn to operate the thing. Sometimes you got no choice. It's a bugger if you can't take a basic photo
without fucking it up.

I can take a photo, I said. Are you sure that's what you want?
You want a close-up of some little kid's grave from back when she

was murdered? I weighed my hands back and forth like they were scales. Maybe a big establishing shot of a bunch of graves, I said.

Angie looked up from her postmortem. Nah, she said. I want something specific. Your job isn't establishing shots. Go break someone's heart. Go break my heart with gravestones. Little murdered kid gravestones. *Capisce?*

Sheesh, I said. Ca-peesh. I slung the strap of the camera bag over one shoulder like a pro. See what I did there? I said. The magic of rhyme, right to your doorstep. I'm like a treasure, Angie. I'm pure rhyming diamonds.

She had her head down in the paper again and didn't offer any opinions pro or contra my rhyme value. I called David from my desk.

How would you like to spend an affable afternoon at the cemetery? I said.

Mount Pleasant Cemetery is really close to the house where I grew up. It's a place kids go to fool around. Lianne and I had used the trails as bike paths, which is odd to think of, given everything that happened later. When you're in high school, kids jump the fence and go in there to make out, or smoke pot, or just to feel cool being in the cemetery at midnight, and I did those things, too. In a studied way.

I walked down from Davisville Station and stopped in front of the gates to wait for David to show up. There was a No Loitering sign on the fence and I tried to strike the best loitering-type pose I could think of, leaning up against an electrical pole. Like the cemetery was a fancy house and I was casing the joint. The camera bag was cutting hard into my shoulder and I put it down at my feet. I had a handful of lily of the valley that I'd picked up from the subway florist for no reason. Except that walking into a graveyard with a camera and an assignment, looking only to take something away, was mercenary.

Whatever trick I'd pulled on my own mind in high school had worked. I realized that I hadn't thought of Mount Pleasant as a place for dead people for a long time. It was part of the neighborhood, like the Dominion store or Maurice Cody school or the Barmaid's Arms. Lianne may as well have been buried in a different city. I didn't remember any trees or grass or anything the day they buried her. I remembered it white and plain, as if it were wintertime, even though I know her funeral was in June and there was sun and it must have been warm because I hadn't worn any stockings.

In the year or so immediately afterward I always wanted to go to the cemetery and bring flowers and say prayers. My mother said I was morbid. I wasn't. It was more like a deal you make with God. If you do everything right, all the time, you're protected. Nothing bad can happen to you.

I knew that there were certain expectations placed upon a sad person. Bringing a flower to your dead friend seemed no different to me than bowing your head when you touched your grandmother's rosary: something that looked great, but you didn't have to think too much about. I didn't have a grandmother, of course, but Cecilia Chan's grandmother kept her rosary in a dresser drawer that was crammed with Oil of Olay and costume jewelry. She lived in the back room at Cecilia's house. While I handled the beads I took stock of myself in her vanity mirror. I liked to look very pious. Cecilia taught me the Lord's Prayer and the Nicene Creed and parts of the Hail Mary. I wore big clip-on imitation pearl earrings when I prayed, and asked Mary to make Cecilia's grandmother give me her white cold cream to smooth over my cheeks.

I brought a hand to my own cold cheek, remembering this, and then there was someone beside me.

Hey.

He touched my shoulder and I jumped back. David.

You okay? I said hello like three times.

I said I was. Okay, I mean.

Daydreamy, he said. He motioned toward the flowers. Nice touch.

I picked up the camera bag.

Let's go, I said.

There's close to no point trying to find a grave in winter. That bears mentioning. Everything is covered up. The snow kills all the flowers people leave. But there we were, anyway. Doing the right things.

The cemetery office is near the Mount Pleasant entrance, inside the gates. They have maps of the whole place and about a million filing cabinets, so you can give them the name of someone who's buried there and they tell you the code number for their gravesite and mark your map with an X.

Lily of the valley, I told David. Because they'll be hardy in the snow. Don't you think?

There was a black-haired woman behind the counter and she had thin eyebrows and her blush had been put on with a sponge. She was wearing a blue blouse with one of those scarfy bows at the collar.

I'm trying to locate a few graves, I said. I went through my list out loud: Alison Parrott, Sharin' Keenan, Lizzie Tomlinson . . .

I figure in high season a cemetery clerk probably has to deal with about a hundred people every day.

In high school we used this place as a running route, David said. I guess lots of people do, hey? I realized he was talking to the clerk, not me. I stepped back.

You mean us? Like me and you?

You don't remember that? You used to steal my yellow sports Walkman and run up ahead and not talk to me.

Sort of?

I'm finding you weird right now, he said. He turned to the clerk: Don't worry about her, she takes me for granted all the time.

Har, I said. For real. This is something I wanted to do?

For real. We used to follow the paths all the way from Bayview up to Yonge Street. There's a lot to look at. All the big Chinese mausoleums, you know? Seriously, you don't remember this? You loved those things.

The clerk looked at me with her lip half-curled, but in a nice way. The way you smile at a little kid when they're being funny and they don't even know.

The jogging seemed vaguely familiar. And the mausoleums. They're all green and gray and raw looking, with lions outside them. I'd kind of forgotten.

The clerk leaned over the desk and handed me a map of the cemetery. Here, she said, drawing in a couple of X's in red pen. Can you find your way?

I didn't move, or say thank you or anything. David went over to the doorway and held it open, waiting.

Anything else? She had her red pen in hand, ready for action.

And Lianne Gagnon.

I hadn't planned on this, but as soon as I said Lianne's name the clerk gave me a nice smile and marked the map in a third spot. She didn't even have to look it up. People must come looking for murdered girls all the time.

Thanks, I said, turning back toward the door. David was half out already, with his hand up in the air like he was checking the weather.

Be careful, the clerk said.

I turned to look at her. She had her head down in a Rolodex of the dead, and didn't look like she'd said anything at all.

Landscaping-wise, a cemetery is just a big, gentle park. That's why kids like them. If this were a movie, right now we'd have a sunny moment of children bike riding up the path, between the grass and the tombstones. The music would be a little off. Or else it would just be happy music, but with the sound of bees mixed in really low to give you a feeling of dread like in *The Exorcist*.

Lianne and I used to play all kinds of places that weren't for playing in. We climbed the crab apple trees in the Bethel Baptist churchyard after Girl Guides. The church was across the road from Cecilia Chan's house. Her sheepdog, Dusty, raced around scaring the other girls while Lianne and I scraped our legs up sitting in the branches. We made Heather Bowman stand guard under the tree. We were climbing in our blue uniform dresses and didn't want anyone coming along and looking at our underwear.

We walked along the tops of the garages in the alley behind Lianne's house, and lit matches up there when we could get them. The garage roofs were all shingled with tar. It was a soft, warm place to sit in the summertime. When you got up, you had black smudges all over your fingers and on the bum of your shorts. Lianne said if we held our hands against the hot tar for long enough, our fingerprints would burn smooth. You could commit any crime and never get caught.

My parents thought Lianne's family were a bunch of hippies. In the first grade, she came to school on picture day with a rip in her pink nylons and the teacher told her she looked like a welfare kid. Doesn't your mother have any clean clothes for you? She had three brothers and a baby sister and when you went to her house, there was always old food and plates on the kitchen counter, like they were all in the middle of making dinner when a tornado warning happened and everyone had to go sit in the bathtub. Her parents were the superintendents of a nice low-rise, which gave them free rent. The kids shared the bedrooms and the parents slept on a pullout couch in the living room. All the boys in her family were named after famous cowboys: Jesse, Cody, and Wyatt. Lianne said, Why didn't her parents give her a cool Old West name? Like Zerelda after Jesse James's mother, or Bonney, which was Billy the Kid's last name. The baby's name was Clementine. When she turned seven, Lianne had a sprinkler party. I wasn't allowed to go because my mother said no one would be watching us and we'd run out in the street and get smacked by a bus.

In the springtime, right before Lianne disappeared, her mom gave us her Bay card and told us to take the baby for a walk and buy ourselves cheeseburgers in the store cafeteria. We walked up Davisville to the subway and bumped the stroller down the stairs to the train platform. Downtown we used the credit card for lunch and tried on lacy bras and pretended we were teen moms. At my house, I couldn't go into my own bedroom for longer than five minutes without someone knocking on the door and asking if I was okay.

David and I followed the curve of the road, taking turns pushing a fingertip against the map. There are no sidewalks in a cemetery and you don't need them. The gravestones bled into one another. David unpacked the camera and took pictures of whatever seemed oldest, or crumbling. We found the green lions and I posed against one, leaning back like I was Tawny Kitaen on a car hood and this was a music video instead of a graveyard on the coldest day of the year.

They shoot those videos when it's cold, David said. For the nipple action.

What, I said. What is that.

So the girl's nipples will stand out. It's strategic. There's a direct correlation between Tawny Kitaen's nipple definition and album sales. I'm pretty sure you can read the stats on this. There's pie charts, David said. He had the camera over one eye. It made him look squinty. I dropped my arms.

So some poor girl has to strip down and freeze her ass so her nipples can get guys off?

So her nipples can sell records, David said. Marketing. Now do that thing again.

I'm going to hell, I said. There was a white Mary Mother of Pietà shining her countenance down on me from the top of an Italian mausoleum. I pointed at her. There's a witness and everything, I said.

Swish your hair more. You were already going to hell anyway.

About five minutes later we finally found one of the girls on my list.

We done? David said. I'd taken a bunch of shots. We stood there a minute, looking down at the map. What's this other X? he said.

Lianne, I said. That X is Lianne. I just thought, I'm here, right?

I'd gone looking for Lianne's grave once before. Sometime before high school started, or before I set a premium on learning how to feel totally normal in the cemetery again.

Her area doesn't have the kind of tombstones that stand up straight so you can see them, I said. She's in the poverty section. The stones are all small and dull and lie flat on the ground and then the crabgrass and the weeds grow on top of them.

Okay, David said.

I remembered walking up and down the rows of markers and kicking at the grass around the stones, but none of the stones said the right thing.

No matter what I did, her name didn't show up, I said. It was like she'd disappeared. What kind of cemetery would move a little dead girl?

David looked pretty disappointed by all this.

I'm sorry, I said.

I get it, he said. It's like, when in Rome.

But Lianne's X was on the other side of cemetery. Not, as I had remembered it, down near the Bayview gate, but up in the opposite corner, closer to Moore, in the center of that other section.

Maybe they really did move her, David said.

Here, I said. I'll go back and ask. I'll run back to the office.

No, just wait, David said. I'll go. I'll be fast. Just wait here. He jogged off in the direction we'd come from.

I looked down at the map again and walked a little farther.

Hey! David called out. Hey, Evie! He'd stopped and turned back to look at me. Don't wander off, he said.

I'm sure you'll find me, I said. There was no one else around.

Helpful hint, I yelled back. I'll be the one moving around and breathing. Okay?

He looked a little skeptical.

Just don't go far.

In the year after she died, I used to dream I was visiting Lianne's grave. I was always there alone, wearing a white dress and my good sandals. Sometimes I just talked to her about everything that had happened and told her all my secrets, which made me feel really good, like she was the best friend I'll ever have. Sometimes I was just very quiet in the sunshine.

Off in one corner of the dream, there was a man. Half-behind a tree, watching me just as quietly.

I knew this man. He'd been there the day of Lianne's funeral. He'd watched me looking down into her casket at the church, and followed us to the cemetery. He saw me fall into her grave. I knew I couldn't stay in the cemetery for too long. He would push me into that grave hole and no one would pull me out.

I went a little farther around the bend in the roadway, toeing the edge of the grass line, or where grass would be if this were spring. My shoulder brushed up against a low-hanging branch and the whole tree lifted into the sky. A cloud of black starlings. Startled. They spread out thin as smoke and then curled again into a tight fist and settled in the forks of a new tree. It had been both snowing and windy. There was a two-inch layer of that glittery-light powder you get in February, with no footprints and no tire tracks. It could have been sand. It could have been sugar spilled across a table and it made the black trees look vulgar and lanky. I stopped moving and lifted my head. David was gone. I was somewhere in the center of the map, as far as you can be from either road. There weren't even traffic sounds.

Ahead of me was a field of eroded limestone statues, angels and saints. Tall white grave markers, broken down over time. Somewhere between them, something was moving. I froze for a second. The sway of a loping willow, hanging low between other branches and other trees. I tossed a quick look over my shoulder. Nobody. I turned back and the field of starlings rose up again, from within the willow this time, and fanned and turned with one body and then knotted themselves into a new shape. They were a whale and they were escaping a whale.

I thought of the clerk who'd marked my map so readily. As though people came looking for this one grave all the time. *Be careful.* Just ahead of me, at the edge of the path, a place where the snow was rippled. Rough ground or gravel underneath, or the marks of someone walking through, some time ago, now slurred by the low wind. Lianne's grave was somewhere in there, beyond the white statues.

I can help you.

A man, standing just to my left. Six feet away.

I jumped sideways. A security guard: uniform, badge, stick. I did the inventory in a practiced way, before I'd even had a chance to ask myself: Who? What? Safe?

Doing my rounds, the guard said. Are you lost?

I looked around to see where he'd come from. The mausoleums? Behind me just more graves, trees, the fence somewhere far off, beyond my view.

No, I said. I like the quiet here. His uniform was buttoned wrong, like he'd been in a hurry. I could see the rim of a white T-shirt under his collar. There was a security badge but nothing identifying him as belonging to the cemetery and it occurred to me that in winter the guards probably coasted around in a car.

I can help you, he said again. You looking for someone? Famous people in this cemetery: Billy Burch, Glenn Gould. I give tours on the side. Billy Burch, you know him? Hall of Famer. The guard had both hands in his jacket pockets and gestured down the pathway with his body, with one elbow and a shoulder.

Nah, I said. My boyfriend's grandfather is buried here. We

parked at the center. He just went back. He forgot his flowers in the car and went back to get them.

The guard flicked his chin at me.

Got your flowers right there, he said. I was still holding the lily of the valley. Why can I never just put flowers down on a grave?

He'll be back in a minute, I said. So. No tour.

I was betting on standing there until someone came along in a car. It was after four and the sky was already dull: another hour and there'd be no light left. The guard shrugged but didn't smile. He was tricky to place. Some people look like hard living.

I turned and walked back the way I'd come, slowly, using strong, long strides. I watched myself go, all the way toward Merton Street. When I got to the walkway tunnel that passes under Mount Pleasant Road, I turned and looked back. No one was there. If the guy was a guard, and the guard was on his rounds, he'd kept moving.

I walked back toward the visitor's center. There was a security vehicle behind the building, and two guards smoking cigarettes. One of them lifted a foot and stubbed out his butt on the bottom of his shoe.

A door opened and David came out of the building. I waited while he jogged over.

The gates are closing in about twenty minutes, he said. So we need to be fast.

No, I said.

What? We were almost there! X marks the spot, David said. He held the map out at me.

I think we don't want to get locked inside, I said. I wasn't looking at the map. I was watching the guards over next to the car. Did you get a look at those guards? I said.

Sure, David said. What about them?

They look okay to you? Security tag, photo ID? Up and up? I said.

Yeah, sure. David said. What about it? Big business, burying the dead.

I talked to one of them when you were gone.

One of those guys?

No, I said. No, some other guy. Didn't seem right to me.

It's a graveyard, David said. And it's getting dark. You spooked yourself. Here, he said. He took the camera bag off my shoulder. I'll sling your pack, Pancho.

We turned and walked up the main path to the road. It was rush hour. A steady stream of cars moved efficiently along, north from downtown, heading home. For a moment I watched us go. What we would look like, if someone else were watching. We went through the gate and then paced the whole length of the wrought-iron fence, south to Moore Avenue. I watched us just like the man in the cemetery dream had watched me. I watched my every move.

CHAPTER 7

I met David when he was only ten years old. You kind of have to keep that in mind. I've known him longer now than any of my girlfriends, aside from maybe Melissa. David took the babysitter thing really seriously in those days. He lay in the bottom bunk at night and conned me into reading three or four chapters of a book. Out loud. In some ways he acted a lot younger than he really was. He peeled back the covers and said, Why don't you get in, Evie? Like I was his mom. He said it in a really soft way that made me want to back out of the room slowly, before he could grab my wrist. One time my fingers started shaking and I actually had to get up and leave.

I didn't like the way he'd looked at me, like he wanted something. I didn't feel like a grown-up and I was supposed to be in charge. I wished I were tiny, so tiny that I could curl up like a hard snail shell and fit into my own pocket. I wished I were anywhere else.

I stood out in the hall for a while, waiting for David to fall asleep, but he didn't. He yelled: Hey! Are we finishing this story or what? When I went back in, I used my fingertips to draw an arc through the air, out from his shoulders to about six inches in front of my body.

David, I said. This is your umbrella space. Then I drew another arc out from my own body that stopped about six inches in front of him.

This is my umbrella space. You stay in your space and I stay in mine.

Do you know any ghost stories? David said.

I know about the Penetang Maniac, I said. I knew that one off by heart from Girl Guide camp. I know one about Hamilton Mountain, I said, and a guy with a hook for a hand and something about a car window.

Do you know the one about the babysitter? David was sitting up now, cross-legged, covers thrown back.

Is it lame? I said. I actually didn't want to hear a scary story about a babysitter. I hadn't liked the Penetang Maniac story when I first heard it and the last thing I wanted to do was get into this, alone in a strange house.

My friend told me this one, David said. Okay, so there's this girl, she's like thirteen and really pretty with skinny legs and long brown curly hair, and she's babysitting late at night.

He pulled a pillow into his lap and pressed down on it with his fists, hard.

The parents have gone away for a wedding, he said. They won't be back until the morning, but the girl is used to that, she stays overnight places sometimes. The baby is asleep on the third floor. The girl is in the kitchen getting some ice cream. There's a big storm outside, so she can't watch TV and it's really quiet in the house. There's just these big black windows all around the kitchen and living room.

David paused for a moment, like he was looking out through those windows. The house is an old farmhouse, he said, it's at the edge of the suburb, so outside the windows there are no other houses. Just fields and fields and sky. And then the lights go out.

He leaned out to switch off the light and I grabbed his hand.

Nope, I said.

David curled his hand up, away from mine, and flicked the switch. We sat quiet for a minute, our eyes adjusting. There was a thin blue linen curtain draped over his window and it let a sheen of streetlight through, plus the crack where the door to the lit-up hallway wasn't quite shut.

The phone rings, he said. And it's a high, high man's voice that says just one thing: Have you checked the children?

Umbrella space, I said. You're leaning.

So she hangs up the phone, because it's a crank caller. People do that when it's a stormy night. But then the phone rings again.

David stopped for a second, then twisted his face a little:

Have you checked the children?

I don't know this one, I said. I realized I'd grabbed his hand again and I was squeezing it in my own two hands, high up against my collarbone. I let go and the hand dropped down onto my knee.

Have you checked the children? And the phone keeps ringing, and it's always the same voice.

Quit it, I said.

David's voice got higher and louder. He sounded out of control. Have you checked the children? He was yelling now. So finally the girl is really mad and she calls the operator to report a crank caller. She tells the operator what's going on and the operator says, Hold on. I'll trace the call. And the girl hangs up.

David leaned back a moment and stared at me.

One minute later the operator calls her back. She says: Get out of the house. Get out of the house! The call is coming from the third floor.

What? I said. Oh, ew. Oh, yuck. Thanks for that. I wrung my hands like I could shake the story out of them. David just smiled a quiet smile, the kind with no teeth.

I got up and went downstairs. The Pattons didn't have a TV in their living room: it was down in the basement rec room. I opened the basement door and the stairs were dark and soundless and caked in soft pink shag. I closed the door again and sat on the couch instead. There were windows on both ends of the house but just a wall in front of me. I looked at the wall, at a painting of a boat on a moon-lit night, at the tall bookshelf. They didn't have a dog. There was a sound in the stairway, a creaking noise, but I couldn't tell if it was coming from the stairs above me or the ones down to the basement. I'd already decided the basement was bad news.

Have you checked the children?

David's feet on the stairs.

Don't do that! I said.

Evie? Did that really scare you? Did I really?

I'm all creeped out now, I said.

I can't sleep, he said.

You have to go back upstairs, I said. No. Wait.

Do I have to go back to bed?

I wish you had a TV here in this room.

David came the rest of the way down the stairs and stood on just the last one, looking at me and holding on to the railing with both hands.

Want some ice cream? he said.

There's no question that it was much, much nicer with another person in the room, even if that person was too small to help me in the event of a psychopath. David on the stairs made me stop thinking about a psychopath.

He scooped two bowls of ice cream and I combed through the records and put on Carly Simon and tried singing like I was having a great old time. I pointed at David: *I'll bet you think this song is about you.* He spun me around so I was singing to the black windows.

We sat down on the carpet in the living room with our backs against the couch.

I didn't think you'd really get scared, David said.

It's stupid, I said. It'll pass, I'm just being stupid.

Is it true your friend got killed? Evie?

Who told you that?

My dad says you're jumpy because your friend got killed.

I'm jumpy? I said. I mean, it's true. I was jumpy, but it's not the kind of thing you want other people thinking about you. You want other people to think you're super together all the time, and just be jumpy in a secret, private way.

My mom wants a different babysitter.

Your dad's a creepo, that's why, I said.

My cousin drowned when I was two, David said, that's why I have to do swimming lessons until I'm eighteen.

Well, my friend didn't get drowned, I said. Someone stole her off the street and killed her and left her body in a park.

The Penetang Maniac, David said.

No, I said. It wasn't. It was just a regular maniac and they never caught him. It was the Unknown Maniac. It was the Maniac Who Won.

David considered this a moment.

I hate getting in the car with your dad, I said. I wish my dad would come pick me up.

We sucked on our spoons. I thought about, How mad will his parents be to find David still awake when they get home? versus, How freaked will I be if I have to sit down here alone?

Am I going to get in trouble for letting you stay up late? I said.

We'll see the headlights, David said. I'll just run up when I see the headlights and pretend to be asleep. That way I don't have to see them. He stopped for a minute. Are you afraid of my dad? Is that what you mean, about getting in the car with him?

I'm not *afraid* of your dad. He's just creepy. He's always asking me stuff like we're pals.

It's okay if you are. My mom is. My mom's afraid of him. He makes her cry a lot. David had his eyes down and he scraped back and forth against the ice-cream bowl with his spoon.

My mom's not really a crier, I said.

Yeah. Your parents aren't like mine.

They fight, I said. I mustered up all my kindly babysitter tone for this. Everyone's parents fight sometimes.

Nah. Not like this. My dad does some stuff downstairs. David stopped for a moment. He takes pictures of girls, right? He says it's like a job. I'm not allowed to tell my mom but sometimes she finds out. They scream and scream at each other, like he's pulling her hair or something.

David had the spoon wrapped in his hand and he stabbed away inside the empty bowl and didn't look at me.

But he's not pulling her hair, right? I said. Not actually.

I thought of my own father, who was probably doing a crossword puzzle in front of the hockey game at home.

I don't know, David said. Sometimes he gets mad. I mean, I get hit. I guess just like any dad hits a kid. This one time he pushed my mother and she fell down the stairs, but he ran right down after her to make sure she was okay. David set the bowl down on the floor and it rolled to one side because the carpet was so soft.

I should stop him, he said. When he yells like that. My mother cries so hard. I should do something, but I just stay upstairs.

I'm sorry, I said. David looked up.

I'd save you, Evie, he said. If anyone ever tried to hurt you.

Even if they were pulling my hair? I flipped my bangs. I have extra nice hair, you know.

Especially that. David dropped the spoon and it clinked in the bowl. Except my hair might be nicer than yours. He shook his head around. Seriously, check it out.

I put my own empty bowl down on the carpet and leaned in.

The Penetang Maniac was up in jail at Penetanguishene, I said. He was in the part of the jail that's for the criminally insane. I heard this story when I was camping up near Midland, I said. So imagine we're out in a tent.

I can make us a tent, David said.

It doesn't matter. I picked up my spoon and held it out in front of me. He has a sharpened hook on one arm instead of a hand, I said. He can slice a tent open. After he escaped they found him in the woods, huddled over a deer, eating its guts raw. He had to lead them to the bodies. He'd chopped them up that small.

David sucked on his teeth. He was wearing pajamas with cars on them. I was wearing jeans and shoes inside the house, like a grown-up.

If you have to get into this kind of competition, you want to make sure you win.

Eventually even David's parents had to admit he was too old for me to be babysitting him. When he was twelve they split up. For a while he barely saw his father at all, but as David got older they started meeting up more often. Every now and then I'd hear about it: My dad called. I have to go drink my bimonthly lunch date.

We went to the same high school and David still hung out with me, but secretly. He came into the ninth grade when I was in eleventh. The first day of school he walked over and gave me a big smile, and I had to remind him that our friendship was more of a private-type friendship, and not a public-spaces type friendship.

At home, he'd double me on his bike up and down the alley and through the side streets. I sat on the seat and he stood on the pedals with his skinny body curved around me like a banana. David always made me feel like a kid, a real kid, not a my-friend-got-murdered kid. The bike swung back and forth across the road in wild zigzags and old ladies honked and swore at us. We crashed on the grass, on other people's front lawns. In a bush, once. Minor injuries. I was getting ready to apply to university.

Almost all the rest of the time I was pretending to be way older than I was. In the most basic ways I grew up anxious, with an anxious family. That makes it tempting to be a show-off and prove how brave you are all the time. This is how my mother has lived her whole life, like the best way to show you're not afraid is to pick the scariest situation and purposefully put yourself right in the middle of that. Then you can save yourself.

Compared to everything else around me, David was relief.

CHAPTER 8

What kind of psycho would assign you a research piece on little dead girls?

My mother had the long-handled garden spade in her hand and plunged it into the slushy ice lining the driveway, then stepped down on the edge of the blade to break it into chunks. I'd been telling her about LexisNexis and how my finger was now on the pulse of international happenings.

You're missing the point, I said. I can find out anything now. I'm like the ultimate snoop. I stomped some ice for her like I was Godzilla. I'm She-Ra of the News, I said. And I'm fine. Plus it's my job. Plus? I'm fine.

Your father worries about you.

Well, I said. It's a good thing you don't. Otherwise I'd have no one to talk to.

Grab a shovel, my mother said. There's a bottle of Baileys inside the house with my name on it. I'm willing to add yours, she said.

There are two kinds of snow shovelers in this world: meticulous, pickax shovelers like my mother, and then high-efficiency shovelers. My mother would be fine to stay out in the fresh air, working away for hours, so she uses a small shovel. The only other shovel my parents own is trademarked for maximum capacity. It's capable of moving upward of thirty liters of snow at a time. I mean, if you can find someone with the muscle to push it.

It's the Back-Breaker™.

My father's car was missing, leaving a bald patch in the snowy driveway.

I'll start there, I said.

He went in to deal with an emergency, my mother said. Six-year-old knocked his new tooth out ice-skating and your dad's yelling, Throw it in a glass of milk! Throw it in a glass of milk! And this poor woman is on the other end of the line. Milk? Milk? They never speak any English.

I gave a solid push to the mound of snow I'd collected and tried to heft it against the side of the path, next to the garden. The shovel flipped up to show its underbelly: frozen garden earth, some limp chives, a dead sparrow.

Bird, I said.

My mother came over for a peek.

Still got its head on, she said.

My parents own a cat that's famous for bird decapitation. You wake up with a chickadee's head next to you on your pillow, like the cat is some kind of sharp-nosed feline mafioso and this tiny bird is his way of calling in debts, the warning before he blows out your kneecaps. Once my mother found him with a goldfinch cornered in the back pantry. The finch had two broken wings but it was still alive, bobbing and weaving like a shaky Muhammad Ali fighting The Hulk.

She scooped the stiff little body up with her spade and moved it off the path, dropping it into the softer, fresh snow in the flower garden.

So who've you got, she said. She gave her shoulders a little stretch back. Her head tilted up toward the sky. Besides Lianne.

Lianne is old guard, I said. Lianne is from the time before. Toronto officially goes bad in 1983. Did you know that?

Long list?

I skim through, I said. I don't read the details. Names and dates and basics. I only read the stuff I need to report, I said.

Basics, she said. Just the facts. She took hold of the spade with both hands and shook the snow off it a little. Just the facts ma'am, she said. Okay, let's finish up and go inside. You going home to work?

I have this standard, amiable-type nod I can pull out at a time like this, where people know Yes I have to work, but also Yes I'm still good for one drink.

The look on your father's face when he walks in and finds us rip-roaring drunk in the middle of the afternoon. She threw her shoulders into a final, radical ice-chopping pose.

I scooped another shovelful of snow off the sidewalk and glanced over to where my mother had set the sparrow. It was gone. In its place there was a little sinkhole in the snow where the weight of the body had borne it down and away, through the top layer of powder. Out of our sight.

I came in the downstairs entrance and up the skinny flight of steps to my own front door. I was dragging a white ceramic sink I'd found on the way home from my parents'. I saw the sink from the bus window, on the curb at the corner of Dufferin and Dragon Alley, and I jumped out and grabbed it, which meant maneuvering the rest of my way home with some ingenuity and a fierce stubbornness besides. Someone had put it out for garbage along with a few other renovation castoffs: a sky-blue toilet, an old brown cabinet with a chipped-off knob, a roll of once-creamy, greasy linoleum.

It was in good shape. A country sink, almost square. During my first year of j-school I'd had a strong, one-day crush on a nineteen-year-old fine arts student I met in the park behind the Art Gallery on Dundas Street. He'd also had a wide white sink. He was using it for a project he called Loss and Foundling, art in a found object, and painting a water scene inside the basin, lilies and fish and whatnot. He was quiet while he worked and I watched him. The whole process was deeply pleasurable. I had a bar of Toblerone in my bag, along with a copy of Joan Didion's *The White Album,* two pens, and my wallet. We ate the chocolate and made out for a while in the park and when he suggested I come home and let him cook dinner for me, I surprised myself and said no.

Since then I've turned this plan over and over in my mind about a found sink. The gentleness of his hands, doing that fine work, left me with a jealous longing. You can want to touch someone and not want them, but instead want to inhabit them.

The idea was to paint the thing and mount it on the wall, inside the front door, and use it as a convenient place to keep small objects. My keys, for instance. I mean, you'd have to keep the plug in, or lodge something in the bottom drain. So your things wouldn't all roll down and fall out through the hole. The idea of a wall-mount sink that's not attached to any plumbing appealed to me. A dry sink. I'd paint it to feel like sand.

I leaned it against the wall in the place I planned to put it later, if in fact I could figure out how to mount something as heavy as that without tearing a hole through the plaster. There was some ice jammed up inside the drain and I stuffed a tea towel under it to catch the melt. I waited for the toaster to finish with the last of an old baguette and dotted cold butter onto it in pieces, and went to work.

My home computer lives in the kitchen. I recognize this isn't the best place to keep electronics. It's like keeping a piano in your bathroom. There's a fan over the stove but it doesn't vent outside. It just blows the steam around. All the same, I try to keep my work and my private life separate, and seeing how the only other room in the apartment is my bedroom, there's not much choice. My kitchen has a small café table against the window and a gas stove, and the computer sits on a desk in the corner near the door. It's very light during the day and private at night. There's a fridge, too, just where the door leads out to the fire escape.

In fairness, the computer itself is a hand-me-down from my father's dental office, and I've never felt attached. Remnants of his secretary's sandwiches—vintage lunch crumbs—stuck in the keyboard and a half-sticky leftover smear on the CPU where someone once applied and removed a packing-tape label.

LexisNexis.

Nexis Search.

Evie Jones, *Toronto Free Press*, 1992.

Come on. Tell me that's not the first thing you'd do.

Here you go, yo. Green type on a black screen, all my "with files from" over the previous year or so, every instance of my name in the news. Abra-abracadabra. I shook my head a little. Because, hey: Check That Out.

```
DECEMBER 30 1992: Cash for Kids shoots, scores
DECEMBER 28 1992: Legal woes loom in police shooting
    case
DECEMBER 27 1992: Recession-weary Canucks take trou-
    bles down south
DECEMBER 21 1992: City-wide mobile phones set to take
    over
DECEMBER 18 1992: Court says alimony still needed, 19
    years later
```

I scrolled down through a retrospective of my eight-month career. From Angie's point of view, the dead-girls list was a huge promotion. Back in July I'd been working on *Community picnic goes on despite rainout, pD7.*

Then this, from before my time:

```
MARCH 30 1992: Fraudsters used phone, mail to lure
    victims
MARCH 29 1992: Woman charged in senior fraud
```

Well, hello. Evie Jones, reporter? Meet Evie Jones, victim-lurer. I tried searching my name from the year before and found her again. This time I cruised through to the whole article.

FEBRUARY 15 1991: Assault, gaming charges laid in
Lovers' Lookout scheme

Be my valentine? As many as four elderly males are
thought to be among the victims of a con artist operating a Valentine's Day investment scheme in Etobicoke's Mimico district. Officers from 22 Division
were called to the scene late yesterday afternoon
after an altercation broke out in the parking lot of
a strip mall. Charged is 44-year-old Evie Jones of
Lake Shore Boulevard in Etobicoke. Jones had been
operating as a psychic and fortune-teller. Initial
reports say she may also have been running an illegal gambling room at the same address.

Evie Jones, perpetrator, was hard to resist. I wanted to know this
woman. She turned up again in 1989, operating a common bawdy
house out of a bungalow in an Italian neighborhood in the east end:

Neighbor Ottavia Primi said the revelation came as
no shock. "We sure saw a lot of comings and goings
over at that house, especially late at night. I'm
not surprised at all."

Then this, further down in the same article:

Police were alerted to the high-traffic address after
a Neighborhood Watch program was instituted in the
area. Spokesperson Pino Arrabia said the Watch was
put in place as a safeguard in light of recent sex attacks in nearby Scarborough. "It's a dangerous place
for girls now," Arrabia said. The local community
association has installed additional lighting and is
applying to City Hall for permission to mount video

surveillance cameras near bus stops. The so-called
Scarborough Rapist is suspected in more than a dozen
vicious attacks over the last 20 months, many of
them lasting half an hour or longer. One week ago a
22-year-old woman was admitted to the hospital after
being attacked inside her apartment building. The
victim stated she noticed a man outside her window
the previous night. It's unclear if the same man is
the attacker in this case. No charges have been laid.

Poof. Evie Jones, con artist, disappeared. The Scarborough
rapes were on my current to-do list. I sat up a little straighter. You
could say they'd been on and off my radar since I was about sixteen.
That was the year bus drivers started dropping women off in front
of their own houses, off-route, because the attacker used to wait for
girls at bus stops in the east end, late at night.

When you hear that, you get a picture, right? It's dark and there's
the sigh of the doors closing and the bus drives away. We're out in
Scarborough so the roads are really empty. Guy jumps out and attacks the girl while she's walking home, or drags her behind a bush
or something.

Only that's not how it was. This guy followed the girls all the
way home. He tracked them like scurrying animals. He liked to
rape a girl right in her own backyard, under her bedroom window,
or her little brother's bedroom window. You think about how scared
you can make yourself at night on a dark, lonely street. Those girls
stepped down off the bus and walked home listening for every little
sound behind them. There's a way of listening in the dark that's so
intense for girls. You can feel the insides of your ears. He waited
until the moment they thought they were home, safe. That takes a
special kind of interest.

I knew he used a knife. The attacks were singular in their dura-
tion. No rush. He held one girl for more than two hours. As a teen-

aged girl, reading that shit has a marked effect on your sanity. The first time my parents left me alone in the house overnight, I came up with a foolproof, go-to solution.

I'm just sleeping with a butcher knife under my pillow the whole time, I told David.

He said that was the stupidest thing he'd ever heard.

Anyone who breaks into your house is going to be stronger than you, he said. The guy will take the knife away and use it against you in about two seconds. All you did was give him a weapon he didn't have before.

Thanks, Detective, I said. Now how will I sleep?

Between the Scarborough Rapist and the AIDS scare, we'd all grown up on edge. In this way you can say the '80s were kind of the opposite of the '60s in flavor: the problem was that we still all had to keep up. Every girl I knew had a repertoire of raucous, horrifying rape jokes. One way to own it, I guess. We made strange choices. Sex was scary. We wanted to own that, too. I'd lost my virginity that same year I was sixteen, during a New England road trip with my family. My parents were sitting out on a patio drinking beers with a few couples we'd met at the beach and I was down by the creek with the one single guy of the group, a thirty-one-year-old pro Frisbee player from Quebec with dark hair and green eyes who looked like he knew how to use a condom. I was sure I'd never see him again and I asked him to confirm that. He asked me the last thing I'd read and I told the truth, *Gourmet* magazine.

His name was Jean-Marie. He'd spent a year working in Lake Tahoe and he told me how anytime he had to deal with an Anglophone government they assumed he was a woman, but that it was a very common man's name where he was from. I said I thought it was a good name for a man.

So I won't work outside Quebec anymore, he said.

But you could rob banks, I said.

What?

You could defraud the system. Because they'd be looking for a woman, see? I said he had two identities in one and how handy that could be.

But only outside Quebec, he said, as though this negated the argument.

He'd made a water pipe by punching a hole in the bottom of a beer can and we smoked a little hash that way, and then he broke up the rest into crumbs. He held his cupped hand to my mouth and I licked the hash crumbs. We sat and watched the creek and your body feels very good with a little hash in it. Your muscles all buzz and relax. It's like a massage from the inside.

Jean-Marie asked how old I was and I lied and said eighteen and he said, Let's pretend you are, but he was laughing a little, and then he hooked his thumbs into my bikini top. He pulled the bandeau part down so that it sat just under my breasts and they were propped there on a little balcony that was my swimsuit and he sat back and looked at me and told me he was very lucky to have met me. I wanted to kiss him or push forward and on with it. The hash slowed us down. I got up on my knees and fed my breast into his mouth with one hand around the back of his head and he played along and everything sped up. The sound of the water in the creek was faster. I wanted to make all the first moves so he wouldn't guess it was my first time. The pain shocked me. I realized suddenly that I had a foot on his shoulder and the foot was trying to push him away and I had to work to override that.

So I didn't have to worry about it, the one-special-guy-who-took-your-virginity thing. I didn't want anyone to have that on me. It was something I wanted to get rid of, both the fear and the label. This made me not unlike a lot of other girls I knew. Melissa lost her virginity to a guy she met at Sandbanks Provincial Park when she was camping with three other girlfriends. It's this thing to be disposed of but then later you can't change the story. The story sticks.

I wish now that I'd had one nice soccer player boyfriend for a year in the eleventh grade and done it with him after months of making out in the front seat of his mother's Toyota Corolla. David had a girlfriend named Emmeline when I was busy at university. Emmeline had long brown hair and she was studying piano and they had absolutely nothing in common but when they did it for the first time it was on Emmeline's parents' bed while the parents were out shopping at IKEA with her four-year-old sister. Her family came home and she and David pretended like they'd been watching TV the whole time and the sister had a face full of cheap IKEA ice cream and they had those frozen meatballs for dinner, with lingonberry sauce. Then David went home and called me and told me all about it.

I liked watching Emmeline. She was slim but she had a softness to her body I admired. She had gentle thoughts. David was laughing and I thought of how he'd buy her a chocolate chip cookie in the mall the next day at lunch. I envied her the softness.

Emmeline Hawco. I'd almost forgotten her name.

B y nine o'clock that night, I'd been running practice searches for three hours in a row. The sky was full-on dark and I was a full-on Nexis expert. I wanted to pick up where I'd left off in the archives, which landed me somewhere in the early '80s.

Lianne Gagnon went missing in 1982. Surely she deserved the same attention as every other girl. In the spirit of equality, I looked her up.

```
NEXIS SEARCH: LIANNE GAGNON, TORONTO, 1982


[SEARCH LIMITATION: A1-A10]
[SEARCH LIMITATION: 23 months]
DECEMBER 10 1983: Amateur sleuths receive top marks at
    Police Board awards
```

JUNE 4 1983: Got a tip? Half million in rewards for tips on these killers

MAY 23 1983: Police still hunt for killer of 11-year-old girl

AUGUST 18 1982: Mother of slain Lianne Gagnon charged after row with police

AUGUST 4 1982: Police set reward for capture of Lianne's killer

AUGUST 4 1982: $50,000 reward set in Lianne's slaying

JULY 17 1982: Lianne suspect fingered in Abbot murder

JULY 11 1982: Lianne suspect wanted for parole breach

JULY 9 1982: Lianne tip came from hostel worker

JULY 5 1982: Toronto police search for American suspect in girl's death

JULY 5 1982: Warrant issued for Lianne killer

JULY 3 1982: Suspect identified in slaying of 11-year-old Lianne Gagnon

JULY 3 1982: Police name suspect in Lianne slaying

JULY 3 1982: Lianne killer named

June 5 1982: Who murdered Lianne Gagnon?

June 5 1982: Missing girl, 11, found dead in city park

MAY 27 1982: "Lianne, please call home": distraught mother appeals to public for help

MAY 26 1982: Police on the hunt for missing East York girl

MAY 25 1982: Search widens for schoolgirl Lianne Gagnon

MAY 24 1982: Have you seen Lianne?

MAY 24 1982: Girl, 11, missing

You can see how quickly her own name moves from being a thing that identifies Lianne herself to a thing that identifies the guy they think killed her, Robert Cameron. There's a subtle shift between saying, Police Search For Lianne's Killer, and Lianne Suspect Wanted For This Other Thing. A staff sergeant was quoted talking about other murders Cameron might have committed. A York University cheerleader named Charlene Abbot had been killed the previous fall and it's suspected that was also him.

> "We don't know anything for sure," the staff sergeant told reporters. "But I can say that we'll be having a long talk with Cameron about Abbot's death."

That's how sure they were that they'd find him.

I have to be honest here: I thought there'd be more. More headlines, more front-page space, more search lines. She moved from A1 to A7 in forty-eight hours. By the time the cops had sent out the dogs, she was City News, not national.

A few months after they found her body, police were called to Lianne's parents' place. Some tenants had called in a disturbance; the mother raged at the cops. They'd fucked it up, she said. They thought Lianne was a runaway and that's how they treated it. They waited to see if she'd turn up for school the next day before they brought in the dogs and did a house-to-house.

You waited! You just left her there, you left her with him!

As though they'd always known where she was but had other things on the go for the first couple of days.

How could you.

By that time Cameron was long gone, maybe in Thunder Bay, maybe in the Sault. Maybe back in the States.

I don't know if Lianne's mother really had a breakdown or if she just needed a reason to get a captive audience with police. They talked to her on her porch and she screamed and cried and then she ran into the street and kicked in the cruiser headlights and they arrested her for that. About a year later, she packed up the rest of the kids with their cowboy names and went to the West Coast. I don't know where her father lives now. I remember how they used to make corn fritters, and his guitar in the kitchen at breakfast.

A woman got a civilian award the next December for drawing a great composite picture of Cameron in the first days of the investigation, when Lianne was still missing. Before they knew who he was, when he was just a collection of aliases. There were anniversary articles on the one-year mark of the day she went missing, and a new reward set for Cameron's capture on the anniversary of the day she was found.

The next year there were new cold cases, and Lianne had become an old case, something from a previous year, a mess that no one had managed to clean up.

And just like that, she was a stat. A bad start to the new decade, to be sure.

NEXIS SEARCH: ROBERT NELSON CAMERON, ALIAS

JULY 3 1982: Police name suspect in Lianne slaying

Cameron has a history of swapping ID when the timing suits him both here and in his native United States, where he has previously been incarcerated for armed robbery, assault, and defacing public property. Names Robert Nelson Cameron has been known to use include Wade Oxford, Arthur Lewis Sawchuk, Lee Ellingham, John James McMurtry, Len Lester.

The phone rang as soon as I plugged it back into the wall. I'd come across this handy list of Cameron's aliases and copied the names in a long row down the page—alphabetically, no less—before pulling the cable on my borrowed *Free Press* modem out of the jack. I looked over at the telephone where it was hanging on the kitchen wall and watched it ring out, as though it could tell me who was calling. I counted. Only my father lets the phone ring more than ten times. I gave in and picked up.

Your mother tells me they have you working on some pretty intense stuff, he said.

I'm working right now, actually, I said.

There was a pause while he tried to remember which number he'd reached me at, home or newsroom extension.

From home?

It's kind of super cool, I said. I'm kind of loving it.

You have access to the whole archive like that?

No, I said. Better than that. Not just the *Free Press* but everything. All papers everywhere.

And you're okay?

Okay how?

Okay-not-upset.

It's just a big long list, I said. I don't have to go interview weeping grandmothers or anything.

It's a brutal chronology, he said. Try to remember that I know you a little bit, Evie. This is going to leave you spinning.

When I was young, my father was the parent on nightmare duty. If I woke up at three in the morning convinced that there were vampires hanging upside down in my closet, he was the guy who came running. He kept a spray bottle of water under my bed and swore it was monster repellant. Once when I was a teenager I had an irrational AIDS panic after reading a story about a sixteen-year-old party girl in Manhattan who was dying of the disease. She'd written a personal essay that ran in the Sunday *New York Times Magazine*. I had zero connection to this girl or her lifestyle, but her stupid death felt convincing and intimate.

She'd made an irreversible bad choice that spiraled and I spiraled, too, reading about it. My dad spent a couple of hours talking me down.

If you're in the middle of an anxiety attack, he's the medical professional you want on your side. A master of calm deductive reasoning. The legacy of this relationship is that there's a piece of him that feels most comfortable in this role. Or, comforted by Evie in distress.

Just the opposite! I said. I sang it out. I'm good. I'm feeling sharply focused. I live in the future now.

For a moment my father didn't say anything. Then:

Just the opposite. He said this quietly. This list is all past life.

We had a soft moment together on the telephone. Each of us in our own kitchen, not speaking but listening to the silence.

I won't let them break my heart, I said. Promise.

Most of what I'd found in the Lianne files was stuff I already knew: Cameron was the only suspect, he was American, he'd disappeared right after she went missing, he was a known felon with a handful of aliases. I had the list of names now, the fake names he was best known to have used. Plus a few new things. I sketched out another list, details I hadn't known before.

Things they found in Robert Nelson Cameron's room:

Three pairs of track pants.

One old running shoe with no laces.

A vest and suit jacket, matching. Simpson's price tags still attached.

Bedding, still on the bed.

A few threaded towels. Two gray ones, and one pink.

In the cupboards: Three mugs, some white CorningWare, the plates and bowls with blue and white flowers that came with the room.

A hot plate but no stove.

Plastic glasses.

Three cans of beans, two cans of chili, two Chunky soups (chicken and beef). Two cans of corn niblets.

A hardback copy of *Helter Skelter*, the Charles Manson true crime, stolen from the Leaside Public Library, one corner turned down sharply on a photo of key witness Linda Kasabian and her quote, *I'm not you, Charlie. I can't kill anybody.*

In the fridge: one pot of leftover macaroni, some milk, two potatoes.

In the crisper: one head lettuce, a few carrots, two apples. No one had been in that place for a couple of weeks. The perishable foods must have been in bad shape.

On the counter: two large terrariums, each containing one large rat and the remains of some others. Like the lettuce and macaroni in the fridge, the rats had been left on their own after Cameron split. But rats are resourceful. After a while, hunger is hunger, and a rat will eat another dying rat.

In the freezer: a few Ziploc bags with dead rats in them. Some of the rats were whole, and some of them had parts removed: ears and legs. Other bags contained just the parts.

We don't know if Cameron was dissecting the rats, or if the rats injured one another. That was the quote from police headquarters in the *Free Press*. The contact was Staff Sergeant Phillip Lacey.

Lacey said: It's just that most people, you know. They don't put their dead pets in the freezer.

The clothes and bedding were all removed for testing.

They didn't find a suitcase or a passport.

I pulled the phone cord out of the wall and swapped it for the modem again. There was a mild clunking sound, the hum from the fridge kicking on. I looked over my shoulder by instinct. Down on the floor I had a loose pile of books that included my own paperback *Helter Skelter*—the ratty copy I'd bought with my mother at the St. Lawrence Flea. I'd cruised through it since, looking at photos, but hadn't read more than the captions. Linda Kasabian was a Manson girl who turned star witness in exchange for immunity. She'd been along for the ride the night they killed Sharon Tate, eight months pregnant and tied to a chair, along with a handful of her guests. It was Kasabian who gave the prosecution the play-by-play. She had a small face, framed by pigtails, and strong bones. I picked up the book and let the pages run through my fingers a few times, then laid it facedown on the far corner of my desk. The title shone out at me from the book's spine and I twisted it a few degrees to make it stop.

The apartment was dark and I had to resist the urge to get up and walk around, flipping lights on and off and verifying that I was alone and no one was hiding out and waiting for my guard to fall.

David had been right, back in high school, about sleeping with a knife under my pillow. It's no way to live.

I've since come up with a way of dealing with nights like that, where you're really worried about someone knowing you're all alone. It's simple. Stay awake and do things until about 5:00 a.m. Think about it. All the horror stories you read in the newspaper? You never hear about anything that happened after five. It's pretty much morning. The sun's almost up. It's like a rule.

Even if it's still dark, or deep winter, criminals know the light is coming. That's why nothing bad can ever happen to you. Five o'clock is a very safe time to sleep.

I reached forward and pulled the little chain on the lamp. The two new lists were laid out in front of me, side by side on the desk. My window faced north and there was just a streak of streetlight in the corner, keening in from the west. Reflected in the actual window, I could see the line of my jaw, my cheekbone, the glowing search window just below my face. A window in a window. The garden was quiet. I turned back to the screen.

I had so much to look for.

CHAPTER 9

Robert Cameron drove into Toronto from Creve Coeur, Missouri. That much we know for sure: he'd been hauled in for a police lineup in April of 1982 and there's a record of it. The next day or so gets sketchy, but you can put a pretty good picture together if you cross-reference for a few hours or so, alone in your kitchen.

We know Cameron left town in a 1974 Mustang II, the gas-crisis car, and came roaring through St. Louis on the I-64. I like to imagine that under the arch he passed some other car, overturned and the undercarriage burned out. It's a rough town now, and would have been worse back then. No one around, or showing their face, that time of day. He'd left Creve Coeur at three in the morning. He had a briefcase and a long blue Anheuser-Busch duffel bag on the passenger seat. The briefcase was full of knives. It belonged to John James McMurtry, a Cutco regional salesman from Okemos, Michigan. McMurtry was a poor drunk and an even worse fighter and Cameron had John James's brown leather wallet tucked safe in his own breast pocket, as well.

The car he'd got in Kansas City six months previous, off a black man named Leo Delaine who owed him money. The duffel bag had some clothes in it and loose cash, not too much, no drugs.

In the trunk of the Mustang II were two glass terrariums, capped with heavy rubber lids, hole-punched for air exchange. Cameron only liked white rats.

He crossed the border at Fort Frances and slept the night in Thunder Bay, then drove down through northern Ontario in one long haul, stopping over briefly at Whitefish Falls to buy tobacco from a man who called himself Smokey Joe. Every reservation in North America has a Smokey Joe. Cameron said it was a poor alias, and Joe said: But how you gonna trace us?

The American guard at the border had waved him through, but the Canadian guard was under strict orders to follow search protocol. The week before, this same guard had allowed a curly-haired woman named Marina Dubuque onto the Canadian side with a steamer trunk of hash bricks in the back of her navy-blue Buick. She was wearing a pink headband and playing Olivia Newton-John's *Xanadu* out the car's eight-track speakers. The guard told this to Cameron while they were standing around waiting for the search team.

Who the fuck was she trafficking for? The PTA?

The woman had disappeared but left the car parked in the loosestrife about ten miles up the access road where a dog unit out on a training run had come upon it by pure accident. Two bikers were chopping up the drugs to fit them into saddlebags, and in the mix a patrol guard was shot twice in the shoulder.

So that's why random checks, and that's why there was a guard who remembered a man of Cameron's description at all, later on when the police and reporters came around.

Cameron didn't smell of drugs or have any on him, but the search team stripped out the trunk and the backseats, just to be sure. There was still a trace of snow on the ground. Fort Frances is far enough north that the snow stays most years till May, the guard told him. The guard had a few white rats at home himself. Pets. The wife had a blue budgie.

They cracked open the briefcase and Cameron told them he was a door-to-door knife salesman.

Really? And folks let you in the door with a bag full of knives?

Oh, yeah, Cameron said. You just got to smile. You boys all

done? He leaned into the car and bolted the backseat in tight. The guard helped him lift a lidded terrarium onto the seat.

You want an open door, Cameron said. You just got to tell folks what they want to hear.

D o you think it's possible to attract evil?

What do you mean? David said. He'd been experimenting with a new beard and raised his hand to rub it in a thoughtful manner. We were sitting on milk crates on my kitchen floor. It was early enough the next evening and David was trying to put together a Scandinavian bookshelf. The instructions had no words. Just pictures of the parts we were supposed to have, and arrows showing how they fit together. The screws were long and skinny and two of them had already rolled under the stove and been lost to time. I'd been in the archives all day, doing halfhearted background on an airline merger that would top the business section in the morning. Basically, an airline runs on a debt-based system and the conditional optimism of venture capitalists. Once you understand that, there's not much else to say.

My feature research on the dead-girls weekend section was due and I still had the '70s and '90s to comb through. I'd told Angie that I had a thorough working knowledge of 1980 to '85. She said I'd done an amazing quarter of a job.

I got down on my knees with a wire hanger from the dry cleaners and tried to fish out the lost screws.

Do you think that wherever he is—the guy who killed Lianne—he knows? I said. I dragged the hanger out and it brought no hardware with it. There was a greasy dust bunny wrapped around the hook. I sat up. I mean: Do you think he knows that I think about him.

If you think it, he will come, David said.

Stop that.

Or more like the Eye of Sauron?

I'm sorry I tell you anything, I said.

He'd brought in a couple of takeout coffees with him when he arrived and they were sitting on the floor next to us with the skinny wooden stir sticks pointing up and through the little holes in the lids. We had a cinnamon bun between us on a plate.

I picked my coffee up and swished it around. He rubbed at his beard again.

Good choice on the facial hair, I said. You look incredibly wise.

David fit the end cap onto the shelf with a click and set the shelf down on the ground in front of him.

I was thinking it would make me look gentlemanly, he said. But I have to shave it. I'm starting to look too much like my father.

I squinted in his direction. I guess that's true, I said. Have you seen him lately?

Last week. Lucky me.

He brushed the screws into a neat pile with his fingers.

Want to talk about it?

Nope. He picked up his coffee and gave me a tight smile. He was asking about you, actually. How's Evie doing? I see she's working for the paper. . . . So lucky you, too. You're just his type now.

Ew. Does that mean you have a new reporter stepmom?

Nah. He's got a new girlfriend, though. She's a year younger than me and doesn't speak English. He met her outside the refugee center on Queen. Illegal in every possible sense of the word. Either she's a Russian hooker, or I don't know. I mean, this girl has a mother somewhere. So, yeah. Time to get rid of the beard.

There was a little silence between us. David started taking apart the bottom end of the shelf where he'd put a piece on backward. I picked up the pile of screws and weighed them in my hand.

They don't know Cameron did it, I said. They can't. They don't know anything.

David stopped and set down the screwdriver.

Yeah they do, he said.

I mean, if they found her body out in the park, how do they know it was him?

Is this a work thing? Is that where this is coming from, all your dead-girls reading? They just know, David said. He pulled the stir stick out of his coffee and sucked on the end of it. The guy was an offender down in the States, and then they know he was up here, and he was doing weird shit, and then he disappears right after Lianne died.

But what if that's a coincidence? I said.

Why are you doing this to yourself?

I just want to know, that's all. What if it's all a coincidence?

David put the stick between his teeth like it was a cigar.

Ottam's arzor, he said. It sounded like he had a mouth full of marbles.

What's an arzor? I said.

Occam's Razor, David said. He put the stick down on a napkin. Occam was a monk. He said, The simplest answer is usually the correct one.

About religion.

I ripped off the outside curl of the cinnamon bun.

It's about evidence, David said. Monks did all the science and philosophy and art and everything, so he wasn't talking about religion. He was talking about science, about knowledge. Occam's Razor is just that, the simplest answer is usually the correct one. David leaned back and pulled a dollar out of his pocket. He laid it out flat in his hand and pushed the hand toward me.

Look, he said. You have a dollar in your pocket. He closed up his fist and whisked it away behind his back. Later the dollar is gone, and you notice there's a hole in your pocket. Are you going to go looking for a burglar?

What if there's a simpler answer that we don't see? What if there's something really easy, really important, but we don't know about it yet?

David tucked the money back in his pocket.

Your dollar fell out through the hole, Evie. It was lost.

He leaned in toward me and I thought he was going to try to take my hand, but he reached for the cinnamon bun instead. He tore it into pieces, into little strips, and laid them out in rows across the plate.

I'm so sorry Lianne was lost, David said. It's a long time ago.

Nothing else Cameron did fits this profile, I said. They know all about him. He used lots of names. I reached over and pulled my printouts off my computer desk. Look, I said. I shoved the papers at him. The sheets were all still attached along thin perforated lines. David unfurled them like a road map.

Look, I said again. Armed Robbery. Assault. Assault and Battery. Vandalism. I ran my hand down the page. Pedophiles are pedophiles, David. This guy was a robber, a cheat, an asshole.

The guy cut up rats, David said. You told me that. He cut up his pets.

Yeah? I said.

That's it. That's how they know it's him.

I didn't say anything. David held a hand out to me, like he was waiting for me to cross over and join him on the path to reason.

If it was someone else, I said. Then maybe that person is already caught. Maybe that person is in jail for raping some other girl. They don't really know anything about Cameron, I said. They know they don't know where he is.

David flipped through the papers on the floor.

What's this one?

I leaned over his arm.

I wanted to see his past record, I said. That's the first time any of his names come up.

NEXIS SEARCH: ROBERT NELSON CAMERON, WADE OXFORD, ARTHUR LEWIS SAWCHUK, LEE ELLINGHAM, JOHN JAMES MCMURTRY, LEN LESTER

TORONTO, 1970

[SEARCH LIMITATION: 10 years]
MARCH 4 1970: No charges in Kensington area raid

FREE PRESS, MARCH 4, 1970
Three men were detained and released Tuesday night
in relation to a suspected drug raid on Brunswick
Avenue. Edgar Fanning, 21, and Oral Alphonse, 20,
are thought to be residents of Rochdale College on
Bloor Street in Toronto. Francis Edds, 21, resides
on Brunswick Avenue. 14th Division spokesman Jim
Belanger declined to comment on the incident, stat-
ing only that the house is known to police. [IMAGE]
[CAPTION]

Hold on a sec, David said. His name isn't here.

I know. I figure he's in the picture. See? There's supposed to be an image.

Where is it? David said.

No pictures on Nexis, I said. I have to look it up at work.

I took my sheaf of printouts into the office with me the next morning. The goal was to finish Angie's list, and maybe dig up a few photos while I was at it.

I switched on my headlamp and held it out in my hand like a flashlight, pushing hard with my shoulder to get the archive door to swing open. Inside it was cool and dark. The door to the archives is never locked, because there's always someone at work on the news. The building is never completely empty. There was no sound. The soles of my shoes squeaked a little against the linoleum floor tiles and then the sudden hum of the furnace kicking in next door.

I had the lion's share of the list on a floppy disk in my purse upstairs. There were still a few things I wanted to check out on the film reader. I tightened the hiker's lamp around my head and walked back through the stacks. It kept my hands free and I was happy to have the spotlight. It felt safer. I'd know if someone else was in there with me. They'd have to carry their own light.

The dead girls' names had changed over time like a most-popular name list from each year. Linda and Karen and Susan in the '60s and '70s, Jenny and Heather in the '80s, Kristen and Amber in the '90s. There were girls found in ditches or lost from bike rides home after school, girls taken to movies and never seen again, girls lost at the playground. Girls taken by their uncles or neighbors, or sometimes their own fathers. It's almost always someone you know. Except in Lianne's case, where Robert Cameron is really just some random drifter. Leave it to me to know the one little girl who was actually abducted by a stranger with candy.

I skimmed a finger along the shelves, shining the light on the date stickers: 1970 January, 1970 February, 1970 March, 1970 April, 1970 May, and etcetera. I pulled a stack of files off the shelf and rifled through them in my hands, keeping them in order. Basically the list I had was '80s and '90s heavy and I needed to flesh it out a little, so to speak, in the earlier decades. I knew Angie's point was to show things getting worse—not better, not just the same—but I wasn't sure that was true. I'd already learned that I could pick any year, any time, any place, and run a search that included the term "missing girl" with good success. With the history of national news wide open before you, all you need to do is close your eyes and let your finger fall on a random date.

There was a noise near the floor, one row over. My light jerked in that direction. My hands were full.

Mouse, I said out loud. The sound of my own voice surprised me.

I picked one of the readers in the center of the room and threaded a reel through the machine. It clicked heavily into place and the machine whirred as it warmed up and I sent the film spinning through.

O
ctober 1970. A girl named Katherine May Wilson goes missing in Kirkland Lake. She'd been sent out to pick up a few groceries and called home from the store to ask her mother if she was allowed to spend the leftover change on a treat for herself. A can of pop or something. Her mom says yes. Katherine is twelve.

She has some younger sisters who walk out to meet her halfway, but when Katherine doesn't show up, I guess they go home. I don't know how long those two little girls stood around waiting, or playing by the side of the road.

When they got home, did they tell the mother immediately or did they just resume their game in the yard? Did the mother know to worry right away? Or was she irritated that Katherine had dilly-dallied instead of walking straight home? It was 5:00 p.m. when she called from the store. Her mother would have needed the groceries for supper. They never found Katherine's body.

The case went cold. It's the second-biggest cold case since the '50s. What makes Lianne's case larger is only the fact that they know who did it but never tracked him down. In Katherine's case, there were no leads, no warrants, no arrests. Every news report about an unsolved case of a missing girl includes the insinuation that police botched the investigation. For an anxious public, it's a good trick to blame investigators. Of course public safety doesn't depend on well-executed arrests. It depends on girls not being killed. Which depends on men not killing them. Every cold case at one time or another headlines as the country's biggest.

Someone reported last seeing Katherine in the passenger side of her cousin's pickup truck. If we believe Report Femicide, this is the most likely scenario. Someone she knew, something familiar. Maybe he'd offered her a ride home before.

Kirkland Lake is way up north. Today, it's got a population of just over eight thousand, down from a high of almost twenty-five thousand before World War II. It's famous for forests and open-pit mining. Driving, they would have been well out of town in a couple of minutes. Maybe he asked nicely. Maybe he just wanted a blow job.

But then she said, No. She said, Take me home. She said she'd tell her parents.

Maybe Katherine kicked him off. She got the door of the truck open. She started running. It's October so there's a deep layer of fallen leaves on the ground, and under the leaves, tree roots trip her up. She's wearing sneakers and the toes of the sneakers are catching under the roots. The thin, bare branches whipping at her as she runs. She has lash marks on her face and arms from the branches. Katherine is only four-foot-nine and her cousin is already a grown man and faster than she is. She is running and the branches hurt her face and her lungs are burning. What she's thinking about is her mother.

I wanted this list to be an honor roll, but every girl was only famous for what someone else did.

finished up my notes and stripped out the film and loaded a new one: 1970, March 1–15. I was keen to see the image that went with the news item I'd shown David the day before, the drug raid. The reel sped up as it wound backward, making a progressively louder whining noise through each date start to finish until I got back to March 4. It's a steady enough noise when it's right next to your ear, loud enough to dull any other quick sounds. I hadn't noticed the furnace shut off. When I stopped the film, the silence was sudden and hard around me and my breath tightened up. I glanced quick over my shoulder and the light from the headlamp swept across the room, lighting up a streak of floor and another table and chair to the left of me. I took off the headlamp and laid it on the desk and stood up. On my feet for a moment I turned slowly around. No other lights. I sat down and threaded my wrist through the strap on the light.

I found it on page A27.

It was a small piece toward the back of the front section, bordered by ads and business information for the paper. The bottom third of the page is just the detailed weather map. There's a large black-and-white photo accompanying the article and this is the thing I'm looking for.

NO CHARGES IN KENSINGTON AREA RAID

FREE PRESS, MARCH 4, 1970

Caption: No arrests in Kensington raid. The house is registered to one Arthur Lewis Sawchuk.

It's a picture of a semidetached brick two-story. There's an alley on one side and a strip of sidewalk, and it's a familiar place. It looks like downtown Toronto. There's what seems to be the remains of a party on the front lawn, bottles and some dirty-looking guys with long hair and a few girls, too, also with long hair. One of the men has a black ponytail. One has lighter, tangled hair that he's tucked just behind one ear on the left side. He's got a beard, and fringe coming off his arms and shoulders. A leather jacket. It's a grainy photo.

This is supposed to be a photo of Arthur Lewis Sawchuk. Also known as Wade Oxford, Lee Ellingham, John James McMurtry, Len Lester, Robert Nelson Cameron. It's a picture of the man who killed Lianne.

I didn't know what he would have looked like in 1970. I leaned close into the screen. What I needed was the photo of Cameron from later on, something to compare this one to. His mug shot, the have-you-seen-this-man photo the paper ran a dozen years later, when Lianne was killed.

I didn't see him, but I was squinting hard enough to make out the house number, 102, on the front door. Which is why the place looked so familiar.

The house my mother once lived in was 102 Brunswick, next to the alley near Kensington Market. Just out of the frame, to the left, was the parkette I'd sat in a few days earlier.

I picked up my light and held it over the screen. Three girls with long hair were standing on the front porch. One of them, a tiny blonde, held one hand lightly against her face, a pose I've often seen my mother strike when she's feeling tired. Her eyes, too. My mother's eyes take up half her face, you'd say. They're that big. She has high, Finnish cheekbones and the kind of brow line that makes her look as though she's always a little surprised. I sat still, my fingers curling around the strap on my lamp.

Maybe I was wrong.

I hit Print, capturing the entire page, then focused in on the text of the article and then just the picture and printed those off, too. The printer, housed on a lower shelf at my right knee, pulled three sheets of paper through, one after the other, and I stripped the microfilm out of the reader and snapped it back into its case. I still had some work I was supposed to finish up, but staying seemed unimaginable. I wanted to go home.

I pulled the prints off the machine and aimed my light straight down on the close-up photograph. The zoom had made it impossibly blurry. The girls on the porch had rope for hair. Their eyes and mouths were smeared. Someone had dragged a hand across their faces, long smudged lines of mascara and lipstick. I folded the papers in half and in half again and stuffed them into the back pocket of my jeans. Carrying the light in my hand, I walked quickly back to the stacks to reshelve the pile of films I'd pulled out. I had to set the light down on the shelf to sort them. The light shone off, distant and ambient, and I was sorry I hadn't just left the thing on my head.

There was a heavy thud from the back corner of the room. A

door swinging shut in the furnace room next door. Something falling to the ground. Someone.

My hands shook as I pushed the films back into their slots on the
shelf. The light knocked to the ground and shone off down the row,
illuminating a long, slim triangle of floor. Shadows rose up on either
side of the beam, the shelves growing taller, white to gray to black. I
dropped to my knees to get the light and there was a scuffing sound
from behind me. I spun around, flashing the light in a wide circle.

If someone was in there with me, he'd been there since before I
came in. He'd been there the whole time, waiting, from the moment
I first opened the door. I remembered the mouse sound from when
I'd stood in the stacks before. He'd been watching me quietly since
then. I raised the light so that it shone across the row of film readers
and tables to the doorway. The light switch on the wall. I needed to
get to the light, to the door, to get out.

Another sound from deeper into the stacks. Behind me, the tick
or creak of the shelves settling. Then again in the next row over.

He was moving around. I pushed my back against the shelf and
swept a slow arc of light from way down the row on my left all the
way through the shelf directly in front of me. Whoever was there
was just on the other side of that shelf. He could see me silhouetted
between the rows of microfilm. I let the light drift to the tables and
readers again. To the door. I aimed the light down and covered it
with one hand. No other lights.

I started toward the door. He was only a few feet away, I was
sure now. The sound of his shoes, the light skid of footsteps on the
other side of the shelf. I came out of the row and started running,
banging my thigh hard against the arm of Vinh's wheelchair. It spun
around and smacked me again and my light dropped to the ground,
shining a path behind me, back into the stacks. Between me and
where I was headed, the room turned hazy and then pure black. I
could see a table and a chair in front of me. I couldn't see the wall. I
couldn't see the door.

I felt along from table to table with my hands out in front in the dark, tripping on chair legs. If he came after me, I'd start pushing the microfilm readers down behind me, anything to put a barrier between me and him until I made it to the wall. I was crashing. I was staggering like a drunk. I was a bear in the woods and he was steady behind me. There was no rush. There was nowhere for me to go. He'd already locked the door.

My hands hit the wall and then the nubs of the light switch and I pushed them up all at once, the fluorescents flickering and spitting for a few seconds and then the room came up sudden and bright and blinding and empty.

Empty.

Just me. I scanned the place from end to end and then again. With the lights on, the vacancy of the room was stark and shiny and seasick. The ceiling stretching out high above me and the walls closing in tighter, then breathing out again. I didn't want to sit down. Everything was the same color, the same dirty white. I put my hand on my chest and I could feel my heart moving there, through my ribs, like I'd just come off a hard bike ride. My lamp was still on the ground, shining back toward the shelves, about eighteen feet away.

Whoever had been there, he was gone.

An alarm sounded. My ear rang. The wall. The phone. There was a green phone on the wall with a curly cord, ringing.

I stood and looked at it and it rang a few more times before I picked up.

You down there? Angie's voice.

I'm fine, I said. I'm leaving. I think I'm sick.

Get up here fast, she said. Shit just hit the fan. They arrested one guy for everything: French, Mahaffy. Scarborough Rapist. It's the same guy. He did all of it. One guy. It was one guy.

CHAPTER 10

He's twenty-eight, blond, cute, boy-next-door, Angie said. I ran along beside her. He's an accountant, for Christ's sake. She slapped a file at me.

Of course he is, I said.

There'd been a leak a few hours earlier and she'd been sitting on the story since then, office door closed.

We've had guys parked out back of Task Force headquarters since this morning, Angie said. The government had put together the Green Ribbon Task Force the year before, to look after the St. Catherines murder investigation.

I sent Mike down there to look at the house, she said. You're going to Scarborough, go knock on some doors, get the family to open up. Angie stopped short in the hall in front of the stairwell. I'm doing a press con down in Niagara. I'll see you here at midnight. File by two. Go!

Paul Kenneth Bernardo, a twenty-eight-year-old high-school heartthrob turned chartered accountant. A guy who wore a suit, and ate at nice restaurants, and on weekends cruised around in a golden sports car looking for teenaged girls curious enough to peer in his window, blithe enough to stop and get in.

———

took the train out to Guildwood, an upscale suburb built in the late '60s. Side-splits and chalet bungalows, big lots, lawn tractors and snowblowers. Three cars to a driveway. Bernardo's father was also an accountant. Paul had gone to the local high school, Sir Wilfrid Laurier Collegiate, and graduated six years before I did. He was about my age, twenty-one, when he started stalking girls home from Scarborough bus stops.

Metro police had set up a tip hotline right away and the line never stopped ringing. At one point they had 1,500 suspects on file. One guy they caught driving around in his car, hanging out near bus stops, waiting. The car was full of aerial maps of Scarborough; he knew every corner of the place.

But it wasn't Bernardo, Angie said. It was just some sick asshole who followed the news.

Angie's rapid-fire brief had included only the main points: the deal was sealed on DNA, there was a match between the rapist and the murder victims, police had interviewed Bernardo years ago and taken samples, but something went wrong, nothing got tested till this month. They'd been staking him out for days. There was already infighting between Metro police who'd grabbed him for the Scarborough rapes and the murder Task Force in Niagara who had wanted to hold off. There was a warrant for the arrest but no warrant for a search.

hit the parents' house first. The door swung open viciously and slammed again. A brother, already used to reporters knocking:

You know about as much as I do!

I hadn't been first. It was still early but I could imagine the steady stream of phone calls and in-person visits like mine.

There was an older man across the street in a green parka, breathing hard and leaning on a shovel. The walk was half-cleared. He watched me pick my way across the road.

Lot of action this evening? I said. He pushed at the pile of snow in front of him and shook his head.

You know this guy? he said.

I'm with the *Free Press*, I said.

It don't make sense, the man said. He straightened up and pulled off his gloves. Jesus.

I thought of the roster of background questions I was supposed to be asking.

Have you lived here long?

He said his name was Tom Bouw. He'd lived there since the houses were built. There were no sidewalks for a long time, he said. Just dirt ditches, like in the country.

Living out here, it used to be the country. His head tilted back like he was checking the coming weather.

A quiet kid, Tom Bouw said. Never caused no trouble. Never made no commotion on the street.

He hung his shovel on a rack in the garage and went inside. For a moment I was completely alone. No traffic. Falling snow. I turned my body so that my back was to the wind and noticed a teenaged girl on her front porch, looking at me from across the road. She was standing there with one hand pressed against her face and the pose made me think of the photograph I'd found, my mother at seventeen. She was processing something, taking it all in. This girl had lived two doors down from the country's most famous rapist. I started to walk toward her and she turned suddenly and went inside. No one answered when I knocked on the door.

Two blocks away I found a guy shoveling out the box of his pickup who said he'd gone to school with Bernardo at Wilfrid Laurier. His mother asked me inside and gave me a cup of tea while her son stamped his boots on the mat. She dug out a cardboard file box of school photos and report cards. The son was called Geoff and he had red hair and sideburns and wore a lumberjack shirt with snap buttons out in the cold. Geoff pulled a few things out of the box for me and spread them out on the living-room shag rug. We sat on the floor and I drank my tea.

In the 1982 yearbook, Paul Bernardo is on the graduate page.

Blond and clean-cut, wearing a tie and a jacket. He says the only way to get ahead in life is to Go For It.

I was back at the paper by eleven o'clock. Angie mashed my notes in with files from the other reporter, a guy named Mike Nelligan. She'd sent him off to St. Catherines to do basically what I'd done in Scarborough. Knock on doors, get people to cough up readable copy. Files went in just after two and by two-fifteen we were lining them up along the bar downstairs. It was after last call but the door was unlocked. The closest bar to the newsroom and there's an understanding sometimes.

Beside the door-knocking, I'd handed in a compiled list of expected charges against Bernardo to go in a box on A6. Forty-five charges so far.

FIRST-DEGREE MURDER, 2

SEXUAL ASSAULT, 9

BUGGERY, 3

ASSAULT CAUSING BODILY HARM, 2

SEXUAL ASSAULT, 1

FORCIBLE CONFINEMENT, 8

CHOKING, 3

ROBBERY, 8

ANAL INTERCOURSE, 5

AGGRAVATED SEXUAL ASSAULT, 2

SEXUAL ASSAULT CAUSING BODILY HARM, 1

SEXUAL INTERCOURSE WITH A FEMALE BETWEEN 14 AND 16 YEARS OF AGE, 1

The bartender lined up a row of shots and Mike sent them down the bar to where we were sitting. One at a time, *ping ping ping.*

I dipped my pinky into my glass and sucked the rye off it. I was three shots in after only twenty minutes and trying to find ways to slow myself down. Mike leaned against the bar next to where I was sitting.

Here's a handy rule of thumb for you, I said. When you get attacked, it'll be someone you know. So that's comforting, right? I was explaining this to him since in a future lifetime he might have to be a girl, and if I didn't tell him this stuff, how would he protect himself? Intimate partners = forty-five percent of assaults. Once you add in your pals, that guy who handed you a beer at the party, and creepy great-uncle Joseph, there's almost no room left for strangers.

Mike picked up my glass and handed it to me. I lifted it in salute.

For kids, that's still true, I said. Times about a hundred. If it seems random, it's not. It just looks random.

I gave him an amicable little cheers. The booze was warm and softened everyone's edges, but I could still feel them there.

Angie said she'd done a famous interview with a victim who sued the police force, because they knew a serial rapist was at work and didn't warn the women in that neighborhood. They were waiting to catch him red-handed. Like those women were bait. In her statement to the press, she'd said: We know our rapists. They are the men we know.

The guy they arrested lived right around the corner from her, Angie said. With his wife and his eight-year-old daughter.

Now, you see? I said. This is what makes a guy like Bernardo so interesting. Bus stop girls! Random strangers! Girls he found sitting out on the curb, right in front of their parents' houses like whiny cats locked out for the night. Girls alone. I'd emptied my glass for a fourth time and pushed it off down the bar, never to return. I'd love to find the girl Paul Bernardo took to the eighth-grade dance, I said. Now there's an interview.

The bartender asked if I wanted another one.

Another round, Angie said. Keep them coming.

Mike's second job had been a list of unsolveds from the last ten years. Other girls who were found raped and burned or strangled or cut up. Because maybe those were Bernardo, too. That's the hope. Make it the devil you know.

CHAPTER 11

I showed up at David's at seven in the morning with a copy of the morning paper.

Man, twenty-eight, arrested in schoolgirl slayings, I said.

You look like shit.

Do I look like a nap and two cups of coffee? I said. Because those are things I want.

He made me drink four glasses of water and eat an egg right in front of him. I lay down on his couch till noon with a scratchy plaid blanket on my feet and sat up again feeling no better.

You get a real byline and everything, David said. He was sitting on the carpet with a mug of coffee, the newspaper spread out all around him.

Suspect grew up in Scarborough, I said.

It's huge. All those years they never caught him.

I know.

They could have got him years ago, David said. They had him in for questioning and everything.

I'm not going in today, I said. Mike's going back. But I'm not.

For a moment neither of us said anything.

I leaned down and dug into my shoulder bag. There's something you need to see. Look at this. I smoothed out the picture I'd printed off the archive at work, my teen runaway mother in front of the house on Brunswick Avenue. I found this like five minutes before Bernardo got arrested, I said. I've been carrying it around.

What am I looking for?

My mother. I pointed. This is the picture of that house, remember? That news item I showed you, the drug raid house with Cameron's alias attached to it, Arthur Sawchuk. It's *her* house, it's the house where she lived. Arthur Sawchuk's house.

David shrugged. So?

So the guy just happened to have the same name? I fingered the picture. It's a weird thing, David.

Unless the guy was using some big long foreign name that no one else has, total coincidence. And even then. He looked down at the photo again. I don't know that I would have recognized her, he said. This is pretty lo-fi. He slid the printout along the table and leaned back to look at me. You had a heavy night, Evie. Isn't this supposed to be your day off?

It's freaking me out, I said. I folded the picture in half, image side in.

What you need is fresh air, David said. He handed me a pint glass of lemon water. I think we should go skating.

David's the one guy in the whole country who didn't grow up playing hockey. His mother took him skiing. She put him on a bus every Saturday morning at six and sent him up to Blue Mountain and he spent the day on the mogul runs. As a result I find him to be a bit of a skating pansy, if you know what I mean. I say that more positively than you think. He's got hockey skates but doesn't have hockey speed. Overall it makes him a better companion, although whenever we've gone skiing I don't see him for the entire day.

We walked down from Davisville Station with our skates hanging by their laces, over our shoulders so the heavy blades kept bumping against my rib cage. I didn't have skate guards and I held my elbow out so that the blades wouldn't slap against my arm and damage my coat or leave it streaked with rust. I hadn't had them sharpened yet, either. The weight on my shoulder zipped up my neck into my brain. I had a stinging hangover and I kept moving the skates from one side to the other until David finally pulled them out of my hand and carried them himself.

The skating rink is a longish walk from the subway. Behind the library, halfway between David's mother's place and the house where I grew up on Bessborough Drive. On the way past my old street there was an Open House sign tethered to the light post on the corner, so that it wouldn't blow out into the street or fall over and get swamped with snow.

You wanna go?

David meant to the house, whatever House was Open. It's a thing we sometimes do, starting a couple of years back. It's a way to get inside new places. Sometimes you go for a walk in the evening and find yourself gazing into living rooms that have their lights on. Just in a cursory way. Not creepy. I have my favorites in every neighborhood. The ones with great giant paintings, or antique mantels. You see those houses where there's zero art on the walls and you know it's either students or old people who live there.

What if it's my actual house? I said. I squinted down the street as we went by. David had never been there. We'd moved from Bessborough to Inglewood Drive the year before his mother hired me as a babysitter, before I'd ever met him.

We sat down in the penalty box to lace up and went around and around in circles for a while. The ice was fresh and smooth on the hockey side, and knobbly on the leisure rink. Leisure rink or pleasure rink? I never remember. I used the lumps in the ice to scrape the rust off my blades. I had a Walkman in my pocket with a tape of Gershwin's "Rhapsody in Blue" and I put my earphones on and David went over and shot some pucks with a couple of guys who were about his age and also about a hundred times better than him. I'm shocked no one ever uses "Rhapsody in Blue" at the Olympics. It's perfect. Slow-fast-slow-dramatic.

So? I called out to David from across the boards that separated his side of the rink from mine. I pointed down the block with my mittened hand. I meant the open house, although I was generally ready to get the skates off my feet, too.

What if it's the house I grew up in? I said again. What if this is an open house at my own house?

I'm telling, David said. I'm telling the agent you don't have any money. Also? I'm totally going to hang out in your bedroom. Your mom will never find out.

I waved my fingers at him in a spooky way. Old houses are ghost houses, I said.

He held a hand out to ward me off.

You're a lousy ghost, he said. I can never see through you at all.

I don't hang around the old 'hood a whole lot. Once a year or so, in the fall when the trees are pretty, or if David's mother forces us over for dinner. The year before we'd gone to play tennis using the courts at my old junior high. We walked up Millwood and through the catwalk and found the courts empty.

It was July, and the middle of the day. No one else was dumb enough to be out in the sun. We'd rallied for a while and then played a couple of slow games, stopping every twenty minutes or so to bend low and drink water from the kid-size fountain just outside the chain-link fence. Before we left I'd gone inside the school to pee. There was an unlocked door just off the asphalt courtyard. The playground, I guess, for whatever kind of playing takes place when you're twelve or thirteen. David waited outside. I opened the door into what I suddenly recognized as the seventh-grade hallway. There was a long line of orange lockers, full-length. Halfway down the hall they'd had to replace one and the new locker was green.

Memory works on random cues. A sound, or some visual blip, something you'd never be able to identify in advance. There's a girls' bathroom in that hall. The toilets were clean because it was summer. I sat down and looked up through the gap between the cubicle door and its frame. A space the size of my index and middle fingers together, a peepshow view of the bathroom mirror, the sinks, and the empty paper towel dispenser.

There's the blip. Sitting there peeing and staring through the one-inch gap at a strip of mirror over the sink. My heart suddenly pounding. *Someone could see me.*

Not a stranger. Not some follower-in-the-dark. Other girls. The twelve-year-old girls who would have been there in 1983, in the bathroom, checking their lip gloss and spraying their hair and cutting one another down with gossip in front of the mirror, the year I was twelve and Lianne was dead and I went to that school. And how easy it was, from that point of view, to watch them back.

I thought of this as we walked down the circular drive, down and away from the Leaside Library rink. Try going back to the park where you used to play every afternoon when you were a kid, or your babysitter's front yard, or the steps up to your nursery school. Now take a look at the way the streets all branch out and the trees hang down and the kind of light in the sky. The familiarity will make you seasick. It's not about nostalgia. Nostalgia is a place you *want* to go back to. I'm talking about the opposite of that. A view that casts you out of your own, grown-up body and back into a place where someone leads you around by the hand and chooses what you eat and when you sleep.

We walked up Bessborough Drive a few blocks. I could see the For Sale sign sticking out of a snowy lawn up ahead and for a moment blanked on which house was mine and which ones weren't. It's an old neighborhood. A lot of the houses look the same. The windows were a different color, I thought, or at least the trim around them was different.

When we got close, David grabbed on to my hand. It was a light and casual gesture, like we did this all the time.

It's not my actual house, I said. It looks like it, but it's two doors down. My house was number forty-one; this is forty-five.

The real estate agent was perched up high on a bar stool near the entrance, with a wool shawl wrapped around her shoulders. The door was halfway open and it must have been cold sitting there, trying to run an open house in February. There were two names on the sign out front, but only one agent inside. She was a fiftyish false brunette. Her card said Antonina Argos.

Is this your first house? Antonina said. She rolled her R's only slightly. Not quite enough to make her foreign. She hopped off the stool and I saw that she stood about four-foot-eleven.

Yes, I said, prying off the heel of one wet sneaker with my other foot. It definitely looks that way.

The steps up to the front door, the entranceway, the landing and staircase to the second floor: everything was identical to the house I'd grown up in. The whole street had been built on the same plan.

There was a pile of shoes at the door and David hunched down to unlace his boots. We weren't the only lovely young couple out touring neighborhood open houses. When he stood up, Antonina folded back her shawl and her blouse parted in a deep and scandalous manner. She'd missed a few buttons for professional reasons.

Antonina waited for David to be done with his boots and then handed him the information sheet, gesturing to the highlights of the place like she was a tour guide at the Louvre. Her grammar was off-and-on. You'd call it practiced foreign charm: Three bedroom up, living, dining, eat-in kitchen. One-and-half bath. Hardwood throughout.

I slipped the sheet out of his hand. Antonina looked at David.

Now, honey. David gave my shoulder a condescending rub. Why don't you go on ahead and look around upstairs?

He turned to Antonina:

I'd like to take a look at the electrical panel.

We had our routine down pat.

———

You hear about tragedy tearing families apart rather than bonding them together. A baby gets cancer and the parents just can't manage all that grief and their own relationship, too.

This is understandable, because it must take everything in you to keep walking around, wearing clothes, starting the car with a key, and pretending to be the person-who-has-your-name. What's left for the other partner? It turns out the other partner is also full of grief and actually wants more from you, not less. Like everything else, mourning is only about power. You watch the baby struggle through and then die and nothing in you can change any of it. Suddenly you're the infant, power-wise. It's bad enough you can't protect your own kid. You're also handed a neat reminder that it could have been you, and that it was unstoppable. In the face of freakish disease or freakish murder, all of us are just babbling. We're on our backs.

The wider extension of this is how tragedy affects a community. You could see a low tremor run through the neighborhood—after Lianne, I mean. Kids didn't play outside on their own anymore. Nobody said, Why don't you go down to Trace Manes Park and see who's there? Nobody wanted to know that *who's there* was some guy in a long coat, or a man just hanging around in his car with a Polaroid.

Our spring fund-raiser at school was a raffle. Kids competed to sell the most tickets and went door to door. You'd sell a ticket to anyone: your mom's dry cleaner, the cashier at the corner store, other parents at the park. When the police called and talked to me in the middle of the night, they wanted to know, was Lianne selling raffle tickets? This is what her mother thought might have happened. That she went into someone's house, someone who told her they had money for her just inside. Later on, the school canceled the fund-raiser. Now they just ask parents to straight-up donate instead. Who knows? Maybe she did sell a ticket to the wrong guy. Maybe it happened on the way to the track, like everyone thought.

There were multiple theories. The police ask you a lot of very specific questions and all the questions need to be answered yes or no.

In the end, three families moved away—mine, Allison Lockyer's, and Herbert Wong's. Three-and-a-half, because a couple of years later, David Patton's father Graham moved out. David saw him on weekends, and then every second weekend, and then in the last few years, only once every couple of months or so. All I ever heard was that he'd moved downtown, but I couldn't tell you where, and it wasn't the kind of divorce where the father still comes over for dinner sometimes or hangs around the old house, having coffee. I never saw him again.

I grazed another couple coming down the stairs as I was going up. All our sock feet on the carpeted landing at once. A tall, real-looking blonde and a man in a crew neck sweater with a tiny polo player over his heart. The man had a back-to-front comb-over and was so much older that I hoped he was her father. I noticed the woman had not removed her shoes and I secretly cheered this act of insubordination. Maybe Antonina had come on to her fake husband, too.

Bathroom, she whispered. You gotta add ten grand for that. She passed me a little card and I saw that her name was Laila Bawshyn and that she worked for a different real estate firm. The fake husband had a line of pinprick holes across the toes of his navy socks.

Upstairs, the aesthetic wasn't much different from what you'd expect. Carpets over wood floors. Curtains instead of blinds. It was another one-child family. A crib in one bedroom, two desks in another. The baby's window, looking out on the backyard. I moved the crib gently against the wall, to get it out of my way. The yard was landscaped, with perennial beds at the edges and a central patio instead of a vegetable garden. I counted two lots over, to what must have been my old house, and saw that the yard there had also been converted to a patio. My parents had always let the grass grow long under the crab apple tree and for a moment I could almost see myself and Lianne out there, building a tepee out of loose sticks for the cat to live in, then letting it collapse into firewood, a campfire my parents wouldn't allow us to light up with matches. The better part of a day spent rubbing sticks together and the warm blisters on our hands. I turned back to the room.

The closet. Lianne the way I'd imagined her once, knees drawn up high, hidden away behind those doors.

There'd been a house-to-house search that extended over to the next street when Lianne was missing, but not quite to here. Our street, like Bernardo's in Guildwood, was occupied by professional people. Large driveways and garages. It occurred to me that if I went back and searched the archives, I'd find basically the same door-to-door piece I'd done the night before, only about a different murder and written by a different reporter. I wondered if my mother had let her in.

The bathroom was plain and clean, and there was a queen-size bed in the room the parents used. The place was antiseptic. It offered nothing about the occupants. This is purposeful, so that a new person can inject themselves into that space and not be bothered by questions or nagging ghosts, but there's an aspect of that kind of whitewashing that verges on sinister. I was thinking of the scene in *Lolita* where she's got the money hidden in a hole behind a painting, and he finds it and takes it away, and how awful that is and I stopped and unhooked a plaque-mounted replica of a Kandinsky and pulled it down off the wall. No holes behind the art.

There were no big indicators, no obvious reasons for the move. New baby on the way? Job transfer? Divorce? There must have been an open house when we moved away, too, and I realized other people walking through would have asked these same questions about my own parents.

I ran my fingers around the window ledge, looking for loose edges. The flats of my hands smooth against the wall, looking for anything, any lip, a painted-over trace. An odd, uneven panel. I crouched down and checked the wood parquet floor for any pieces out of place. The edges were all flush. Out in the hall, the walls were smooth and vacant. Just faux Parisian prints from the poster shops on Bloor Street and etcetera. No real art. No secrets.

I turned and started back down the stairs. From the landing I could see into the living room: a bowed window overlooking the front yard on one side and on the facing wall, a long mirror. My father had bought a similar thing for our old living room, a mirror to catch the light and open the room up. We'd left it behind. Too heavy to move. In this mirror, from this perspective, there was someone familiar standing in front of the window. David, waiting for me, stalling with Antonina. Rubbing at his dumb beard.

And then one of those strange sensory blips, a memory laid down over top of what was really there. Another time I'd stood on the stairs and seen a man reflected in the mirror, a man standing in my living room. Like that moment in the girls' bathroom at my old junior high, I could almost hear his voice. I took the rest of the stairs nice and slow, allowing the rug in the living room to blur and spread out into the red Persian that had been there in our house. Our red carpet, our couch, our mirror. My mother's things.

The day before Lianne disappeared, I'd come running home to find the front door locked, my mother arguing with a man in the living room, someone I didn't know and never saw.

Only I did see him.

For just a moment, just like this, I saw him reflected in the mirror. I could see him now. This memory of a man's face in the mirror. I stopped and squinted at it. Someone who wasn't really there. Not-David.

David's father. Graham Patton.

But you didn't start babysitting for me until you were twelve, David said. He pulled the zipper on his jacket up against the wind. He'd had to practically chase me down the street. That's the whole point, he said. Remember? You were twelve and I wasn't. My mom wouldn't let me stay alone, so why would she let some ten- or eleven-year-old kid babysit for me?

She didn't, I said.

I still don't get it, David said. You're saying you remember my father in your living room. You met me when you were twelve. You didn't meet me until after you moved out of that house.

We were hustling back toward the subway now. I stopped and grabbed David's arm and the skates slid down off my shoulder and landed hard on my bent wrist.

So I remembered something. I remember your father, I said. I remember him from before I used to babysit you. In the house, arguing with my mother.

What are you even talking about?

He was in the living room and they were fighting about something. I wanted to ask my mother a question and she told me to go back upstairs. I wanted to go someplace, Lianne was going and I wanted to go, too. Lianne got to do everything cool.

Evie? Do you think this could be another one of those, what do you call them? Reconsolidations. Maybe you're reconsolidating my father.

We'd started walking again, only slower. David switched sides so that he was walking closer to the curb and I was on the inside.

It's not, I said. It's not, I know it's not. That kind of memory trick is there to make you feel like you're answering a question. Confabulation, reconsolidation—that's to give you a solution.

I think you're looking for solutions, David said. You had a bad night at work. You found an old picture of maybe-your-mother and now you're tying her down to anything—first Robert Cameron, now my father. That wasn't even your house! You're just working yourself up. Evie. This Bernardo shit is fucking you up, that's all.

I know I saw your father there, I said. I know because it's making me more confused, not less.

CHAPTER 12

Here's what happened. Not the way I'd remembered it the week before, or the month before, or any month in the past eleven years, but the way I remembered it standing on the landing halfway between the bedrooms and the front door in that house on Bessborough Drive, looking down at the reflection of a man in the long, wood-framed mirror. A man who looked like David, but was not David. A man in the living room who was not my father.

I'd been out around the neighborhood with Lianne. It was springtime, Toronto spring. We were wearing cutoff shorts and jelly bracelets. Saturday morning, the real beginning of the weekend. We took a couple of grape Popsicles out of the freezer and went out wandering. The purple juice stained our lips and we used the Popsicles like icy Magic Markers, like lip gloss wands to make sure the stain set. We walked down past the library to visit the ocelot at the Endangered Animal Sanctuary on Millwood Road, and almost had to leave because the smell in that place, the pet-store smell, wood shavings and animal poop, was making me gag. Lianne would have stayed for hours. Lianne wanted a houseful of endangered animals. The owner was a thin, quiet man who seemed old to us. He probably wasn't even forty. He wore a baseball cap and his hair stuck out of it on all sides. He smoked. You could smell it on him, even over the animal smell.

What he had at the shop were animals that had been adopted

or smuggled into the country as pets, but then grew unruly. Too hard to tame. The ocelot in its square glass enclosure, tarantulas, a few big snakes. Furry creatures that looked cute and came with sharp teeth: ferrets, minks. Once, a chinchilla. The owner's name was Frank Churchill. He pulled the mink out of its cage, one hand gripping it behind the ears, where the jaw connects to the skull, so he could control the movement of its teeth. With the other hand he brushed wood shavings out of its fur. Then he stretched the animal's full length out in front of us.

That, girls, is the cat's meow, Frank Churchill said. You know how much money changes hands over mink coats? Number one Valentine's Day gift you can get a lady, that's a mink coat.

Lianne said she'd never wear a coat made of anything living.

How about cow? Frank said. You wear leather shoes, don't you.

Lianne said she didn't. This was true: she wore hand-me-down sneakers and rubber boots in the spring and fall, and snow boots in the winter. I doubt she'd ever had to buckle up a pair of Mary Janes in her life.

Plus they've figured out how to turn old tires into shoes and purses now, Lianne said. It's the wave of the future. Petroleum products. Now put it on me.

What, Frank said.

The mink, of course. I want it over my shoulders like a stole.

Stoles are usually made of fox, I said. A fox stole. No one says *a mink stole*.

Lianne raised her eyebrow at me.

Even better. Give me a fox stole made of live mink. Come on, she said.

Frank Churchill held the mink out toward her and shimmied it up and down softly, like a wave.

They bite, he said.

So do I, Lianne said.

Frank told her to turn around. He held the mink's body against the back of her neck.

If I do this, he said, you can't tell your mother. This is between you and me.

Okay, Lianne said.

If it bites you, you have to say you stuck your hand in the cage, Frank said. You can't say I put the thing all over you.

Okay, Lianne said. Go.

Frank lowered the mink's back end over Lianne's right shoulder and showed her how to grip its jaw with her left hand just under its chin.

He's shaking a little, Frank said.

Lianne moved slowly toward the front desk. She walked like a girl balancing a slim stack of books on the top of her head. Frank and I just watched her go.

There's the mirror, I said.

She stopped about a foot and a half away from a tall mirror that was leaned up against the wall next to a Komodo dragon. The lizard's terrarium was the size of my bed frame at home.

He likes me, Lianne said. He sounds like he's clucking. She dropped her hand away from the mink's jaw. A moment later she screamed.

The thing had gone for her immediately, catching her collar and a chunk of her hair in its teeth before Frank grabbed it off her and swung it out like a pendulum by the tail, upside down.

They're vicious fuckers, I told you, he said.

It didn't hurt, Lianne said. It didn't hurt, I'm fine. She ran her hand up and down her neck and pulled her shirt off the shoulder a little in front of the mirror, to check. Look. Look, she said. It didn't get me.

The thing about Lianne is that she knew how to draw attention. People remembered her. Frank Churchill called her a prime suspect.

We came out of the storefront and walked back through the park, toward my house. I had purple streaks on my legs where my Popsicle had dripped. There were bits of wood shavings in the toes of our sandals. In front of the library, a man was getting into his car. He turned and saw us and stood against the open door. I thought he was airing it out, trying to cool down the vinyl seats before driving off.

Hey, girls.

We didn't stop because why would that guy be talking to us, right?

He shut the door and walked toward us. He was tall with wide shoulders but maybe not much meat on him. Dark hair and most of a beard. Or else long hair and a full beard. I don't know. I was mostly looking at Lianne. She stuck out her chin like she was getting ready to argue. We stopped. There was something about him that made me feel like I'd done something wrong. Now I was caught.

Hey, girls, he said again, taking a few half-jog steps and arriving on the grass where we were waiting. You seen a dog running around here?

Neither of us answered. Sometimes when you're a kid, you get that stun on when adults ask you a question.

Big guy, he said. Black and white. Ears like this, see? He leaned forward and held his hands up to his temples and flapped them at us. Lianne cracked a smile.

He's real friendly, the guy said. But he don't stay on his leash.

Where did you lose him? Lianne stepped forward. She was interested now. Lost dog? Her specialty. Almost as good as a chinchilla, when it comes to that.

Oh, like over that way. The guy waved his arm vaguely in the direction of my house.

Were you in the school yard? Lianne said.

What's your dog's name? I said.

It was the first time I'd spoken. I was losing the attention battle to Lianne again. There was nothing about this that felt different to me from any other day at school. That was the way Lianne moved through the world. It was the effect she had on boys. At recess, there was always some boy who wanted to spray her with water from the fountain or tell her the name of his favorite band or race her the four hundred meters around the goal posts in the field. I was along for the ride at recess time. I got to be the audience. I was the witness in a blue sweatshirt.

Yeah, he was running around in the school yard, the man said. He was talking only to Lianne now. He stepped forward so close that the tips of his shoes almost touched her sneakers and he ran a hand through his hair, making it stand up and look spiky. He's a real sweet dog, he said. I rescued him from some bad people that used to beat him with a broom. Stupid mutt, he's still afraid of brooms.

What's your dog's name? I said again.

Lianne tucked a piece of hair behind her ear.

Maybe we can help you find him, she said slowly. We're walking that way, anyhow.

I was just going to take a drive around, the man said. He paused and then stepped back and pointed to his car like he was showing us what *drive around* meant.

We have to go, I said. There was a flavor to this interaction that irritated me and also made me ashamed, the beginning of something I was feeling more and more at school. I didn't want to waste my afternoon riding around looking for a dog, but I didn't want to be left on the sidewalk, either. If Lianne had survived and we'd gone on to high school together and stayed friends, this is pretty much how I imagine it: Lianne getting to ride around in cars, and me being left on the sidewalk. The logical extension of our recess routine.

We could go for a while, Lianne said. Looking at me. Then: But I've gotta ask first anyway, she said. In case my mom needs me to babysit or something.

She was pretty used to catching hell for not being home when she was needed.

A woman came out of the library holding her two-year-old under one arm like a football and a bag of books in the other hand. Behind her a sulky-faced older kid trailed along, crunching a lollipop. I hate kids who crunch lollipops. You know they're going to be hard to deal with, because they can't even wait for candy to melt in their mouths.

The man flinched, like he couldn't deal with the noise of the screaming toddler. He bounced on the balls of his feet.

Okay, yeah, I'll be at the school yard, he said. If you see him, you gotta catch him for me, right? He moved back toward his car and gave Lianne a little salute, like she was his right-hand man. He threw himself into the front seat in a lazy way.

We totally have to find this dog, Lianne said. That would be so awesome if we were the ones to save it.

Save it from what? I said. He says he already rescued it.

But Lianne was moving off, backward, jogging like she was a boxer in training. She was hopping on one foot. We were just young enough to be able to skip in public. We still made hopscotches on the sidewalk in front of my house.

Call me! she yelled. She turned around and started running.

I looked back and the man in the car was gone.

I started running, too. If I didn't show up, Lianne would go on and find the dog without me and have some fun time with ice cream and then she'd get in the guy's car and open up the glove compartment and find a necklace and wear it to school on Monday. The *Town Crier* would print a picture of her with the black-and-white dog. Girl Hero Finds Rescue Dog, Enlists Help of Trained Mink.

The *Town Crier* isn't a real paper. It's like the neighborhood paper that reports on the church bazaar every Christmas at St. Cuthbert's Anglican. It lists events at the high school and sales at Bruno's Fine Foods and reviews any new restaurants on Bayview Avenue. But somehow Lianne's picture made it in about three times a year, for one thing or another, and I wanted a piece of that action.

I came bounding up the concrete steps in front of the house and grabbed the door handle and pulled. The door didn't swing open and the force of my bounding and pulling made my hand slip and

I fell backward down the stairs. I landed on the little flagstone path that led to our front door.

The real door was wide open inside. It was the screen door, the little lock on the interior handle. The screen door was never locked.

My mother came to the screen and flicked the little switch and opened it up, but instead of saying something nice, she said: What are you doing?

Like my falling was something I'd done on purpose to embarrass her or to make her life hard. I came inside with my elbow bleeding and started talking right away.

There's this dog lost! I said. A lost dog, Lianne and me are going to go find it.

No, she said. No, you need to go upstairs. My mother stood with her back half-turned, facing the living room instead of me, like she was keeping half an eye on something there, a pot in danger of boiling over.

I'll only be gone for a little while, I said. I'll only be gone for an hour. I'll be home for dinner. It's this black-and-white dog. What if it gets hit by a car? What if it falls down into the ravine and breaks its leg?

I'd read a story the year before about a cat that had fallen down into Moore Ravine and broken two legs and was amazingly found by a lady and her two little kids. It had probably been lying there, starving and fighting off skunks, for a few days. The cat had fallen out of a tree but I didn't see why the situation couldn't occur to a dog, especially a big galumphing dog that was a rescue and used to being alone and too stupid to stay near its owner.

Evie! My mother spun around and pointed up to the second floor. Upstairs.

What are you so mad for? I said.

Get a Band-Aid on. Look after yourself. Read a book or something, Jesus fuck, I don't care, just get up there.

I walked slowly up the stairs. I was on the landing when I heard a man's voice calling out for my mother. Impatient, like she was a kid and he was sending her to her room.

From where I stood I could see only the interior wall, the long wall mirror my father had put up over the couch. He'd put it there to reflect the window, to make the room feel twice as big and shiny and surrounded by glass and light.

My mother walked quickly from the hall into the living room.

When you're a kid, there's heavy investment in the status quo. You like it best when there are no surprises. What you want is to come home every day to the same house and the same parent and have the same snack. When I was nine I read *Harriet the Spy* and envied her, how lucky she was to have that cake and milk every day after school. And she knows it, she sings a little cake-and-milk song to herself. If your mother yells at you for no reason, you don't apply logic to the situation. You don't think, Why is she in this terrible mood that clearly has nothing to do with me?

You just want her to stop screaming at you and give you a kiss on the forehead. You want what's bad to go away and for things to be good and normal again. I waited on the landing for my mother to come back and hug me but she didn't come.

There was a man standing just inside the living room, a tall man with a brown beard and a leather jacket. Not my father. I could see him reflected in the mirror. I don't know if I thought about the locked screen door and my mother's mood or even the man I'd just seen at the park. I know this man wasn't in the house later, when I came down for dinner at the regular kitchen table with my regular parents.

I didn't ask any questions. I went upstairs and never thought of him again.

CHAPTER 13

I made you something.

David pulled up a chair next to mine. I was in a study room at the university library, looking at the morning edition of the *Free Press*. There was no new information on the Bernardo case, just a rehash of what we'd already reported on the day before. We'd agreed to meet at the library so David could do some field research on Higher Education: Why David Patton Keeps Avoiding It. I'd slept twelve hours and was fully recovered from the hangover but hadn't been able to talk myself back into the newsroom.

I called in sick, I told David.

I hear Bernardo's still in jail. So you're not missing much. He passed me a little black notebook. Like Hemingway's, he said. See? I get you. Reporter and etcetera.

He was a sports reporter, I said.

Baseball to bullrings, David said.

I flipped the book open. On the inside front cover, David had neatly printed out a list for me:

TOP TEN JOB OPPORTUNITIES FOR GIRLS WITH SOMETHING TO PROVE

1. High Park Personal Trainer, Midnight Shift
2. Improv Coach at the Don Jail
3. Amateur Sherpa

4. Handler, John McEnroe
5. Bullfight Cheerleader
6. Getaway Driver for the Rainbow Warrior
7. Grizzly Tagger
8. Underwater Scout, Swim with the Sharks
9. Competitor, Pro Hitchhiking Circuit
10. Frontline Reporter, Vicious Murder Unit

I could absolutely be a Sherpa, I said.
I think you'd be happier as a Sherpa, David said.
I'm a clam.
You're making yourself crazy.
I'm onto something! I said.
I know, David said. You got a Nexis pass for Christmas and you haven't been the same since.
I turned the little notebook over in my hand.
How long are you going to be here? I said. Student grazing.
I'll be here. Why?
I want to go down to the archives and flip through city records, I said. I want to look at pictures.
Of course you do.
Don't be like that.
Like what?
I had the drug raid photo in my hand, with Robert Cameron's alias—Arthur Sawchuk—written on the back of it. My mother standing on the front porch of the house. I looked at the two men in the picture, out on the front yard.
I just need an old mug shot of Cameron, I said. Something from the States. Then I could compare it to these two guys.
Here's a wild and crazy thought: How about you just ask your mom?
We looked at each other for a hard moment.
I want to see what I can find by myself.

I stood up and David leaned over and hung his coat on the back of my chair.

You can't control this, Evie.

I flipped the notebook open on the table and carefully folded the first page over and creased the fold with my hand, hiding his list.

They found Robert Cameron's car in a factory parking lot in East York, I said. I didn't know that before. A couple days after they found Lianne. Someone reported it abandoned, stripped like it was stolen. That's information Nexis gave me.

You can't own this, David said. You can't research it away. It doesn't matter how much you know or what new thing you find. You can't write it over. You can't make it not have happened.

He pulled a notebook of his own out of his pocket and tossed it on the table. The two notebooks matched. I closed mine up and slid it into my bag, then slung the bag over my shoulder. When I was at the door, David looked up and called after me:

Happy climbing, Sherpa.

I still carried my expired j-school student card from the year before. I'd fashioned a fake registration date sticker for the back that showed I was a student for two more years, until 1995. A student card is a handy thing. Cheap movies, cheap transit, student rates at the Y. Library access on my day off. Where I had dial-up Internet at home, only the universities had high-speed service. I came down the escalator and flashed my card at the security guard and he leaned in and pushed the heavy door open for me.

Inside, there was a retrieval desk for archived paper and a wall of microfilm readers like I had at work, plus two computer stations. I sat down and reached around to the back of a monitor and flipped it on, then opened up the Telnet and waited to log on to LexisNexis. There was a dribble of traffic in and out of the room, picking up holds from the archive desk. I pulled everything out of my bag and laid it all out in front of me: the photo, a few other printouts from home, bits and pieces of information about Robert Cameron. Taking stock. What might have happened versus What we know for sure. The screen blinked at me.

L et's say Cameron ditched the Mustang himself, behind the industrial mall on Laird Drive.

He could have busted in the windows with a piece of scrap he found lying around out there. He popped the hood and ripped out the battery, stashing it underneath an overturned grocery cart, then maybe he changed his mind and hauled the cart to its wheels, threw the battery inside, and pushed the whole assembly off into the ravine. It would have made more noise on the pavement than it did down in the bush. It was about three in the morning, but hot for May, and sweat ran down his back as he worked. He had another car waiting in the parking lot at the east end of Taylor Creek. A '72 Caprice, olive green with beige panels that he'd bought off a Portuguese junk dealer in Etobicoke for three hundred bucks and a few cartons of American cigarettes.

This part we know for sure: He hiked out through the park, along the bike trails in the woods. There were a handful of teenagers drinking down in a gully. He walked along the ridge just above them. As he walked the branches brushed his shoulders and snapped back. He had heavy jeans on but his arms and face were getting scratched. The bag he was carrying caught in a bush and he heaved it forward.

He was moving steady, not turning his head. The soil on the trail crumbled away and dropped and rolled downhill, off the ridge. Cameron probably weighed two-ten, two-twenty. The group of kids flattened themselves to one side of their hiding place. Cameron knew they were there. He'd smelled the cheap pot they were smoking from a hundred feet away.

Shut up! Seriously!

The girls were afraid he was a cop.

He'd gone on another fifty yards or so when he decided to turn back. He was holding the bag on his shoulder with one arm over the top of it. The thing was getting heavy. He pitched it long and low off the trail, into the underbrush. The kids heard him coming back again.

He dropped down into the pit.

Who's got a smoke for Smokey Joe?

They were caught red-handed with the weed and Cameron relieved them of most of it. One of the boys started making a fuss and Cameron cuffed him hard across the jaw and then he sat down and regarded them all.

He never said he was a cop, one of the girls said later. The only person she told was her sister, alone in their basement rec room at home. I thought we were all toast.

He stayed with them for maybe twenty minutes, puffing on a joint, then got up and climbed back onto the trail.

He had these awful ragged fingernails, the girl said. I couldn't stop looking at his hands. He was just dirty. I don't know if he lives out there or what.

Lives in the park? the sister said.

He'd climbed back up onto the trail and looked down at them all. The girl said she was halfway home in her mind. As soon as he leaves, we're outta here, that's what I'm thinking.

He just stood there stoned.

Lotta pretty girls out in the woods tonight.

That's what he said.

NEXIS SEARCH: ROBERT NELSON CAMERON ARREST 1969

I fooled around like that for a while, moving backward and forward in time. Nothing Cameron did prior to 1975 was big news. Every search led to a stream of birth and obit pages, other Robert Camerons, born in other cities to other parents, but no A-section items. A single image, but it turned out to be a photo of the list of inmates released from the American prison Terminal Island in 1967, and the article itself was about one of the other prisoners on that list: Charles Manson.

I hadn't been able to talk myself into reading my own copy of *Helter Skelter* yet. There was a fat photo section in the middle of the book that I'd spent some time with, mug shots and press clippings and court evidence photo records, the weird white outlines when the victims' injuries were too graphic for a paperback you could buy off any newsstand in the country. They'd found a copy of the same book in Cameron's room, stolen from the library, I remembered. After Lianne died. Just his way of catching up with an old pal?

New slogan: All the best psychos do time at Terminal Island.

I pulled out the photo I'd shown David and gave it another look. Chewing on it. The corners were already a little ragged. In 1970 my mother was seventeen years old. The age of bad decisions, I guess. Her hair seemed lighter or straighter than now, or maybe both. Would she have known my father yet? Yes, almost certainly. Although maybe not quite.

I tried to imagine a pre-motherhood version of her, stomping cockroaches and going on dates and listening to music and making rent month to month. The way she talked about those days, like a place she'd rather put behind her. It occurred to me she must have been frightened. Seventeen is young. The kind of fear she'd lived with on Brunswick linked up in my mind with how she'd seemed after Lianne died. Disappearing for hours. On high alert. She must have been scared then, too. Not a thing you associate with adults, until you are one. I couldn't picture hitting her straight-up with all my weird questions, the way David suggested. Hey, Mom? So, remember Robert Cameron? The guy who killed my friend Lianne? Was he by any chance your roomie? Oh, and while we're here on memory lane: I don't suppose you can recall having a screaming fight with David's bad dad in our living room, one time?

I didn't want to open her up to that again. Not unless it was necessary. If I was honest, I didn't want to open myself up to it. I needed her on my side.

I folded the photo in half and tucked it inside the notebook David had given me. My bag was in my lap. It was a little past noon. I leaned into the keyboard. I figured there was time for one last kick at the can.

Without a birthdate or middle name or mother's maiden name, my search on David's father came up like this:

NEXIS SEARCH: GRAHAM PATTON, TEACHER, TORONTO

MARCH 4 1991: Local school hosts western science fair
winners
OCTOBER 10 1990: Secondary school teachers' strike
looms for Toronto
FEBRUARY 17 1989: Computers in shop class? New world
order for Toronto high schools
AUGUST 27 1984: School renovations a boon for industrial arts teacher
JUNE 3 1983: Inner City Angels balloon race lights up
summer sky
MAY 11 1978: York grads whoop it up on Alumni Day

Nice. Nothing I didn't know.

NEXIS SEARCH: GRAHAM PATTON, LEASIDE, TORONTO

OCTOBER 10 1990: Local teachers on strike

Thank you, *Town Crier.*

NEXIS SEARCH: GRAHAM PATTON, TORONTO
Nil.

```
NEXIS SEARCH: GRAHAM PATTON, TEACHER, TORONTO, CRIMI-
NAL RECORD
```
Nil.

```
NEXIS SEARCH: GRAHAM PATTON, TORONTO POLICE


MARCH 4 1970: No charges in Kensington area raid
```

Hold up.

I looked over my shoulder like someone was playing a joke. There was a printer behind the archive desk and I added a new copy of the drug raid news item to my growing collection.

Look at this, I said.

David was poring over a thin-leafed course calendar in the study room where I'd left him a couple of hours before. He waved me off.

Let's get a coffee, he said. No. A falafel. Let's get a shawarma.

I waited while he packed up and we came out of the building and walked north to Bloor Street.

Remember how I've been running those searches on Robert Cameron?

Wait. David stopped cold in the street. Are you telling me you have an interest in Robert Cameron, too? he said. Man! I love that guy.

I know, he's the best, I said. And you're a master of sarcasm.

All whimsy, all the time!

Now listen.

What's next for us, Evie? David said. He strolled out ahead, opening his arms up wide and almost clotheslining a couple of old ladies out for their daily. Don't tell me. You also like long walks on the beach? Piña coladas?

I caught up to him and struggled to match my stride to his.

Look, I was thinking about the open house yesterday. Your father, I said.

Oh, fuck you with this, David said.

I had the search result printout in my hand and while we stood in line at Sarah's Shawarma I ripped the printer tracks off the sides and wound them around my fingers.

I'm not saying I know what the connection is, I said. But don't you think that's weird? Don't you think it's strange that I run a search on your father's name and come up with an address where my mother once lived?

I think it's strange that someone obsessed with a child molester ran a search on my father, David said. That's what I think.

We got our food and sat down at a table in the back and I smoothed the news file out next to his tray.

David held up one hand.

For the record, I'm going to say that I am a staunch supporter of the work of the Metro Toronto Police in this matter. While it's a shame they didn't catch him, they had Robert Cameron nailed. They don't need new detectives. They're not hiring.

Look: the thing about Robert Cameron is that it doesn't fit. He's not a child molester, that's not the history, I said. The things he was arrested for, they were weapons charges, all of them. Armed robberies. Violent crime, sure, but no kid stuff. No little girls.

David took a fork and pushed around at the splotch of hot sauce inside his falafel, spreading it out.

This is ridiculous now, he said. You're making things harder than they need to be. This doesn't fit, that doesn't fit. The guy was a violent maniac, a psycho. You're not going to find logic here. You're not going to find anything.

I'm saying the last day I saw Lianne alive, I also saw your father in my living room, I said.

The fork and sandwich froze in David's hands.

What the fuck is that supposed to mean? he said. Did you actually just say what I think you said?

I shook the printout. All I'm saying is, This. What I'm saying is, Now. This.

David grabbed the news file and scanned it.

My father's not in here, he said.

I know, I said.

Like, not at all. He looked from the page back to me and then tossed the printout onto the table.

But this article came up in association with his name, I said. And that's the part I need to know about. Maybe he knows something about the photo.

He's not in the picture. I saw it.

Are you sure? It's pretty poor quality. You said so yourself.

I saw my father last week, remember? David said. I'm pretty sure I know what he looks like. He finished the sandwich and crumpled the long wrapper in his hand, then tossed it onto the tray.

I managed to coax David home with me. If one of the guys in the picture was really Graham Patton, at least those two dots would be connected. It would give me an opener with my mother. I wanted him to make the ID.

He wasn't interested in talking any more than we already had.

If he's in the picture, I promise to stop bugging you. I'll ask my mother and leave you out of it, I swear. You didn't even really try, I said.

Is this about Lianne or you? David sat down on the corner of my bed, low to the ground.

Just take one more good look and tell me if anyone seems familiar.

I curled a leg under me and leaned against his shoulder. He held the picture in his left hand and traced along the faces with a finger.

There's only two guys, he said. It's a weird picture to run with that piece. It's like it's a picture of the house, like the house says it all.

People hated hippies, I said. No one ever talks about that. They were scared of them. It was way more wrapped up in biker culture and hoboism than anyone wants to remember. People remember, Are you going to San Francisco? They don't remember dirty hitch-hikers.

La-la-la flowers, David said.

I thought of my friend Melissa, living out in that tent squat parking lot in Nashville and then getting dragged home crazy. People get damaged, I said. By drugs and also by other people.

Acid will burn actual holes in your brain, David said. I looked up. True story, he said. I did a biology project on MS and that's what the tech I interviewed told me. People come in for CT scans and have these black spots where the holes are. Blackouts: that's what he called them. The holes from acid don't look any different. He said he had to ask every patient what kind of recreational drugs they use.

My mom's this one, I said, pointing.

Yeah. Skinny.

She had beautiful bones, I said. My father says that. All her bones stuck out.

He's not here, David said.

What do you mean?

My father. I'm telling you he's not in this picture.

Oh.

My head hurt and I leaned it on David's shoulder for a moment.

I don't understand anything, I said. I wanted to stand up but the ground lurched under me. A wave of nausea hit the back of my throat and I leaned forward a little. I would have liked to put my head between my knees. Something's wrong with me all the time, I said.

Maybe there's nothing to understand, David said. He shifted his body so that he was a little closer and held an arm around one of my shoulders. I leaned in. You're pushing really hard right now, he said. Just stop and ask yourself what's this about. Is it Bernardo, or Lianne. Or is it you.

He smoothed the hair at my temples and tucked it behind my

ear. I looked at him. He'd gone home after the open house and trimmed his beard down to a rim of stubble, like Brad Pitt in *Thelma and Louise*. I rubbed the back of my hand against his jaw and it was rough and soft and I realized I wasn't thinking of anything but that, the feel of his no-beard against my skin. My head was airy. I tried to remember if I'd eaten anything at Sarah's.

What, are you gonna slap me now? Relax, I'm joking. Maybe you're just strung out. Ask Angie to make you do something else.

I can't, I said.

They can't fire you over that. It's like a disability, he said. His hair fell over one eye and I could tell by the look of him that he thought he was being pretty funny.

Oh, I'm disabled all right, I said.

Don't I know it.

David's tried to kiss me before, not just once, but maybe a handful of times. Sometimes it works, if we've been drinking, or even just hanging out more than usual, without the buffer of other people. So I knew I was safe. I knew if I kissed him he would kiss me back. I wrapped my hand around the back of his neck and pulled myself forward into his lap and let my mouth brush his and he tightened up immediately, his arm wrapping hard around the back of my waist. We slid down off the futon onto the floor with me straddling him and his hand up under my shirt and then outside it, working at the buttons. His mouth on my shoulder and my neck and I pulled his head up so that his mouth would be just on my mouth. I wanted the moment I'd had with my hand against his beard to extend to my whole body. I didn't want to think or worry about anything and the heat coming off him made me feel full and undamaged and at the same time I was choked by sadness. I was choking. He was wearing a plaid shirt with snap buttons over another shirt and I pulled at the snaps and they were harder to open than I thought. The snaps gave way one after another and under that there was a thin T-shirt and

I slid my hands under it and his whole body was solid and made of bone and would last forever.

We weren't drunk. We hadn't been drinking and he kissed my shoulders and my neck and breasts. I was in my bra and the straps were already coming down off my shoulders and I pulled them up and tried to take a break, with my hand pushing flat against his collarbone.

David pulled away and then I did and he sat me on the floor so that I was next to him but not right on him anymore. He looked at me and he was wary.

Today is not my best day, I said.

What do you want me to do.

I pulled my legs cross-legged in front of me and leaned over sideways against the bed.

I'm sorry, I said.

You don't have to be sorry. It's not a sorry thing.

I smoothed out his shirt for him.

You're all over the place, he said.

My head is just rushing all the time.

I just want to know, David said. I like to know where I stand.

The photograph was still lying there. I stared at it a moment.

I know there's something here, I said. There's something I'm not getting. I tugged the photo closer. Why is your father's name on this if he's not in here, I said.

Are you fucking kidding me, David said.

What?

You're making shit up.

I'm not. I remember it. I remember him.

You don't remember shit. You were a little kid. Your brain is overloaded and you're filling in the blanks.

That's not true, I said.

You don't know what's true. You just jumped on me.

I know. I don't know what I'm doing. I looked at the picture in my hand. What if Robert Cameron had another alias, too, I said.

What if that's why they never found him? What if he's been here all along? Hiding in plain sight.

David looked at me.

Watch your mouth, he said.

David, it makes sense. What if your father is Robert Cameron? It explains everything: the connection to my mother, the photo, everything.

I told you my father is not in that fucking picture.

Why else would I remember him?

Forget you. David got up and went out into the hall. I followed him and watched him prying his boots onto his feet. He hadn't bothered to untie the laces.

I'm the first fucking one to slag my father, David said. I fucking hate that guy. All he ever did was cheat on my mom. We'd get home from the grocery store or my fucking soccer game and he'd send me down to the basement to put something away. I'd go down there with a tub of ice cream and there'd be some girl there, half-naked, hiding out behind the freezer. David slammed his foot down into the boot and looked at me. He sent me down there on purpose, he said. So I'd be proud of him, big man, big score, some girl.

David.

No. No. Just no.

I was standing there with my shirt still half-open.

I'm allowed to say it, David said. It's on me. He's a liar and a shitty father and a shittier guy. But he didn't kill your friend, he didn't rape some little girl and leave her body out in the woods for a dog to find. David threw his arms into his peacoat. I don't want you to say stuff you can't take back. I can't take this back for you, so you just have to keep it to yourself. My father is not Robert Cameron. Get it? You want to make shit up, make things fit? Keep it to yourself.

He kept talking like that and repeating himself. I couldn't get a word in edgewise. He talked himself right out the door and it slammed and clicked and I stood there and listened to his feet on the steps until the downstairs door slammed, too, and he was gone.

CHAPTER 14

You got a driver's license? Angie stuck her head into my cubicle and dropped a file folder on my desk.

I don't have a car, I said. I picked up the folder and leafed through it. A handful of wires and the release about Bernardo's arrest. Plus an address, what looked like an old real estate listing, and a copy of a warrant.

Cops are picking the house apart, she said. Down in St. Catherines. They're not gonna find anything right away. But I want you to go sit and watch them do it.

Angie drives a blue Turismo she bought new in 1982. It's a good car for blending in or hanging around in and it's got a great big hatch so if she needs to she can throw photo equipment in there or haul a few guys around with her.

Last year she was working on a guns-and-gangs feature series where she started following leads around town: squad car chasing, mostly, and also a few gangsters. Modern gangsters are a lot less glam than old movies would have you believe. Nobody wears a fedora or goes to the casino with Myrna Loy. It's hard drugs and guns and sex trade. It's a moneymaking endeavor operated by thugs.

When she was working on the series, the paper rented her a different car every day of the week for a month. So she wouldn't be traced, or tracked.

Because the gangs are stupid that way, Angie said. No one's

going to notice a white lady with big hair happens to be hanging around everywhere they go.

But in fact it must have worked, because the series won an award for investigative journalism, and now Angie has driven every make and model car from economy through to luxury sedans.

The best thing I learned on that job, she said, was that I'll buy Japanese next time. Great pickup, great on gas. Across the board. Now there's an article for you.

I took Angie's Turismo down to Port Dalhousie, Bernardo's high-end neighborhood in the city of St. Catherines, and spent the first afternoon parked too far away to see much of anything. The street was gridlocked with locals taking a leisurely drive past the murder house. It was Saturday, so no one was at work. The police had only just got their search warrant the night before and the best thing that I could see to report on was a transport that showed up around 3:00 p.m. and took away Bernardo's gold sports car. At the end of the day, a couple of officers walked out of the house carrying some white file boxes and a full black garbage bag and that was it. A lot of rubberneckers. Something like this really draws the community together.

I'd seen the details of the warrant and knew they didn't have much recourse to do anything. Angie had said they were picking the place apart, but the truth was that police weren't allowed to take down any walls or do damage to the structure, so they had to be in there looking for stuff that was in plain sight. If they found video, it had to be watched inside the house. What they wanted was to find evidence that the first girl, Leslie Mahaffy, had spent time inside. They knew Kristen French had. They knew she'd been alive for thirteen days. I spent a little time shooting the shit with people as they went by. An old woman stopped and got out of her car but left it running; the driver's door hung open while we talked. She was small and only slightly hunched, wearing a gray-green tweed suit with a long skirt and a matching hat. She had her lipstick on. I thought she might be a retired school principal.

The old lady pointed a finger at the yard. She wanted me to see the way the house and the garage met. You could pull your car into the garage and shut the door and get into the house through the side door, she said, and no one on the street would ever see you.

People love privacy, she said. But now you see what happens out here. High fences on every side. She grabbed on to my hand and then let go. We always knew what our neighbors were up to, she said, and we didn't have this, this, this. She waved her arm in circles at the house and her voice got louder with every *this*. Like it was the house— suburban architecture—and not some human that had done it.

There was nothing to see, but I had to file a story. My job was to keep finding new ways to talk about the same thing. You have to keep feeding it, Angie said, so that when something really breaks people are still paying attention. I listened to the talk stations all day. Every hour there was a sound bite, new or repeated, it didn't matter. Two-minute interviews. A dwindling level of expertise after only a few days. The old lady was my man-on-the-street. Why tenements were safer than suburbs, she said, and then I said it, too.

S unday morning I left the city early because the media crush was going to make it hard to find a good spot, near enough to the house to actually see it. On the way down to St. Catherines I pulled over for coffee and a pee at a diner just off the highway, on a service road between Grimsby and Beamsville. It was about 6:00 a.m. I'd known a theater student in college who was from Beamsville and categorized it as the worst place on Earth. The whole Niagara region has this lovely reputation for Shakespeare and fresh peaches, but you get down there and it's shiny and desolate. Rich grape estates, poor market gardeners. Suburbs where girls go missing and turn up in the lake, chopped in pieces. Beamsville also happened to be Task Force headquarters.

There were two transports and a cop car parked at the diner and inside I saw two truckers and a waitress wearing a pink uniform. She poured my coffee into a Styrofoam cup and added the cream herself before snapping on the lid. Her nails were bitten down ragged but still painted mauve, and I wondered how much nail polish she ingested, doing that. I'd once read a statistic on the amount of lipstick the average woman swallows over the course of her lifetime and it's something like twenty-one tubes. Feel the mash of all those tubes between your teeth for a moment. Dense and slippery. I ordered toast and peanut butter along with the coffee, then waved the waitress back and asked for a club sandwich and an extra coffee to go, because I knew I'd be sitting in front of the house all day and might not be able to get away for something to eat. The cook dinged a bell when my food was ready. The toast was white and square and it came with those packets of jelly on a rack, grape and raspberry and marmalade. I went to open up the raspberry but my thumb slid. The jam rack sat on the counter all day every day and the packets were slick with ambient grease.

While I was waiting for the rest of my order I sat at the counter and sipped the coffee and burned my tongue. There was a copy of a rival daily just lying there and I flipped through the front section to see where we were at. Bernardo was A1 and A6. Like the *Free Press*, this paper was publishing two kinds of articles: A1 pieces that were all hard facts drawn from daily press conferences, and heartstring A6 half pages about the relief in the community and for the victim's families. Some of the articles quoted the fathers of the girls in this case, French and Mahaffy, and some of them quoted a mother in a different case, a six-year-old girl who'd been found dead a little while before and whose murder had been resolved immediately. The papers talked to her because she was an expert on closure and relief.

Today's A6 was a large photograph of a woman who claimed to be Bernardo's ex-girlfriend, wearing sunglasses and heavy lipstick. The quality of the paper made her lips look black. She said the police were wrong, they had the wrong guy. No reporter had interviewed her. She was writing letters to the editor every day.

The two transport drivers were also at the counter, farther down, with a couple of empty stools between them but talking all the same, the way men do in a place like that. One was clean-shaven and older. Early sixties, wearing work pants and boots and he didn't have a jacket or a coat, but a green down vest was slung over a chair behind him and I figured that's what he was wearing against the cold. Bernardo was lucky, he said, that he was safe in jail.

They ever let that fucker out, someone's going to string him up. Cut off his cock and choke him with it. Jam it down his own fucking throat. I'd do it myself, he said. If that was my little girl.

Just then the cop came out of the bathroom. He was still zipping up his fly and looked surprised to see a woman sitting there. He let his gaze rest on me for the count of three and then turned to the truck drivers.

Lot of folks talking like that, he said. He said he'd been on the scene when Kristen French was found and the three men threw around some details for a while. Some of it was stuff I'd heard before. Some of it was brand-new to me. The cop shook his head and drank his coffee. He said he didn't know how much longer he could do this job.

He was married. Bernardo. This was the younger trucker speaking. That's the thing I can't understand. You get the wife, too? It's the wife I want to hear about.

The trucker was ten or fifteen years younger but in worse shape, with a large, hard belly and a ragged beard. He had acne under the beard, with facial hair wispy enough that you could see the pimples through it.

The waitress brought me my sandwich in a Styrofoam clamshell.

She worked for my girlfriend's vet, the waitress said. The wife. My friend knew her. Saw her every time she took her cat in for shots, always said, Hello, how are ya. Real friendly! Young, blond. Clean uniform. Always smiling.

The waitress looked at me. At the vet! Dealing with little animals!

I got back out to the highway and worked my way down into the suburbs and found the street. There were about four other cars already there. There'd been a black Honda behind me all the way down the service road from the diner and now it pulled up to the curb and stopped, too. There was a uniform cop standing around on the porch but nothing else going on. I turned off the engine and tipped my head back and closed my eyes. I was low on sleep. My eyes felt hot and bruised.

I let my neck loosen and rolled my shoulders back and opened my sore eyes again. There was a face in the window. I jumped back and grabbed at the parking brake and also my seat belt. He was crouching low down next to my car and waving a sheet of paper at me. I rolled the window down an inch or two. Mid-fifties, gray flattop, coat open.

I'm with CVQR, he said. He shouted it like my window was still shut and he had to get my attention. I rolled the window down a couple more inches. He handed in the paper. CVQR is all-news radio.

Is something wrong, I said.

No! No, no. I just wanted to let you know, he said. Here. He reached a hand in through my open window. Name's Dave Snodden. I followed you in, see? He pointed back at the black Honda.

You're a reporter?

Not exactly. I do some production, he said. But the thing is, I was born here. I'm from St. Catherines.

Okay, I said.

I'd like to take you around, he said. I mean, if you'll let me.

I looked at the paper he'd handed me. It was divided into eight sections. In each section, he'd written *Dave Snodden* and his phone number.

What do you mean?

Oh! Not like that, Dave Snodden said. Listen. It's just. We're all out here trying to make a buck, right? I grew up here. I'd like to take you around, show you all the places. Take you down to the lake where they found Leslie Mahaffy's body parts, and over to the church lot where he grabbed Kristen French. So you can see how it happened. He gestured back to the Honda again. I got a car right there.

I still had my seat belt on. I told him, Not today. He seemed like the kind of guy you have to be nice to when you're turning him down. Sort of happy-go-lucky but possibly instantly full of rage. When he was a few feet away from the car, I locked the doors. I did that before I rolled the window up even. After that I didn't close my eyes again.

Just after eight a white van rolled in and the forensics squad got out, already dressed for work. They wore white paper suits and black boots and gloves and their faces were obscured enough that I wondered if it was the same team that shipped away the gold car the day before, or a different team, and if the same people had to go in and pick through the cupboards and the toilet tanks and electrical panels every day, no matter how long this took, and if they also dreaded what they were hired to find.

If they found a video, it couldn't leave the house. I thought of the cop I'd seen in the diner, grim and disappointed. I knew they'd likely view it on some Task Force A/V, brought in for the purpose, but instead I pictured them all getting comfortable in Bernardo's living room, slouched forward around his TV, sitting on his couches and beanbag chairs, a bunch of men in space suits watching another man torture girls until they died. I pictured their faces as they watched.

At the end of the day I drove Angie's car back up into the city and left it parked on Sussex Avenue, a few doors down from her house. I threw the keys into her mailbox. The temperature had been dropping solidly since noon. It was snowing now and I remembered that usually means things are getting milder. The worst February days in Ontario are snowless, dry and clear and injurious with cold. I walked up past the Jewish Community Center and down into the subway at Spadina. It was well past rush hour and the platform held only scattered groups of people. A draft blew down the stairway and the farther I wandered down the platform, the warmer it got. I stopped and watched the tracks for rats. David said he often saw rats, running along just parallel to the live track. Some days you see one that's been accidentally fried. It was only three stops to Dufferin Station and then a long wait on the platform for what is arguably the worst bus in the city. Four or five inches of snow on the ground now. When we got down to Dundas, the intersection was blocked off by two cars in a T-bone and one local squad car with an officer trying to stop traffic in all directions. The bus driver levered the front door open and stepped out.

After a few minutes, my compatriots on public transport started getting restless. There was a guy wearing wet sneakers and a track jacket alone in the back row, his arms spread out wide under the window, yelling curses in Portuguese. It doesn't take much to turn the bourgeoisie into the mob. The driver returned with a coffee and a bag of pastries from the Brazil Bakery. I walked up to the front of the bus and asked him to let me off and I hopped down into the snow. I cut along Dundas, down to Gladstone. Stores were closed now and the street was quiet. On Gladstone every second street-light was out. The silence made it feel close. I wanted to look behind me and make sure I was alone, but it wasn't even nine o'clock and that seemed crazy. The tiny lawn at the side of my house was ridged and icy. The snow crumbled down into my boots and burned my ankles. I don't remember if the landlord had cleared the path or not. I crossed the lawn and came into the house quickly because I was hungry and cold and the urgency of the past two days, spent alone and waiting for something grisly, pressed down hard. I know I used my key to get in. The door closed heavy behind me, clicking into place. I couldn't tell you if there were footprints outside the house that were not my own. It did not occur to me to look.

nside, I flipped on the hall light and pulled off my hat and boots and went into the kitchen still wearing my coat. Bits of snow came off the cuffs and fell onto the floor and when I stepped on them, my socks soaked through. I threw a pot of water and rice onto the stove and lit the gas, eager to get to anything hot and meal-like. The stove light from the overhead exhaust spotlit the kitchen and made it seem warmer in the night. I got my coat hung up in the hall and stopped moving for a moment. The larger house was still and quiet. I was the only one at home.

There was a bag of spinach and some cheese in the refrigerator, and I pulled these out along with a container of calabrese olives and ate three of the olives in a row and poured a glass of red wine. The door to the apartment above mine opened and shut and one of the guys upstairs came heavily down the steps. The door downstairs slammed. I picked through the spinach leaves, tossing out any that had gone black or wet looking. I'd thought I was alone in the house. I couldn't shake the feeling I'd had out in the street, of wanting to turn and look behind me.

I'd stopped in at the office the past two evenings and filed what-ever bits and pieces I'd seen at the house. There was more ahead all week. My notes centered mostly on the effect on the community, the strangeness of the forensics team. I hadn't spoken to David for two days, not since the night he walked out, and I missed him. I needed to thrust the stories onward, to push them over to someone else's consciousness and get them out of mine. There were things I'd heard early in the day, the shoptalk in the diner, that I couldn't rid myself of.

The cop had said when they found Kristen French they knew they had a psycho on their hands, but one with an education. There was some knowledge of basic anatomy there. Her Achilles tendons had been sliced through, to make it so she couldn't get away.

The wife, the waitress had said. The wife was a vet assistant and would have known such things.

I had no trouble putting myself in that girl's body, crawling on her elbows because she could not stand.

———

I had a handful of spinach leaves in one hand and the other swirled through the bag, fishing for good ones, and I stopped for a moment and felt how still the place was. A ticking inside the wall that was mice or the tremor of the hot water pipe. I flicked three blackish leaves from the bag to the sink. Outside, something heavy chimed off the metal fire escape and I froze.

A heavy icicle falling from the eaves. A hardy raccoon. I turned my body to the window.

The stove light shone hard and white off the glass, bleaching it. I could see my own reflection, my own fridge and stove. One of my hands was full of spinach and I held it out in front of me with the fist tight and the raw leaves sticking out between all my knuckles. Where the reflection faded, I could see the landing outside my window, a couple of solid black stumps. Boots. Black boots and legs. Someone out on the fire escape, looking in.

I counted in my head, waiting for the boots to move on, a friendly knock, something. Someone from upstairs, having forgotten his key. The boots stayed there. My breathing stopped and I squinted. The window shone a pale and cloudy version of my own kitchen: table, wall, desk, chairs, and under the stove light, a girl, staring. For a moment I didn't recognize myself. I took two long steps to the window.

It can't happen if you've imagined it enough.

My own long hair brushing my shoulders, the V of my sweater, my collarbone standing out white. In another yard, a cat or a raccoon screamed and the neighbor's motion sensor kicked on. The outside lit up all at once.

The raccoon scrambling across the top rail of the yard fence.

The light held for the count of five. Long enough for me to see him there, only a foot or two from the window. Tall, black cap pulled down close, coat, boots, hands huge in black gloves. Eyes deep set. Face half in shadow.

Long enough for him to see me watching.

Then the light flicked off again, leaving just the white walls. Dancing spots. My eyes trying to adjust to the sudden swell of brightness and then the dark again. Just a silhouette where I knew he was standing, a few feet away at most, the window between us.

I tripped backward and switched off the stove light. The clink of breaking glass: I'd knocked my wineglass into the sink. The spinach leaves tumbled out of my hand and my reflection disappeared, the window opening up to a mute view of the backyard, the black fire escape landing. There was nobody there.

I shut the kitchen door and shoved a chair up under the doorknob. Outside, the fancy ironwork over the outside of the windows, and beyond that the snow-covered landing, the steps, the black railing. I was in the dark now.

Could he be inside? Or still out there, watching me do this. I walked over to the window and raised my fist and slammed it. Forehead against the glass, eyes shut.

I know how to work myself up. Heart beating hard through the brain.

They'd cut through her Achilles with a knife, with a band saw, and this slowed her down. It made her easier to hold. She crawled on her knees, on her belly. She wanted home. They held her by the hair.

No. The cop had said they'd cut her long hair off with the same knife.

I opened my eyes.

Fuck you, I whispered. You're so fucking paranoid.

No one there.

The snow put everything to sleep, white and muffled. The raccoon was gone. Outside was clean and gorgeous and I looked down and saw the tracks: boot prints, all up and down the landing, the heavy marks in the snow where he'd stood and stared.

I was still standing against the window, with my back to the blocked kitchen door. I looked at my hands. My fingers were splayed out on the frozen glass.

You don't have David, I said to the hands. You don't have him. Now what?

I turned on every light in the kitchen. While I was doing it, I called out like I was talking to someone in just the next room: Hey, what are you up to? I said. That's hilarious!

I yelled a bunch of stuff like that and tried laughing really loud, so anyone listening would know what a great old time we were having, me and this other person I live with, some other person who loves me to pieces and will never leave me alone. The chair was still wedged under the kitchen doorknob.

If I unwedged it, whoever was out there in the dark apartment would come in. He'd broken in while I was yelling: I was making so much noise I hadn't heard him lean into the crowbar, the soft splintering of the door frame. Now he was inside with me. A guy like that will wait you out.

You can see I have a lot of practice scaring myself.

I thought of walking down to Queen Street and along to the Skyline and ordering some pancakes from the all-night kitchen. I'd be happier if I wasn't at home. The Skyline is owned by a nice old Greek couple who get upset if you don't eat meat, and the idea of being out in the street felt much safer than being trapped in my apartment where someone knew I lived. My head had that pins-and-needles feeling you get in your feet if you sit on your knees for too long. I put on the radio, then turned it right off. The noise of the radio made it so I couldn't hear what was really going on. I wanted the old Greek lady to put her hand on my shoulder and make me eat bacon. The imagined weight of her hand on my shoulder felt so good to me that I started to cry.

I leaned over the sink and gagged a little. Then I sat down on the floor in the middle of the kitchen and called the police.

The problem with leaving the apartment is that you have to come back.

CHAPTER 15

It took dispatch a few hours to send anyone over because in that part of Toronto there's a lot of drugs and sex work, even on a quiet Sunday night. Other problems that are considered high priority. I sat in the bright kitchen on the floor with my knees tucked up to my chest and my back against the cupboard so I could see everything: all the windows, every corner, the door to the hall, jammed shut.

After I'd hung up with 14 Division, I called my parents, and they were the ones who arrived first. I heard the click of a key prying open the front door lock, out in the hall. There was a moment of quiet when their eyes must have been adjusting to the dark. I pictured my mother running her hand along the wall, looking for the light switch. My heart flew up into my throat. What if it's not them?

My father's voice: Where the hell is she? And then a soft knock at the kitchen door, still barricaded with a chair up under the doorknob.

Evie? Evie, we're here.

I had a sudden flash of how foolish this was. How shameful. Trapped in my own kitchen. I stood up and pulled the chair out and my mother pushed the door open and grabbed my shoulders and hugged me.

You okay? She pulled back and held my face, gently, with one hand. What happened? You okay?

I hadn't told them much over the phone. Someone was on the

balcony, I've called the police, he's gone now, but he was there. Someone on the balcony, a man. Looking in.

My father went over to the window and leaned his face into it, cupping his hands like a visor over his eyes.

Did he come back? my mother said. She said this sharply and without anxiety. All business.

He was only there a minute, I said. I feel really stupid for making you come over.

Are you kidding? She turned toward my father, intent on his window surveillance. Anything out there?

Nah, he said. Looks fine to me. He came over and patted my shoulder. All clear, sweetheart.

What did he look like? my mother said. Did you get a look at him?

I don't know, I said. He was tall. He was a tall guy. I feel like an idiot.

How tall? Anything distinguishing? Did he have a beard, or crooked teeth or something?

I don't know.

Annie, stop. It's nothing. She's fine. This was my father. He turned from my mother back to me: Evie, you're fine.

She's not fine. Look at her. Can I make you a cup of tea, sweetie? Something hot. My mother started opening and closing cupboards. She's white as a ghost, look at her. She's not fine.

My father put his arm around me and pulled me in. You're fine, he whispered. Your mother's going into hyperdrive over this. I bet it's nothing at all.

The cops arrived and banged on the downstairs door with their fists. This wasn't uncommon on my street. Police! Open up!

I ran down the dark stairs and made them show me their badges through the peephole. They were both men.

There was a dark-haired young guy and an older cop with gray hair, and the young guy walked around back first to see what he could see. The older guy came upstairs with me and sat down at the kitchen table.

Who's this? he said, pointing at my parents. They were both standing up, leaning against the kitchen counter. My mother had my yellow teapot in her two hands like she was keeping it warm and she held it out to him and he shook his head No. She poured a quick shot of whiskey into a mug, filled the mug with tea, and pressed it into my hand. She'd brought the mickey with her, in her purse.

The cop said his name was Constable Mercer. He asked me if I'd ever seen anyone hanging around my house like that before and I said, No.

It's a lousy area, my mother said. My father made a gesture like, Shh.

I mean, yeah, I said. Yeah there's always guys hanging around in the street, but no one looking in my window like that.

So he was looking in the window?

I nodded.

Yes or no.

Mercer had a little notebook and a pen and he was getting ready to write things down, but not writing anything yet. I found him hard to look in the eye. I was glad to not be alone, but with all three of them in the room, watching me, I felt surrounded. I had a sudden feeling the cop was going to catch me at something.

I think so, I said.

What do you mean, you think so?

Just tell him what happened, Evie. This was my mother again.

I was standing at the stove, I said. And I heard a sound, like someone climbing the stairs out there. But I couldn't see anything, because I had the lights on inside.

You didn't see him climb up?

I heard something, I said. I heard his boots.

What'd he look like? Mercer said. I stared over at the window for a moment before answering.

Something happened next door, I said. Like a cat fight or something. They have a motion-sensor light in the backyard, and it went on. So it got really bright outside.

So then you saw him? Constable Mercer looked at the window and then back at me.

Yes, I said. I was trying to look out the window and tell myself no one was there but then the light went on and he really *was* there.

Then what? Mercer still wasn't writing. I had a weird feeling in my stomach. Then the light went out, I said. And I couldn't tell. I went to the window and he was gone, but you could see where he'd been standing, because of the snow.

Footprints? Mercer finally touched his pen to the notebook.

He left holes, I said. There were holes in the snow where his feet were.

Someone was on the fire escape, knocking on the window.

It was the young cop. Mercer unlocked the fire escape door and the other cop came in and shook the snow off his boots.

Nothing out there, he said.

He was there like three hours ago, I said. It took you a long time to come.

No prints, the young cop said, but it's a lot of snow since then. I realized he wasn't talking to me; he was talking to Mercer. Mercer wrote something in the little book.

You seen anyone out there before? The young cop looked at me. I looked at Mercer, then back at this new guy.

She already answered that, my mother said.

I think we're going to go, my father said. Annie, get your coat on. My mother didn't move. She had the staunch look of determination you might associate with sit-in protesters. She would have been happy to sit down and answer all their questions on my behalf. You've got to let them do their job, my father said.

The new guy asked his question again.

No, I said.

You have a boyfriend, ex-boyfriend, someone might want to give you a scare?

No, I said. No, I don't think so.

The young cop said his name was Job. Like from the Bible, he said. He scraped a chair along the floor and sat on it backward, so he was facing me, but with the spindles between us like a little wall.

What'd he look like?

He was tall, I said. He had boots on, and a hat. And a hoodie, I said. A black hoodie.

Tall, like how tall?

I don't know. Taller than me.

Like six foot?

Okay. Yeah.

What kinda hoodie?

What do you mean? I said. Wait. Black.

Like what brand. Did you see that? Like with a name?

Oh, I said. No.

Mercer sighed and doodled into the notebook.

It's pretty hard for us to do anything, Mercer said. You women never remember what these guys look like. Anyone live upstairs?

I was surprised that he asked that, because I wasn't finished with my part of the story yet. I looked at Job but he was done asking me questions.

Um. Yeah, I said. Yeah. There are three guys up there.

But it wasn't one of them?

I don't think so.

Are you sure, Evie? My mother sat down in the chair next to me.

Did he go up or down? Job said.

I don't know. I didn't see him go.

You didn't see him?

He was there, I said. He was standing there. But then he was gone, I don't know. I don't think it was one of them.

But you don't know for sure, Mercer said.

Why would someone do that? my mother said. Why would someone from upstairs look in her window?

Mercer pushed his chair back and did a thing with his hand like, What do I know?

Who owns the place? he said.

The guy downstairs.

Mercer tipped his chin at me.

He's a mute, I said. You can talk to him but it won't do any good. I thumped my foot on the ground. He can't even walk.

He looked over at Job.

Go see, he said. We'll go shake him up a little. See if maybe he suddenly knows how to walk. Upstairs, too.

My mother had her hand on the back of my chair. In practice the interrogation made the actual incident seem really far away. Like it was something I'd dreamed, or a story I'd read. I was already thinking about what would happen now, when they all left. It was about midnight. There was a lot of night still to go. I felt really young sitting in my kitchen. I felt like the chair was too big for my body. I wondered if the cops were shaking me up, too. What they were hoping I'd suddenly come up with.

I lost my mittens, I said. And then someone left them on the fire escape for me. Is that something?

When was that? Mercer said.

A few days ago. Maybe a week.

He didn't say anything but he opened up his book and marked it down.

Here, Job said. You got a broom? Let me sweep off that snow for you. So you're not thinking about it all night.

He went outside and swept off the landing. Then he came in and handed me the broom and locked up the door. My mother put the teapot in the sink and I realized that everyone was leaving at once.

Mercer closed his little book and got up out of the chair.

That's a good lock, Job said to my father. She's got a good land-lord here. He turned to me: You're okay.

They moved off toward the front door.

What happens now? I said.

Mercer looked surprised.

We'll let you know if we find out something, he said. Call back if he comes around again. But I don't think he will.

You're all right, Job said again. Just lock up. Look out for your-self. Okay?

Okay, I said.

Do you want to come home with us? My mother had her boots on already. Just for tonight, she said. All four of them had crowded into the hallway; Mercer's hand was on the doorknob. I focused on the four bodies, four sets of eyes, instead of the empty shadows in the rest of the apartment. The kitchen and all its windows stretched out behind me.

Or a few nights even. Take a break from this place. You don't need to do this by yourself.

For a moment I imagined packing a quick bag and scurrying down the steps between my parents, waking up in their house instead of my own, drinking coffee at their kitchen table. And then what?

I think I really do, I said. I need to stay.

My father walked the two cops down and I could hear them ex-changing a few words at the front door. My mother got her coat on.

Are you sure? You might feel better if you come home.

I'm okay, I said. This is my home. You don't have to worry about me.

Listen, Evie, she said. She took hold of my face with both hands. No one is coming for you. Okay? I promise. You're safe here. No one's out there. No one's coming to get you.

My father came slowly up the stairs and took another look at the dead bolt before putting his own coat on. He gave me a wink.

I didn't walk them down the stairs because I didn't want to have to come back up alone.

If this had been last month—or let's face it, even last week—I would have known what to do: call David. I'd just call up David, and he'd come over and show me how those weren't footprints, they were something else, and he'd explain how they got there and it would be this totally reasonable phenomenon, and then he'd swing the fire escape door open and shut and also check every place inside my apartment where someone could be hiding. We'd have a few drinks and make popcorn. He'd show me again how the kind of dead bolt I have on my door is the very best kind and then we'd watch a movie. If I still seemed too imaginative he'd just stay over. That's what he did last year, or back when I lived at home. That time my parents left me alone in the house for a weekend and he found out I was staying up all night with a butcher knife hidden under my pillow. In the morning you're a little embarrassed, but it's totally worth it because at least that way you get some sleep.

Something about my mother's reaction had made everything worse instead of better. No one is coming for you, no one is after you. I'd thought of the incident as more of a random thing. It hadn't really occurred to me that this might be specific, that I could be a target. How to Make Your Daughter a Neurotic Mess. I wished she'd offered to do my laundry or take me out for breakfast, the way I imagined other mothers might do.

The key in these situations is to just put the guy right out of your mind. When I say The Guy, I mean whatever it is you're afraid of. Get busy; make your brain do something else. I know this is the right answer, but suddenly all I wanted to do was to demonstrate that I didn't care. I don't even care that you're out there, watching me; I'm going to do everything right here in my kitchen, everything right next to the window. I opened up the freezer door and made a big show of prying two ice cubes out of the tray and let them slide into a glass nice and slow. I added a big splash of my mother's whiskey and watched it swoosh around and raised my glass to the room.

Cheers, sir! I said.

I gave a little curtsey and knocked back half the drink. I was proving something. I was showing him reckless. I put the radio on and slipped on my rubber gloves and commenced dishwashing: little sip of booze, squirt of soap, quick lather. Rinse the plate and repeat. When the sink was empty I let the water suck down the drain and added more whiskey to the ice. There was a dog barking down the street.

The lights were all still on. That's normally the first rule of being on your own: if you don't want to know what's outside the house at night, you switch all your lights on and keep them on. It's brighter inside than out. The garden outside your window becomes black and soft and felty. That makes you feel safe. Or, it used to.

I scooped a little coffee into the pot and put it on the stove. It wasn't even one o'clock yet. I didn't want to be in the kitchen but I also couldn't leave the back door unwatched. The coffee boiled and I turned off the stove but I didn't pour it into a cup. Instead I poured a little more whiskey into the glass and swished it around. I tried counting my blessings, like Rosemary Clooney in *White Christmas*.

Come on, I said to the window. I said this out loud.

I dare you.

CHAPTER 16

David called me at the paper first thing Monday morning.
I've been down in wine country, I said.

I've been reading about it, he said. Jesus. You okay?

Angie had just left for Niagara herself. Press conferences were being held in Beamsville at Task Force headquarters, plus she wanted to go see the house, live and in person. I told David about the truckers and the old lady who'd demonstrated the ill value of high fences.

But are you okay, he said.

Do you remember Mitten Guy? I said.

Your secret admirer?

I think he came and saw me last night.

What'd he leave you this time? A scarf? A fur muff?

Nothing, I said. He didn't bring me anything. He saw me.

What do you mean?

I came home last night and there was a guy on my fire escape, I said. Just looking in. He was just standing there.

Why didn't you call me?

I called the police.

So they got him.

No, I said. There were some footprints but the snow covered them up. They said I should call back if I see him again.

I'd told Angie about it early in the day and she'd said to run a quick search on recent police files, but there was too much going on and I hadn't had a chance.

Can I come by and see you later? David said. What time are you getting home?

I don't really want to know if there's some guy in my neighborhood who does this, I said.

There was a little pause.

Evie? Are you sure you saw something?

What do you mean?

I mean, you're reading about murdered girls all day. They've got you staking out some psycho's house. I'm watching you go through this. Every day you're a little more fixated, it's all Lianne and Robert Cameron and Paul Bernardo and who knows what else. This is a massive trigger for you, right?

You sound like a therapist, I said.

It's just. It's like you're looking for this stuff. This is what you do. You work yourself up. You're spinning.

We were both quiet for a moment.

Spinning, hey? Don't candy coat it for me. Tell me what you really think.

Spinning's a harsh word, David said. I don't mean that. I'm just saying, are you sure there was someone out there? For real?

You think I'm making it up?

I wouldn't say it that way. I'd say, freaking yourself out.

I stopped and looked out the window. My cubicle was on the sixth floor of a thirty-two-story building. There were tall towers all around me, the kind of mirrored windows that kill a thousand birds a year. In a building that size it costs too much to turn the lights off and on every day, or it's just easier to leave them on, and the lights create that shine. I could see a sliver of the lake from where I sat, and then the same sliver a hundred times over, reflected and multiplying off other windows of other buildings.

No, I said. He was right there. I saw him. And then a minute later, he was gone.

———

A gag order had come down from the attorney general's office over the weekend, meaning we weren't getting much new information out of prosecutors or police. Also meaning there was lots to tell, Angie said.

So sit pretty, she told me.

I'd been mucking about in the newsroom all day. Word was that Metro police had jumped into the arrest too soon and now the Task Force was scrambling to catch up. Too many charges laid all at once. With a public that's so invested, you can't really afford to fuck it up.

Angie was back from Niagara early in the afternoon, stopping in at a quick press con with the chief coroner.

The wife's sister, she said. Wifey's little sister dies over Christmas a couple years ago. She's like fifteen. Choked on her own vomit. They know he was in the house at the time, so now they're opening that back up, too. She pointed a finger at me. When they exhume her, I want a picture of that, the digger in the cemetery.

What, I take pictures full-time now?

Just don't let me forget I said it. Angie pulled her hair back and wrapped a plain elastic band around an uneven knot on the top of her head. She shoved me aside at my own desk and flipped on the monitor.

Now, she said. I've got five minutes. Let's find your Peeping Tom.

There's no one there, I told David.

We were sitting in front of the same screen, this time at my kitchen computer. He had all the lights on and every now and then he'd get up and stride over to the window, leaning across the little table or near the fridge, double-checking the dead bolt on the door to the landing.

I'd called up the Peeping Tom search Angie forced on me earlier in the day.

It's less of a downtown thing than you think, I said. Guys in the subway, sure. Or apartment buildings, the ground-floor units with patio doors. But there's way more reports out in the suburbs. Kitchener, Cambridge. It's like these guys need yard space. More bushes.

More bush in the bushes?

Har, I said. I read out a few victim impact statements, girls who were getting out of the shower in their basement apartments, looked up and saw a guy jacking off in the window. If it's summer, he might cut the screen.

But that's for effect, I said. These guys don't want in. Sometimes they're addicts or sometimes they're just mental.

Come on, David said. That would totally freak you out.

I said I didn't know. At least if a guy's spanking, you know what he's about, I said.

Anyone slices through your screen, you'd be upset.

I'd interviewed an ex-stripper-turned-sex-workers'-advocate back before Christmas. She told me she liked the jocks and the frat boys best. Guys come in hooting and hollering and ordering drinks, they're there to have a good time. Nothing wrong with that, she said. It's the hard tickets you watch out for. Guy comes in every day and sits and drinks slow and steady and doesn't talk to nobody and just watches you with his dead eyes. That guy? You point him out to the manager. You watch your back at the stage door.

The guy in the screen-cutting case confessed that he'd been looking in windows at women undressing since he was twelve.

What about your guy? David got up again.

Just standing there, I said.

But was he getting off?

I tried to reimagine him standing there. Everything would be easier if he'd had his dick out. There's something almost benign about a guy like that. It's sad and gross and yeah, the guy should be in jail, but manageable. It's kind of retarded. There'd been nothing easy about the guy on my escape. I realized that while David had paced the room, checking and double-checking, I'd avoided even glancing toward the window all night.

No. It wasn't like that. He was here, I said. It's like he wanted me to know.

David hung around for a few hours trying to find things to do for me. Stuff he could do with his hands, fixing or building or cleaning things. I still had the old sink sitting in my entranceway and he offered to bolt it to the wall.

With what, I said.

Bolts.

I have to rent a drill, I said. Drill-for-hire. Plus I haven't even painted it yet.

The drug raid photo I'd printed from the newspaper was sitting out on my desk. My teenaged mother and the other unknown girls standing next to her on the porch, the two mystery men down on the lawn in front of the house. David glanced at it and then looked away. We didn't talk about the fight, or my accusation about his father, or even the idea that my Lianne investigation was somehow pushing me over the edge. When he first came to the door, I could tell he was turning something over in his mind. The only thing he asked me about was my secret admirer, the details. He made me walk him through.

And now you're standing here, like this?

Yeah.

And then you jammed the door? With a chair?

I nodded.

Why?

Why what.

What'd you do that for? What if he came in your exit? He pointed at the bolted door to outside, next to the fridge.

I don't know. I wasn't thinking that.

That's a trap.

I wanted to know what space I had to worry about, I said. I wanted it to be something I could control.

Around midnight David put on his boots.

You want me to stay?

It was the first thing he'd asked all night that I wanted to answer.

You're already wearing your boots, I said.

I can take them off, David said. If you're worried.

I looked down at the sink on the floor.

I like this place, I said. I like the walls. I'll be sad to punch a hole in the wall to put that thing up, but I'll be glad once it's there.

You can't win, David said.

You really going out to live in the bush and fight fires?

More bush in the bush. Remember? Har har.

Har, I said.

Plus I got to take a break from my mother. I need a new Dave, David said. He slapped his hands to his sides, at attention. New Dave. Different Dave.

I couldn't wait to get out of my parents' house, I said.

New Evie.

New Evie! I said. I'm fucking sick of old Evie. Lianne's friend, alive for now. Sleeping with a butcher knife under my pillow.

Old Evie is still a decent model, David said.

You think you can will yourself to be a different version, I said. Guess what? Turns out you can. You can turn it on and off. Or, it comes on like autopilot, but you can override it. You can switch to manual.

So you're not worried.

About you and the fires?

About you and your special friend on the balcony there.

Nah, I said. I'm not worried.

I won't touch you, David said. That's not why I'm asking.

I said I wasn't worried about that, either.

I wrote up a pro and con list one time, in an effort to figure me and David out. I wanted to contain my range of feelings about him in one neat package, simple and codified. The list only served to prove what I already knew. Some nights nothing made more sense than David's hand on a table next to mine. But the centripetal force of changing the code now, from pal to lover? Thrash us both senseless. I swore off.

The last time we'd kissed had been about a year previous, just after I'd been glamorously dumped by a bike courier named Cort Lindstrom. Cort had a long silver-bleached ponytail and a ropey body from being on the bike all day, and he left a toothbrush and an expired passport at my place when he went to visit his ex-girlfriend in Alaska. They eloped on the black sand beach at Prince William Sound and then sent me a postcard with pictures of ice floes on it.

Sometimes a thing like that happens, you get good and drunk and kiss your best friend. Or you find yourself morbidly stressed by childhood trauma, and ditto. But no sense making a habit of it.

I drew the curtains closed and undressed. I hummed while I did it, folding my jeans neatly and stepping into a pair of sweats and a worn T-shirt I like to sleep in. I went through the order of evening tasks in a way that was both practiced and showy: curtains, undress, dress, sort out the laundry, dim the lights. I smoothed the bedsheets and folded them back, then surveyed the neatness of my handiwork, hands on my hips. To the naked eye, I was very caught up in the act of getting ready for the night. I padded out to the bathroom, brushing and flossing my teeth twice, something my gums were unused to. Little bloody clots of saliva adhered to the sides of the sink and I turned the faucet on high to rinse them away. On my way back to bed I took special care not to bother looking into the kitchen.

There was a muffled quality to the dark of the apartment with the windows blacked out. The whole room had a gag on it. There was no door between the room where I slept and the hall. This is part of the charm of a bachelor apartment. Everything is open concept, even your bedroom. I opened up the curtains again and lay down and closed my eyes and listened. A little ambient streetlight lit up a square patch of floor. Propping myself on my elbows against the pillow, I scanned the room. A car went by and the sheen of its headlights drifted across the bedclothes.

Stop asking for it, I thought. I got up and went out to kitchen with a cardigan sweater over my shoulders.

Without David's company, the overhead light turned the kitchen into a fishbowl. I was like a thing kept under glass for academic purposes, agitated and bumping around from one surface to another. I switched on the stove light and the desk lamp and turned the ceiling fixture off.

I'd walked David to my own door but not down the stairs. He gave me a thumbs-up through my bedroom window. This meant the lock downstairs had clicked tight. The house was as secure as it was going to get.

Results from the last search of Peeping Toms still gleamed on the monitor and I wiped the screen and picked up the drug raid photo. My mother's thin face shone out at me and left me lonely. A bunch of strangers, standing around. I propped the photo so that it stood upright against the wall and fixed it there with a piece of tape. If David was right and the names were all a giant coincidence, then this photo was nothing more than an interesting find. Spoils of the job. Something I could one day put in a little frame and slip into the top of my mother's Christmas stocking.

Either way, I needed a little break from the Lianne story. Who knew? Maybe David was right. Maybe I was too fixated. Maybe a rule of thumb is that you can only deal with one horror story at a time, and I already had the Bernardo show to deal with for work.

David had brought me a present of my own, a plastic mickey of Wild Turkey he'd stolen from a house party over the weekend. I poured a generous few fingers into the bottom of a juice glass and sipped at it neat. Half-a-hand. That's what you call more than two fingers of liquor. Give me half-a-hand of bourbon.

I put down the glass and plugged in a search on Bernardo's sister-in-law, the inquest into her death that the coroner's office had announced earlier in the day. I typed in *Exhumation* and the date, then a range of dates. I was keen to see how sensitive the system was.

Angie had only filed the story a few hours before. It would appear in the morning edition.

What I found was something entirely different.

NEXIS SEARCH: EXHUMATION FEBRUARY 1993

FEBRUARY 19 1993: *THUNDER BAY CHRONICLE*, A6

FEBRUARY 19 1993: *CALGARY HERALD*, A4

FEBRUARY 19 1993: *TORONTO FREE PRESS*, A18

KILLER BELIEVED FOUND IN WHITEFISH FALLS GRAVE
POLICE HOPE EXHUMATION WILL PROVE BODY IS THAT OF
SUSPECTED MURDERER ROBERT CAMERON

Espanola—Toronto police believe they have finally found the man who killed 11-year-old Lianne Gagnon in May of 1982. Authorities will exhume a body from an unmarked grave on Monday to examine it for DNA and possible fingerprint and dental evidence to determine whether the man, who died here three years after Lianne was found dead, was indeed Robert Nelson Cameron.

The unidentified man was using the name Thomas Allen Hargreave when he died of complications related to cancer on August 16, 1985. He was buried under that name. Ontario's deputy coroner, Dr. Georgina Smythe, says she has signed a warrant to exhume the body from an unmarked plot in the Anglican Cemetery in this small, northern Ontario community.

About a year ago, local RCMP alerted Metro police about the unidentified man buried here. They had been trying to put a name to him since the real Thomas Allen Hargreave surfaced at a passport office in

Alberta. He was unable to obtain a Canadian passport since all government records showed him as deceased. He told police that in 1982 his wallet was stolen in Thunder Bay, Ontario, where Cameron is known to have spent time. It's taken Metro police cold squad about 13 months to gather enough evidence to obtain the warrant from the coroner's office.

"There are a number of striking similarities that lead us to believe this may actually be the man (Cameron)," lead investigator Art Laidlaw said. "There's just too many coincidences."

Robert Nelson Cameron was a repeat offender who'd logged jail terms for armed robbery and assault in his native United States and had escaped assault and battery charges here in Canada. There's evidence he crossed the border between Canada and the United States regularly, using a number of aliases. The man known as Thomas Hargreave was described by his former Whitefish Falls employer, Jim Loney, as "a hard ticket. He looked like hard living. He was a chain-smoker with a rotten, lousy cough all the time." Loney's wife, Marietta, added that the man had "smelled bad. He was rude to everyone around." The Loneys had rented Hargreave a room and Marietta Loney refused to clean it out after he died. "We hired office cleaners all the way from the Sault," she said.

Police found similarities between the time when Cameron disappeared from Toronto and Hargreave first arrived in Whitefish Falls, their general appearance and demeanor and most interestingly, the men's interest in keeping rats as pets. Mrs. Loney also stated that cleaners had found a number of odd objects in Hargreave's room. "There was a plastic garbage bag in the freezer," she says. "And they told me it contained two dead rats and some little girl's clothes, a pair of shorts and some underpants." Mrs. Loney says the items were all disposed of at the time of Hargreave's death.

In his application for the order to exhume the body, Laidlaw said that Cameron may have kept a few pieces of Lianne's clothing as a souvenir or trophy of the sex slaying.

Lianne Gagnon went missing May 23, 1982. Her body was found by a dog walker 12 days later, on June 4, in the heavily wooded ravine of Taylor Creek Park in Toronto's east end. She had been raped and strangled. The search for 11-year-old Lianne galvanized and terrorized an entire city and included a door-to-door search and helicopter sweep. It was the first highly publicized child abduction case of its kind, with both television and print media asked to blanket the city with the little girl's image. "We wanted every cop with a pair of eyes," Laidlaw said at yesterday's announcement. "We wanted every father."

Police also said yesterday that Lianne's case may have prevented other similar murders from happening, as terrified parents drew their children in close and the community was alerted to the danger that lurks on city streets.

Buried on A18, at the moment the entire newsroom was fixated on a new killer, a story that blew my mind wide open. I rocked back in my chair and stared.

CHAPTER 17

The news that they were exhuming a suspect in northern Ontario should have got me revved. You'd think I'd be flying. Instead something inside me crumbled. I read the article four or five times, slower and slower each time, and then yanked the modem cable out of the wall and went and put my feet up. It wasn't so much going to bed as a kind of controlled faint. Your body gets a chance to catch up and you're overcome. All through the next day I felt hungover with it. Like I was looking at the world from behind a piece of plexiglass.

There was this little warp to my view. The sharp edges were all muffled.

Since the incident on the balcony my father had started checking on me after-hours. Not every night. He wanted to be sure I'd pick up the phone every time, which I wouldn't do if I thought he was just trying to make me feel better. He didn't want to be trackable.

Whatcha up to, sweetheart?

He's a peach. Boisterous, but contained. The way you'd expect a dental professional to be. You have to make people comfortable before you can go into their mouths with a sharp stick. A little personality goes a long way, but no sense going too far.

Painting my sink, I said. I'd slept fast and hard the night before and spent most of the day trying to pull myself out of it. Anxiety jet lag.

I'd scrubbed the old sink out with bleach before the phone rang and now it was sitting in the middle of the kitchen floor. A taupey base was already layered on in wavy fronds all over the bottom and sides. I had three shades of blond and one white in small, open pots on the floor next to me, plus a roll of paper towels, unfurled, and a small bag of black beach sand I'd been given as a souvenir of my ex-boyfriend's Alaskan wedding. I meant to add the sand into the last coat, to let it set and glitter there.

I cradled the phone between my ear and my shoulder and worked with the other hand, stroking on the darkest shade with a wide, wet brush I'd found at the art store on Spadina. The paint went on thick and sultry and gorgeous.

My father asked a few questions.

This might not work, I said. Because of the painting.

One of the upstairs neighbors arrived home. The door below thudded closed and then his footfalls up the stairs toward my door and then farther up still, and their door closing the same way as he went into his apartment.

Did you get something for dinner?

I threaded some thinner, lighter lines along the dark base where the sink grew wider and more open.

I buy seven quarter-pounders on a Sunday night, I said. I put them all in the freezer and every day at 6:00 p.m. I nuke one. The one I eat on Saturday tastes no different from the first one I ate the Sunday before. The receiver slipped for a moment and I caught it with painty fingers. That's what you were hoping to hear, right?

Now someone was coming down from upstairs. The sound on the steps quieter and more tentative. A girl leaving. Someone trying not to be heard.

My father told me a story about spaghetti he'd made. I have sauce for you, he said. With cremini. I'll put it in the freezer and you can take it next time you're here.

There was a pause while he waited for an answer and I thought of how to add a little skein of white to the sink. Without wrecking the job entirely. I leaned down over it with the skinniest brush in my hand. The ends of my hair dipped into the rim. The thin coat of paint on my hair could have been botched mascara. I was waiting for the sound of the door downstairs, the girl leaving.

My father still said nothing and I leaned in closer.

Is that you? I said.

What? he said.

Hold on. Don't say anything.

I put the brush down on a piece of paper towel and sat completely still. It was the most gentle tapping sound, out in the hall. Out at the front door.

There's this noise, I said. It's like a tapping noise.

Like the pipes?

I think there's someone at the door. I set the receiver down and it rocked on the floor next to me like an open ear.

I crawled out into the hallway and sat up on my knees, listening. The noise was like something cracking, or smacking lightly against the wall. The phone still lay on its back in the kitchen, next to my paint experiment. My father was saying something to me from his end of the line. His voice was thin and distant. He sounded tiny.

Someone had left the downstairs door open. One of the guys from upstairs, when he'd come in, or else the girl or whoever it was leaving, hadn't shut it. I hadn't heard the door shut. The tapping stopped and then started again.

Maybe there wasn't a girl. I'd been buoyed enough by the exhumation news that I hadn't thought of anything else. I'd given myself permission, a whole day off.

Maybe he'd come in through their apartment and down the steps and had been sitting outside my door since then.

Stop it, I whispered. Just stop. It's nothing. You should be embarrassed. God. Jesus. This is no way to live.

My father's voice came louder from the next room. He must have been shouting into the phone. I slid back into the kitchen and grabbed the phone, keeping my eyes on the black windows.

I'm being stupid, I said into the phone.

Evie! Jesus, I was worried. You okay?

I'm feeling, I said. I was going to say *weird*. My throat caught. I'm scared, I said. I think there's someone outside. There's someone at the door.

You're okay, my father said. You're okay. Remember how the pipes shake a little when they heat up in winter?

No, I said. No it's not that.

You think there's someone there?

I stopped. I didn't know if someone was there, or if it was the pipes, or if there was a noise at all. My ears were ringing a little. Fuck it.

I'm good, I said.

You're good?

Why am I like this?

Maybe I'll just come by and see, he said.

Please.

It's sobering. You're twenty-one and your dad is coming over to check for monsters under the bed. I spent fifteen minutes alternately telling myself to grow the fuck up and the other fifteen listening acutely for strange noises in the hall. I sat on my bed so I wouldn't have to look out the kitchen windows at the fire escape. My father has my spare key so he can let himself in.

I heard him come in the downstairs door and the smack of his footsteps up the stairway and I got up and went and stood in the hall. There was the key in the lock and the door made a noise and I stopped cold.

The man from the fire escape. He pushed the door open and let it click behind him. He had his black wool cap on and dark jeans and a black hoodie under his jacket. I could see the pattern of the knit in his cap. The empty eyelet where the cord was missing from the hood of his sweater. He pushed the door open with his head down and then looked up as he came in, one arm reaching out toward me. This was so real I had to catch my breath.

The door swung open and my father walked in. He had a Tupperware container filled with something red.

Put this in the freezer, he said. The spaghetti sauce. Remember I said?

It's possible that my father never actually slept when I was a kid. I never once woke up earlier than he did on a Saturday morning. The first time I slept over at Lianne's I was amazed. Her parents stayed in bed till noon on Sunday. We'd get up early and tiptoe through the living room right beside the sofa bed where they were sleeping. There was a rule where you couldn't stand at the side of the bed, whispering any questions to them. We made toaster waffles with Kraft peanut butter and watched the *Super Friends* and *The Smurfs* on the sixteen-inch TV in her bedroom. Her little brothers got in bed with us. By the time Lianne's mom and dad got up we'd already seen *The Little Rascals. The Three Stooges* was on. The boys liked *The Three Stooges* but if we were lucky there'd be an old Marx Brothers movie on instead. Lianne's mother wore a man's shirt to sleep in and at noon she'd suddenly be up, boiling coffee and frying bacon and corn fritters together in the pan and putting ketchup on the table, and Lianne's father would be doing all this, too, and also somehow strumming a guitar in the corner and wearing a towel on his head.

At my house I'd get up at eight and wander downstairs and my father was already working away out in the garage, his shirt off and a cup of black coffee balanced on the Black & Decker collapsible workbench. Or he was busy in the kitchen, the stand mixer blending pancake batter. Or he was chopping onions for chili, or using a press to make fifty hamburger patties for the freezer, a thin sheet of plastic between each patty. A summer's worth of hamburgers, all made by 9:00 a.m. on a Saturday in early May. Late into the night he'd be sitting downstairs in a double-wide green Naugahyde arm-chair. Hockey Night in Canada. Old Westerns or *The Bridge on the River Kwai*. When I was a teenager, if I wanted to sneak out at night I had to wait until 2:00 a.m. to slide the patio door open. To be safe, I'd have to be back before six.

After Lianne died my father made room for me in the chair and for a year or so I stopped falling asleep in my own bed at night. I fell asleep under a pink blanket while Steve McQueen and his car zoomed around on the screen or Clint Eastwood shot people. I fell asleep while Mike Nykoluk yelled at Börje Salming from behind the boards.

Everything I was going through still had to do with Lianne, my father told me. His opinion. We were sitting at my little café table next to the kitchen window and drinking midnight coffee. All the paints and the sand and the half-finished sink were still spread out on the floor.

Evolution-wise, my father said, what your brain is doing makes perfect sense. He stirred a spoonful of thick honey into his coffee. He said this is how his mother drank it when he was growing up in Vancouver.

The point is to perceive danger wherever it might exist, he said. He held his hands out the width of the table, then brought them together, slamming one fist into the other palm. But you're stuck. See? You're caught in a flight pattern. Hard on the nerves, sweetie. Hard on the heart.

He said I had too much going on. I looked out the window at the empty fire escape. I could still see the man standing there, lit up stark as lightning by the neighbor's floodlights.

Why don't I have a motion sensor? I said.

I told him about a girl I'd seen when I was out running in High Park, back in the fall.

I'd come running along the path, through a curve. When you're running on gravel, there's this thing where the pebbles that your feet kick up shoot back and land behind you, and the sound of the gravel spray hitting the path behind you creates a weird echo. It sounds like an extra set of footsteps. You think there's someone behind you, but you're alone.

Way up ahead there was a kids' soccer game going on and the colored shirts of the players stood out in the distance like orange and yellow petals in a field of grass. There was the sound of a motor running just ahead of me and a machine lying on the edge of the path and then a man in a crossing guard vest about eight feet down from that. The machine was a hedge trimmer. Not a crossing guard. A city worker, a landscaper, working the trail. He was standing right where the chain-link fence comes out of the brush and meets the path. He had large, perfectly round sunglasses and two days' worth of stubble.

I rocketed by, I said. I was really on pace and he looked at me with such an odd smile. And then I saw the girl.

Her back to me, close to the fence. A couple of fingers touching the chain-link fence for balance maybe. I only saw her for a second as I was running by. She was wearing pink jeans.

I said: Her back was to me and I could see her blond ponytail and I thought she might be doing up her jeans and that's why she was turned around. She was saying something but I couldn't hear what. I thought: She was peeing and this guy came along with his hedge trimmer.

My father's face had gone still.

And then the next moment I thought, It's a boy, she's been caught rolling around in the woods with a boy. There might have been another person in there with her, I said, I don't know for sure.

So what was it, my father said.

I don't know. I didn't actually see another kid up there in the brush with her. But I felt like there was someone else. The point is, I said. The point is I should have stopped. The guy had this shruggy smile, you know, but I couldn't see his eyes because of the sunglasses.

You think something bad, he said.

I don't really.

But kind of.

I was probably half a click away when I thought, I really should have stopped and checked in with her. I should have stopped and said, Hey, are you okay?

She probably got caught peeing, my father said.

But that's how this shit happens, I said. And now whenever I read one of these stories, every time there's some guy who says: Oh, I saw a little girl talking to an older man and it seemed a bit off, but then I kept walking. Why do you keep walking? It happens so fast. Your brain gives you the easiest answer.

Did you go back? my father said.

Nah. I shook my head. By that time, who knows? I didn't even slow down.

I had a therapist early on who explained things this way: there's a spectrum. Take that fifth-grade class from 1982. The class list the police spent all night calling. On one end of the spectrum, there are kids who don't even remember that night. There's at least one kid who doesn't remember what happened or how, and if they stumbled upon Lianne's name in the paper tomorrow what they'd think is, Oh yeah . . . I forgot about that. Weird.

The other end of the spectrum is me.

Doesn't that have more to do with how close we were? I said to my father. Rather than my extreme powers of empathy?

Look at what you do for a living, he said. Your job is the anxiety machine. You're mainlining fear.

I have something to show you, I said. I went over to the desk and pulled my mother's photo off the wall.

Look at this.

I smoothed the picture and pushed it at him across the little table. My father regarded it for a moment.

Quite a find, he said.

Do you remember her?

Your mother? I still see her around the house. My father gave me his quiet smile. Is that what you mean?

But do you remember *her*. Not like she is now. *Her*. I stabbed at the picture with my finger, just gently. This version, I said.

She was something else, he said. When I met her she was sick as a dog. He put his hands on the table and moved the picture back and forth between them. I don't know if you've noticed this, but she's kind of a jackass when she's sick. Frankly it's a miracle we ever got together.

He said this kindly. I was very fond of her from the get-go, he said. She wore this kerchief when she came to clean the house. I used to make sure I was cooking something when she came into the kitchen. Because, you know, then I'd have something to offer. He passed the picture back to me, across the table. Plus I'd make a mess in the kitchen so she'd have to stay around longer.

You know how I found this? I said. I was looking for Robert Cameron and this picture came up. Robert Cameron owned the house, I said. Not Robert Cameron. Arthur Sawchuk. But that's his alias. It's one of his names.

What are you doing?

What was she like? I said.

My father stared at me.

What are you doing, he said.

Humor me.

I got up and started moving around for the hell of it, stacking things on the counter and putting other things away in the cupboard over the stove.

She was lovely, my father said. She'd had a rough start. And then you were born and she was fine. When Lianne happened she had a hard time. Hard as you. Harder, maybe.

It was like she disappeared, too, I said.

She didn't, he said. She was holding on.

It felt like she was gone for a long time, I said. I stopped cleaning and turned back to face him. I always wanted her and she never came. She was always in bed. Or else gone.

My father looked sideways out the window.

She used to go for those long walks, I said. Remember? She'd be gone for hours. Everyone else's parents split up.

She couldn't look at you, he said. She told me that. Too close to home. What if it had been you?

There's something else, I said. There's another name that comes up with this picture.

Evie, my dad said. These are common names. That's your mother's house. I didn't know any of the people there. I knew your mother. She needed out.

Graham Patton. That's David's father, I said. Right? Graham Patton's name is buried in this file, too.

My father went silent.

I looked it up, I said. I can't figure out why his name is attached, but hers is and also Cameron's.

These are common names, Evie.

Stop saying that.

He threw his hands up. It's the truth! You're making problems where there are no more problems!

I think I know what happened, I said. I need your help. Which one is he? I spun the photograph back toward him.

If you have a question about David's father, he said, I wish you'd ask your mother, not me.

What if Cameron's been hiding in plain sight the whole time, I said.

Robert Cameron's getting dug out of the ground up north, he said. You just told me yourself.

He stood up.

I'm going to give this place a once-over so you can sleep, he said. Go let your hot water run and then turn it off. I bet we hear that rattling that had you worried.

We looked at each other quietly for a moment, the photo with its raggy edges still lying on the table where I'd left it. I went into the bathroom and my father stood in the hallway with his palms against the wall.

Now go, he said. Throw it on hard.

I cranked the tap. Water spat out at full volume, hitting the sink at a sharp enough angle that I could feel the spray on my forearms, going from cold to hot. In the wall, the pipe throttled and shook with the force of the water. *Tock tock tock tock tock tock tock.* I turned off the water and the tapping in the wall slowed but didn't stop. It ticked and clicked faintly.

I hate being me, I said. My father's cheeks lifted.

I said: I'm too stupid to live.

Hard on the heart, he said.

Sometimes, at moments like that, I think about those other kids in the class. The opposite end of the spectrum, the ones who don't have much recollection, or any at all. There are girls from that class who live alone and don't ever give what happened to Lianne Gagnon a second thought. They don't scan bars for the man sitting darkly in a corner, or turn completely around when they're walking home at night to check the path behind them. Their reality has a different configuration. One of my secret mechanisms is to simply pretend that I am one of those girls. They're allowed to grow up.

I imagine myself in this same apartment but in a different body and my shoulders relax. The tightness in my jaw slacks off and I can feel the relief right across my forehead, down into my cheekbones.

The door closed behind my father and I heard him go down the stairs and I latched the dead bolt and turned around and leaned against the door and imagined myself in this other, parallel body. It's an easy space and it feels good. Let's assume he's right and this is the same old anxiety. It seems crazy that a thing can have that kind of staying power, can keep coming back to give you a regular kick to the head.

The pipes, shaking in the wall.

So you can stop it now, I said out loud to myself. Everything's fine, everything's easy.

I came back into the kitchen and picked up the honey jar from the counter and put it into the cupboard. I was aware of myself doing this as keenly as if I was doing it for a camera. Enter stage right: Regular girl cleans up and gets ready for bed.

Our coffee cups were still on the table and I picked those up, too, and stopped for a minute and leaned my shoulder against the dark window to look out over the patchwork of backyards.

A hand reached out and touched the window from the other side.

I jumped back. My hands popped open and the cups hit the floor, banging hard but not smashing. He was out there on the balcony, his hand pressed against the glass. I grabbed on to the chairback and shoved the chair at the window, between us. His hand on the glass at the level of my shoulder. A thick black glove at my throat, his face half in shadow, the wool cap pulled down low on his brow. A half beard, or thick stubble, the same coat and black hoodie. He pulled back from the window slightly. I couldn't see his eyes.

Had he been there the whole night? Standing back in a shadow, watching me paint, the phone call, my father arrive, everything. How long was it since my father left?

I can see you, I said. I said this out loud and the sound of my voice surprised me.

I leaned forward and touched my own hand to the glass. It matched his, but smaller, finger to finger.

Mercer was back.

We did a quick perimeter check on the way in, he said. Did you get a better look this time?

He has a beard, I said. Like half a beard, or just really unshaven. He wears this wool cap, black gloves, black hoodie. He put his hand on the window.

You sure it's the same guy?

I looked at Job.

Okay, Mercer said. What time was he here?

Job said, I promise you he can't get in through that window.

If I'd been only a year or two younger I would have started crying. I had the prick, the hot threat of tears, and I was sure they could tell and even that was humiliating.

I'm just telling you this, Job said. He can't get in. He can't come in here unless you let him. This is a safe house.

Mercer took down the notes and stats.

I'm really sorry, I said. I really don't want to cry. This is stupid.

You're shaken up, Job said. That's why you're crying. It's an invasion.

Everything's fine, I said.

Geez, I went to see a break-and-enter yesterday. I mean, the occupants weren't even home when it happened but they come home and the door is forced, right? They were in way worse shape than you, he said. The lady, she was like, hysterical. You? You're shook up. He turned to Mercer. Am I right?

Mercer made a shrugging face with his lips and patted his notebook against his fingers.

Job said: You're a little shook up. That's all.

He stayed around for maybe two or three minutes, I said. I don't know. I don't know. Maybe less. Maybe it was longer.

Mercer said: What time was he here?

I don't know. I don't know how long. A long time.

You called 911 at 12:46.

Okay.

Did you call right away?

I thought maybe I was making it up, I said. I thought I was seeing things.

How long was he here?

He had his hand on the window, I said, right here. It was right here and I put my hand on the glass.

Job said: What happened then?

He didn't disappear.

CHAPTER 18

I spent the next day with my feet up on the dash of Angie's car, watching nothing get resolved in St. Catherines. I hadn't slept after the cops left. I sat up finding things to do until it was time to leave for what felt like a better place. Put it that way and it seems crazy. I felt more comfortable sitting outside a murderer's house than inside my own apartment, but it was the crowd that made it safe. I wasn't alone. Not even close. The light and the new surroundings felt good and I was tired and snuggled back into the furry lining of my coat. The house itself was blocked off by police vans. A guy with a flat cap and a gray beard came by early and set up an easel next to where I was. I pulled on my hat and got out of the car. The man told me his name was Rod Carey. Former art college painting prof, retired or fired when he was discovered to be the Phantom Pooper. For two years he'd taken midnight dumps in the school library.

Any section, he said. It wasn't targeted. It was performance.

He took three quick sketches of the house, the high fence, front porch, whatever he could see, and worked them up in watercolor. He had spattered leather gloves on against the cold. The wind came up and he put away the easel and tied the canvas to a pole instead.

Twyla Sweet, he said. You know her? She's queen of Niagara-on-the-Lake. She does watercolors of kids and dogs and those redbrick houses with the gingerbread trim. Cute Ontari-ari-ari-o. He stopped and put down his brush. Two guys wearing paper anti-contamination suits came out of the house carrying cardboard file boxes. They could have been housepainters.

They wear shower caps so their hair won't mix in to the house, the prof said. That last girl, they cut off all her hair. You hear that? In a ditch, with her hair all sawed off. He picked a new brush up and spat on it. I fucking wish Twyla Sweet would paint this house. I'd buy that shit.

By mid-morning, press vehicles had a hard time getting in. Some guys camped out overnight. I was due to start trading off with Mike Nelligan but Angie kept finding other stuff for him to do. I'd been in the car since five in the morning. Around eleven o'clock, a guy I knew from j-school came by and knocked on my window. He works for the Hamilton paper. Any other kind of investigation, he's all boob jokes. I reached over and cranked the window down. He's the kind of guy who'd hand you a dildo and think that was really funny. He'd hand you a vacuum nozzle and call it a dildo. But he just gave me a coffee and it was sweet and full of cream and we didn't talk.

At noon I noticed a tall guy with a half beard and a black leather car coat hanging around too close to my car, for a little too long. There were more cars every day now, reporters I didn't know. Everyone was a stranger. I flipped open my notebook and took down a full description. Fifteen minutes later he was gone, but I started noting any strange man standing around within ten feet of me. Three or four different guys over the course of the day. I measured them quietly against the man from the fire escape: height, build, anything identifiable. I didn't get out of the car again except to line up for the Porta Potty.

The sky was overcast but bright. I'd brought water with me in the car, and some fruit, and trail mix. It's easy to get focused on watching the other reporters watch. I wrote up anything I thought of by hand in a three-hole lined notebook from the drugstore. I had a photo of Rod the painter in my camera.

At the end of the day, I stopped at the office to type up my notes and file them off to Angie. I parked her car down in the garage and then sat there with all the doors locked. There was no one around and I realized I was waiting for someone to make it safe to get out of the car. A locked car in an empty parking garage feels like one of those shark cages that scuba diving explorers use so they can take pictures of the sharks and not get torn to pieces. Park close to the exit and wait inside the cage until it's safe.

Statistically, a garage is where I'm most likely to get raped. It's dark and there's lots of things to hide behind, lots of places to go. Before Bernardo and his wife, I would have been waiting for a woman or a couple to come down for their car. Now I wasn't sure. Who knows what a threat looks like? I got out of the car, carrying my bag and Angie's spare umbrella. A woman is more likely to be attacked if she's got her hair in a ponytail; less likely if she's carrying an umbrella. A ponytail is an easy thing to grab on to.

Job called from 14 Division while I was still at my desk.

I've got news and no-news, he said. The news is, they grabbed up a Peeping Tom in Woodbridge last night, more or less fits your guy. Black hat on, hoodie, a week's worth of beard.

Do you think it's the same guy?

Officially? Maybe, Job said. It's a possibility. He fits the mug and he was doing the same thing, looking in the lady's window off her balcony.

Off the record? I said. What's the no-news?

Off the record, don't count on it.

That sucks, I said.

Yeah. I have to tell you if we arrest a reasonable suspect, but geography is working against you here. Woodbridge is pretty far out of town. Maybe it's him, Job said. But don't go around leaving your windows open, you know?

No news is supposed to be good news, I said.

There was a bunch of broccoli in my fridge at home and I stir-fried it up with lots of garlic and chilis and tamari and sesame oil, and burned my tongue on it, eating. Not from the spice, but because I was impatient. Usually I would have put the radio on, or the television or something, but I'd been in too much of a hurry. Having sat in the quiet of Angie's Turismo all day, the silence didn't seem out of place. No noise from the upstairs apartment.

I chewed.

The police had first interviewed Bernardo in 1990. They brought him in because his friend's wife thought he was weird. He matched the composite for the Scarborough Rapist and he gave them some DNA samples, but no one bothered testing them for two whole years. It was just an interview. No arrest. He seemed like a well-adjusted, well-spoken guy. The quote from the interviewing officer was that no clean-cut young guy like Bernardo could have raped all those girls.

You can get a lot done in two years.

I'd barely noticed feeling hungry through the day. Now I was starving. The garlic was cleaning my blood. I was perfect. I was a perfect broccoli eater. I was good and did good things for my body. I was like an example of how to live.

I'd been leafing through an old issue of *Rolling Stone* on the table while I ate, something to distract myself. Clean the palate of the day. It was Sinead O'Connor on the cover, with her giant green eyes. A tiny part to her lips, just enough to seem vulnerable. She was so engaging. How to be like that. I put down my fork and went into the bathroom and practiced. Just for fun. Making my eyes big in the mirror, hair pulled back tight. I stared in at myself. Lips parted just so. Sexy, but childlike. Because childlike. Someone small and broken, or breakable.

The light in the room changed, as though outside the window, darkness had fallen suddenly, leaving only the overhead fluorescent light. I felt floaty.

It's okay, I told myself. You're okay. You missed a night's sleep, that's all. Bound to catch up with you. I squeezed my eyes shut and then opened them wide again.

The girl in the mirror was both farther away and more in focus. It was like looking at myself through a viewfinder. My peripheral vision dropped away. Above me, the ceiling stretched up higher and higher. I turned my body to leave the bathroom and swung against the tub, banging my shin and almost falling: my perspective was that narrow. I couldn't see any obstacles.

On my way back to the kitchen I trailed my fingers along the wall to keep steady, then found my chair and sat down all at once. A wave of nausea and I bent over, tucking my head between my knees.

Something I ate? Food poisoning. My shoulders swayed. Even bent over like that, my head was swimming.

All I'd had was broccoli. What could be wrong with that? Some kind of mold or fungus on it. Was that it? Or low blood sugar from starving myself all day.

I focused on my breathing: *1-2-3-4-in, 1-2-3-4-out.* Maybe this was an oxygen issue. Carbon monoxide. Something inside the apartment.

Someone.

I sat up, but the light streaming out from the ceiling fixture seemed impossibly bright. It hurt. The light was stabbing at my temples. I lifted one hand to shield my eyes and the other went instinctively to my heart. My heart was coming through my rib cage. I couldn't get any air. *1-2-3-4-IN.*

Someone in the apartment. Not safe. I staggered down the hall to the doorway.

If you're going to pass out, I thought, do it outside. You can't be alone. At least that way, if you pass out, someone will find you, someone will call an ambulance. You'll be lying in the gutter and someone will call.

The way the lock worked, I needed two hands to get out: one to hold the dead bolt open, the other to pull on the handle. Out in the hallway, I pulled the door shut and jumped. There were stairs and with my tunnel vision, I didn't see them until the last second, until I'd turned my head. They were right there. I dropped to the floor and slid down on my bum, struggling with the outer door the same way I had with the door to my own apartment. Outside, I sat down on the curb with my feet in the gutter.

The light was failing now. I tucked my head back between my knees.

If he's in there, he'll come out for you. Eventually he'll come out here.

I lifted my head but stayed leaning over, my elbows heavy against my knees. The street felt like a strange place to me, or like somewhere I'd been once, long ago. Someplace I'm supposed to remember. A thing that should make sense, but doesn't.

All the parts, everything on the block, were dissonant. The sewer grate, just a couple of feet over from where I was sitting. The light standards, the shape of the curb against the road. The swath of road that was black with a wash of fresher tar, the chunky patched places where potholes had been repaired. The red VW parked across from where I sat. Its license plate (A1G H4H Keep It Beautiful), the driveway it was in, the pavers stamp on the sidewalk, *Dufferin Materials 1987*. My head fluttered inside. The sharp ache had dropped away and was now replaced with a steady pressure along my brow line, over the bridge of my nose, like something dull and heavy was trying to push its way out.

Slowly, the street came back together. The curb was part of the sidewalk, which was part of the road, which links to other roads. The neighborhood was like a rose, the streets curving one into the next.

Tell no one about this, I thought. This is what it feels like to lose your mind.

———

I don't know how long I sat there. It was dark. The air was cold but I liked breathing it. The nausea dropped away and after a while I noticed that I wasn't thinking about how I was feeling anymore. I'd started thinking about other things.

There were footsteps behind me and I started to cry.

What are you doing out here?

David was wearing his navy peacoat, and I realized I had no coat on at all.

I think I have food poisoning, I said.

Why are you on the curb?

Someone broke into the apartment, I said, suddenly not believing it. I couldn't breathe inside. I didn't want to pass out by myself.

David reached a hand down and I got up on my feet.

Your mother would say you'll get a kidney infection, sitting on the cold ground like that, he said.

I brushed off my legs.

I won't, I said. Then: I don't know what happened.

Something scared you?

I felt really sick, I said. I couldn't see.

David looked at me. I closed my eyes.

I thought I was going to throw up and pass out all at the same time, I said. I didn't want to do that by myself. Only then I thought I wasn't by myself, I thought someone was in there with me.

Who? David said.

I don't know, I said. Someone, someone, I wasn't alone.

David glanced up at my window.

Like, for real?

I don't know. I don't feel like going back there.

Your secret admirer.

I don't know.

Let's go to The Stem, David said.

I might have food poisoning, I said.

You don't. You'd be puking. I'll get your coat.

He disappeared up into the house. I hugged myself. The streetlights were on now, and all the house lights. Nothing was left of the strangeness I'd felt when I first came out onto the sidewalk. I was surprised to be outside.

There are a few houses on this street I really like. There's one across the way and down a bit with a dining room all painted Chinese Red, and a big yellow brick house at the corner with a round room in front, and two armchairs and a giant cherry bookcase built into the wall. A reading room. If I'm walking home at night, I take stock. I know which houses have the best art on the walls, which families only watch television in the basement. You can see the blue flicker from the tiny ground-level windows.

I looked up at my own window. The light was on, and I could see David moving around the apartment. Searching for something. My wallet, my sweater, whatever he'd decided was needed. From where I stood, looking up, I could see just his head and shoulders, his shoulders in the navy coat. My walls painted creamy yellow. I stepped back into the road. Now I could see my own armchair, bookshelf, my desk. I could see my whole life up there, laid out like candy in a coin-op machine. The shiny glow from the chandelier, lighting the room like the screen at a drive-in movie.

We walked along Queen Street to the restaurant. David linked his arm through mine, which is my favorite thing he does. It makes me feel like this is the '40s and I am wearing spectator pumps and we are watching the warplanes fly overhead.

Do you want a drink? I said.

I can't decide if that's a good idea or a bad idea for you right now, he said.

We sat and waited for our sandwiches. I always order a BLT and he always gets a club. The only difference between these things is turkey. Other than that, it's the same sandwich. There was a little white bowl of condiment packs in the middle of the table: peanut butter, jam, mustard, mayonnaise. Just one packet of marmalade. One bowl for the whole day: breakfast, lunch, supper.

I think you had a panic attack, David said.

Panic about what? I said.

What've you been doing?

Murder house.

Peachy, David said. He passed me a tiny mayonnaise, already peeled open.

And the cops came back last night, I said. I mean I called the cops. He had his hand on the glass, David. He was right there.

Tonight or last night?

Last night.

And then the murder house, David said.

I guess, I said.

Eat your sandwich.

We ordered extra French fries for the salt and beers a half-pint at a time.

I always love when beer comes in a small glass, I said. We're civilized now, we're drinking *glasses of beer*.

And what will you have to drink? David said, pretending to write down my order.

Why, I'll have a glass of beer, if you don't mind!

Oh, you will, will you?

We were many beers in, many small glasses of beer. David counted out the bill, right down to our last dimes and nickels. We celebrated our way back home to my house, pleased to have not drunk ourselves into having to cheat the waitress.

Don't feel so panicky now, do you? David said.

Do you think that was really it? I said. I stopped and he stopped with me, just ahead of where I was. I grabbed his two hands. Really? Just a stupid panic attack? Like a loser?

David took one of his hands back and tucked a little of my hair behind my ear.

I think you had a little anxiety, Evie. That's all. You're working really hard. Don't let the fear take over. Don't let it rule you. He messed up my hair again with his fingers, but softly. Maybe you need a little break.

I twirled around and fell backward against him.

Okay, I said. I closed my eyes and leaned my head back, my chin pointing sharply up at him. Break me.

There was a pause and I opened my eyes. David was looking down at me like I was something small and funny but also damaged in some way. Like a cute kitten, but it's blind.

I think we'll just go home, he said.

Up, up, up the stairs! I charged forward, one arm high in front of me. David had my keys and he nudged me aside so he could get the door open.

Also? I said. Also I'm drunk.

The door swung open and we fell inside.

Coffee! I kicked my boots off and went into the kitchen. David followed behind me, watching as I scooped grounds into the Bialetti with a teaspoon.

Come lie down with me, he said.

Why? I said.

Just do this, he said. Forget the stupid coffee. Let me take care of you.

I should never have kissed you! I said. I should never kiss anyone! I make terrible mistakes!

You make the best mistakes. Come lie down.

He had his face against my neck and it was warm there and nice and I held on to his hands and then I was up on the counter, his thumbs pressing into my hips. His mouth on my neck, collarbone, a hand tugging down at the neckline of my sweater, another hand up inside. His mouth on my mouth.

The Bialetti screeching on the stove.

Wait, wait, I said. I don't want to catch on fire. I had to turn away to see what I was doing, to turn off the gas flame under the coffee. David at the same time pushing up on the sweater, trying to get it over my head.

We found our way into the other room, to where the bed was. My sweater was on the floor now with half of David's clothes and I wriggled out of my jeans and threw them at the pile. David rolled over and we looked at each other like that. Then he reached his arm across my body and slid the drawer of my nightstand open.

I don't have any, I said. He craned his neck anyway, to peer into the drawer. Condoms, I said. That's what you're looking for? I don't have any.

Why not? David shut the drawer. That's totally irresponsible.

Well, why don't you have any?

I'm not going to carry them. I'm not going to just put a couple in my wallet before I come to your house.

Too bad, I said. Closing my eyes and sinking deeper into the pillow.

Wait. I can go out.

As soon as he said this, he was up and balancing on one leg, shoving himself into his pants.

I don't know, I said.

Just wait here!

I live here, I said. Where else can I go?

Just don't move, David said. He threw his coat on and launched himself out the door. I could hear the *bang bang bang* of his feet on my stairway and I did just what he said. I didn't move. I lay there and thought, What happens next?

Now is the chance to change your mind. Usually with guys there isn't a big pause like this, there isn't a big change-your-mind-think-it-over moment. There was a soft thunk from out in the hall. David, back already. But then no other sounds.

You back?

I got to my feet and went out into the hall on tiptoes. It was cold there. There was a draft that rushed all around me. I still had my panties on and I pulled a tank top over my head.

I poked my head through and then one arm after the other and I stretched my arms back behind me. There was still time. I walked into the kitchen to make sure the gas wasn't on, turned on my toes, switched off the light.

He was there. Outside the window. Just standing, a fist against the glass. What I'd thought was the sound of David coming back in, his footsteps on the stairs.

Had he seen me in the hall? Half naked. Slipping the tank top over my head.

The downstairs door slammed and I heard the sound of David's feet on the stairway, and then he was knocking at my door. He'd locked himself out. So he was knocking.

I walked over to the window and spread my hand out against the glass. On the other side, the stranger didn't disappear. He was close enough that I could see the small wrinkles on his face, between his brows, hard lines at the corners of his mouth.

I wanted to be sure enough to make a positive ID, but it was dizzy-making. He uncurled his fist and spread out the hand on the other side of the window, matching mine.

I was surprised he didn't look more angry.

David knocking.

Evie, hey, Evie!

I pressed my other hand against the glass and pushed my body closer, elbows splayed out. Push-ups against the window. I thought of what David had said to me, down in the street. Don't let the fear take over; don't let it rule you.

I'm not yours, I said. Fuck you, I'm not yours. I pushed off the window.

I turned my back and stripped the tank top off again.

Not. Yours.

David knocking louder now, insistent. His fist turned sideways.

I walked out of the room. There was a slam against the glass, or else it was David at the door, banging, banging away with a fist.

Evie!

I opened the door.

What's going on, David said. Cold feet?

All kinda cold parts.

He came inside. I took his navy peacoat off his shoulders and put it on and did up the top buttons, and he left his boots against the wall. We stood around in the hallway for a minute. I danced back and forth a little. David reached for me in his coat and thumbed the buttons open and it slid off and hit the ground.

If you were outside, standing on the fire escape, you'd see just my heels and ankles, my calves, doing this nervous dance. My shoulder. Through the doorway. I started to laugh.

This is a safe house, I have a good lock. I said this out loud.

David switched the hall light off. My tank top was still on the floor.

You look like a little kid, David said. Look at you. In your bare feet.

I bent down and picked up the camisole and stretched it tight, spreading my arms out wide. I stepped half into the kitchen.

Tie me up, I said.

David pressed a hand between my breasts and pushed my back lightly against the door frame. He still had all his clothes on.

I don't need to tie you up, Evie, he said. Plus I like this little dance you do.

His cheek twitched. He had a little white plastic bag from the convenience store in one hand and he swung it back and forth. There was a sound like a branch cleaving away from a tree and David said the wind was wicked and I should be grateful he was so willing to brave it for me.

I pulled him by the hand and we lurched into the other room. I couldn't get his shirt off fast enough. The buttons all stuck and caught in their holes and I fought them with shaky fingers. My mouth on him wherever the skin showed. He was wearing a pair of army pants with a button fly and I fought that, too, and a button came flying off and I had my hands on him. We were on the bed.

David was on the bed and I was over him and he sat up and grabbed my wrists and held them for a moment.

Tell me you want it, he said. My teeth at his throat and his ear and along his jaw and he ducked his head to keep away from me and held me there like that, a foot of space between us. Even a small moment of reflection was going to be too much. I wanted the interior noise of fast motion, of rushing headlong into this. The man on the balcony was coming in. Another minute and he'd be in the room with us. So long as we kept moving I wouldn't panic. I wanted my mouth on David's mouth to stop myself screaming but he held me like that until I'd said it, I want you I want you, David I want you, and we rocked back together so the bed frame smacked the wall.

L ater, when he was sleeping, I got out of bed. We'd left the bedroom curtains open and it was still dark out. Four in the morning. Even at that hour, you can hear the traffic from Queen Street, cabs coasting along. I dragged myself into the kitchen. There was a crack down the pane of the window, as though someone had thrown a stone at it. A stone or some other heavy thing. No moon that I could see. No one was left standing on the escape.

CHAPTER 19

My mother's name as a little girl was Anneliese, although she told me her father had often called her Anja or Annika. Her family had been in the country for a couple of generations already, but they'd all kept their grandparents' ginger-blond hair and light eyes. There's a pocket of Swedes and Danes and Finns up in the north, aside from all the French Canadians. There's one Chinese family in every town in northern Ontario; or, at least, there's one Chinese restaurant. That might be more accurate. In many small places, this restaurant is the only thing open on Sundays, or Easter or Christmas. It's a hub. I don't know if this is true of other places or not.

My own father always called her Annie. She went through a stage where she wanted me to call her Annie, too. This was not an unpopular thing among parents in the '70s and '80s. There's no question that Annie suits her, as a name: it's trim and practical and outdoorsy. *Annie* sounds dependable, too, as a pal, but perhaps not as a mother. I felt that Annie wanted to be more like my fun roommate, and less like the person responsible for my safety and well-being. Annie might spring for an off-road bike ride or teach you to make a gimp bracelet, but she didn't have to hold your hand at night or be home for dinner or take you to Girl Guides. I imagine my mother also knew this about Annie, and that's why it appealed to her.

She's a Pisces. You can see this in her, if you believe in that sort of thing. She's a vivid dreamer. I've seen her sit straight up in bed and talk to me as though she were wide awake, only the words she's stringing together don't make sense. The words are all English, but she's put them together wrong. It sounds like an incantation. When I was a teenager I thought she was possessed. Pisces are also escapists, which is connected to the dreaming.

We were at a second-floor pool hall on the Danforth. I'd said good-bye to David outside my house that morning and jogged through the snow to the newsroom. It was Mike's turn on Murder House Watch, so I stayed in town all day and then came straight out to meet my mother after work. There were twelve or sixteen tables with lights hanging over them and a guy sitting in a corner window booth who'll sell you beers and balls by the hour. There wasn't any separate bar. He had a row of highball glasses hanging from a dusty bracket over his head and two refrigerators and stacks of triangles on the counter. The beer all came in bottles: 50, Blue, Ex, Canadian. There was a swimsuit pinup calendar sitting flat on the counter next to the stack of triangles and when I paid for the beer I noticed he'd drawn a long arrow in pen to the girl's vagina. In case anyone missed it.

You've never slept with David before? My mother leaned hard over the green felt table. Really? All this time?

I've known him too long, I said.

And he's hung around. She shook her head like she couldn't believe David's incredible resilience.

On the wall next to our rack of cues there was an oil painting of dark men wearing hats, playing cards around a table. There was a dog on the floor with a long tongue hanging out and one of the card players had his foot on the dog's back. The walls were all covered in these paintings. The owner's son, an *artiste*. It was Friday night. We were the only women there.

I said: I can be quite nice, you know.

My mother laid her cue out across the table, measuring the angle between the white ball and yellow-stripe number 9.

Off the seven, she said. The white smacked her target smartly and spun back, leaving me boxed in a sea of stripes. She stood up straight with her cue planted next to her like a hiker's pole. So what now?

I'm trapped. I pointed at the table. You trapped me.

What now with David. You think this is what you do now?

I don't know.

What does he think?

He's a guy.

What does he think, Evie.

We were drunk, I said.

I hadn't said anything to David about the man at the window. There were branches down in the yard and in the light of day the crack in the glass seemed barely noticeable. Had it always been there? In the morning David dusted the spilled coffee grounds off the counter into his hand and practiced a little Michael Jackson spin to throw them into the sink. He whistled and I watched him. I'd gone to sleep thinking how much I loved this new Evie, an Evie who didn't let anxiety rule her life. We made coffee on the gas flame and I didn't mention that I'd seen the man out there, watching us.

By mid-morning I had a banger of a headache and a nail hole of guilt and fear in my stomach. What if he'd come through the window? What about tonight, or the night after? If I'm there alone, if I'm not in the mood to put on a show?

I wasn't home alone now. I was out shooting pool with my mother. I'd come with the idea that I'd confess about the man outside the window, his heavy fist against the glass.

I also had the drug bust photo in my shoulder bag—so, make that two things I was too nervous to talk about. For better or for worse, she couldn't seem to get beyond David.

He stayed, I said. He kissed my forehead this morning.

David would sort your dirty laundry if you'd let him, my mother said. He'd drink your bathwater.

I looked down at the table, the white ball cornered by stripes. My own solids tragically shut off.

I can't get out of that.

The leave, see? my mother said. The leave always beats the play.

O n our way down the stairs her feet went out from under her and she flew. The steps were covered in the kind of used-up carpet that slides and too many wet boots had been up and down them over the course of the night. I grabbed her elbow and her shoulder slammed against the rail. My mother rubbed her arm and laughed. Outside it was pelting freezing rain and we pulled our jackets up over our heads and looked for a cab but nothing came.

Go one more? she said.

We ducked into a place two doors down with a picture of burning charcoal in the window. The owner brought us a couple of shots of ouzo before we'd had a chance to get our wet coats off. She was small and squat with dyed auburn hair tied back in an elaborate swirl and she clacked over in a pair of violently colored burgundy heels. The veins and little bones of her feet bulged out the sides of the shoes. Her husband had a thick mustache and sat behind the bar reading the Greek newspaper.

Weather makes for bad business, she said. You want eat?

Nice to see you, nice to see you. This was the husband, but he didn't look up from the paper when he spoke. He waved a vague hand in our direction.

My mother stacked the menus neatly at the corner of the table.

Here's something, I said. I pulled out the photo of the house on Brunswick from where it was buried under my wallet and a couple of books in my shoulder bag. It had a vintage look now, folded over and generally dragged around. I showed it to Dad already, I said. He said to ask you.

Where did you find this? my mother said. She'd put back her shot all at once and her cheeks glowed pink. I ordered two more.

It's you, I said. Her eyes lifted. The wife clattered back and forth in her swollen shoes.

This is a long time ago, my mother said. I don't know if I'd even met your father yet. She peered down at the picture. This is me. Here. She pointed at the blond girl on the porch, straight hair hanging down below her shoulders. This one, she said.

Who are the other people? I said. Who's this. I pointed at one of the other girls, a tall brunette with a little more curve to her body.

Mary Bramer. She was from Saskatchewan. And this here, this is Ted Fanning. He was fine. He was a sweetheart. He smoked too much pot and it made him stupid, but besides. She drew a line around Ted's face with a fingernail.

Which one is Arthur Sawchuk?

She looked at me, sharp, but also slow.

The caption only lists a few names, I said. It lists the guys who were arrested and the guy who owned the house.

Art Sawchuk didn't own the house, my mother said. He had the line on the place and we all paid him. But he didn't own it.

It says the house is registered to Arthur Lewis Sawchuk.

Sawchuk. My mother shrugged. He used a lot of different names. He ran drugs through the house, drugs and some other stuff. He had a bunch of names. He got away with it. In those days it was easier. I don't know who owned the place. She took a sip off the top of her second ouzo. It was a squat, she said. There were always fifteen kids living there. When Mary didn't have the rent he'd make her give blow jobs to all his friends. He'd hold her by the hair.

My mother grabbed at the back of her own head and pulled back hard.

That's the kind of place it was. You'd have to watch that. I always had the money, she said. And I got out. I would have been next.

How'd you know him?

I knew Ted Fanning, she said. That's who brought me in. I knew him from home, his brother was my sister's boyfriend. The one that went through the ice.

But Ted didn't live there, I said.

No. My mother ran a hand back through her hair and a few drops of rainwater came off the tips and hit the table.

What other names did he use? I said. Your landlord Art.

I don't know. Art Sawchuk, I don't remember what else. She passed the photo back to me across the table. He wasn't from here. He was an American.

She said Art Sawchuk had been all through the Southwest before coming up to Canada and who knows what he'd done down there. He told stories but maybe they were lies and maybe they were true. He liked to scare you, she said.

Scare you how?

She took a long breath. He had a mean streak, I guess. He'd tell all kinds of lies. Ted told me he'd driven up from California, or hitchhiked, and walked over the border somewhere in Manitoba. He'd slept a lot of places. He'd sleep in barns or out in fields. One time he told me he'd sleep out in a barn and any animals out there with him, he'd cut their throats in the morning. Sawchuk told me that himself. So the farmer would come in and just find his lambs and calves slashed and bleeding and not know what happened. He liked to terrorize you, she said. Mary was scared of him and she got it the worst.

You weren't.

I wasn't what.

You weren't scared.

I stayed away, my mother said. I put Mary and any other girls in the room with me and locked the door. Her shot glass was empty now and she flipped it upside down and banged it on the table. That's not true, she said. Sometimes I let her take it. We were all fucking terrified.

We sat there a moment. I finished my shot and set the glass quietly upside down to match hers.

He said a lot of things, you have to keep that in mind. He told me he was a personal friend of Charles Manson, she said. He'd met him in jail. Later on, hitching through the desert, he'd ended up at Spahn Ranch, where they all lived, for a night or two. Sheer accident. He called them a bunch of dirty hippies. She leaned toward me. When I knew Art Sawchuk, Manson had just been arrested for killing a house full of strangers. Two houses. A pregnant woman. In the most horrible ways. So it was very much a threat, you understand. I know it doesn't mean much to you now.

Actually, I find that connection pretty interesting, I said.

The owner came over with another set of shots and my mother turned and said, Light these on fire, would you?

She turned back to me: We're talking '69, '70. It's not like it is now. It wasn't flowers and peace signs. Hippies were more like drifters. The bikers were crime, they were gunrunners and murderers. That's why regular people were afraid. It wasn't about long hair. It was about morality and power. There was this awful heavy tide turning down in the States but now we only think of the fun parts, she said. Or we think about the anti-war stuff, whatever pieces of it were good and nice.

The heels clacked back to us with a green BIC lighter. Her thumb flicked. There wasn't much lighter fluid left and her thumb flicked and flicked. The two shots flamed up.

Let it burn, my mother said. We're already drunk.

So you and Charles Manson, I said. Two degrees of separation.

My mother held her hands high in the air like a preacher.

You have to hand it to Manson, he got them all believing in the end of the world. That was Sawchuk's thinking. He said no one else had soldiers like that. Tex Watson, he said. Now that was a soldier! She boomed this out. The Greek husband looked at us over the top of his newspaper as if we were regulars arguing about the soccer game.

And all of them wearing dresses, my mother said. Sawchuk said that, too. Because of those robes they wore. She leaned forward and blew out the flame on her shot.

That's what he wanted for your house, then. I pointed down to the photograph again. My mother's eyes in that photo.

No, she said. I don't think so. He didn't want to convince you. He was very secretive or else he was bragging, all the time. Two modes. She stopped short and looked at me. I don't know, she said. A few months after I moved out, there were all these photographs in the paper, Manson's girls heading to testify.

Linda Kasabian, I said. Remember I bought that book about it? At the Flea. She was the star of the show.

Yeah, with her little pigtails. She slept with all of them, that was her role. I saw her picture and I thought, Mary Bramer. That was Mary's role in our house, that's what she was for. My mother fingered the dark-haired girl in the picture again. She tapped a finger on the girl's face. By that time I was living out with your father.

You left clean.

I left owing some money. She looked up at me. It seemed like a good time for me to disappear. Down in the States, that trial was revving up. Sawchuk was worried about getting caught, I think. He was ready to split. Everyone down there was naming names. Worst mistake Manson ever made was taking on Linda Kasabian. That's what Sawchuk used to say, she sold them all out. He followed the whole story in the papers. Every day he'd go out and buy three papers, *Toronto, New York, LA Times*. He sat in the back kitchen smoking and he'd read the A-section of all three of them, one after the other. He couldn't get enough.

He was afraid, then?

Of Manson?

Of you.

You think? Maybe. Or else it was part of the act, I don't know. He hated women. In June of '70 your dad got a job offer in Orillia and I was rotted that he wouldn't take it. I wanted to get away. Sawchuk never let a debt die, she said.

What about Graham Patton? I said.

My mother jerked back slightly.

You're in full-on reporter mode here, aren't you?

His name comes up on this photo, I said. I don't know if I'd recognize him.

Who?

Graham Patton. David's father, right?

My mother pulled out her wallet.

That's a common name, Evie. Who knows?

Did you know him?

Back then? She looked down at the bill and counted through her money. I met David when you did.

Is it possible that Art Sawchuk also went by that name? Graham Patton?

No. My mother laid the money down and smoothed it with her hand. No, I don't think so. And don't go saying that out loud again.

Robert Cameron also went by the name Arthur Sawchuk, I said. And Cameron was in jail with Charles Manson, too. I found a list.

I thought you were working on this Bernardo thing.

I'm finding out a lot of things, I said. Some of this is for work. Some of it I'm doing on my own.

You're working too hard.

Cameron was American.

My mother closed her eyes and when she opened them again her face had relaxed.

I knew Graham back then, she said. Before I knew your father. You can't imagine. We were a bunch of kids in over our heads, she said. You all done?

Last question.

Let's go home. You're making me feel ancient.

Which one is Sawchuk? I pushed the picture at her again.

She shook her head. He's not in here, she said.

Oh.

She turned her glass upside down again and it smacked off the tabletop.

I really wish we'd moved to Orillia, she said. All that fresh air.

CHAPTER 20

My mother taught me how to ice-skate when I was four, at the little ice rink in the center courtyard at Hazelton Lanes. In the summer you can have coffee and pastry at the tables there, when you need a break from shopping for designer shoes and jewels. In the winter, they close all the glass doors and the courtyard becomes a tiny, perfect ice rink, with a tree growing up out of the middle of it. My mother held out her hands and skated backward, away from me. Slowly.

I'm not moving! she said. I promise. Skate to me!

Then she'd glide another foot or two away.

I wonder if she really thought she was fooling me, or if it just seemed like the right thing to say. Metaphorically, she was not leaving me behind. She was imbuing me with a new and valuable pleasure. This is my mother in a nutshell: when faced with the possibility of preschooler tears, employ metaphor.

She also taught me to ride a bike in one shot, on the grass behind Maurice Cody school yard. On the grass so that if I fell (more likely to happen if you're riding over a bumpy field, for the record) it would hurt less. She gave the bike seat a solid push from behind and then jogged just out of reach, screaming, You're sitting half-assed! You're sitting half-assed!

Compare and contrast at will.

If you leave Hazelton Lanes on the Yorkville side, you can walk down a little cobblestone pathway that runs between Remy's bar at one end and Hemingway's at the other. These are both stockbroker bars, guys-in-their-thirties-wearing-suits bars. The kind of place a guy like Paul Bernardo might have hung out, when you think of it. Remy's sometimes had a dance floor and a bad DJ, too, with a video screen. Music videos were still exciting. People wanted to show off this new technology.

Keep going and you end up right on Bloor Street, where all the richest stores are. William Ashley if you're getting married, Creed's for fur, Holt Renfrew for everything else. I spent half of high school skipping off so I could spend my afternoons riding up the Holt's escalator and trying on Christian Lacroix bustiers. Inside, it's a comforting place. Bright white and swank. There's a nice old doorman who knows my name. His own name is Leonard, like the poet. You can go into Holt's and Leonard always has a nice smile for you and he's wearing a carnation in his buttonhole, but it's always a different color. You waste a few hours manhandling all the clothes and it's like you're growing up rich in New York City. Then you come out and go down into the grotty subway and buy one of those big Treats cookies and there's a guy with one leg sitting on the ground playing violin and he's not even very good and those things all feel okay again.

I walked into Holt's the next afternoon holding a Styrofoam cup of hot chocolate in one hand. The other hand stayed in my pocket to keep warm. Hot chocolate doesn't seem like what you want for a hangover but you'd be surprised. It tastes like a warm bed and someone's hand on your forehead, checking to see if you have a fever. After the pool hall, I'd spent the night at my parents' instead of going home.

I was keen to do anything frivolous and normal. Allow foreign ladies to spray me with perfume. You can't bring Leonard a coffee or a cup of tea or anything because both his hands have to be free, contractually: ready in their thin leather gloves to open the door and close the door and hail cabs as required. So we smile and whatnot, but no congenial exchange of goods.

I was playing around in the second-floor dressing room mirror, wearing a green skirt with no price tag on it when the fire alarm started up. At first it was just *ding ding ding,* and no big deal because probably someone's fooling around. But it kept going. I figured if it got serious, someone would knock on the door of my little room. Then it changed.

Attention please, attention. Please leave the building immediately. The fire department is on its way. Please leave the building by the nearest exit.

The fire bell rang three or four more times and then the evacuation message repeated. I left the skirt on the ground and started hopping to put on my regular pants. By the time I'd slung my bag on my shoulder, there was no one left on the entire floor. The escalator was stopped. The announcement played over and over again.

In elementary school, they showed us a movie about two girls who get locked in a fur coat warehouse overnight. At first the girls really like it, they're trying on all the coats and wrapping themselves up and posing. But the stillness and the racks of coats, hanging there like animals, get progressively creepier until the girls have to escape. I don't think there was any talking in that movie, or if there was, it was in French. This is what an empty department store makes you think of.

I stood there between two display shelves of ultra-high heels, listening to the bell and the moment of silence whenever the message paused. A black-and-white Versace poster stretched across the wall over my head: an angry brunette holding her stiletto like a dagger, stabbing at a prone, laughing blond. Then I kicked my shoes off and slid my feet into a pair of alligator Vivienne Westwoods.

I was about four inches taller in the heels. Like a giant. For a moment I really thought I'd walk out of there in these stolen shoes, stopped escalator and all. There was no one around. I glanced up to where I thought the security camera's eye might be, hidden among the pot lights. Someone was watching.

The alarm bell rang and rang. I kicked the shoes off and jammed my feet halfway into my own Converse and ran down the toothy metal steps of the escalator like that, stepping on the backs of the sneakers.

The tall glass doors at the front of the store were all shut. Leonard was still standing there in his coat and gloves and when he saw me he pointed with both arms toward the back of the store. From somewhere under the alarm there was a low crowd sound, feet and voices, from people who seemed far away.

Is this for real? I yelled to Leonard. He shrugged. The big epaulets on his coat flounced.

Bomb threat, he yelled back. But I don't know. Go, go! Get going!

Outside, a few cars and vans stood around in a clump. Two fire trucks blocked Bloor Street, and the men in their heavy jackets and hip waders came pouring off. Police sirens mixed with a car alarm. A red hatchback was pulled up on the sidewalk outside the plate glass window. The driver's door left open, like whoever parked that car was in a hurry to get gone.

I turned down between the stalls in makeup alley, stepping quickly to try to catch the tail end of the line, other people somewhere up ahead. I could hear them but not see them, heading farther downstairs and through into the underground pathway.

Then another set of footsteps, too. Over to my right.

I looked back and Leonard was still standing where I'd seen him last, halfway between the escalator and the doors.

I'd thought I was the only one left. There hadn't been anyone else upstairs.

Someone was pacing me. Just to the other side of the row of cosmetic counters, the blockade of Shiseido and Elizabeth Arden and Clinique. There was a shimmery chime of breaking glass and then the heavy wash of perfume through the air; my own arm brushing against the tester perfume bottles, sending them flying off the shelves. I pushed myself along faster.

The PA announcement and the bells and the whoosh of my own pulse hammered through my ears. My vision narrowed to a white tunnel: the glossy floor and pale countertops. The perfume smell covered everything.

What if someone else had been watching those screens? Watched me pull clothes off the racks. Pose in the mirror. Someone following me now.

My knees buckled a little and I caught myself, skittering out into the open and sliding toward the doorway.

I caught up to the edge of the crowd and lost the sound of him. The annex opened up and I looked over my shoulder one last time, the border of makeup alley. No other person came out from between the stalls.

I was the last one.

The crush of escaping shoppers moved like a hot wave. I shoved my body through. There was that stink in the air, a subway stink, like animals in a tunnel, all sweating. We went down a wide set of six or seven steps and a woman fell and no one helped her up. She pushed against the wall and swung back out, grabbing onto my wrist for a second. I shook her off and hurtled my way down the stairs. As we came down into the underground mall the walkway widened out and people started to run.

I walked through, taking long strides, my bag hanging off one shoulder. The last thing you want to do is seem panicky, easy to pick off. Or, worse: fall. We were far from any possible car-bomb danger now, but people were still flooding out of the smaller stores and down the hall, on toward the entrance to the subway.

A few others slowed down the way I had and fell into walking just ahead of me. A spontaneous emergency response station was setting up: workers wearing those orange vests. A man with a megaphone. Water for anyone who needed it.

If you're lost, find a policeman. That's what they tell small children. Corollary: If you think someone's following you, make sure to never be alone, even in a crowd. Draw attention to yourself.

I stopped where the paramedics were standing.

Hey! I said. Hey, is that water?

What you want to do is talk loud, seem eccentric, swing your bag around and accidentally hit a few people. Something that calls you out. Something that people will turn toward, someone that people want to look at. Be memorable.

I sipped my water from a white Dixie cup with a pointy bottom.

Standing there against the wall, facing out, I could see everything. No one else had stopped. No one was behind me. A group of firefighters cordoned off the entranceway I'd just come out of. They were tall guys moving fast and dressed in the same hip-wader uniforms, but one of them laughed and I thought, Threat over.

It was like I'd taken off a set of earmuffs. I'd come in from a snowstorm into a warm house full of people. A loose crowd is a safe thing. You're surrounded by witnesses.

I rounded the corner and started up the steps to street level. I was walking bent over, trying to use my finger like a shoehorn and jam my heels into my sneakers and someone yelled out, *Evie.*

Evie. A man's voice.

My toe caught on the top step and I pitched forward onto my hands, my right knee slamming down hard.

I thought it was you—

I was still on the ground, rubbing my sore knee. I looked up. Black cords, black boots, brown beard. Some gray in it.

I couldn't catch you, he said.

Later on, I thought what an odd way this was to begin.

He didn't offer an arm to help me up. Both his hands stayed low in his pockets. Graham Patton, David's father.

Speak of the devil.

What are you doing on the ground like that, Evie? His attempt at reestablishing the comfort zone. My body shrunk back against the steps for a moment. It really was Patton. I brushed off my hands and struggled to push up off the floor, trying to keep my knees together. Not easy. As I got onto my feet, he finally took his hand from his pocket and stretched it out to help.

Big panic over nothing, he said.

They thought there was a bomb, I said.

Yeah, Toronto is not New York, he said. Not yet. He was wearing a leather jacket, unzipped, and a shirt with no tie. A moss-green sweater with a crew neck. He put his hands back in his pockets. You hear about that?

He told me there'd been a bomb a few hours earlier under the World Trade Center in Manhattan.

Still smoking, he said. Still getting people out.

I said I'd left work at noon, but I was picturing the newsroom as I said it, the wire coming in and everyone crowded around the television, watching for angles.

I heard you were working for the paper now, Patton said. You must love that.

I was going home, I said. I don't want to take the subway.

I hadn't actually been thinking about going home or the subway, or what I was going to do next at all. I wanted a good look at Graham Patton, the set of his jaw. How tall was he, the size of his hands. I wanted an identifier. I was thinking about David, what he would say about all this, and about my mother's reaction to my question the night before.

Subway'll stay shut down now for a few hours, Graham Patton said. They're not letting anyone into that tunnel. I was supposed to teach a photo course, but that's all shut down, too. Come on, he said. I'll give you a lift home.

I was standing with my back to the wall, halfway between the escalator up to the shopping concourse and the doors onto Bloor Street.

I used to do some photo work for the *Free Press*, he said. A million years ago, geez. You should come by the house. I'll make you a coffee, get you over the shock. He leaned his body back toward where all the fuss had been.

I looked around. It was almost five o'clock. There was nothing remarkable. It was like nothing had happened at all. People were still rushing by us.

Anyone looking would have thought I was perfectly fine. Graham Patton looked like someone's father. I thought of how paranoid I'd been, the rush of anxiety in Holt's. How quickly I'd jumped to thinking someone was chasing me. Lianne's killer was half out of his grave in northern Ontario. What if I was wrong about everything?

Graham Patton smiled at me and his smile was like David's.

No one was watching a man in his late forties talking to a girl half his age. We walked together over to the Cumberland parking lot across the street and I got into his car, a silver Toyota. We got in and I wrapped the seat belt around the front of my body. There was the thunk of the door locks all engaging at once.

You can't be too careful, David's father said. He popped the gearshift into reverse and laid an arm across the top of my seat to back out of the parking spot. The windshield fan pumped hot air at high volume.

There was a man in the next car over, a green station wagon, writing something in a file folder. His pen jammed and he shook it violently between every word. He never gave us a second look.

CHAPTER 21

David's father stood on one side of an L-shaped kitchen counter and I stood on the other.

Grab a seat, he said, gesturing to a couple of bar stools lined up along my side. Cop a squat.

The house had been newly renovated back in the '80s and the kitchen was still decorated in what you could call '80s gray. A soft gray, meant for pink accents, like a '50s diner. The kitchen counter had since been done over in blue glass tiles. Patton pulled a couple of coffee cups out of the cupboard. He dislodged the filter cup from an espresso machine on the counter and smacked it sharply over the garbage and I noticed a spray of dry coffee grounds in the corner where he'd missed the garbage another time. There was a Lavazza package on the back of the stove. The window gave onto a tiny backyard with a few raised beds and half a wooden swing set. An A-frame with a slide and one swing, brackets along the top bar where the other swings should have been. A kit you buy at Home Hardware.

Do you have other kids? I said. I didn't sit. We were both staring out the window.

Not yet, he said.

The answer surprised me. I thought of David's story about the new Russian girlfriend and caught myself glancing around, looking for some sign of her in the house. A pink umbrella. *Glamour* on the coffee table. I realized that aside from my recent interest, David almost never talked about his father.

A black Lab had greeted us at the door with a long whip of a tail and now it was lying in the middle of the wood floor, on its side with its legs straight out, relaxed but also ready for the next thing, and I could see it had a long scar along the belly where the fur didn't grow in right.

What did you want to ask me? he said.

What?

You had questions.

I didn't remember saying that and I stared at him. He pushed the portafilter firmly into the machine and pulled down on the lever.

Upstairs is where I work, he said.

The main floor was designed open concept, with the kitchen at the back door where we'd come in opening out to a dining room and then a living room that faced the front of the house. He took the two coffees and walked around the counter. The stairs led up from the center of the house, with a stringy red oriental runner tacked all the way up to the second floor. There was a skylight overhead blocked with snow and a small stained-glass window on the landing that let in some light. On my way up, I stopped and leaned my face against the rosettes. A shadow moved by outside the house. You could see shapes but nothing defined. I wondered if anyone could see in through a window like that. I took two steps down to look out the window on the ground level and a woman walked by with a dog. David's father was waiting on the next floor.

Photos ran staggered up the wall: black-and-whites near the bottom, men and women that must have been David's grandparents or great-grandparents. David's baby pictures. Leaning on his elbows, propped there for a studio shot; I'd seen the same picture at his mother's house. Some '70s Technicolor. At the top of the stairs,

David with his mother outside the white house on Rumsey Road, and then in front of another house. High grass and barn board and a long gravel drive. David down low beside her, on a tricycle.

It was a shock to find her there. Wincing against the sun with her hair in a blue kerchief. A windy day: you could see it in the set of her face and David's short hair, all pushing up at the same angle. She was wearing a white pantsuit, her hands flat and calm against her thighs. A country house.

Do you still see her? I said. I crossed slowly to where David's father had set the coffee down on a table by the front window. He was sitting back on an olive-green couch and he shook his head and shrugged at the same time.

You like pictures? he said.

I thought the couch was leather, but when I got close I saw it was made of something else and I reached down and rubbed it with the back of my hand. It was fine and silky and dry. Graham Patton sat at one end with his legs stretched out almost the length of the couch. I expected him to shift as I sat down but he didn't and I curled up at my end.

Parachute material, he said. Army surplus. I got it made. It's wildly expensive. Then look here. He pointed to a spot near his own knee. Two tiny burn holes in the fabric. She did it on purpose, he said. With her cigarette. Told me she wanted to see if it would burn.

For a moment I thought he meant David's mother.

Susanna, he said. My girlfriend.

I'd already forgotten that he had a woman living there, or somewhere, that there was a woman and that he was thinking of more children.

His foot rested heavily against mine now. In the chaos of the shopping center I'd been so keyed up. All I could think about was showing that I wasn't afraid. Getting into his car was meant to be fearless and pointed.

I probably haven't seen you since you were, what? Twelve? Thirteen?

Sounds right, I said.

You were the one who knew that little girl, he said. Leslie.

I nodded. *That little girl* is modern code. The thing I'm famous for, knowing a dead girl.

No, wait, he said. What was her name again? You remember?

Lianne, I said. Like he might mean some other little girl. Lianne Gagnon.

That's right. The French girl. Lianne Gagnon. Shame. He rubbed his beard and smiled over at the dog. That was the one left out in the woods, he said. In a hockey bag. Right? Or the one in the fridge?

Down in the kitchen I'd felt like I was in control. I moved down onto the floor to make a little space between us and leaned against the couch sideways, with my shoulder and elbow.

No, I said. No, the one in the fridge was later on.

I didn't want him touching me. He moved along the couch a little but it was only to set his coffee down on the table. I had a surge of pins and needles across my forehead. I realized the point of coming here had been to prove myself wrong, to find him avuncular and harmless and simple.

The dog came over and collapsed against my hip and I reached out and laid a hand on her side. I could feel my blood moving and tried to catch my breath.

Is it a girl? I said. The words came out in a gasp.

Maxie, he said. I got her from a rescue up in Sudbury four years ago. He pointed at her belly. She had a barn accident. Someone dumped her at the shelter.

Maxie laid her head in my lap and when she sighed and shifted David's father leaned in from where he was sitting, over my shoulder, and brushed a hand across her muzzle. He stayed like that, bent over and close enough that I could feel his breath against my cheek when he spoke.

You know I could reach down and snap that dog's leg, he said. His voice was steady and instructive. She'd let me. She trusts people that much. He clicked his tongue softly. A dog trusts you like that, you can do anything you please.

I stiffened up and snaked an arm around Maxie's neck.

What did you come here for, he said.

I turned toward him, shifting my body so that I was facing the couch and not leaning on it. Which one's mine? I said. The coffee.

He pointed and I picked a cup up off the table and then stood up with it, looking first out the window and then strolling along one side of the room.

You don't see much of David I guess.

The second floor was more or less a giant loft and Graham Patton didn't answer but watched me walk around it. There was a door off to one side. I stopped in the doorway and looked in. It was a tiny room, almost entirely taken up with photography equipment: two umbrellas and a big soft box in one corner, lights on legs in another, a pile of tripods all folded up and leaning against a tall black filing cabinet. An unmade bed sat low to the ground. Some clothes on the floor, a pair of running shoes and a black bra.

Another door led out to a balcony off the back of the house. A row of heavy bookcases along the wall. Books in piles on the floor. A couple of big open boxes of old photographs. I'd gotten myself back to the open staircase where we'd come up. David's father had his feet on the floor now. I looked down at the landing below.

How long would it take to get back to the door. I squatted down and ran my thumb along the tops of the photos.

You like pictures? Patton said again.

You must have quite a collection. A lot of years.

I keep most of the archive at my place up north, he said. Here, I've got a little darkroom set up. A workspace. Down in the basement.

I didn't say anything. The boxes were full of contact sheets, I could see that now. Not photos, per se. The tops of the sheets rippled under my thumb and made a little sound of their own. Patton had them neatly organized by place or by publication, little colorful file separators stuck between each group: Chicago, 1978; Yorkville, 1976; *Saturday Night*; *Evening Telegram*; *Free Press*. The second box looked more personal: Rumsey Road, Linsmore Crescent, Cabin.

David tells me about you, Patton said.

David tells me you've been asking, I said. I turned my head. Do you spend much time on the balcony?

It's winter, he said. I guess it would be too cold.

I picked out a few random handfuls of contact sheets from the boxes, five or six from each category, and glanced over to see if mixing them up like this bothered him. More black-and-whites, David and his mother. David cold by a creek, hugging himself, his bathing trunks plastered to his legs. All his ribs sticking out and his bony knees. David's mother in a plastic-weave lawn chair in the high grass, wood slat exterior of a house casting a shadow on the picture.

Where's this? I said.

Bring them here. Patton was sitting straight up on the couch now, knees apart. He set his coffee down on the table and held a hand out to me. When I offered him the sheet he patted the spot next to him. It seemed tight and too cozy and I leaned on the arm of the couch instead. A half-sit. He held the photo with one hand and leaned his body against my knee. It was familiar. Almost-but-not-quite paternal.

That's the cabin, he said. It's fantastic. No neighbors. Deer. You should come up in the summer. Couple kayaks. Go out and get a few salmon. If you want to hunt, I'll take you out. Get a moose. Twenty-five years of photographs stored up there, too. He handed the photo back to me. You and David, of course.

I had a dim recollection of David going north during the summertimes. Something he liked or didn't like but had to do. His father had given him a hunting gun and taught him to shoot. I remembered that part. A Crickett 22 target rifle with walnut finish: I'd seen photographs of that as well, ten-year-old David with the gun in the crook of his arm. Patton taught him to shoot tin cans and then told him to try his luck with squirrels. Told him, Come back with a squirrel.

The shot from a .22 will strip the pelt right off an animal that small. Something David told me years ago, when we were alone in his house on Rumsey Road.

I skimmed through the other contact sheets I'd pulled out of the box. More cottage pics. Lots of black-and-white. A few city views I recognized, panoramas of Yorkville in the '60s. The Sears Tower. Kensington Market.

Hasn't changed much, has it? Patton said.

I buy coffee there all the time. I showed him with a finger. This place on the corner. You can see the bins of stuff in front of the spice vendor next door.

The last sheet had four wide-angle shots on it, each one extending the whole width of the page. Crop marks drawn on in thick black marker.

What are these? I squinted.

I used to sell to local press, Patton said. Freelance this and that. Neighborhood shots.

Kind of like that.

Each thumbnail was cut off, a smaller rectangle or square drawn around a given section to show which part of the photo to print. The rest of the shot had been blacked out with an X or scribbled line. I looked closer. The top two were street scenes. The two on the bottom were of a bunch of kids in front of a house. Printed small like that, the kids looked like heads on sticks. They looked like puppets. I angled the sheet to catch better light. More like teenagers than kids.

The drug raid photo from the newspaper. The same photo I had sitting on my desk at home.

You took all these, I said.

You caught me.

I twitched. Nothing about his face had changed. He looked like a guy in a bar, trying to buy you drinks you don't want. No. Trying to get you to want them. I shifted slightly away and looked back at the sheet in my hands.

Photo credit. That's why Patton's name had come up on the search. A thick crop line boxed off the part of the picture I knew. To the right of where my mother stood, a black X obscured whatever else had been in the original shot.

Whomever else.

I shuffled the page quickly to the bottom of the pile and held up the cabin pictures again. Something about his look made me want to hide.

These are nice, I said. You're in Muskoka, right?

Fuck no. He shook his head like I'd said something laughable. No, Muskoka's all city people. We're up past Manitoulin. You take the boat over to Manitoulin and drive off, north, toward Sudbury. I'm between Espanola and Manitoulin.

I know Espanola, I said. Patton shrugged.

It occurred to me as I said it that Espanola was where the news of Cameron's exhumation had been reported, that's why it was familiar.

Little place up there, he said. Not in town. Near the Indian res. Place called Whitefish Falls.

My fingers went cold. Whitefish Falls. Where the dead man had been living. I got up and laid the pile of contact sheets back on top of the box where I'd found them.

Maxie! The dog got heavily to her feet and padded over to me. I can let her see me out, I said. I held on to the dog's collar and led her down the stairs. David's father followed me down and I held the dog between us.

Your cup, he said.

I handed him the coffee cup and he bent and set it down on the lowest step. I had to let go of the dog to pick up my coat and bag. As soon as I dropped her collar Maxie left me and went to the kitchen and started lapping up water from a bowl. The light had started to flag outside. There were red stains on the wood floor next to my bag. I looked up the stairs, toward the landing window. The sun was lower in the sky now and it burned through the rosettes in the stained glass and the red light was projecting onto the hardwood. Patton wasn't speaking. The sound of the dog's tongue, slapping against the water in the bowl, and the bowl sliding around on the tile floor, drowned out everything in the house. I slung my bag over my head so the strap would cross my body and looked around to find my shoes. The backs were still pressed flat where I'd stepped on them in the escape from Holt Renfrew. Graham Patton stood and watched me.

Nice shoes, he said. How much you have to pay for those?

I stared at him.

They're sneakers, I said. So, you know. Average cost.

Sneakers. But you must like grown-up shoes. Don't you, Evie?

I slid the shoes on and bent down to hook the crushed backs around my heels.

He sat down on the steps and spread his feet out on the wood floor and cocked his head at me. Lucky you didn't walk out of Holt's in those heels, he said. Those high heels you tried on. Make you flip and kill yourself in that crowd. His voice dropped. You see? I worry about you, Evie.

My body stiffened. Patton rubbed his knees and stood up. He walked up two steps and stood there, looking down at me. He raised two fingers to his temple, like a salute.

Back door's unlocked, he said. You look like someone who wants to leave.

He turned and walked up the stairs, leaving me standing in his living room.

I picked my used cup off the steps and walked over and set it down on the blue-tiled kitchen counter. There was a six-burner gas stove wedged in the corner and the espresso machine and a bar-sized fridge. If Graham Patton had a real refrigerator, it was hidden away in a pantry or down in the basement, next to the darkroom door. With less sunlight now the gray of the walls could have been concrete.

A joist creaked in the ceiling overhead. I listened for his feet on the stairs but the sound didn't come. Maxie hadn't followed him up.

The door closed behind me with a click. There was a rough path to the back gate tramped down in the snow. The worn tread on my shoes slid. Halfway across the yard I stopped and turned. Maxie had her paws up on the kitchen windowsill, nose against the glass. The second-floor window was dark. The dog threw out a couple of warning barks. If Patton was up there, watching me leave, I couldn't see him.

CHAPTER 22

Angie wasn't in the newsroom. Vinh was stretched out at my desk, listening to the police scanner. It was after six. There was a half-empty two-liter bottle of Pepsi on the floor next to his chair. Condensation had loosened the label and he'd been peeling away at it piece by piece. It said PEP. I knew I was on deck to go back down to Niagara the next day but I wanted to talk to Angie first.

Nah, she's home for the night, Vinh said.

He handed me two phone messages, scrawled on the little pad in his all-caps style and written using the last dying moment of a pen, by the looks of it:

Call Police Constable Job at 14 Division. He likes walks along the beach and wants to get laid.

Job from 14 Division. Dude seriously wants to see you naked.

Thanks for these, I said. You're extraordinary. She leave me her keys?

He pulled open the desk drawers one by one. Take a look yourself, he said. I don't see keys.

I rifled through the jumble of pens and paper clips and notecards in the top drawer.

Maybe we should divide up these drawers, I said. You take three and I'll take three. Make it easier to keep stuff organized. We'd been sharing the desk since Christmas and this was the first time the idea had occurred to either of us.

I hear you got a peeper giving you a hard time, he said.

I looked at him. Oh?

He pointed at the scanner.

I hear all, I know all, Vinh said.

They say my name?

I just put two and two together, he said. You're near Gladstone, right?

You're really creeping me out right now.

Vinh threw his legs up on the desk.

I'm just fucking with you, he said. Angie told me.

I found a spot a few cubicles over where I could make some calls, the phone cradled between my ear and shoulder. I laid the two messages from Police Constable Job side by side. Along the far edge of the desk there was a row of paper cups turned upside down, each with a pencil stabbed down through it. I didn't remember who the owner of the desk was. The cup installation piece made me want to root through the desk drawers to see what other treasures might be hiding, but everything was locked up tight.

Where were you last night? David said.

Out ripping it up with my mom, I said. I slept at their place.

I would have come over, he said. What about tonight, what are you doing now?

There was a minimal evening crew in the newsroom. I'd offered to stay late and write a firsthand account of the bomb scare, but Angie said a pretend bomb at a Bloor Street department store wasn't a high-urgency story. She'd told me this also by phone, from her house. Traffic terrorism, she called it.

Took me an hour and a half to get home. They wouldn't let us out, she said. I could have walked in less time. We're running a single paragraph about the subway shutdown. It's A7, A6 tops. This isn't New York. And I need you on Bernardo.

I told David about the bomb scare and he laughed.

When's the last time you saw your father?

Silence.

I told you, David said. A week ago? Two weeks? And also: fuck you with this. Don't do this.

I hadn't mentioned seeing Graham Patton or being at the house or any of it.

I'm slammed here, I said. Can we do tomorrow?

Are you going to be able to sleep?

I crumpled the two messages from Job in my hand and fired them into the trash.

I'm a prize-winning sleeper, I said. Sleeping is actually the thing I do best.

I left the newsroom and meant to head home. With the safety of a few hours between us, I kept looping the visit at Patton's over in my mind. His cabin up in Whitefish Falls: the coincidence was upsetting. If Robert Cameron was the dead man they'd just dug up in northern Ontario, then there was nothing to worry about. Then it really was coincidence. So what? Patton has a cabin in the same place. So what.

Suddenly I was sorry I hadn't found a way to pocket that contact sheet. If Patton was the kind of player he made himself out to be, he wouldn't be sitting home on a Friday night. And if he wasn't at home, then there couldn't be much harm in checking to see if that sheet was still available. Plus whatever else I might find in his studio. A decent shot of Patton himself, something from the '80s, something to compare against a mug shot of Cameron. I stopped thinking about where I was going and just went.

There was no car in the alley behind Patton's house in the east end. The lights were all down.

I picked my way through the backyard. With evening, the

temperature had dropped a few degrees. All the slushy places had turned to ice and my feet slid around and caught in the ruts. There was a bang and a face in the door, but it was only Maxie. I tried the backdoor knob and it clicked a few times but stayed firm.

Two possibilities: find a hidden key, or else something more drastic. A crowbar. A garden implement. One of those fork things.

I had a mag light attached to my own key ring and I cast about near the doorway. Where do people stash keys? Under the mat. In the garden gnome's mouth. Behind the smoothest rock in the garden, next to where the peonies come up in the summer. Maxie jumped around on her side of the door. If Patton was home, he'd have heard me by now. I stretched high on my toes and groped around above my head. Taped to the upper edge of the door frame. Under a loose piece of siding.

Hidden on top of the porch light.

And voilà. We have contact.

The click of the latch. The many clicks of Maxie's nails on the kitchen tile, dancing out a greeting. I stepped inside and closed the door behind me. The place was dark. There was light from outside, from the street, filtered through the blinds and landing in stripes on the wood floor of the living room. I passed by the kitchen counter and the door to the basement and aimed for the stairs to the second floor. No lights on up there, either. A kind of incandescence from the stained glass, the streetlight glowing through the rosettes. Not light, exactly. A glimmer. Embers.

There was no one upstairs. Maxie followed me and I dropped down and aimed my key ring flashlight at the box of contact sheets. The sound of Maxie's panting in my ear. Uneven. Her breath regular but then studded with pauses. My pile from the afternoon was still on top and I pulled the sheet with the drug raid shot and set it aside so I wouldn't forget. The second box held single prints, eight by tens. I turned my head to look at the dog.

What else has he got for us, Maxie? I started from the back, hoping the photos were chronological, not random.

David's mother. The same series of country house pictures. Graham Patton himself in some of the shots. Patton in hip waders in front of the cabin, the wood facade. An A-frame. One floor with a tiny loft, the tip of the A.

David's mother in black and white, in an evening dress, cooking in a house I didn't know. Cooking because she was wearing an apron. Then with no apron, wearing nothing but splayed comfortably on a floor, on a bed. Her eyes wide, smiling for the camera. And then less easily lain out, blindfolded. David's mother again? The blindfold made it harder to identify. It could have been any woman.

He hadn't stopped me from looking through these. Knowing what I'd find.

I went back to the shots of Patton and pulled out a few that looked best—close-ups where his face was clear and a wide angle that showed the look of the house and the gravel drive. I had what I'd come for but I ran my hand over the second box again to be sure. Near the front of this box the photos were older, the women in them all different, thinner, their hair longer and center parted. A row of men at a long table in a beer hall. The women to one side. Everyone smoking, thin cigarettes in every hand. The packs out on the table along with the bottles.

The aftermath of a few parties. Girls on a porch. Girls swinging in a hammock on the front porch of a house. The lawn and porch of the house on Brunswick, and my mother in the hammock, my mother at seventeen, holding a cigarette in one hand and posing for the camera. I pulled that one, too. Then the same picture I'd found from the paper, the house on Brunswick, my mother and Ted Fanning and Mary Bramer. Cropped according to the marks on the contact sheet.

Wedged in the bottom of the second box, a different picture of that front porch. Patton and another man. I squinted and tried to direct the light more keenly on Patton's face. Younger. A little more meat on him, maybe. His eyes dark and hard. Both men with beards, longish hair. Nothing excessive. I laid the two photos side by side. In the new photo, the second man had a black, fringed leather jacket over his shoulder. His face was turned away from the camera. He could have been anyone. Ted Fanning again.

Graham Patton standing next to him. Also living there? Or the house simply known to him?

I set the three pictures, Patton and my mother and the drug raid one I knew so well, on top of the contact sheet and gave the boxes a little shake to make them look more natural. Less searched. There was a hum and the heat came on, warm air suddenly moving up through the ducts. I sat still a moment, listening, and then moved quickly into the other room, the studio. The umbrellas and soft box I'd seen earlier made big, grotesque shapes in the dark.

The file cabinet. I pulled at a drawer but it wouldn't budge. There was a lock on the top drawer that I knew would control all the rest of them. Trip the one lock and the whole cabinet is your oyster. One of those times I wished I were the sort of girl who wore hairpins. I dug into my bag and rooted around. Something brushed my leg and I pulled in my breath. Maxie's tail. She went where I went. Wagging.

There was a small blue toolbox against the wall, down underneath the umbrellas. I flipped it open, looking for something usable. A file cabinet lock is not a complex thing. You can jimmy it with a butter knife. I found a small flathead screwdriver and spent a minute or so playing with the lock before it gave. You want to go in carefully. You don't want to leave marks on the lock.

The top drawer was contracts only, and in the next one there were no files at all but small, stacked boxes of negatives. I didn't know how long I'd been in the house already. It could have been ten minutes or an hour, and I didn't want to put the light on or waste time holding negatives to the bulb, trying to decipher content. Third drawer down was where the photos started, more contact sheets and full prints, mostly work for hire, nothing exceptional. I found a few family pictures and the same blindfolded mystery woman in the bottom drawer and got down on my knees to take stock. David's mother but not only her: other women, too. I shuffled through with my thumb, like they were a deck of cards. Black-and-white mostly, or that high-grain fade-out that's left from color film shot in the '70s and '80s. Naked and curled into a hammock, sitting on a wood floor and painting her toes. Seminudes in black-and-white. A blonde wearing a kerchief and unhooked garter, no stockings, legs folded demurely on a rolling office chair. Shading her eyes with her fingers, like a toddler's game of peekaboo. They were lovely. A little art house porn in sepia tones.

My thumb stopped. There she was.

My mother. Sitting on the corner of a bed, a wry and patient look to her lips. Smoking. Liking and not liking being photographed. Not my seventeen-year-old mother. In color, her nipples faded out to a brick brown. The mother I knew. Patton had a date stamp on all his photos. My mother in 1982.

Back behind the nudes he'd jammed a large manila envelope and I unfastened the string tie closure and shook out another set of photos. No faces in these ones. The same unfastened garters, ankles bound tightly to a headboard, to a radiator; a torso, breasts, leather strap pulling at her neck. Ass and pussy, fingers spreading her own thighs, or wrists tied behind her back. No faces.

I pulled the photo of my mother and stacked it with the others in my collection, sliding them carefully into a notebook to keep them flat and put the whole thing away in my shoulder bag and slung it over my head, across my body. I paused for a moment with the screwdriver in my hand, then slipped that into the bag, too. I looked around. Maxie was gone.

Maxie had gone downstairs while I was busy with the pictures and now I heard her toenails on the tile floor, her slight whine from the kitchen. On the landing the stained-glass rosettes flashed with a passing car. I came down the stairs soft and fast. In the backyard there was a burst of white and then darkness again. Not the backyard. Back behind the house, in the alley. The headlights of a car as it parked. The darkness when the driver killed the motor.

Maxie jumped up against the door. I froze. Outside I saw the gate swing open and bang shut again and the crunching sound of someone navigating the backyard, the ridges of frozen snow.

The front door was too far away now. There was an expanse of open floor I'd have to cross to get there and it wouldn't work, I'd be seen and trapped. Beside me the door to the basement was shut tight. I grabbed the doorknob and pulled and I was down on the wooden stairs, door closed firm behind me. The furnace thrummed on. The sound of it lighting up. There were a few small windows at the other side of the room and the darkroom door with its fat, red bulb. I lowered myself to sitting and slid down the stairs like that, so that I wouldn't lose my footing in the dark. Just above me I heard the door open, footsteps and the dog whining and barking, a man's voice. I got to the bottom of the stairs and crossed the room. There was a row of basement windows here, up at street level, giving onto the path at the side of the house. They were high up. Underneath them a row of tool shelves, and then a chest freezer.

The footsteps were all right overhead. He was right above me but it sounded like he was on the stairs. He was on the stairs and the light would go on and I'd be caught. I heard voices and every voice was a man. I climbed up on the chest freezer and pulled out my key chain with the flashlight on it and it dropped and bounced off the freezer onto the floor. It made a noise doing this and I dropped down, too, running my hands back and forth over the concrete floor in the dark. The floor was covered in something, dirt or grime or sawdust, something dry and gritty. My hands on something cold and sharp. The keys. My key ring. I switched on the flashlight and got back up on the freezer and worked on the window latch. If he went up to bed I could get out. The footsteps came and went on the main floor. Once he stopped just over my head and I stopped, too, afraid that he could hear me. The latch was frozen and stuck in the cold and I held my hand against it to thaw it out until my skin burned.

I pushed and the window slid open suddenly, banging against the frame. The footsteps had moved on. I heard the door to the basement open and suddenly he was on the stairs and then he was down there with me. The light flipped on. I heard Patton call out but he sounded far away.

It was David on the stairs. He didn't move. He looked at me like I was stealing from him. He looked at me like I'd taken off a mask and he didn't know my name.

My breath came back to me.

I'm so sorry, I mouthed at him. I'm sorry.

Patton at the top of the stairs, calling down:

Hey, Dave. What's up. Is there a raccoon down there or what?

David stared at me.

There's nothing down here, he said. His voice was flat. Nothing at all. He turned and walked slowly back up the stairs. The basement door shut hard.

I listened to the steps retreating, toward the front of the house. The TV went on. I turned back to the window.

There was a screen and I plunged the end of my house key into the top of the mesh to rip it through, then ripped out the rectangle with a few clean strokes. I took off my shoulder bag and shoved it out onto the path. It was a tight fit. My hand slipped as I levered my body through and my cheek hit a chunk of ice and scraped up against it as I pulled myself out. The side of the house was quiet. I stood there a moment to catch my breath. The back door slammed shut. I leaned up against the wall to stay hidden. The back of David's head, walking past the swing set, through the gate and away.

I found my way down to Gerrard Street through the alleys and blew twenty bucks on a cab to my parents' house, riding the feeling that if David ever spoke to me again, I could at least say I'd done what he told me in the first place: Just ask your mother. On the way there I pulled the photos out of my bag and looked them all over. The print of the drug raid shot was crystal clear. If there'd ever been any doubt, it was put to rest. My mother's wide, sad eyes and fair skin were unmistakable. She was wearing a sleeveless dress. You could see the freckles on her arms.

I traded it in my hands for the nude portrait. It was taken the year I turned eleven, and my mother was still a young woman, even then. Twenty-nine. The same pale freckles across her collarbone, her breasts. The photograph walked a weird line. Not quite artful. But not candid, either.

I tucked the pictures away and paid the cabbie and climbed out. There were two cars in the drive and lights on in three rooms. It occurred to me for the first time that my father, too, would be home at this time. There were some cat prints on the porch in the snow and I tried the door before searching for my key. It gave. I shook my hair and called out.

Evie? My mother came out of the kitchen. She was wearing jeans and a soft sweater with the sleeves rolled high. In her sock feet, she barely made five-two. You missed your dad, she said. He's out for his walk.

I didn't say anything and pressed my lips together.

Sweetie, what's wrong? Did something happen? Did that guy come back?

No, I said. No, I just need to talk to you.

She'd been getting tomato seedlings started in the kitchen. The round table was covered over in newspaper. On top of that there were fifty or sixty tiny brown starter pots and a handful of paper bags of seeds.

I got them at the health food store, she said. Heirloom! A bit more work. But they'll be beautiful. They'll be like jewels.

I sat down. How long will Dad be gone?

She glanced at the stove clock. I don't know. Another half hour. Maybe a bit more.

I need to ask you some things, I said.

Okay. She'd rolled her thin gardener's gloves on and was ruffling about with the paper seed bags.

I found some more photos and I need to know what they're about.

She looked up.

Just sit down a moment, I said.

Okay, Evie. What's up. What happened?

I don't want you to ask me where I got these. I just need to know what's going on.

She sat down slowly. Her hair was in her eyes and when she brushed at it, the glove left a dirt streak above her eyebrow.

What do you mean?

What's the connection between you and Graham Patton?

I told you, Evie. She shook her head. We all knew each other a long time ago. It was rough times.

That photo I showed you, remember? From the paper. I have the original here. I took the stack of photos out of my bag and pulled the drug raid shot and the contact sheet. Look.

Okay.

It's definitely you.

I told you it's me, Evie.

Graham Patton took the photo. I found this in his house.

My mother's face went still.

What are you doing in his house, she said.

It's his photo. He took it. That's why his name is attached to it, but he's not there.

Evie, my mother said. What are you doing in that man's house?

But look. It's not the whole shot. There's something else that wasn't printed.

I see that.

Who else was there?

What do you mean?

Who else was in this picture? What's he hiding?

My mother picked up the contact sheet and gave it a squint. She shrugged. I don't know.

You do know.

I don't. I don't know. It was a long time ago.

I pulled out the other photos, Patton at his cabin. My mother's nude.

This is you, too.

She was quiet.

It's you, isn't it? When I was a kid.

Jesus, Evie. What if your father was home.

He doesn't know?

She picked up the photo and ran her finger along the edge of it. I don't know, she said. In the end I don't know what he knows. She looked at me. I worked very hard to keep some things from him, trouble I was in. I owed Patton money, a lot of money.

You said you owed Sawchuk money.

I owed Patton.

Are Patton and Robert Cameron the same man?

Evie.

Sawchuk is Cameron. I already know that. I pushed aside the pots and earth and seeds and spread all the photos out on the dirty table-top. You can keep trying to hide this from me, Mom, but I am so close to figuring this out. So close. I saw Patton in our house, in the living room, arguing with you the day before Lianne disappeared. I know I did. You can't hide this forever. Is Patton really Cameron? Is he?

My mother stood up suddenly. You have no idea, she said. Her mouth was set tight and grim. You have no idea what you're talking about. You think you're close? I paid him back, every cent. I worked very hard to keep you away from this, I did whatever it took. I flattered him. Don't go over to Patton's. There's nothing for you there.

There was a sound from the front entrance, the door creaking open. My father coming in, kicking off his snowy boots.

And as for Cameron, my mother said. He's dead. He's in the ground in Whitefish Falls. You told me that yourself. Her photo was on the table and she flipped it over, facedown. I'm glad. Whatever killed him, I hope it hurt.

CHAPTER 23

Don't hang up.

I'd left my parents' house and spent a half hour walking north up to Yonge Street before ducking into a doughnut shop to use the bathroom and the pay phone.

There was a pause on the other end of the line. I could feel David's hand hovering over the phone cradle.

You're right. Okay? I'm an asshole.

I don't care.

You do care, I said. Please don't hang up. Please listen. Please.

I don't want to.

David.

Look, whatever, David said. I went over to see my father to help you out. Because you're so crazy these days, I thought maybe I could ask him some questions. For you. I went there for you.

You don't have to do that, I said. I don't know what's wrong with me.

I fucking hate my father, he said. I go out for beers with him, for you, a thing I do for you, and you know what he tells me? He tells me you're visiting him for coffee times this afternoon. You're over at his place snuggling up for coffee. And what a hot piece of ass, that's what I'm listening to.

That's not true, I said. I mean. I was over there, but you're not listening.

You're just lying to me all the time, Evie.

I was over there trying to figure shit out.

And then I come in and you're hiding in the fucking basement like one of his girlfriends.

You don't believe that.

What am I supposed to think.

Don't think. Just listen. I broke in.

For fuck's sake.

I saw no one was home and I went in the back door. I found a bunch of photographs. David, you have to see these. They all knew each other back then. I know there's a connection, I said. I'm almost there. I am so close, David.

There was no answer.

David.

Where are you, he said.

At Eglinton Station. In the Coffee Plus.

It's late.

I have to talk to Angie. And I need to go talk to the coroner, I said. In Espanola.

When's the last time you were home?

I was trying to talk to my mother. See? Just like you said. I asked her everything. David, something's really wrong. You'd know that if you'd just listen.

It's late, Evie. Go home.

If it's Cameron in that grave, everything goes back to normal. I just need to know.

David said I'd lost track of normal. You don't even know what normal is, he said.

There's a guy out on my fire escape every night of the week and the police aren't helping, I said. I just need to know. I need to know if it's Cameron. David, I said. You get this, right?

I don't know if I can help you anymore, Evie. I need a little break. Go home. Get some sleep. Call me tomorrow.

I'll be gone tomorrow.

You're already gone, David said.

I went down into the subway, heading south to Angie's, hoping to railroad my way through to a different assignment, or at least to get her car keys. It was close to midnight and the platform already felt deserted at that time of night. Eglinton is too far uptown. People get up early and go to work in the morning. I stood next to the emergency pole, waiting for the train.

I took stock.

Here's what we know for sure:

On May 23, 1982, my friend Lianne Gagnon went missing in Toronto. She told her parents she was on her way to Varsity Stadium to practice for a track meet. Her body was found twelve days later in a city ravine. Lianne's murder was traced to an American named Robert Cameron—a repeat offender with a Charles Manson fixation who was known to keep rats as pets and occasionally mutilate them. The day before she disappeared, a man we didn't know asked Lianne to get in his car and help him find a lost dog. This now seems a terrible coincidence. Cameron was never apprehended.

We know that Cameron operated under several aliases, including Arthur Sawchuk. We know that a man named Arthur Sawchuk also ran a kind of flophouse for hippie runaways in Toronto in 1969 and 1970, and that my mother, Annie, was one of those teenagers. This Arthur Sawchuk also had a Manson fixation. He was known for a kind of cruelty toward women. He kept rodents mostly to torture them. We know my mother owed him money when she left. Sawchuk never forgave a debt.

David's father, Graham Patton, was also connected to the house, and to my mother, both in 1970 and then again in 1982. My mother also owed him money. They were intimate enough for Patton to have a nude photo of her stored in his studio, or else that's how she paid him back. He was almost certainly in my mother's living room the day before Lianne disappeared—the same day the man with the lost dog approached Lianne and me in the park, only a few blocks away. There are photographs of Patton in connection with the house that Arthur Sawchuk ran on Brunswick Avenue in 1970. There is no photo that shows both Patton and Sawchuk together.

In 1982, a man named Thomas Hargreave had his wallet stolen in Thunder Bay, Ontario. Later that year a man posing as Hargreave rented a room and took a job near Espanola. He died in 1985 and was buried under that name in Whitefish Falls. It's now suspected that this man was actually Robert Cameron. The real Thomas Hargreave lives in Calgary and was surprised to find federal records listed him as deceased.

Graham Patton has a cabin, a summer house, in Whitefish Falls. It's where he stores most of his photo archive of the last twenty-five years or so. It's a house he's owned since at least 1980.

W here do you get off telling Vinh Nguyen my personal life? I'd charged over to Angie's place to con her into giving me her car keys, and the exchange with Vinh over the Peeping Tom was a good enough excuse to come out swinging. The way he'd thrown his feet up on the desk, like he worked on Wall Street and cared about things like the year on a bottle of wine, or Egyptian thread count, instead of living on salty snacks and staying up all night listening to the scanner in case something dirty or violent cropped up.

Angie came to the door wearing a bathrobe and a pair of dirty red high-tops. I hadn't even taken off my shoes and she was throwing questions at me. So I hit her back about Vinh.

It's not your personal life, she said. That's where you're wrong. It's a matter of public record. If a couple more cases like this come in you can write a firsthand account about how victimized you are and get nominated for a prize. She walked away from the door and back toward her own kitchen. The minute you call the police, you're in open country, she said. Wide, wide open. You are a free-range girl.

She hadn't asked me in but she hadn't given me the keys, either. I followed her back. There was an old Formica table in the middle of the kitchen floor with a handful of mismatched chairs around it that looked like they'd been stolen out of a junkyard or else from the alley behind a TV talk-show set on garbage day. She had a tweedy couch with wood armrests up against the wall under the window in a spot that looked like cabinets had once been there. You could see the mark where the old countertop had met the wall.

Angie collapsed. Kitchen couch, she said. Get yourself a drink. Get me one, too. While you're at it, yeah?

I'd never been this far into Angie's house before. She looked like someone who'd been through a rough divorce. It looked like half her stuff was missing: half the pots and pans, half the dishes, half the household appliances. This wasn't the case. Angie was a confirmed bachelor. *Bachelor* because *bachelorette* sounds like someone who wears kitten heels and wants to get married.

The area around the kitchen sink operated as a wet bar. There was a high cabinet over the faucet that stretched to the ceiling, where most people store dish soap and dishwasher powder and extra rubber gloves, only this one was filled with bottles. She had a wine fridge on the counter that also held a little container of cut limes and I used these to make up a nice-looking tray of tequila shots. The tray had an altered photo of a flying fish on it and a recipe. The fish was laughing and wearing a chef's hat. It had been produced by the Trade Commission of Barbados.

I put the tray on the table and we fooled around with the salt and the shot glasses a few times.

They're not gonna find anything down in St. Catherines, I said.

Nope, Angie said.

Because the warrant is shit, I said.

The warrant is indeed shit. Angie threw a few loping nods in my direction. She'd had a few, or more than a few, before I got there.

There's something else I'd rather do.

No way.

It's a fascinating story with a personal connection, I said. Hear me out. You cannot turn this down.

Officer, Angie said. Officer, sometimes I hang around in my dark, dark apartment late at night, just wearing this little negligee, see? And the big bad wolf comes to my door.

Hey, fuck you, Angie.

No, fuck you. I really mean that. Fuck you. You're not going to get anywhere in this business playing the fool like that, so shut the fuck up.

I lay back against the couch and let my head rest on the hard wooden arm. She'd gone mean on me and now I'd have to wait it out.

They're digging up a dead guy, I said to the ceiling. Up near Espanola. They dug him up on Monday.

I know, Angie said.

They think it's Robert Cameron.

I know.

Robert Cameron, Have You Seen This Man? Most Wanted Criminals Robert Cameron. I sat up and took a better look at her.

Yeah, I know. I know all that.

So it's a story, I said.

No story, Angie said. She seemed to have cursed the booze right out of herself. She got up and made four more shots. You would have sworn she was cold sober.

Come on, I said. Way more of a story than sitting down in St. Catherines watching a bunch of guys in paper suits walk in and out of a house. You said it yourself. The warrant is shit. Their hands are fucking tied down there.

Doesn't matter, Angie said. *That's* the story. That house, that guy. You know why?

I didn't answer. I lay back down and let the armrest make a bruise on the back of my skull.

That's the story because we still remember those girls. That's why, Angie said. Leslie Mahaffy, that's almost old news already. But at least she was chopped up. At least he put her in concrete and sunk her into a lake. There's a killer. There's a psycho for you. She handed me a shot. I plugged my nose and threw it down, still lying back like that.

Nobody the fuck remembers some little girl from 1982, Angie said. Case closed. Maybe it's him. Maybe it's some jerk-off hobo. What the fuck do I know? If it's him, trust me: the cops' PR will be on the phone to us first. They'll be dying to let us know. She handed me a shot glass and a slice of lime. Stop living in the past, Evie. Time to get on with it.

I woke up at six, still on Angie's kitchen couch. Someone—me or else Angie—had moved my head off the armrest and onto the cushion. The tweed pattern pressed into my cheek. The room stank. I looked over at the counter and there were three bottles of booze standing there open, adding to the air quality. I had a blanket over my legs and my head hurt enough to make me rummage through the liner of my purse for a couple of Tylenol before I even tried to get up. I lay there, waiting for the pills to kick in.

When I managed to get on my feet, I locked myself in the powder room and brushed my teeth using a mini-sized travel toothpaste I found under the sink and a wadded-up facecloth. Because fuck you, too, Angie Cavallo. A story is a story.

I had to go through her purse to find the right keys. It was still dark out. I shut the door soft and locked it. Out on the sidewalk I turned left. The Turismo was out there on the street somewhere. I figured I'd better get looking.

CHAPTER 24

By the time I got home the few sunrise streaks were already widening out. The sky shone white. Lit through a high, thin veil of winter cloud. I found a spot on Gladstone and left the car and crossed over to the house. I hadn't been home in two days. It hadn't felt like I was avoiding it on purpose, but now that I posed myself the question I was left feeling embarrassed, or somehow pressingly young. I could barely remember what it had been like to live there before everything went to hell. Something about the fear made it feel like I'd just been pretending to be a grown-up. It felt like a place I used to visit wearing shoes that were too big for me. Like wearing your mother's best dress to play house. Only I got caught.

In the early morning sunshine, it was a nice enough building. I looked up at my own bedroom window. The curtains were drawn tight, as though whoever lived there was still sleeping. The day was going to be warmer and you could already tell. A slight drip from the icicles, the sound of little droplets falling from every high eave on the street and hitting the ice below.

Once when I was thirteen, I arrived home from school with no key in my pocket. I did that thing where you check every possible spot, the tiny coin pocket at the front of your jeans. The inside flaps of your backpack. Places you would never put a key because, in fact, you always put it in the same place. Almost always. You just don't want to face up to what you already know: the key is on your nightstand, next to a box of tissues and two pencils and the wrapper from a pack of Swedish Berries. My parents were both out, at work or whatever it was my mother got up to when she wasn't at home. There had been at one time a tire swing on a rope in the backyard, but this was the year we'd taken it down, and where the swing had been there were high ferns, fresh and splayed and untrampled.

I had this idea that it would be hilarious to climb up onto the second-floor balcony. We were not a family that left doors and windows unlocked. I didn't fool myself about that. There would be no getting in. But the joke of it, my father arriving home from work and me sitting out on the balcony in a lounge chair, taking my ease. I had to wear my backpack properly, on both shoulders, to do this, and I accomplished it by first stepping up onto the large rusty-orange air-conditioning unit and from there grabbing hold of the balcony railing and walking myself up the fence, then performing a last-minute twist that allowed me to wedge a toe onto the balcony ledge. It was simple. I'd stood up like that, on the outer edge, and swung my legs over. Ta-da.

I thought of this in the context of my own fire escape now. A kind of balcony. I wondered how he was getting up there.

Instead of heading straight up to my apartment for a change of clothes, I walked around the back of the house. I'd never been in the backyard before. It wasn't a garden. It looked like someone had dug a few holes for geraniums and cherry tomatoes and then they gave up on life and filled them all in again. I don't know who had rights to it. It hadn't been shown to me the day I took the place. There was a strip of bare and stony earth around the fence line and some limp green showed through the melty snow. Earth with scattered weeds. I looked up. The stairs to the fire escape wound down along one side of the house. From where I was standing I could already see the door to my kitchen. I couldn't see my fridge but I knew it was there, on the other side.

I had to grab tight to the railing to get up the steps. There was a tapering layer of clear ice on each one. The ice was slick with melt.

Up on the escape my feet slid around in a pleasant way, like when you're fooling around on a rink at recess time and you haven't brought your skates. I let them slip side to side like I was doing a vaudeville number. The railing was high and strong, and the balcony itself was higher than the one at my parents' place. I thought about my mute landlord, his weird whines and clicks echoing in the high-ceilinged rooms on the main floor. At suppertime, when he called for the cats. Maybe he was the lapsed gardener. I realized that in all this time I had never suspected him. The clubfoot could never have carried him up the steps. He was a cripple. The crippled quality in him weighed more than anything else. He might have had the sickest mind of anyone. His foot couldn't close the deal.

I skated forward and peered through the window. There was a crack down one of the outer panes and I ran my finger over it. You can look at a thing a million times and never notice a crack like that. Was it old or new? Maybe it had been broken for years. The window, propped for fresh air one summer, falls with a smack and the pane cracks.

Or else it was new. I remembered his fist on the glass. Then that's much more serious.

I looked in at the kitchen. It didn't look like mine. It didn't look like a place where I lived. For a moment I couldn't remember where I lived, or what I was doing there, with the icicles dripping all around me. I imagined standing there and watching a girl come into the kitchen, open the fridge, pour a drink, sit down to write a letter or read the newspaper. She was tall and thin and wearing a man's striped shirt and a pair of slippers meant to look like a ballerina's. She was going to bed, or else she was getting up in the morning. I could see her but she wasn't aware of me. She flipped the page on the newspaper and stubbed out a cigarette in an ashtray on the table. When I blinked hard she was gone. I was cold. My hands against the frozen pane of glass, my hands with no gloves on them.

And then it was my house again. I could identify all my things in it: the wrinkled blue tea towel hung on the handle of the oven door, the pale yellow egg cups in the shape of chicks along the back wall of the counter. A mustard jar, emptied out and washed clean on the drainboard. The sink I'd been painting the night my father came over, pulled to one side of the room, its center piled with the tiny pots of paint.

For a moment I saw the man from the escape. My secret admirer. He was pacing the hallway like someone in a prison. I was on the outside and he was in there, waiting. He stopped pacing and looked straight at me.

Trapped in my apartment, a thing of my own making. What if I'd imagined it every time? Someplace to put the fear, someone concrete to pin it on. What if it was just, as my father might say, a little anxiety?

I shook my hair out to get rid of this.

The way down was treacherous and I turned around to take it backward, one step at a time, hands out. One on the railing, one against the brick wall. There would be no way to do this quickly. My eyes flicked up and I noticed the ladder on the other side of the escape, and I climbed back to the landing. At the opposite corner a new set of steps stretched higher still, to the third floor. Below these there was a gap in the high railing where a retractable ladder sat open against the wall and ran down to the ground, or almost. There was no ice on it. It held my weight fine. I hopped from the last rung to the ground, a drop of maybe three feet, and gave it a shake. No way to fold it back up from there.

There was a scuff of feet on the snow behind me and another sound, high-pitched. When I turned it was the landlord. He was in shirtsleeves in the cold, and shorter than me. He gestured and made his noise again. I glanced behind me at the fence.

When he handed me his little notepad, it said, Police? Okay?

Yeah, the police have been here, I said. Asking you questions? He nodded. There was a grave look to him. Anxious, even.

I thought I saw someone up there. I pointed. Looking in my windows and stuff. The landlord snapped his fingers at me.

Police-Friend-Family, he wrote.

Like, asking if you know anyone, I said. Or do you mean, they're asking your family? About you? I stopped myself. I already told them it couldn't be you, I said.

He bleated at me. Combined with his sad look, the whole thing was dangerously close to a clown routine.

I have to go, I said. He pushed the notepad into my hand.

No More Police.

I get it, I said.

The stairwell inside was dark enough that I almost didn't notice the door. It took a minute to wrestle the key out of my purse. Then I held back. Something was wrong. The angle looked off. Instead of sitting flush, the door was resting there, touching the frame but just slightly ajar. I gave it a gentle kick and it swung wide. The strike plate wedged out two or three centimeters. I had a heavy steel door and a heavy dead bolt, but a cheap wooden door frame. That's a good combination for a crackhead with a jones and a crowbar. A few good wails and the door would have just sprung open. A good combination for anyone, if you think about it.

I kicked at the door again and let it bang back against the wall before walking in. It occurred to me that I wasn't touching it with my hands. In case of fingerprints, something the cops would ask about later. The hall looked undisturbed. I thought back to when I was standing out on the escape, looking in. The kitchen had looked fine. The computer was still there. Nothing was out of line. The number one thing you'll lose in an addict break-and-enter is gold. Rings, earrings, whatever: gold with no stones in it, gold you can melt down fast. The second thing is CDs. These are both items that convert to cash readily. An addict doesn't want your TV or your electronics. They want ten dollars for the next fix and they want it ten minutes ago. I was working hard to believe this was a standard

B&E, executed by one of my desperate neighbors over the past two nights sometime.

I had a quick flash of fire escape man as I'd imagined him, pacing the hall, waiting for me to get home.

He was behind me. Any moment I'd feel him there, his hand over my mouth. Quick. What will you do then. Bite down. Get your elbows back. If you can turn around, you can break his nose with the hard base of your hand. You can go for the eyes. The eyes are soft and will hurt him.

He was in the bathtub, bleeding to death. He'd sliced himself open in my house, knife marks scored long down the veins from inner elbow to wrist.

Deep breath.

checked the kitchen first and then the bathroom. Everything was in order. Soap in the soap dish. The floss I'd used a few nights earlier still in a tangled pile on the edge of the sink. The kitchen just as I'd seen it from outside. Untouched. The little red light on the answering machine blinking. Five missed calls.

In the bedroom the dresser drawers were all shut and inside, the shirts and pants and underwear in piles. Folded. Nothing taken from the closet. All the CDs in the rack, or strewn on the floor near the stereo, wherever I'd left them. Not a thing was out of place. If he'd picked up a trinket to feel the weight of it in his hand, he'd put it back exactly where he'd found it. Nothing was missing. It was like someone had broken in just to teach me a lesson, and the lesson was, *I can*.

Or the lesson was, *You break into my house. I break into yours.*

If Robert Cameron was dead in Whitefish Falls, then he wasn't hiding out as Graham Patton. Then the man on the fire escape was just a Peeping Tom, then the break-in was a crackhead. There is such a thing as coincidence.

I lay down along the edge of the bed.

This is fucking stupid, I said. You probably left the door open yourself. I said this aloud, to test the theory.

Option A: Graham Patton is actually Robert Cameron and has been stalking me on my balcony. Hiding in plain sight for eleven years. Until now. My mother knows this, or at the very least, suspects it to be true.

Option B: Graham Patton knows both Robert Cameron and my mother. My mother knows Graham Patton awfully well. The dead man in Whitefish Falls is not Robert Cameron. Robert Cameron has returned and is stalking me, and has maybe broken into my house.

Option C: Robert Cameron is dead and has been so since 1985. Whatever exchange occurred between my mother and Graham Patton, over past debts, is old news. The guy on my balcony is a coincidence. The break-in is also a coincidence.

Option D: I could keep going but what's the point. If Robert Cameron is dead, shouldn't I feel safer?

At that moment, the phone rang next to my head. I sat up and stared at it. I'd forgotten I keep a phone in the bedroom.

The first thing Job said was, I've been trying to reach you since last night. He said he'd spoken to my landlord. And the guys upstairs, he said. I thought you should know. In case any of them change their behavior.

This didn't make a lot of sense to me, since if he'd wanted to warn me about it, he would have done it in advance. But it felt nice to have a voice on the other end of the line. My front door was still standing wide open.

Yeah, I said. I saw my landlord. He doesn't like having the police around.

I wanted to give you the heads-up yesterday, Job said. So you wouldn't be surprised.

I've been away, I said.

I almost said: I crashed at my friend's house instead of coming home, but suddenly thought better of it. *Away* seemed like enough information.

I banged on the door, Job said. But you didn't answer.

Hold on, I said. You were here yesterday?

Yeah, he said. On my way into the station. You sure you were away? You're not afraid to answer the door or anything, are you?

What door, I said.

Your door. Do you answer the door still?

No, I mean, what door did you bang on, upstairs or downstairs.

Down on the ground. Right? Even in uniform I can't just go walking into houses like that.

Okay.

So, do you answer your door?

It took me a second to register this.

What? I said. Oh, yeah, I guess I do. Yeah.

This was a lie. If I'd been home the night before and he'd banged on the door without calling first, no way would I have gone downstairs to answer it.

Someone forced the door here, I said. But it's the upstairs door. I don't know. I might have left it open myself, but I don't think so.

Did you file a report?

I didn't answer.

Evie? There was a kindness to his voice that made me uncomfortable, the way a guy can sound before he touches your hair or tries to put a hand on your shoulder.

If someone was in here, I said. He didn't take anything. So there's nothing to report.

We can't do anything unless you file a report, Job said.

I wanted off the phone.

Any more information on the guy up in Woodbridge?

We're working on it. This is why filing a report is really useful.

I'm sick of feeling like this, I said. I just made a mistake. Forget I said anything at all.

I hung up. It was almost 7:00 a.m. An hour from now, a team of men in paper suits would be hard at work, paring away at a house in Niagara. That was where I was supposed to be. I was already late for that show. The break-in had delayed me. They start work early.

Six hours north of the city, there was a coroner who'd been assigned the job of figuring out once and for all who the dead man buried as Thomas Hargreave really was.

I picked up Angie's keys.

CHAPTER 25

The day after he dumped Lianne's body in the woods, Robert Cameron drove the Caprice up to Tobermory. Let's imagine the plan had been to jump on the ferry to Manitoulin Island and head off toward the Sault from there—this would be the fastest route— but the heat and good weather had meant a shotgun start to tourist season. Cameron wouldn't have liked the idea of sitting in a long ferry line. Maybe he'd passed three cop cars between Little Cove Park and the ferry dock and skimmed through a speed trap before he knew it was there. He changed his plan and backtracked all the way down to Owen Sound and around the harbor and came up the long way, on the road, through Sudbury. About five miles out of Tobermory he'd passed a sign for a place called Cameron Lake. The name must have given him a smile. He got off the highway, stopped the car, and threw his old ID into the water. We know this part for sure. Cameron's American driver's license was found washed ashore when the lake receded later that summer, the hottest on record for forty years.

Let's say he stopped at a diner in Espanola around twelve or one o'clock and ordered a hot hamburger with gravy. He'd been driving since maybe 4:00 a.m. on a few cigarettes and the remains of the pot he'd taken off the kids back in Toronto. He finished his plate and ordered a second and a side of onion rings. When the waitress brought him his bill he pulled out a wallet he'd been saving in his back pocket for a few weeks. The stolen credit cards had gone into the lake with his own ID but he was holding on to the driver's license and anything else with a name on it. He counted out the girl's money in cash.

Thanks, mister.

I'm Tom, he said. Tom Hargreave. Practicing the new name. But keep on calling me mister. He curled his lips up at her like he was friendly. The girl was maybe fifteen or sixteen and had been waiting on truckers for a year already, so bad come-ons didn't faze her. Bad tips did.

We know from recent police files that a man named Thomas Hargreave was in the diner that day and that he stopped to gas the car on his way out. We know because he got to chatting with the man at the next pump over. Jim Loney needed a driver for long runs north, into Quebec. Rouyn-Noranda, Abitibi, mostly. Mining supplier. Did Hargreave know of anyone looking for that kind of work?

Loney gave Tom Hargreave the job on the spot and rented him a room besides. The Loneys lived in Espanola but they had a place in Whitefish Falls and that's where the room was. Hargreave drove for Loney for almost three years. Then he got unreliable and Loney contracted the trucking out to a guy in Timmins, name of Mario Laplante. Laplante got on better with the Frenchies anyhow, Loney said.

About four days before he died, Hargreave walked into Loney's office looking for him to sign some disability forms. He needed money.

Hargreave turned around and pulled up his shirt, Loney said. He'd told his wife, Marietta, about the visit when he got home that evening. Marietta was shoveling creamed peas into the baby's mouth. When Loney told her about Hargreave pulling up his shirt she made a face.

Man's got a lump half the size of his own head, Loney said, growing out of his back. Right here. He twisted an arm around to his own spine to show her where the lump was.

He's only just applying now? Marietta said. Government's in no hurry to help you out. It'll be six weeks before he sees a check. How's he going to pay the rent?

Jim Loney dropped into a chair and took the spoon from Marietta's hand. He made the spoon an airplane for the baby's peas. He said they might as well start looking for a new tenant, anyhow.

Hargreave didn't have six weeks left in him, Loney said.

Setting out for Espanola, I had a case of nerves that was not much different from playing hooky in high school, where every time you start to relax you think you see your mother or your vice principal out of the corner of your eye and your whole body freezes up again. In senior year we'd skip school and ride the Queen car all the way out to the Beaches for the day so there was no chance of getting busted. We sat in the bandstand in Kew Gardens and did party tricks. Melissa learned to hold a lit Zippo lighter to her open mouth and inhale so the flame sucked back into her throat and circled around and came out again. It was a thing the boys wanted to learn. She called it Breathing Fire. Fear me, she said.

Traffic was crawling down into the city on the other side of the median. Fifteen minutes north a high, looping silhouette rose into the sky, and another swell behind it. An outline of waves, curling and rolling, backlit. I came up on it fast. Roller coasters. The Minebuster. The Bat. There's a moment where you think the road will take you through the amusement park, right under the spiral of track. In winter, the coasters draw a line between ghost town and city's edge, white and skeletal and abandoned, but once you get up beyond Newmarket it's easy to settle in.

The commuters slowly disappeared. There are ski hills near Barrie; the lifts were moving like worker ants, up and then back down in an even stream. You could see the moguls, with specks starting and falling back; the specks were early morning skiers. Farmers' fields on both sides of the highway. They hadn't had the same thaw up there and where there was no stand of trees to one side or another a sheer and equal curtain of light snow blew across the windshield.

The fastest way to Espanola is to take the boat to Manitoulin and then drive off the land bridge on the north side, but the boat doesn't run over the winter. The other way is to stay on the 400, up past Honey Harbour. You let it turn into the 69 at Killbear, and then on and up through Sudbury. It's close to six hours if you drive straight through. At French River I pulled over on the big bridge and got out of the car and looked down. There's another bridge farther down inside the park. Two snowmobiles zipped along it and I could see them because they were red in all that snow, but I couldn't hear them. The river was frozen, with a thin current of running water straight down the center of it and more snowmobile tracks at the edges. A transport truck blared past me going highway speed and I turned around and held my back to the bridge rail and stretched my arms out. There was another truck in the distance and I stayed like that and let that one rush past me, too, stray snow swirling off the top of the cab. The snow looked like confetti but it stung.

If they'd dug up the right body, Robert Cameron had been dead since 1985. I wondered how long the lump had taken to grow, how much it hurt, if he'd been afraid.

The waitress was wearing a blue Fight Like a Brave T-shirt with another long-sleeve underneath it, and jean shorts and black tights underneath those. It was almost eleven and the place looked like it was in the off-hour, before a lunch crowd came in. I sat at a booth and then changed my mind and moved to the counter and sat near the pie under a glass cover. I had a bacon sandwich and coffee and I opened up the sandwich and spread a layer of strawberry jam inside and closed it up again before taking a bite.

I never seen that before, the waitress said. She was wiping down the chalkboard with a wet dishcloth and then turned her back and wrote out the afternoon specials. Soup: *Mushroom*. Sandwich: *Roast Beef au Jus*. Blue Plate: *Roast Turkey/Pots/Mixed Veg*.

How far to Espanola? I folded up the receipt and added it to my wallet.

Another hour to Sudbury, she said. And then an hour after that. She wiped her hands on her jean shorts and they left chalky finger marks there, like she'd been dancing with a schoolteacher, or been pickpocketed and they'd dusted her body for prints. Depends on weather, she said. Looks good now, but snow's coming in this afternoon.

I plugged a handful of quarters into the pay phone by the door and called David's number. It rang ten times and I hung up and all the quarters came tumbling out like I was playing slots. I plugged them all back in and dialed again. This time I let it ring twelve times, until the answering machine picked up. At the sound of the tone, I blanked a little and stumbled through another apology. There was a click but no tone.

Hey, I'm here, David said. I picked up.

Oh, I said. I just left you a message.

Yeah, I heard it. I'm lying here not answering Evie's calls.

Got it, I said.

Where are you?

Two hours out of Espanola.

You alone?

David, I miss you.

Yeah? Because you're really fucking me around.

I'm just going up there to figure this out, I said. I'm going up there, and if the coroner says, Yes it's him, then I never have to think about this again.

What if it's not him.

It's him, I said. I'm ninety percent sure on this.

That's a big fat leftover ten percent.

It will be so good if it's him, David. Imagine how good that will be.

There was a silence and I threw another quarter into the phone to be sure it wouldn't cut out.

David said: I don't want to watch you do this to yourself. I don't want you to put yourself through it anymore.

Someone broke into my place, I said. I went home and the door was broken. Who would kick in my door? Why would anyone do that?

I was staring out the glass door of the diner. There was a gas bar on the other side of the highway with a full-serve sign out in front of it and on my side the restaurant with about ten spots for cars. A silver sedan was parked at the south end, nearest the bridge. It didn't have any snow cover on it. I couldn't remember if I'd driven past it coming in or if it was new. Neither of us said anything and I threw in another quarter.

You think my father's in this? David said.

I said I'm sorry, David.

I'm asking.

I don't know.

He was quiet for a moment.

I'm worried about you, he said.

I don't want to go home anymore.

Okay.

Okay?

Try and be careful up there, Sherpa, David said. Come straight here when you get back. Do that, okay? Come straight back here.

Okay.

For real.

I said okay.

Evie.

Yeah?

Don't go snooping around up there after him.

Who, Cameron? That's the whole point. He's a dead man now, remember?

I mean my father, David said. My father's still alive.

CHAPTER 26

There was no one sitting behind the information desk at the hospital in Espanola. I almost walked in the emergency entrance because that's the only place I'd ever aimed for at a hospital, then checked myself and found the main door. There was a map of the two floors pinned to the wall next to the desk and some pamphlets sitting on a rack next to that. The pamphlets looked like ads for pregnancy. Each one featured a pregnant woman or else a woman with a new baby and they were about all the ways things could go wrong: Fetal Alcohol Syndrome, Postpartum Depression, Pregnant and Abused? Along the bottom row someone had stuck some tourist brochures for cabins and the A.Y. Jackson Lookout. While you're in town.

I could go to the switchboard and ask for someone or I could poke around till I found the right place. There was a set of elevators with a stairwell next to it and a red Exit sign over top and I half expected an alarm to ring out when I opened the door, but there was nothing. Half a level down from me, two women were hanging around on the landing. I heard the voices as though they were far away. As soon as I turned the first corner I fell into them. One of them had a real bathrobe on and black Nikes and she was sitting down and lighting a cigarette. The other was standing up, attached to an IV pole. She was wearing a hospital gown over a pair of green track pants. She was already smoking and tapped her cigarette into a tinfoil cup in the palm of her hand. I almost tripped over the woman sitting down. I had to grab on to something and I was glad I hit the banister and not the IV pole. The women weren't surprised to be tripped over.

Nothing downstairs but the morgue, said the one with the foil ashtray. And the janitor.

Downstairs there was a set of heavy doors and a schedule on the wall in a plexiglass cover. I hadn't known for sure the morgue would be in the basement but that's where it is on television.

The regional coroner's office is actually in Sudbury.

This was the doctor, looking down at me. I'd been sitting on the floor of the hallway waiting for her when she arrived according to schedule, at four. Normally I don't come all the way out here, the doctor said.

I stood up and rubbed my pants with my hands and showed her my press card. Her name was Georgina Smythe. I was in luck because she was the right person to talk to, she said. Just in town filing some paperwork.

Inside the morgue there was a desk and she sat on one side of it and I sat on the other in the same kind of chair you might find in a regular waiting room, with metal legs and armrests and half-worn, royal-blue upholstery. The back of the room extended around a corner. When Georgina Smythe turned around, I leaned out of my chair a little but I couldn't see much beyond the filing cabinets. It was a small place. I could see the wide doors that led into the cold room.

She was the right person to talk to, but there wasn't much to tell, she said. They'd taken some samples and sent them off for DNA testing. That was another thing altogether.

It'll be close to four weeks before I can get a positive ID, she said. You're not the first person to ask about this. When I'm in Sudbury I get two calls a day from Toronto.

I only just caught wind of the story, I said.

Jumping the gun a little, Georgina said. She rolled open a file drawer and pulled out a small stack of folders and flopped them onto the desk in front of me. Whoever he was, he was scared shitless.

Shitless how, I said.

He never came in for treatment, she said. No record of a visit here or in Sudbury or even in the community clinic on the Res. They found him dead in a room down in Whitefish Falls. Cancer all through him. She opened up a file and shoved it at me. Everything would have been shutting down. You're talking about someone who couldn't eat or pee or anything. Renal failure, liver failure. The biggest tumor was on his spine. That would have hurt like a mother.

What else, I said.

Poor general health to start with, probably. Hard to say because the cancer would have stripped him down.

So to be that sick and not want help, you have to want to keep a secret even more.

I'd say that sounds right, she said. Preliminary forensic reports are here. Teeth, mostly. I could tell she'd been expecting something different from me. She looked relieved and started to gather up her folders again. That's how we know it's not Cameron, she said.

I threw a hand out and stopped the folders on the desk.

What do you mean?

That was the first thing Toronto wanted to know: Is this guy Robert Cameron. Cameron's wanted for a murder back in '82. He—

I know, I said. What do you mean it's not him. Everything fits.

That's the ID they were pushing for.

I pulled the open file over and stared down at it. What she was showing me were dental maps. Notes. X-rays. How is this not Cameron. How. I didn't know what I was looking at.

You just said you didn't know anything, I said.

I thought you wanted an ID, she said. We don't know who this guy is. We've got no clue.

Who's this? I held up the X-ray.

The real Thomas Hargreave.

This is the guy out west.

Yeah.

And you know the dead guy's not Cameron how?

Georgina pulled the folder back over toward her side of the desk and swapped it for another one.

They don't know a lot about Cameron, she said. But they know he was circumspect. He was good at hiding and not being found.

He was an old hand at new aliases, I said.

That's in all the APBs that went out at the time and it's one of the reasons he's been hard to track. She flipped open the new folder. A guy has bad teeth, she said, eventually he's going to a dentist.

The open folder held a few original Wanted APBs from the United States and Canada, starting in the '70s. Grainy mug shots and lists of physical attributes. Dark hair, six-foot-three, one hundred eighty-five pounds. Six-foot-three, dark hair and full beard, two hundred pounds.

Cameron didn't want to be found, she said. He had every tooth pulled out of his head by 1975. It's here, see? Subject wears false teeth, full set. That's something they knew for sure. She opened the first folder again. This guy they pulled out of the ground down in the Falls? Bad teeth all right. But they were all still attached to his head. Georgina stacked up the folders in front of her. This is off the record until we get a release out, she said. But as far as Cameron's concerned, I can give you a No. For sure. Robert Cameron made himself impossible to track. He may as well have burned off his fingertips.

I came out the stairwell door into waning daylight. I was in an alley off to one side of the hospital, next to the service door, and I realized it was there to give access to the dead. This is where the funeral home comes for pickup.

I'd been expecting to walk out of that office clean and free and new. New Evie. Instead, nothing had changed at all. The list of options I'd fashioned for myself, lying on my bed at home, was waning fast. Robert Cameron was not dead. Graham Patton either knew

Cameron or he was Cameron, and Cameron was or else wasn't the man stalking me on the fire escape. I'd driven six hours north in a stolen car and if I went home now, all I'd find waiting was the same list of unanswered questions. Everything was unsolved. Whatever my mother knew, she wasn't telling.

I pulled out the contact sheet in my bag, the photo of my mother and the house on Brunswick with its heavy crop marks. The key was hidden under those marks. Whatever Patton had chosen not to print, to keep secret. The town of Whitefish Falls and the cabin where he stored his photo archive were maybe twenty clicks up the road. Twenty-five years' worth of photos, he'd said.

There was a good chunk of cloud in the sky. Georgina Smythe had told me to hurry it up if I was hoping to get ahead of the new weather.

Snow moves in quick up here, she said. If you're not used to the driving. Big stretches between towns, and no one living in between. She asked where I was staying and I lied and said I had an aunt living in Kagawong.

Assuming city hall wasn't also trying to get on the road before the snow, I had fifteen minutes before the district clerk went home for the day.

The clerk was sitting sideways in his roller chair and sliding a pair of rubber galoshes over his dress shoes. A bell rang when I opened the door and he looked up and then down again, sharp and disappointed. His overshoe was stuck and he tugged on it in a grim way. The sign on his desk told me his name was Albrecht Köhning.

Albrecht, I said. My man. I need a quick solid. Albrecht looked to be within three months of retirement, and without much interest in solids.

In ten minutes I am in my car, he said. The door will be locked. He stood up. He had a gold-colored pen clipped to the breast pocket of his shirt.

Fair. I plunked my bag down on the desk and pulled out a half page I'd ripped from my notebook. I need you to check some names against your property records for the district. Ready?

Albrecht pulled out his own notebook and removed the gold pen from his pocket.

Robert Cameron.

Lee Ellingham.

Len Lester.

John McMurtry.

Wade Oxford.

Arthur Sawchuk.

Albrecht paused. How many more?

Graham Patton, I said. That's it. Those seven.

He went over to a sidewall lined with gray medical filing cabinets. It's almost alphabetical, what you give me.

The drawers opened and closed. Albrecht checked his watch between each name.

Only one, he said. Patton. What you need to know?

Is it still registered to him?

He pulled out the file. What you need to know?

He's offered it to me in a private sale, I said. But my instinct is he doesn't own the land he says he does. Is there a survey on file?

Albrecht didn't move.

This is my inheritance, I said. From my grandfather. I don't want to blow it.

He put the survey down in front of me.

He owns this land since 1971. You have one minute.

If you give me a photocopy, I said. We can both get out of here right now.

I could see the house for a full five minutes before I pulled around the back of it. It was a gray board A-frame with a slanting, mossy roof off the tip of Huron. Fields cut into the forest in patches. Hay left out to freeze in bales. You could see the place where the lake ends. The road wound down to the north channel in quiet switchbacks and the house disappeared and reappeared between stands of bush as I followed it down. I hadn't really meant to get close. I thought I'd have to leave the car and walk in from the road, but there was a tire rut through the snow and I followed that around the back of the property. There was a tire rut but no other car.

I got up on my toes and peered in the back window. I was losing the light fast now. My fingers and the tips of my ears buzzed with cold and when I leaned into the window it fogged with the wash of my breath. The place had been built for wind and bad winters and had only small windows giving onto the lake side of the property. The back door was frozen shut but unlocked.

I reached into my bag for the screwdriver I'd taken from Patton's house in the city and jammed it into the door frame and threw my hip against it and then kicked back hard with my heel and it gave. I was inside. My fingers wrapped hard around the cast-bronze knob, burning through the laced-on frost. Nothing moved. No one.

The house smelled of dust and ash and wet wool and a little bit like dog, but not much. I leaned on the door to shut it behind me. It was dry inside. A collection of fishing rods and nets leaned up against one wall of the kitchen and next to it, a small birch table with a couple of chairs pushed in tight. There was a woodstove against the interior wall for cooking and for heat, and the stovepipe widened on its way up through the ceiling to the second floor. The woodbin sat near the door and there were only a few bits and pieces left in it.

I took a couple of steps into the kitchen. A film of light came in through the window and gave the counter a soft look. There were a few dishes upside down on a tea towel but nothing dirty in the sink. I could hear my own breath.

I wondered how often Patton came up in winter. There were a few personal things near the sink: a drinking cup, the case for a pair of eyeglasses. No toothbrush. In the cup, there was a little powdery residue. Toothpaste? Or denture cleaner?

I could hear my breath, but not see it. The dishes didn't look dusty and I ran a finger along the edge of a teacup. It came away clean and my gut stitched up tighter.

There wasn't much to the house. By the look of it, I figured Patton used it for a little fishing and hunting and not much else. From where I stood in the kitchen I could see the whole place, the back door where I'd come in, a couple of big windows across the living room, on the land side, looking into a mix of fields and bush. You could see the road from the windows there, standing out in black patches against the snow cover.

In the living room there was a stone fireplace with a low shelf next to it and another small woodbin. The ceiling was board and beam, like a farmhouse, with a set of notches in the beams so they fit together. The shelf with a few books on it, field guides to Manitoulin and Algoma, and a jigsaw puzzle in a box. I pulled the box down. The puzzle was called Heidi, and she stood there with the tips of her blond hair just long enough to reach her rosy nipples. Almost long enough. I remembered David making jokes about this, how his father had a puzzle of a naked woman called Heidi, and then once dated a woman named Heidi and brought her up to the cabin and she'd stormed out. She hitched all the way to Sudbury, David said. To catch the train back to the city.

Your father wouldn't drive her?

Fuck no, David said. My dad took the boat out a few days later. He didn't even watch her go.

Maybe he thought she'd give up, I said.

The puzzle had a hundred pieces. It wasn't engineered to try your patience. I slid it back onto the shelf and drew the field guides out to have a look at them. The covers were worn at the corners, cottony with use. Peeling. I thumbed at them and the sound of the paper rippled out and surprised me and I turned back to the door for a quick second but no one was there. The stillness filled up all the space and I wanted to laugh, that kind of nervous laughing that makes you feel better and not so alone. It was like being underwater, or in a house buried in a landslide. I found myself counting things to hear the tone of my own voice, whispering the numbers just under my breath: how many shelves, or fat chunks of firewood and splintered kindling in the bin, how many floorboards. Somewhere in the cabin Patton kept his treasure trove of photos. There was a set of thin wooden steps and I counted them before starting up. Heavy through both my feet. The stairs were sharp and steep to conserve space. They functioned like a stylized ladder, a railing on both sides.

Upstairs, there were two tiny rooms without curtains. I could see the room that had once been David's, his skinny bed with a blue comforter, all jammed up under the little square window. A pair of old hockey skates in the corner, a cardboard LEGO box with a flattened lid. How long since he'd been up here? I took a step in and switched on the bedside lamp and the bulb spat a couple of times and then glowed out orange under its autumn leaves lampshade. The stovepipe ran up between the rooms like a chimney. I went to lean a hand against it and pulled back, expecting the sting of frozen metal, but it wasn't cold.

I wrapped my fingers around the pipe, gauging how warm it was. Not hot, but kind to the touch. Someone had been here, stoking a fire, sometime in the last day.

Out the eastern-facing window, the sky was entirely black now. If you were outside in the night, this house and me in it would be the only light on the horizon. I dove forward and switched off the lamp. The highway was far enough away that there was no ambient light and I pulled out my key chain and lit the flashlight. The beam shone a spotlight on the floor and I got down and scanned under the bed, then froze there, crouched and listening. The tire tracks I'd followed in were recent enough. He was here, or had been. Was maybe on his way back. I sat up and glanced at the window for new light, some sign.

David's room was spare and empty. No boxes, no closet. Nothing stacked against the wall or under the bed. There was a chest of drawers and I wrenched them open one by one and rummaged under the clothes, running my fingers along the seams in the wood. The bottom drawer was empty. A few safety pins, the manual from an old humidifier, a broken coat hook. When I pulled my hands back I had tiny splinters in my fingertips and I sucked them out.

The answer to every question I had was hidden somewhere in this house.

In the second bedroom there was a nightstand with a stuck drawer and just one small, curtained-off closet. I pulled back the curtain and a few empty hangers swayed there with the force of it, as though someone had just grabbed the shirts off them. There was a ceiling light but I didn't see a switch. There were no books in the room. High over the closet there was a wide cupboard that ran the length of the wall. I unzipped my coat and let it fall off me, then dragged the bed to one side of the room so that I could stand on the footboard and open the latch. I was moving too fast and the bed frame groaned and scraped against the floor. Every noise I made surprised me and I went faster and crashed into things.

Inside the cupboard, a crawl space extended back about five feet, into the eaves. A few dozen storage bins were pushed up to one side and on the other, an infant's lifejacket hung off a nail sunk into the roof beam. Tufts of pink insulation where the mice had been at it. I dragged the closest bins forward and ripped off the first lid and it fell and rang out a little spiral on the floor and I jumped down after it.

Hold on now. I pulled back and stood there, holding my breath.

Be methodical. If he comes back, you're done. There is no controlling this.

I climbed onto the footboard again. There was wallpaper on just one wall of the room and I could see where it was peeling, up near the ceiling, out of the corner of my eye.

The first bin was all emergency supplies: three flares, a first aid kit, candles. Behind the bins Patton had stashed two jugs of water and a bottle of Polish vodka. The second bin was heavier. I had to use both hands to pull it closer and this time I pried up the lid and tossed it gently down onto the mattress. Inside, there was a cardboard box stacked with paper. Files or photos or Patton's tax records. I rifled through it all, trying to get a feel for what might be in there.

What I wanted was hard evidence that Patton was or wasn't actually Robert Cameron. Did or didn't know his whereabouts. Was or wasn't the man on my balcony. I thought about a man who'd have all his teeth pulled out rather than ever be tracked down because of a dental record. What else would you alter? What face would you hide behind?

There was enough paperwork in the box to keep me busy for a few hours and I pulled it down onto the floor with me and started sorting. The temperature in the house had been falling steadily and I shivered and pulled my coat off the floor and up over my knees like a blanket. The deed to the property was folded and stuck in between an envelope full of gas receipts and the brown cover of an old, unlabeled 45. I pulled out a stiff sheet of yellow construction paper and opened it out to show a greasy oil pastel drawing. King of the Dads.

David.

Something he'd once drawn. Stuck to the back of the card was a paper clipped folder. I peeled it off and opened it up. News clippings. Girl, 11, missing since Sunday. Family hoping for miracle in case of missing girl. Have you seen Lianne?

Like souvenirs.

There was a flash out the west-facing window and for a moment I was glad I had my mag light in use already, before the storm took the power out. I paused, my hands sunk into the box. I thought of how you can count, from lightning strike to the crack of thunder, to calculate how close you are to a storm. From the other side of the house, the flash came and went again.

There are no electrical storms in winter. I switched off the flashlight and stood up. Out the window in the other bedroom, a skinny beam of light moved slowly downhill. Someone was on his way home.

CHAPTER 27

The car came down nice and slow, snaking its way through the curves as though the driver had eyes trained on the house instead of the road. Now and then the headlights snuffed out and I realized this was where the trees created a blind. The vista went dark, then shone suddenly on again as the vehicle swung back around a bend. The car was being repeatedly swallowed by the earth and forcing its way out of the chasm. It kept coming. There was just the one road down to the house. There was no sneaking out now.

I took the stairs softly, listening for engine sounds or a trunk slamming. Back in the kitchen, I pulled the longest carving knife from the block, then chose a spot far from the door, back in the corner of the living room, between the window and the woodpile. I thought of what David had said, that a knife would be useless protection, but I didn't like to be empty-handed. Somewhere outside I heard the thunk of a car door closing but it was muffled and distant. He was walking in. I counted in my head, trying to match my pace to a measure of strides. By now he'd seen Angie's Turismo parked beside the back door. Fair's fair. No surprises for anyone. I waited for the sound of the stuck latch in the kitchen, where I'd had to kick the door to pop it open, but nothing came.

I was standing close enough to the window that the heat of my breath left little patches of fog on the glass and I could feel the moisture rising off it, against my cheek. The fog bloomed out with every exhalation. My lungs were working quick and shallow and I held my breath to slow things down. The film of mist on the window shrank back toward the center. By the time I inhaled again, the pane was clear.

He was right there. Outside, looking in. On the other side of the glass.

Put down the knife, Evie.

Graham Patton's hand on my shoulder, fingernails digging in. Not outside the glass. Behind me. His reflection.

I spun around, arm raised and he grabbed my wrist and the knife hit the floor.

Let me help you with that, he said. Before you hurt yourself. He kept hold of my wrist with one hand, twisting it so that I leaned hard to one side.

I moved my shoulder to try to give myself more leverage or at least the possibility of getting my arm free.

You invited me. Remember?

Funny, he said. You didn't seem too eager. He placed a foot on the handle of the knife where it sat on the floor and pushed me back toward the little couch. Have a seat, he said. Relax. Stay awhile.

He bent down and picked up the knife and walked away into the kitchen and I heard the clatter of it as he tossed it into the sink. In a moment a light came on and then shone brighter. Patton came back into the room carrying a lantern. There was a thick smell that came with it, the kerosene smoking a little.

I just drove up this morning, he said. Our little talk yesterday reminded me I hadn't been here in a while. I guess I was homesick for the place.

Where's your dog?

She's off on a run-around.

Outside? Now? In the dark?

In the new lamplight there was something formless and crisp-edged inside the stone fireplace and I saw that it was newspaper, bunched up to be fire-starter. Patton struck a match as long as his hand and lit the paper in four places, then crisscrossed a few sticks of kindling over top of that. He sat crouched in front of the fire with a block of scrap wood in his hand, waiting for the kindling to burn high enough. He didn't turn around.

If you're planning to run or push me into the fire, he said, best make up your mind soon. Sooner rather than later. He threw on the scrap wood and pushed up to stand. The lantern was on the floor at the other end of the couch, away from the fire, and it flickered and sputtered. Patton sat down in a wood rocking chair opposite me.

Romantic, he said. Wouldn't you agree?

I realized that no one else knew where I was. Not my parents, not Angie. Would David guess? The city clerk? It would be at least a day before someone started asking questions. The cabin closed in over me and shut tight.

What's your name? I said.

The edges of Patton's mouth lightened. He stuck out his hand, like we were being introduced. Graham Patton. Haven't we met?

Your real name.

My elbows were tucked in tight against the sides of my body, to stay warm, but it made me feel small and tense.

Got something to say? Patton said. You ought to spit it out.

I leaned forward over my knees.

I am spitting it out, I said. I asked if that's your real name.

Who do you think I am.

I think you killed Lianne Gagnon, I said. Then you disappeared.

I'm pretty easy to find.

You changed into someone else.

Patton's brow lifted a little and it made him look grim and amused.

You must be hard up for copy at the *Free Press,* he said.

Nothing else makes sense.

He leaned back and pulled a pack of Lucky Strike out of his chest pocket and lit one up using the same long matches. The match burned in his hand like a candle and when it was half gone he threw it over into the fire.

Patton drew on the cigarette and exhaled and shook his head in a friendly way.

It's an old story, isn't it, Evie? he said. And a sad one. I heard they just dug someone up out of the cemetery, though. Is that a lead? Can you use that?

But it wasn't you.

Well, I'm sitting right here, he said. So, no. It wasn't me. Tom Hargreave, wasn't it? He rocked a little in his chair. The north is just a magnet for anyone with something to hide. Poor old Tom. How about you, Evie? Learn anything new, doing all your research? Get a description? No? How about fingerprints? Or dental records? I hear those can be useful. He leaned in toward me with his feet flat on the floor and the rocking stopped. Because the police around here, they just don't seem to know what's going on. All that time and they never found him. Imagine. He clicked his tongue. His teeth were straight and completely even. Poor little . . . what was her name again?

Lianne. You know that.

That's right. Lianne.

A piece of newspaper in the fireplace shot a few sparks into the air and then crumbled away. He got up out of the chair. Excuse me a moment, he said. I realize I haven't even offered you a drink.

He walked into the kitchen again and came back with a bottle of rye and two short glasses. He set the glasses on the floor and uncapped the bottle and poured a couple of fingers of booze down into each glass.

Tell you what, he said. You ask me a question, and if I don't know the answer, I'll take a drink. And then I'll ask you a question, and if you don't know the answer, you take a drink.

I'm not getting drunk with you.

Who said you have to get drunk? Patton said. You just have to answer your questions correctly.

All right, I said. Then I'm not playing games with you.

Patton raised his glass.

Look, he said. I'll give you a handicap. First one's on me. He took a sip, then lowered the glass and let it rest on his thigh. I think you'll find that I'm a good sport.

My face felt tight and stretched. Between the lantern and the fireplace, there was enough light now that I had a clear view of the room. There was almost no furniture and only a coiled rag rug.

Not much of a homemaker, are you? I said.

Patton took another sip.

That's the first question for me, he said. You do want to play! Answer: Hunting cabin, mostly. Hard to keep the floor clean. All that dirt and blood comes in on your shoes, see?

I looked down at his feet. He had a solid pair of black boots on. Army issue, meant for weather. There was a long moment while I considered if these were the boots I'd seen on my balcony.

When I lifted my eyes again he was staring at me.

What did you come here for, Evie?

I found some pictures in your house in the city, I said. You and my mother used to live in a squat on Brunswick Avenue. You used a different name then. You called yourself Arthur Sawchuk.

I was right. You do like pictures.

I came looking for the one that pegs you as Lianne's killer.

You hunted me down! Evie, I'm impressed. Don't get me wrong. But the man you're looking for is Robert Cameron, he said. You know that part, don't you?

I looked at him hard.

Show me your teeth.

That made him laugh a little and he refilled his glass.

I wish you'd have a drink with me, he said.

My wrist still hurt and he'd stopped talking now and just watched me. There was some wind outside. The night was dark enough to feel soundproof. Patton took the pack of cigarettes out again and this time he offered me one and I took it to have something in my hand. He struck another long match and put a cigarette between his lips and let it flare. He sat and smoked and it was quiet. Better to keep him talking. I thought of what my mother had said. Flatter him. I worked up a smile.

Here's what I know, I said. Cameron was a drifter. You couldn't tie him down. He'd been in prison at Terminal Island when Charles Manson was there and when he came up to Canada and Manson started to get attention, he used that fact to scare people.

Patton gave an appreciative nod. Maybe. Maybe he ran that house like a branch of the Manson family. Your mother tell you that? Maybe it's true.

Nah, I said. Cameron was too smart for that. The hippie kids were just a cover. Right? Like a distraction. He had his eye on California. He saw what was happening down in the States, how the cops got focused on a bunch of kids with long hair. The kids were afraid of Cameron and the neighbors were afraid of the kids. From the outside it looked like a cult. I leaned toward Patton. If I were Cameron, even later on, I would have left Manson paraphernalia just lying around. Make people think you're crazier than you really are. He told stories about being locked up with Manson because those stories were true. But it wouldn't matter if they'd never met.

Patton's eyebrows lifted.

Oh, they met, he said. They were cellmates at Terminal Island. Bet you didn't know that. He'd lit both our cigarettes off the same long match and left it burning in his fingers, and suddenly he wrapped the match into his fist to put out the flame. Manson asked the warden to keep him in there. He'd been in and out of prison his whole life. Didn't know what to do with himself on the outside. Warden turned him down, of course. He was supposed to be released, that's why they send you there.

That's a remarkable piece of information to have at your fingertips, I said.

I have it on authority. He opened up his hand and pressed down on my leg. The burned match tip was still hot enough that I could feel it through my jeans and I leaned my body back and away from him.

Evie. I need to remind you that I'm not Cameron. I knew him.

We had a gentlemen's agreement of kinds. I stayed out of his way. Even made a buck off him now and then. Let's talk about something else. Here I was hoping you'd come to see me.

There was a space of no more than five inches between our knees. It was a tiny room, meant only for intimacy or loneliness.

I said I didn't see any kind of agreement, gentlemanly or otherwise, with a man who cut up his pet rats for fun.

You don't believe me? Okay. Then how'd I get away with it, Evie? Patton had a look to him that I recognized. Like an old guy in a bar, patronizing but too forward, his ego tempered by a kind of carnal desperation. If I'm Cameron, how'd I do it?

I didn't know if he was mocking me or just trying to wear me down.

Robert Cameron was already well known to police on both sides of the border, I said. So the easiest thing was to find a new identity. Instead of going back to the United States, you invented Graham Patton. In 1971, you bought a swath of land up here and built a place to hide in case things ever got too problematic. But a couple of years passed and no one came looking for you.

Nineteen seventy-one. Now *that's* a remarkable piece of information to have at your fingertips.

I'm a pro, I said. You came back down to the city and fit right in. You got married. You tracked my mother down. You never forgave a debt.

That's Cameron's rep all right. What about Lianne? How does she fit in?

Something about the conversation had turned Lianne into a thing, no more alive than a glove left at the scene of the crime, or a canceled train ticket. Evidence. I stopped talking for a moment. When I started up again it was quieter.

After you killed Lianne, you came up here to wait out the manhunt. You picked up a hitchhiker on the way. He looked enough like you and you could see he had a few things to hide. You had a wallet you'd stolen sitting out in the car and you let him take it, thinking that with his description and the stolen ID, he'd be an easy mark to take the rap for Lianne. But no one ever came looking up here, not for him and not for you. Not till this year.

Patton nodded slightly. Sure, that could have happened, he said. But you're missing the why. Why would I kill that girl. His voice had gone quiet as well, but also dark.

My cigarette had burnt down in my hand and I threw it into the fireplace.

You've got quite a souvenir collection upstairs, don't you? I said. I would have guessed antlers, or a big mounted fish or something. But you must have every news item ever printed about Lianne Gagnon's murder. It's stunning. I figure you think about it almost as much as I do.

Patton's eyes narrowed slightly, then relaxed again.

You like pictures, hey, Evie? He slowed his voice down around my name like it was a new language or a toy he'd bought and wanted to show off. He stood up and pulled me by the hand.

I've got something you're going to want to see, he said. Come on with me.

Patton walked me over to the base of the steps and held an arm out, gesturing to let me pass. The answer to everything was almost certainly hidden away upstairs. The thing I'd come for, once and for all: the proof. The story. My own theory had made me fearless, or bold enough that I'd forgotten how trapped I was. His tone worked as a reminder. My toe caught on the bottom step and I used it as an excuse to grab the railing and steady myself a moment.

Come on, now.

He had the bottle in one hand and he tipped his head back and took a long swallow. I went up slow, with Patton following close behind me. A hand on my back so I wouldn't change my mind. Once we were up there, I would have no easy way down.

———

n the second bedroom, the cupboard door was still standing open. The box of papers on the floor.

You disappoint me, Evie.

You need to stop using my name like that, I said.

Like how? Evie?

I went to turn back toward the stairs and he caught me by the wrist and squeezed. I whipped around to face him. Take a seat, he said. I see you've already made yourself comfortable. He pushed me toward the bed I'd dragged around like a footstool an hour or so earlier. His body was between me and the door. There was no phone anywhere in the cabin. It was the first thing I'd looked for.

Patton took a key from his pocket and opened up the drawer of the nightstand. I'd thought it was stuck and hadn't wasted time on it. He thumbed through the drawer for a moment and then drew out a long yellow envelope. He tossed it at me. The same kind of envelope I'd found in his file cabinet back in the city, stacked with faceless bondage shots.

No thanks.

Evie. You said that's what you came for. You told me you like pictures. You going to chicken out now?

I thought of the news clippings he'd saved and the little girl's clothes and underwear they found in Hargreave's room. Trophies, the police had called them. I tossed the envelope back at him. I told you I don't want to open that, I said.

Patton sat down close beside me on the bed and fiddled with the string that held the envelope closed, then drew out one long photo. Half as long as my arm.

Not snuff. The real shot of the house, the drug raid photo. Without cropping. My mother out front. A half dozen more people.

I took the photo from him and held it up close. I didn't have to ask if Patton was in the photo himself. I could see him, at the front of the lawn. It could have been David standing there. I put the picture down in my lap.

That's your mother, Patton said.

He pointed to a man, now standing next to her on the porch: And that's him.

The man he showed me was dark-haired and lumbering. An easy foot taller than my mother with straight shoulders and tangled hair that fell below his chin. A kind of ragged, unplanned beard on him.

Robert Cameron, I said.

You ever seen him before?

He's the man with the dog, I said. The guy who lost his dog. He was a little heavier than the man I remembered, with slightly longer hair. Memory is a strange thing. I couldn't have described the man if anyone had ever asked. But the breadth of his shoulders, his stance, his black eyes and the set of his jaw, a kind of swagger to him. I knew him.

You're right that he went by Sawchuk, Patton said. He'd come up from the States, running a tight ship for a gang of bikers. So he had a lot of names.

And you're not him.

No. I keep telling you. I'm much, much more pleasant. He flicked the photo with the tip of one finger. Robert Cameron wouldn't ever lie to you, Evie. If you've been doing your research, you know that. He'd be standing here, bragging. He'd want you to know. He'd want you to know everything he's ever done. He'd tell you the last ten words she said before she died. Maybe make you say the same words back to him, nice and easy, before he killed you, too.

I was holding all the pieces, but somehow I'd arranged them wrong. I looked at the photo again, my mother and then Patton and then Cameron, and I couldn't make them fit.

You're right about some of it, he said. But you made it so complicated. Patton lit a new cigarette and handed it to me. Your mother owed Cameron a lot of money. True. Back in the day, on Brunswick. She split owing him three months' rent. Cameron wouldn't let a man owe him a red cent, not even for a moment. But the girls? He took it in trade. He let them rack it up. Mary Bramer was so high most of the time she didn't know whose dick was up her ass. Your mother paid her own debts. She paid in cash. But then she got sick, see?

Patton massaged my leg with his hand. I wanted to keep him talking and let him do it. The police were cracking down and it was an easy time to get out of there, he said. I think she really believed she could get away without paying him, too.

I flicked the end of my cigarette. The ash scattered all over my leg and the blue bedspread and I took a quick drag on what was left. Patton brushed the ash off his hand.

She thought she was leaving, I said. She thought she was moving to Orillia.

Cameron tracked her down where she was living, with Jones, uptown someplace.

My father.

Patton nodded. He sat outside that place, out on the curb, and watched them for a week, he said. Made sure they knew he was there. He wanted her terrified. Every day he moved closer, till he was sitting on the front porch. Hanging around, looking in the window when your mother was home alone.

I still had the picture in my hand and I looked sharply at the man who was Robert Cameron.

He wasn't much taller than my father, I said.

No, Patton said. But with Cameron it wouldn't have been a fist-fight. He was cruel. He had no regret in him. This is what, 1970.

Patton lifted a hand and ran his fingers down my jaw. I pushed him off.

Don't touch me.

I'm trying to tell you the story! Evie! He lifted his hands in mock innocence. Look, your mother didn't have the money. Cameron had a mouthful of rotten teeth. So Jones found a way to call it even.

That stopped me for a second. What could my father do for a man like Cameron? I rubbed at my own face, brushing away the feel of Patton's hand on me. A mouthful of rotten teeth.

He pulled Cameron's teeth out, I said. So he couldn't be found. So he'd never see another dentist again. That's what you're saying.

Every fucking tooth out of his head.

So that paid off the rent, I said.

I didn't hear from him again, Patton said. Years. I'm at the grocery store one day and there's your mother. Small world! Hey, Evie? He put his hand down on my thigh again. Chances we live in the same neighborhood. I thought she moved up north.

I need a little space, I said.

By all means. Patton moved back no more than an inch or two. She told me Orillia, like you say. Imagine my surprise.

There was a sudden noise from downstairs, someone kicking at the wooden door. Splintering. Someone trying to get in. I pressed my back against the wall behind me and brought my knees up to my chest.

Who else knows you're here? I said. Patton's cheeks twitched. He'd been drinking steadily the whole time and I could see his collegiality was starting to fade.

Me? No one would have followed me up here, Evie. This is my home. This is my place.

I turned in the direction of the sound just as it stopped.

Now Evie you need to relax, Patton said. That's just Maxie outside, trying to get in.

The dog. I slid along the wall, trying to make a little space between us and get closer to the door without pissing him off, either. He reached out and grabbed me by the shoulder.

You came here to my home for answers and I'm playing real nice with you, I'm telling you the whole story. I could feel the pressure of his thumb in my shoulder socket. He was drunk and it occurred to me that this is what he wanted, a chance to hold me down. A reason for it to go that way. My fault.

Okay, I said. Okay, you're right. Just go ahead and tell your story. You're hurting me, I said. Please.

Patton slacked off a little and regarded me from there for a minute or two. Even a minute seemed long. Then his grip tightened up again.

Evie, someone should have told you this story a long time ago, he said. This is the part you'll really like.

You're hurting me, I said. I just need some space.

Okay. He took the hand off me and held it up. Looking to see what I'd do. I didn't move.

Cameron turns up back in Toronto in '82, Patton said. Driving a Mustang. Skinny fucker. Lost a bunch of weight. Looking for money so he comes after me. He doesn't have a fucking thing on me, but he's bluffing. Your mother, now that's a different story. Says he never got what she owed him. He wants cash. Tells me he knows she's got a daughter. He'd been watching your house for days, he said. That house on Bessborough. And there's Annie trying to raise the money to make him go away.

What about my father?

Jones never saw him that time. He made sure of that. Cameron wanted something from the lady in particular. He wanted her to give in. Started following her around, waiting for her in the driveway, in the parking lot at the bank. Whatever he said, he scared the shit out of her. That's why she came to me. She wanted it to go away. I offered to give her a loan.

What a gentleman.

I gave her a couple thou in cash.

And she paid you back. I've seen the photos, I said. That makes you no better than him.

His brows lifted. You think? Over a few photos? Your mother and I have known each other a long time, he said. Those were lonely days. Seems a small price to keep you safe.

You were in my house, I said. You came to the house on Bessborough Drive. I saw you there.

Patton said: I helped her out.

Did she sleep with you? I said. I'm not asking her. I'm asking you.

Then? On Bessborough? Evie, you were so sweet then. Like a different person. Remember when I used to drive you home at night? So sweet. You were so keen to be a big girl, start babysitting, and your mom was so worried he'd come back.

I had the cigarette he'd given me in one hand, resting on my knee with about a half inch of ash hanging off it. I thought for a moment about bringing it up to his eyeball, the sizzle of that burning ash against his eye. Making a run for it down the stairs.

I grew up, I said.

Huh, Patton said. Did you. He took the last drag off his smoke and crushed it under his heel.

I wrapped my arms around my body. The smell of kerosene from the lamp drifted up from downstairs. It made my head hurt.

Cameron was watching me, I said. Not Lianne. He was watching me.

We saved you, Patton said. Think of it that way.

No, I said. You don't understand. He wasn't watching Lianne. She wasn't part of it. None of this had anything to do with her.

I told you: he liked to make people afraid. He wanted to show your mom he meant business. Or else he just had his mind set on it by that time, he said. I guess. He was mostly an animal, but a clever animal.

But she paid him the money, I said. She thought he was after me.

None of us even noticed there was another girl, Patton said.

But Cameron did, I said. Cameron saw her.

The dog landed against the outside door again and Patton stood up suddenly and looked out the window. The room was starting to close in on me. I was out in the middle of nowhere, alone. Worse than alone. Trapped at the edge of real wilderness. I wanted to lie down on the floor.

Your mom never let Cameron fuck her. That's what he said. She wouldn't stay in the room if he was there. One time he got too close and she scratched the fuck out of him. In front of people. It pissed him off. He never forgot. For all I know, he couldn't tell you and Lianne apart. Maybe it wasn't a threat. Maybe he thought she was you.

There was a high, sharp whine between my temples and I dropped my head like you do to keep from fainting. I held my hands together in my lap and looked at them and pressed my fingers hard into each knuckle. The little stab of pain felt good and brought me back.

I'm going to throw up, I said. I grabbed my coat and bag off the floor and staggered out and down the stairs, my back against the railing. Patton followed close behind, a hand at the back of my neck, and I held him off with one arm. When we got to the kitchen I leaned over the sink. The stupid knife was still in there where Patton had thrown it when he first came in. I wanted to laugh. I coughed and spat on it. His arm was around my back. I shrugged it off and tried to push him away. I wanted to look sicker than I was and I gagged until I vomited a little. Outside it was black and I could hear Maxie, still there, scratching and whining at the door. Patton grabbed my chin and turned my face toward him. He took his thumb and wiped at my mouth, hard. His other arm was wrapped tight around the small of my back.

Why are you here, Evie? he said.

I want to go home, I said. I went to steady myself against the counter and my hand slipped down into the sink. It was wet with spit and vomit and my stomach turned again. I twisted and leaned down into it. Patton grabbed my hair like he was holding it away from my face, but rough.

You want to know what I think? I think you've got a sick fascination. I think there's a little part of you that lives what he did to Lianne every day of your life. Driving out here like the sheriff, he said. You want to know what happened? You want to act it out? Keep it up. He pulled back hard on my hair. He had his other hand on the counter for balance. His body so close that I could feel him pressing into me from behind.

I want to go home, I said. I shifted and my fingers slid in the sink, bumping up against the wet wood handle of the knife. His mouth on my neck like I was his girlfriend. I could see my own reflection in the window and Patton's hand next to me on the counter. I grabbed the knife out of the sink and stabbed it through the hand.

Jesus fuck! Patton tried to get a hold on the knife and I bore down with all my weight on the butt end of the handle, keeping it there, hammering it into the counter. I wanted to pin him down. He jacked his other elbow up against my shoulder, sending me back a few steps.

Blood seeped out from under the hand. He was already working the knife out.

I said I want to go home.

Outside, Maxie had stopped whining. Something slammed hard against the door. I turned and watched the door frame tremble.

Patton was hunched over the counter. His body jerked up all at once. He looked at me, the knife in one hand; the other hand was bleeding freely now. He had a fine sweat across his forehead. His hair was damp with it. From the door, another slam.

That's no dog, doing that, he said. His lips curled up a little like he might laugh, but he didn't. You expecting someone, Evie? Who else have you been tracking down.

I stepped back a little farther.

Who's after you, Evie?

The frame shook again.

There was a different way out of the cabin, through the living room, but I couldn't get to the car from there. Out front there was only snow and more snow. At least a hundred yards to the tree line. I looked at Patton. He was breathing heavy, hand pressed tight against his shirt.

The only sure way home was through that door. I spun around and pulled hard on the handle, throwing myself past whatever was out there. The dog rushed into the room and then, almost as fast, David.

David. David knew I was here. He reached for me and I stopped short, grabbing at his arm, his wrist. My shoulder smacked into the door frame.

There'd been no flash of headlights, no crunch of tires on the ice. Or if there was I hadn't noticed. I'd been aware only of the dog, scratching at the door. I held on to David's wrist with both hands. I could feel the flush of his pulse through my fingertips.

Patton leaned hard on the counter and threw the knife back in the sink. The hole in his hand was ragged and bloody: a pinker, more watery look to the blood than I expected.

I got this feeling that I'm supposed to kill you now, David said. Or beat the shit out of you anyway.

Patton pulled a cloth out of the drawer and wrapped it around his hand a few times.

Over that? He gestured to me with the cloth.

Thing is, I don't want to touch you, David said.

Let's go, I said. Let's get out of here. I let go of his arm and shifted my body a little closer to outside.

I don't want to catch what you have, David said.

Patton looked up at him.

Get out of here before I beat the shit out of you myself.

Maxie whined and paced between us, pawing at the ground a little. Her nails on the wood floor.

I found your dog, David said. Hiding out from coyotes. He looked at me for a second, then back at his father.

Maxie, come on, I said. I snapped my fingers down low against my leg and the dog came over and rubbed her face on me and I grabbed on to her collar.

I'm going now, I said.

You think I won't let you? Patton said. He kicked at my coat where it sat on the floor of the cabin. Shows how much you know.

CHAPTER 28

Here's the final score:

Robert Cameron crossed the border into Canada at Fort Frances on or about May 3, 1982, using a stolen passport and the name John James McMurtry. He slept the night in Thunder Bay before heading down to Toronto, where he spent several weeks locating and threatening a handful of people whom he thought owed him money, including but not limited to my mother, Annie Jones.

He wore a full set of false teeth.

He'd lost weight recently and his jeans hung off him and he needed a belt.

Annie paid the sum of two thousand dollars in secret. The money was given to her by Graham Patton, a man they both knew. She paid out the money in secret but made Cameron sign for it in Patton's presence, for what it was worth. She wanted a guarantee that he would stay away from her and her family. This all happened early in the day on May 22, 1982.

A few hours later, Cameron approached two girls in the park surrounding a community library. He knew one of the girls to be Annie Jones's daughter. He told the girls a story about a lost dog and solicited their help. The girls returned home safely. But sometime the next day, eleven-year-old Lianne Gagnon got into Cameron's car and disappeared.

Her body was discovered twelve days later in the wooded area of Taylor Creek ravine in Toronto's East York suburb. Her leg had been severed from her body and was sticking out of a blue Anheuser-Busch duffel bag. There was a dog walker, and the dog found the leg.

Lianne's parents divorced a year later. Her mother moved to Vancouver Island with her remaining children, as far as she could get from Toronto without actually leaving the country behind. What happened to Lianne's father is unknown.

Robert Cameron became the subject of the longest and most extensive cold case manhunt in Canadian history. There's very little that's complicated about his story. Despite repeated sightings and the exhumation of an unknown man who fit his description neatly, he was never seen again.

Lianne Gagnon was buried in Mount Pleasant Cemetery. She's easy to find.

W e drove back down to the 400 in the early hours of the morning, David in the van he'd taken from his mother's driveway and me in Angie's Turismo with Maxie shedding and drooling on the seat next to me. That country is as much water as it is land. There was fog almost down to ground level and we drove slow till past Espanola because of it. Ice on the road. There were three deer standing at the edge of the woods at Willisville and I thought Maxie might see them and kick up a fuss but either she didn't or she didn't care. We went gliding by and none of us made a sound. It was that time of day, low light. About half a mile farther, another one, lying dead where a driver hadn't seen it coming and the ice and road salt around it all stained.

Patton hadn't moved to stop me while I gathered my things. He stared at his own son and wrapped the cloth tighter and tighter around his bleeding hand and knotted it firm. I almost wanted to apologize but I didn't. There was no reading his expression. We didn't talk. I left the photograph where he'd dropped it upstairs. He shook his head a little as we moved toward the door.

Outside, the deep freeze was on its way. David and I paused out back of the house.

You take the dog, he said. So you won't be alone.

There was a temptation to just abandon Angie's car and climb into the van, the three of us together, but neither of us said it out loud.

There's a gas station in Espanola, I said. Texaco. With a coffee machine. And a diner near French River.

I'll race you, David said.

I opened up the driver's door and Maxie jumped in and flounced her wet paws all up and down the seats. David had his engine running and he was waiting behind the wheel of the van, rubbing his hands together and blowing on them. I threw my bag over into the back and looked up for a moment, just before getting in myself and driving away.

The one thing I'd always thought of as random, Lianne's abduction, was the one thing that was calculated. It was no coincidence at all.

The speed of the clouds. Weather moves faster in the north. Ten times, a hundred times faster. You stand still and watch it streak in and it's hypnotic and then it's upon you. So fast that nothing can catch it.

We came back down through Sudbury, taking risks, as the light came up and no one else was on the road. We drove too fast or too slow, or side by side, waving to each other, David chancing the oncoming lane in the van. The dog barking and licking the glass. Once he slowed down and I passed him, kicking in the fantastic pickup that little car had and zooming way out in front. A game. To cheer us up, except for a second over a hill I lost sight of him and the Turismo skidded out faster, the road black and empty as if I'd driven out onto the middle of a frozen lake. I took my foot off the gas and let the car decelerate and spin a slow 360. A moment later David crested the hill, driving sensibly. A thing to make me laugh.

We stopped for eggs and greasy potatoes on the near side of French River. The same pay phone where I'd called David, maybe eighteen hours before. How could it be less than a day? There was a new waitress on shift wearing a different version of the same uniform. Tight jeans and a Dolly Parton T-shirt. On the back of the shirt there was a list of dates and places, none of them in Canada. She was a few years older. She'd dyed her hair red and had some trouble with the dye. While we waited for more coffee I played with the jams and the waitress sat swiveling on a counter stool and told David what she'd done.

I didn't think enough dye was up top, she said. I just kept rubbing it in and rubbing it in!

Her roots were a wild salmon color. The rest of the hair hung plain and gingery and straight down off her head.

We didn't talk about what happened at the cabin. I dipped my toast in a pool of cooling egg yolk and drew a smiley face to one side of my plate. David stood up and checked every table until he found a little rack with a grape jelly on it and he peeled off the seal and ate it with a spoon. On the way out he noticed the pay phone near the door and said, This where you called me from? And I said, Yeah, it was. That was as big as the discussion got.

Maxie stayed in the car. We had a bacon sandwich wrapped in a napkin and I made her get out, into the snow, and we fed it to her there in pieces.

Does this make us dog thieves? I said.

You don't look unhappy, David said. Do you, girl? To the dog, not me.

Then Huntsville and Gravenhurst and past Barrie to the city and I couldn't bear to drive home so we went to his house instead. We took turns in a hot shower and when that was done I sat and replayed the story for him in detail like it was a debt I owed him, like it was reparations.

Aside from everything else, I basically stole Angie's car, I said.

You're so fired.

David stood around in his boxers and made me drink hot, sweet coffee under a blanket. He shook his fist at me in mock frustration. You'll never work for a paper in this town again! You hear me?

I felt quiet. Settled in my skin. I could see this reflected in David. Gleeful and relieved and ignoring the bigger issues we'd have to talk about later.

Maybe, I said. Maybe this job is not for me.

There's still time to become a Sherpa, he said. He pulled a sweater over his head.

I said: David, I'm sorry.

I knew something was up when I got that call, he said.

The search at Bernardo's house in Niagara went on for seventy-one days, but Angie pulled me off the story and swore she'd never loan me her car again. Within a month I'd left the job and moved on to a different city in a different province, anyway. A judge handed down a publication ban that meant that for almost two years only police, media, and the victims' families had any real awareness of what would be uncovered in that house. People were dying to know the details. My father's hygienist drove from Toronto to Buffalo for a copy of the local paper because she'd heard they were publishing what Canada couldn't. A kind of horror the public only thought it wanted access to. Mike Nelligan, the other first-year reporter, stayed on the story and told me later he became a fast alcoholic, drinking hard every night of the trial.

Despite a handful of updated warrants, that search squad never found a thing. In late April they called it quits. On May 6, Bernardo's lawyer, a newbie with little experience in criminal law, retrieved a set of videotapes Bernardo told him were hidden behind the light fixture in the bathroom of the house. They'd been there the whole time. It would be more than a year before these tapes were finally handed over to the presiding judge as evidence. By that time Bernardo's ex-wife had brokered a successful plea bargain. Paul

Bernardo himself was sentenced to life in prison in 1995. For what it's worth, they declared him a dangerous offender. He goes by Paul Teale now, a name he stole from a fictional serial killer in a movie he used to like.

The house in St. Catherines was bulldozed. They've built a new house there instead.

A month after that night in his father's cabin, David left to train as a wildfire fighter in northern Quebec and I quit my job and went along for the ride. The ride was a blue VW van with a pop-up bunk built into the roof. He found it in a parking lot on Dundas West with a For Sale By Owner sign in the window. If you wanted to lie down you had to step up onto the driver's seat and hoist yourself up like you were hopping a fence.

We went back to the apartment on Gladstone just once, with a vanload of empty boxes and garbage bags and I folded up my clothes and fit them tightly into two suitcases. I had a few boxes of books. We left the shelves and the old bed frame on the curb and when we drove by the next morning I saw that someone had already hauled them away. There was no damage, no evidence of any new break-in. A few months after I left the city Angie sent me a clipping from the *Free Press*: Balcony Stalker Attacks Two Women in Parkdale. There was a police sketch and a limited statement from police that used vague terms to describe the assaults. Angie had written in the margin in pink pen:

Your guy?

I don't know. It seems hard to believe I've walked away twice.

There are things I've kept to myself, parts of the story I withheld when I was relating it, later on, to my parents. Whatever the truth is about my mother and Graham Patton, for one. Whether it was a simple exchange of goods, money for a set of nudie pics, or a more complicated affair. This has required careful reconstruction on my part. Some secrets are worth keeping.

It's possible my mother is aware that I know.

The day we drove home from Whitefish Falls, David and I curled up under the blanket at his house, down in the basement, and slept for three hours straight. Then we got up and went to see my parents. The house was warm. They had all the lights on, like they were expecting a visit from strangers. I shouted a warning as we came in, because of the dog, but their cat was already high on a bookshelf, hissing back. Maxie lay down with her ears flat and they watched each other.

My parents were making dinner and we sat at the table near the kitchen window and David reached over and drew little pictures on the steamed-up glass with his finger. I said we'd been to Espanola and back and my father was surprised. My mother had her back to me, stirring a pot of water so the noodles wouldn't stick, and when I said this she turned slightly in my direction. Her head over one shoulder. Wary.

It's not him, I said, and her eyes closed a moment and she turned away.

The radio was going on top of the fridge and it was someone talking about the symphony, what to expect, coming up next.

I told them what I knew: that the real Tom Hargreave had surfaced out west but this other man in the ground was not Cameron. The dead man was unidentified, at least for the moment. My father had been sitting at the table with us and he got up and pushed in his chair and moved closer to my mother.

The description fit, I said. Everything fit. Height, weight, personality. The timing of his arrival, even. Everything.

That doesn't make him Cameron, my mother said. A description.

The coroner told me it's not him, I said. It turns out the north is just a good place to hide.

More than one guy's thought of it, David said. Over time.

My father reached over and around my mother's body to get

a cutting board and they stood at the stove for a moment with their backs to us but slightly touching at the arms and shoulders, working on their separate tasks. My father inclined his head and said something to her that I couldn't hear. On the radio there was music now, something loud and happy and Austrian-sounding, a waltz. My mother let her spoon rest on the pot's edge for a moment and turned to him and touched his arm at the elbow. She let her forehead rest against his shoulder. They stayed there a moment and then she picked up the pot and poured the noodles and boiling water out over a colander in the sink. The steam rising fast enough that for a moment her face disappeared. She surfaced out of it like a long-held breath, her hair curling here and there in tendrils, at her ears and the edges of her cheeks.

It was February 28, 1993. Early that morning, while David and I cruised down the highway, a hundred and fifty federal agents stormed a compound in a place called Waco, Texas. This is what we watched on television in my parents' living room that night, eating bowls of chicken Marengo and my mother's buttered noodles off our laps. David and I cross-legged on the floor like children.

The agents had trained for the assault for eight months and they approached undercover, hiding out in livestock trailers. The siege was not a surprise. The cult leader, a man who went by the name David Koresh, had been tipped off by the presence of a hapless reporter who'd lost his way and stopped to ask directions. We didn't know it that night, but the result would be a fifty-one day standoff.

On April 19, an M-728 tank with a battering ram punched an eight-foot hole in the front of the cult's base of operations, a place known as Mount Carmel Center. The tank broke through and pumped tear gas directly into the building. There were undercover operatives in place at Mount Carmel Center and David Koresh himself could easily have been arrested by one of these men. He'd thought of them as his friends. The Davidians had no clean water or electricity for six weeks and the gas and subsequent explosions killed at least eighty civilians, twenty of them children.

That kind of fear, the power of the word *cult*, is Charles Manson's legacy.

Later still, a famous chemistry professor testified at the Waco hearings, comparing the resulting conditions to a Nazi gas chamber. He said the kids would most likely have been suffocated by the gas right away. Little was ever reported about the manner in which these children died. What you'll mostly find are accounts of Koresh's depravity, his child brides and guns. How young the girls were when he married them, how many there were, what kind of sex acts the little girls were told to perform.

We were still getting used to the narrative that constant, live coverage affords. A year earlier, we'd learned to watch missiles striking Baghdad targets in real time.

After a little while, David got up and took his plate into the kitchen and put Maxie on her leash. My father followed him out into the yard, and then David poked his head back in for just a moment like he was worried about leaving us alone.

Koresh himself was interviewed by CNN from inside the standoff before nightfall. I was in the living room with my mother when the broadcast aired and I saw her lean forward for just a moment and I realized she was studying his face.

He's too young, I told her.

She shrugged.

Bad teeth, she said.

ACKNOWLEDGMENTS

I could not have written this book without the love and support and incredible smarts of the people close to me. George Murray, who read and reread and listened and talked-through and hand-held more than you'd think a human possibly could. My children, Nora and Desmond, Silas and August, who forgave my constant state of distraction and occasional absences. Nora, also, for her keen reading and enthusiasm. My parents, who never fail to support my writing life. My early readers—Miranda Hill, Sandra Ridley, and Lisa Moore. How lucky I am to count such a fine group of writers among my friends. My agent, Samantha Haywood, who brought me through the whirlwind of early drafting, and my editors, Patrick Crean and Sally Kim, whose close attention and support and faith were invaluable.

While the Bernardo case serves as a backdrop, *The Devil You Know* is not meant to be a factual depiction or police procedural of events at that time. The *Toronto Star* archives were very useful to my research, as was the public document "Bernardo Investigation Review—Report of Mr. Justice Archie Campbell." Both of these resources pinpoint some dates and events that were of interest to the novel. It's important to note that the death of Terri Anderson was never tied to Bernardo or his wife, Karla Homolka—although at the time of Kristen

French's disappearance, the missing girls were most certainly linked in the media and within the general climate of fear. A few other real stories make an appearance in the novel, including those of Sharin' Morningstar Keenan, Nicole Morin, Alison Parrott, and Lizzie Tomlinson. Katherine May Wilson's murderer was apprehended and convicted in 2009.

Finally, I owe great thanks to a handful of funding bodies in two provinces. The Canada Council for the Arts, Ontario Arts Council, Toronto Arts Council, Newfoundland and Labrador Arts Council, and the city of St. John's all supported the writing of this book, and I am very grateful.

ABOUT THE AUTHOR

Elisabeth de Mariaffi is the critically acclaimed author of one previous collection of short stories, *How to Get Along with Women,* which was nominated for the prestigious Giller Prize. A long-distance runner and dog lover, she has juggled a surprising range of day jobs, from marketing professional to flight attendant. Born and raised in Toronto, Elisabeth now makes her home on an island in the middle of the North Atlantic—she lives in St. John's, Canada, with the poet George Murray and their combined brood of four children. Find her at www.elisabethdemariaffi.com.